WHERE WE'VE MADE IT DARK

NICHOLAS CRAWFORD

Printed in the United States of America. Imprint: Curtain Literary Press

Contact info: www.nicholascrawfordauthor.com

ISBN 978-1-968096-02-1 (paperback)

First edition: October 2025

Electronic edition: ASIN B0F7GV8LTW (ebook)

Front cover design: Naomi Clark

Front cover art: Christina Kent

Author photo: Carolyn Fong

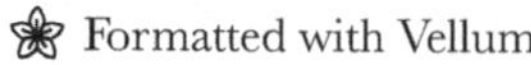 Formatted with Vellum

To Liara and Elspeth, forever and always

PART I

BREAKOUT NEWS

I'M open on the concave slopes of an as yet unslept in morning. It's too much, but it doesn't stop. No one part of me takes the lead against it. All at once I'm out and stumbling as the hand on my chest crumbles to carpet quicksand and I'm there. Swiped through on that sun-kissed smile and silent again in the cuddle.

Brighter now through the blinds as celestial neon takes the wainscoting. Nothing's left that aches. The carpet scrunches around my feet until I'm out on the tile, then it's back to safety at the bath mat. Close the door and crank it on. There's that shrill whistle. Some princesses get birds, I get old pipes that sing for me. It's a dog's pitch intoning down before it gets spat fully out, a pebble on its way, only me to catch it. And whoever else is in the house.

The same soft-pink slippers bounce me down the stairs like they've done since junior high. Something's on and blaring that's not daytime TV. A lone, greasy tangle of bed head's watching it.

— What, are you like Mom and Dad now?

He doesn't turn.

— I'm not the one who pretends to be an adult. It was all over, look.

Breakout News. Deadly protests erupt in Indonesia, leaving hospitals overrun, urban chaos. Could this be the start of ethnic cleansing?

— Did Mom get yogurt?

The following images may be disturbing to some viewers.

— I forgot to change my alarm.

— Good for you.

A man is lying on his back. His face is blurred away, but he's definitely dead. The angle hides the wound. He's gutshot, maybe. A flat madder red muddies the details. The photo is at night, and another man stands to the side with his hands resting on his head as though he's just walked off from a car accident. Dirt on the street, figures gathered in the distance.

Two women in skirts lie facedown on top of each other. The flash glares on their butts, narrow, one in almost that same shade of red, the other washed-out purple. But their hair is what's caught together in a mess. No purses or the like. Only one heel's left between them.

— Well, that's more than I wanted before breakfast.

— Then go eat.

No yogurt, but there is granola. The bananas are songbird green, and I keep looking for better fruit.

He's still turned for what's next. More people and more of their insides.

— What is it?

— Zombies.

I smirk and flip the hot water kettle on.

— Oh, yeah?

— That's what people are saying, anyway. All the posts are about how everyone's biting each other. People actually getting eaten alive.

— Sounds serious.

I hook a handmade mug. The ceramic pit looks back at me, surprised.

— Yeah, there's just nothing good. They were talking earlier about some sort of disease, but that's dropped now completely.

I leave it waiting as I pour cereal. The hearty flakes are doused, and I'm sitting next to Jake.

— They looked pretty normal dead to me.

I'm thrown a crowd on knees together in the street. A few look hurt in places. They're reaching down, but it's hidden. This one's at dusk.

— What, you think that's helping someone?

— It's not exactly eating them either.

— But it's close, right? It's like they're trying to keep it boring. It's a riot with no rioters. A virus with no symptoms. Everything's all small and sanitized.

There's a real bite against the cereal, just a bit sweet. Maybe it's the same from last time.

— I'm just waiting for them to use the Z word. Call it what it is.

His smile splits the upstart sketch of his Vandyke with jagged teeth. It holds its blackness tight.

Stone cracks under us; my phone's back to life and rattling from its plastic. I pull it up, close and far, buzzing angrily. Dodge the notification and go to Aidan.

So my brother thinks there are zombies now.
Welcome home to me. Woo!

I swallow a mouthful too quickly. It stays with me, rough on the way down.

Hey Babe!

Well, it's pretty intense.

Watch **REAL ZOMBIE ATTACK** Indonesia, Location Unknown on YouTube.

— Here, Jake. Present for you.

— Oh, awesome!

I hold for us to hover.

It takes a moment to play. The video starts with blackness, noise on the street. Voices speaking, screaming, shrieking on top of each other. It's rhythmic, coming out in its own buried waves. The camera and others are running in the dark as mopeds zoom right by. Everyone in the same direction. The video is two and a half minutes long. A lot of it is feet hitting against a flow of pavement and dirt and grass. The camera swings through the scuffling of torsos and jerks to a doorway passed by. A form stands there, taking it in. It steps forward slowly, stumbling to join. Others come behind. There's breathing in choked spasms and something in Indonesian. The screams that rear awaken to something else, free now of melody. The video ends.

— Man, still nothing.

— You don't think that was weird?

— I mean, it was all running.

Crude CG and makeup zombies reach out in plastic gestures against toy guns and amusement park grins until they go black. Subscribe.

— Yeah, but that didn't sound normal.

— Probably the audio. What's a normal scream anyway?

Did you see it?

— This is so annoying. Just one clip of someone getting eaten is all I want.

He goes back to his phone, and I'm back to mine.

> Yeah, that did seem like more than just panic.
> What do you think?

— Should I text Mom and Dad?

He smirks.

— You really want to do that?

— Well, it is news.

— Sure, if you want to get them worked up over how gullible you are.

— You mean like you?

— Hey, I'm just having fun, remember? You want to tell them how maybe zombies are real, be my guest.

— Fine.

The chat bar pulses ocean blue in wait. Its line goes too short in either direction beneath the used up words of another time zone. Here. Happy little buzzes cascade through on their own.

> Same.

> I'm finishing up at the gym.

> Miss you, Imy.

The next bite is all limp, lasagna layers of bran mush that go squish in your mouth. A couple more bites and it'll be buried at sink. The water's been ready.

> Hey, Imogen.

> How'd I do?

A photo of Crissy's sexy, cute, but also undead unicorn from Halloween. My thumbs thwack back the words from seeing, not clicking the link that follows.

> <3
> Hi Crissy! Lol. Yeah, it's pretty freaky.

Are you started yet?

The Mom and Dad group chat is still empty with its words.

TV drops its people giving reactions to their reactions for a roadside swell of bodies surging on foot. They're all coming to the camera and hurrying past like there's a gate. The feeling of something charging down sticks with them.

<3

Yeah, this internship is AWESOME.

Loving NYC! :D

Sorry, Jim, we've just received word that the president is about to address the nation. We'll go to there now.

There's a blank podium and a slow, suited walking up in camera shutters.

My fellow Americans. As many of you may know, last night, crisis struck the island nation of Indonesia. A new kind of disease has emerged there, bringing with it pure chaos. People turned berserk against each other in ruthless acts of violence. Neighbor against neighbor. Family member against family. And those who try to help only become its next victim.

With the information that we have, I can with certainty confirm to you, the American public, the serious nature of this situation. Thus far, anyone affected appears to fall into a senseless rage, losing their will, their very self, as they go on to attack and to kill others indiscriminately. Loved ones. Young and old alike.

What we are witnessing is something worse than a civil war. Our hearts go out to the good people of Indonesia. And to them I have one message: We are here to help.

Whatever the cause, which we will find, the entire world now faces something that can strip away our very humanity. It's an enemy armed only with hands and teeth. An enemy that tears its victims limb from limb. We're seeing cities turned into armies overnight. Armies of.

He swallows, wrinkles unyielding.

Of regular people.

But I am also here to give hope. Hope against this dread news. We will not stand idly by. We will not leave this problem to someone else. We will treat this as the threat that it is. For the good of the world, this bedlam must not continue. And it must never be allowed to set foot on American soil.

We will act swiftly. We will gather the world's brightest minds to find a cure. We will mobilize the most carefully orchestrated aid deployment history has ever seen. And we will use the full strength of the American military as necessary to keep the world we live in safe.

The people of Indonesia are suffering terribly, and our hearts go out to them.

Thank you.

A roar of flashes and questions takes him as he fails to wave.

— He meant zombies. He meant to say zombies there, didn't he?

The brown, sogged bowl is still ready to go. New voices are picking up.

My screen's still black.

SHOPPING

THE PEOPLE past the glass try their way down Geary. There's no downtown purpose or the staggered leisure of Fillmore, Noe. The street-bound doing's tight to overcast and cement.

We come stopped where someone old and half a ball is readying to cross. Her cart's nudged by her nose, face beneath a derby with some sort of flower on it. The beauty's there and gone in the constant shuffling for vegetables.

We drive before she does anything.

— So where did you want to go?

— I don't know. Where do you need to go?

— I don't need to go anywhere. I'm doing this for you. Don't you want some summer clothes?

The temperature's left on cold.

— Yeah.

— You okay? Did you get enough to eat?

— Yeah, I'm fine.

The door doesn't give much room.

— I'm just distracted.

— Distracted by what? Are you really too brain-dead to spend some time with me?

She looks.

— It's not like you were exactly pushing yourself this semester.

— Geez, Mom. It's just weird with the whole outbreak thing.

The road hands us one part of town for another.

— Oh, that. It sounds bad, really unfortunate. But what a stupid reason to make us go to war. They can't even say what it is they're fighting.

— Wait, war?

— Did you hear what that guy said? He called it a civil war, and now we're involved. It's none of our business if people are causing trouble over there.

— I mean, it's a metaphor, Mom. The thing's contagious.

Her fingers splay dark and flaying.

— Yes, a mysterious disease. Better go rally the troops. If there's something that really makes people go crazy, what good will soldiers do anyway? All they can do is kill the sick people. And what happens when they get infected? They'll start shooting each other. It's fuel to the fire either way. No, it's just some sort of power grab. They only do what makes them more money.

The brushstrokes over her eyes arch as sharply as they can to me, brow taut from furrows.

— But it needs to be contained.

— It already is. But no, our big, macho president wants to send our people. Our boats and planes. See? It doesn't make sense. They just want us scared while we cheer them on like idiots. It's people fighting like always, you'll see.

Mom's knuckles are tight and white where they are. There's a slight jitter with her elbows winnowed alone at the base of the wheel.

— Yeah, maybe.

Oil black jacket. Hoodie that's embedded with brown and brown. A puffy coat and the sheen of a penny nobody's touched. The way bodies stay bent with no one to turn the hanger back again.

Shouting starts down the street. Someone hobbled locks all face to someone who might have recently been called young, now a mix of lost identity. It's a sound I've never used or had used towards me. The hailing's there to slip as easily into cackles as it can blows. The exhaust-parched throat keeps on, and Mom and I are on our way to spend a few hundred dollars. At least it'll be on something I like.

The sun cuts out as we drop into the garage, and Mom rushes through the gap where there's no telling if someone is right there in front of you.

The golden doors of the first store are too heavy to stop from coming back at me.

— Is there anything that I can help you find?

— We're just looking.

— Sure, just let me know.

Mom shoulders her bag forward, keeping it tight to her chest.

— Actually, we'd like to see your day dresses. And the material shouldn't be too thin. It's for my daughter.

— Sure! I'd say most of our newest designs have a nice bit of summer flow to them. Rustic, peasanty patterns are what's in right now. They're really fun. But if that's not enough, you'd probably like what's over here.

They look to me.

— Sounds good.

She goes in a bounce.

— You know, I really like these pimpernel ones. They're enough to shield you from the wind. But don't they just drape too? They really look great with some brown stockings.

Her eyes beam darkly at me while parts reach in whisker twitches. Above's a mane that takes living with. The red shape has the rest down to a strain.

— What about that one, white with the leather, what is that, a gorget?

Her laugh breathes quick.

— We just call it a bib, although I like the way you think. It's faux. Rather Grecian huntress, isn't it? That one's on sale too since it's still from our winter collection, but here you could really keep wearing it all year round. Looks great with the right jacket too.

— Can I try it on?

— Sure, what size are you?

— Two.

— Okay, we might still have that. Let me set you up in a room.

I step past the curtain and pull my way out of jacket, boots, shirt, and jeans. They hang on the hook like pelts, ready to get me through snow again. There's something greasy all over about me in the mirror, my lacy, worn-down underwear and strangers taking up the same air a few steps away. Feet go through first, and what's left of the nail polish from Brunswick looks back, a scraped and outgrown orange red. They make an uneven smile, clownish up through the circle of otherworldly white. I wriggle each stretch of the dress up past my hips and onto my waist, and the heavy golden zipper bites me snugly in.

The gorget's old and new, something kept already there from before. Tight to a turtleneck as Mom's wedding cheongsam. A milk chocolate layer splits in spiderwebs of cappuccino. There's a weight, fingers to collarbone. The black of my hair lashes at the surface and cuts its own profile, adding something new. Something mine.

The ripples take each of my movements. The bust has an added texture, close to houndstooth, luminescent and chiseled from ivory and pearls. Its firmness gives me a nice shape beneath the brown. I feel the dress up and down, something saved for a hidden moment when Aidan is here.

— Wow, you look like an Amazon.

— Neat, huh?

— Where are you going to go dressed like that?

— Mom, it's really cute.

— You look good. I just don't understand when you are going to wear something like that.

— I don't know, just whenever.

— If I get that, it'll sit in your closet.

I keep her from turning aside.

— No it won't, I promise. I'll wear it out of the store if you want.

— Oh God, not in those shoes.

Her laughing is more of an eheh than a heheh, still a world away from haha. The worn-in space of it bears down, but there's nothing cutting, even if it comes at my expense. Her chin dips through watermarked cheeks, making her smile wax fuller and still small at the angle. She looks up from the slant as though it's my joke that's caught her unawares.

— Okay, but don't you want something more? Like this?

— No, I really like it.

She looks back at what's in her hand.

— This one's nice too.

I set up to take a picture back in the room. The marionette strut of my arm puts only the dress in frame. It's downward and accentuating. The last bit of mobility clicks. Send to Aidan. ;-)

They're all at the register with no one on the floor. The rest of the store is empty as people dart in the aquarium outside. One of the girls is caught on nothing, another relaying it all. The one who helped us is barely smiling in our direction. She stays the whole way over until the dress is there on the counter.

— So it's a match?

— She likes it.

Mom puckers over a smile.

— I bet you look stunning!

— Thanks.

She begins the dance of folding, bagging, card taking, receipt pulling, receipt giving. Her pile of freckles leaves her bordering on palomino. The others smile back at us evenly, lips tight, eyes red at the rims. A phone is on the counter, and one fingers at it lightly. The other taps nearby with annoyance at anything. I arch my eyebrow, but she doesn't see or care. The girl from Rossetti hands us the bag. We get a wordless crinkle of lips and teeth that's moused its way out. But her eyes still aren't at either of ours.

My home screen stays empty on smiling Aidan.

DE YOUNG

— So how the hell do we have zombies now?

— I know.

— I mean, it's bad enough that every show is zombies this and world ending that. Now it's actually happening?

— I still don't get how it's real.

— Right? Like what, is it a parasite? Does the virus come with a little defibrillator? And are we really that appetizing to them? I mean, you and me, sure. Who wouldn't want a bite of us? But hordes of corpse-monsters ready to consume all of society as we know it? Now that's going a bit far.

The flat stretch he makes of far knocks my laughter out in bubbles.

— I don't know about you, but I'd prefer to remain uneaten.

— Oh, me too, but won't fault them. Of course we'd get those pulseless hearts pounding.

— So that's your great plan; you and I get the zombies hot and bothered?

— I wouldn't knock it till you've tried it.

A phone's thrown across the room and a woman just bends without it. When she doesn't move, someone old and local brings it back to her, balancing his tray.

— So how'd you find out, Imogen?

My slouch doesn't take me anywhere.

— Nothing special, just a dozen notifications shouting that the world was over.

— Oh, well, my story is funnier. I was taking a shower, and my mom starts pounding on the door, saying that if I don't hurry up and get out right now, I'll make her late for work. And she doesn't stop either when I yell back for her to just tell me what it is. So I jump into a towel with conditioner in my hair, and she just tells me that it's zombies. They say it's zombies now in Indonesia. And then she hugs me while I'm wet and trying to keep my towel up. So I just say, "Oh, I'm sure they're not that bad," like it's the flu or something. And she looks at me like I'm her idiot son and tells me I'm probably right. And then she runs off to work with her shirt wet.

— Well, that's, um, touching.

— You know, if she could have waited for just, like, five minutes, I think I still might have her respect. And that hug would have been so much better than the one that's burned into me now.

The rubbery curl of his lips catches on his smile.

— Aw, Wes, I can hug you if that'll make you feel better.

— Well, you did just give me one. But okay, I'll take seconds.

We get up from the cafeteria chairs and let them make their awkward screeches. The hug's chest forward with our arms doing most of the work. The childishness goes to the others around us, and their audience makes it hum.

— So tell me, how's boyfriended life?

— It's good. Aidan's fine; he's Aidan.

— What does that mean? He's Aidan?

The woman at the table is still there.

— It means long distance sucks. All the good, new parts of you are frozen.

— Aw, well, aren't you the smitten kitten?

The move builds pillars into his shoulders that stay crossed with his arms.

— You said he's coming here?

— He'd better.

— Well, we should meet up. Just tell him to get flight insurance.

Air puffs out across my teeth.

— He's waiting to figure out his schedule since he's helping out at his dad's firm. At least he has something to do.

— I don't know about you, but right now all I'm good for is a few months of absolute nothing.

The chair doesn't give, and he slips back from leaning with a start. Our giggle brambles over the hard, geometric surfaces around us and slips out of sight.

— So, what, does that make him the prelaw type?

— What do you mean? Like, litigious?

— Yes, Imogen, would you call him litigious?

I enunciate my words back at him.

— No, I would not call him litigious, Wesley.

— No? Because I've been getting some real straitlaced vibes from the guy so far. He hasn't been too into the rules of a party game or talking about any Supreme Court decisions, has he?

— No.

— Really? No SCOTUS or POTUS talk yet?

— What's that?

He leans back.

— Oh dear.

— I mean, he's been taking econ and poli sci.

— Okay, I get it. So you've been dating your mother.

— Oh God, you're bad!

I swat at him, and the air is ready for much more.

— Wait, how is it that you don't know SCOTUS?

— I don't know. She never talks about work. And if anything, I'm more into my dad's stuff.

Servers bring and carry off food, black as houseflies.

— Okay, fine, you just tell me what he's like, then.

— He's great! I think you'd like him.

— Well, he must be a lot of fun if he can keep up with you.

— Yeah, he is. He's sweet. I don't know. We just click. Like, close without it taking any kind of effort click. You know?

He shocks nacreous at me.

— Oh love, it's always effort to win people over this hard.

— Well, you are charming.

— I am, thank you.

— But he's, I don't know, someone I feel at home with.

— That sounds cozy.

— Yeah, he's my old leather chair.

— Old?

— Well, familiar.

— Okay, so we're smoking cigars and drinking brandy in the dorm room, then?

Long fingers twirl the air into a snifter. He laughs too much.

— No, he's a regular guy. Sometimes he parties with his guy friends and I stay out with my girls. Or we go off on little adventures together. Normal college stuff.

— Play sleepovers too?

— Yes.

My eyebrows join in the answer.

— Well good, you need some shiny new fun in your life now that we're on different coasts.

— I have fun, Wes.

The white undersides of his eyes roll wild.

— Imogen, you asked that we meet at a museum.

— Oh shut up, you know you wanted to come too.

— I did. I just also want to get you out. Have a drink?

— No ID.

— Oh, come on. I know a guy.

— You know a guy.

— I know plenty. Of guys.

He bubbles and I bubble into laughter. I ditch the empty coffee for the crumbs of carrot cake that Wes got to have more of than me.

His fingers run through the length of his hair, and he looks down briefly as the blades flop back along his scalp. He stays there, blond as the sun.

— So do you want to actually go see some art now?

— Well, we did pay to be here.

— But who says money matters anymore?

— I think the zombies have to actually be here, Wes.

The woman just looks normal now. I could check my phone but follow Wes to the hallway, where the Wayne Thiebauds can be seen by everyone exiting the bathroom.

We walk over the muddy agriculture and get straight to the cityscape. The way he dodges the responsibility to actually paint the city is just funny. We're thrown out by a triangle that has the painting half filled with warm, steel-blue highway. In a bad seat, and we lost the view. The interesting bits are left to scuffle over each other for our attention, the ruddy hillside, the other curve of high-way, the tower that's made from bathroom blocks of blue-green glass.

The bit of road that's there is a delightfully impossible vertical stretch that stands right up like another tower. Only the roads here can drive straight into the sky or deep down to the earth like that. The street anchors everything. All the angles sink into it, make it a pit. I have to fight away the rest of the painting just to get there. Everything else keeps buzzing around me, wanting to be let in. If I could just rip the highway from the canvas, I might get to what matters here. Where everything's headed.

— Where do you think those trucks are going?

— The trucks? I don't know. Nowhere. They're right where they are.

— Yeah, but, okay, fine, don't play my game.

Wes looks sour to the coats of people not far off.

— They're going to deliver Campbell's soup cans to Andy Warhol.

Ooh, well, I think they're full of toys, but they're all defective rejects. Makes it nice and gritty, right?

— That'd make for a great title. Gritty Defective Reject Toys Headed to Orphanage.

— You should be an artist, Imogen.

— Right, because that makes sense now.

His buoyancy comes adrift at the center, elbows to fingertips.

— Well, we're still here.

He jumps back close.

— You want to go play Indiana Jones in the Mayan and Aztec art?

— You have your bullwhip?

— Oh, you know it.

The lighting grows warm and dim in the plasticization of some used-up ritual. The room is brown with vessels, figures, everything detailed over and over with the same slugs of clay. Wes pulls me to the stub of a ceremonial knife that shows obsidian and turquoise.

— Hey, maybe they're white walkers. Should we take it?

My laugh lingers in the hollow till the pieces fall back into dustiness.

— I don't know, the blade is well-set, but it's pretty much an old tooth.

— But magic.

— Well, if what it is melted itself free out of Antarctica, we're coming back.

— Deal.

We continue in the artifacts. Wes leans close but doesn't whisper.

— Won't take much for these pots and wall chunks to slip back into ruin.

He stays between joke and regret. I go to the next piece.

— Well, it's not like we haven't seen the movies. Where's it actually end? Bombs can't stop what could always happen. And a cure's not going to ever get worldwide.

A clay dog stays on prongs between us.

— I mean, do you see how people've been? No one wants to even be here. It's like we're all afraid of each other.

— Okay.

Wes shines wet at me in the temple lighting. I move into his ribs and merge us along, coupled.

— Anyway, I guess this would be a funny site for whoever survives.

He squeezes me back, and the next room's clogged with colors and saurian twists of glass. It's all play, and no part of it shakes the weight of a price tag sticking somewhere underneath.

A Klimt blanket of metal tabs weaves the wall in ripples. In my face is a cube of suspended char, stopping me. Each black piece hangs from its own absent string, shattered and filling the space of a cell.

— Speaking of ruins.

— Yeah.

Wes fingers the placard on the wall.

— It says it's from a burnt-down church in the South. Arson.

We can't move to its sides, but we try.

— I really like how it raises everything up in a way you could never see. It all belongs in a dump from decades ago, right? But here it is.

— It's the junkyard Matrix.

— I kind of wish I could just walk right through it.

— Uh, I see nails.

He gulps the would-be pain as I'm still at the edge. Every part's smashed.

— It's like that woven foil. I think that's made from wrappers or something. It's all violence, waste that they're creating from. They found a way to make something ruined work, right? Maybe we can too.

Wes's eyes explode back at me.

— So we hash together installation art from zombie parts? Ooh, I know. We put half a dozen disembodied zombie heads on the wall so people can watch them snap and stuff. Seven deadly sins? Wait, that is what happens to them, right? The heads stay alive?

— Ugh, I hope not.

What's ahead is too small and simple to get us forward. We turn back.

— There's just got to be a way to adapt, right?

— I'm fine so long as we don't end up in a gallery ourselves.

He stays for more from me, all soft in the gap.

— I'm sure that we can find a way to make it through whatever this is, Imogen.

Something tugs at my pocket.

— Oh, that's my dad.

— Ooh, good luck.

The buzzing grows until the foyer swallows it and me in its leviathan din. Everything is scrubbed clear to white, ahead and above.

— Hi Dad.

— Imogen, hi.

His voice becomes a tunneled storm.

— I imagine you know the news now.

— Yeah, it's pretty crazy.

— Yes, crazy's a good word for it. So are you at the de Young right now?

— Yeah, I'm out here with Wes.

— Oh, I hope he's doing well.

— He's fine.

— What about you? Are you doing okay?

People break their color again and again into the greyed white.

— Yeah, sure, I'm fine. It's not like the zombies are actually here, right?

I stop face-to-the-brightest-part, leaving the glare where it comes.

— Right, well, good. Don't stay out late, okay? We need to all be here for dinner.

— Yeah, that sounds good.

— Good, okay, well I just wanted to check in on you. We haven't had the chance to talk much since yesterday, but I want you to know that everything's fine. Okay?

— Okay Dad, I know. We'll figure it out.

— We will.

The burrowed noise circles in on itself.

— Okay, enjoy yourself. Tell Wes I say hi.

— I will.

— I love you.

— Love you too.

Wes is waiting with his smile spread to its corners.

— Good?

— Yeah, he's just checking in. Get to have a family meeting tonight.

— Fun.

He doesn't let the word end.

— Just remember to bring your serious face. They don't like it when you have more fun than them.

We head out.

— Yes, must not joke ourselves to death. First rule of the new era that I guess we have to get set in stone.

We leave behind the complex that's its own copper monument. The tower winds above the tree line like something built for the future.

FAMILY MEETING

— I REALLY THINK that everything is going to be just fine.

He keeps us both in the same look.

— Dad, you don't have to sugarcoat it. We know how zombies work.

— Oh, and just how do they work?

— They take over one way or another. Things break down and we have to be ready to live in a world where it's every man for himself.

The smile lies forgotten in the undergrowth of his beard.

— Well, yes, they do love showing us that in movies. And I'll grant you, Jake, that we do have to prepare for some of that possibility. But have you stopped to consider our own real circumstances here?

The wire frames are parentheses around his eyes.

— Just because they're on the other side of the world right now doesn't mean they won't get here.

— It doesn't, but we aren't dealing with something intelligent enough to chase us all down by boat or plane, right? They can't wage a global war. They're stupid and slow because all their good parts have died. And more importantly, they're completely isolated from the rest of the world. So how are the zombies actually going to get here? The second something smells bad you know they'll pull a kill switch somehow. It's not like they're counting who's innocent.

The words stay past their saying.

— Have either of you ever looked at what actually happens to the human body in modern warfare? I don't. Recommend it. But trust me, it gets obliterated. There won't be anything left that's biting.

And it would take an extraordinary string of bad luck for this epidemic to spread anyway. Perhaps it slips into the rest of Indonesia, and that would be terrible. But do you think mainland China or Australia or Japan are going to just let it come to them? Not a chance. Obviously it's a humanitarian issue, but an actual apocalypse? We love to think about it, but that won't make it happen.

Dad sits back for us to say something. Jake stays clenched with listening, and it's me.

— But anything could still go wrong. And it's not like anyone has experience with this. Fighting zombies.

— I do. I mean, online and stuff. And there's that CDC zombie containment strategy. Might have been a joke, but I know it's real.

Jake smiles unlooking at us. The weight in Dad's fingers splits fanned.

— Nothing is ever perfect. We still have to trust that everyone involved is doing the best they can.

— Either way, we're just watching.

He swells closer.

— And that's difficult to admit. But I think that we can let ourselves feel confident in the hands that it's in. All that ridiculous military spending has got to be good for something, right?

Dad's mouth is on the cusp of a laugh that he keeps onto.

— I mean, I think Jake and I mostly just don't want to be left in the rush.

Dad drones back in, half to himself.

— Don't worry, the world's not about to run out of canned goods. Even if supply chains are stalled, we'll still be getting whatever's vital; it's fine. The corporations understand that this isn't a going-out-of-business sale for them. It never is. Zombie preparedness will just be a new and exciting shopping category. It's a fad.

He's unmoored in his stillness.

— Well, what are we going to get?

— Food, water, outdoor supplies. You don't need me to tell you what will be good to have lying around. But it's not going to matter, you'll see. People will find some staple to freak out about. Then the media will keep shaking the same stick at us until they get something else.

— So, what, we should do nothing?

His lips get to his teeth.

— No, it's important for you both to feel safe. But I do not want either of you to get caught up in the panic right now; that's my point.

— Okay, so when are we going?

He winces.

— Well, unfortunately, this little crisis has made things hectic for both your mother and me. Hopefully she'll be home soon, but she has too many clients suddenly trying to change things. People backing out when they shouldn't. I don't know, but it's not fun. And I'm already getting calls from concerned parents trying to bump up their sessions and get more hours in. It's going to be a lot worse, but I'll do what I can. Everyone will have to make sense of a world in which zombies exist. Children are no exception.

— Or maybe it'll be bad for business. Depressed kids will become what's normal.

Dad holds the O of his mouth back from curling.

— Now why would you make a joke like that, Imogen?

His face narrows to a page-worn point.

— You and Jake have nothing but free time without school. You can take the SUV tomorrow for whatever it is that you think we need. I'll leave plenty of cash. But if people are being stupid in any way at all, you leave.

— We will.

A fingered T comes gelled to his brow.

— Just think of this as another earthquake emergency kit. And that's never been a big deal, right? Zombies will be the same, we just need time. No one's preparing for the end of the world. We just have to weather the mania for now.

A smile grazes across his lips. He's ready to go.

— So where?

— Honestly, I think you two can figure it out.

Jake and I look without seeing each other.

— What about guns?

— What about them?

— How are we going to get them?

Dad sighs and rubs behind his glasses. His sand-and-earth beard is made ruddy in the dining room light.

— I've been watching, Jake, things aren't going that bad. Even with the disease here, we wouldn't fall into anarchy and martial law right away. There are steps. And the barriers are insurmountable.

— But regardless, self-defense is, like, the main thing, right? All we have are kitchen knives.

I fill forward too.

— And we can learn proper gun safety; it's not like we're going to be playing with them or anything.

— Then get an axe or something tomorrow. Don't worry about guns.

— But now could be our only chance.

He gets up without the room to pace.

— I don't think either of you realize where you are. If things do get bad, do you really think that the city's the worst place to be? Sure, if the disease appears right here, right now, then yes, we'll be in incredible danger. But that's not happening. We have plenty of time to prepare, and we moreover have the infrastructure and the social impetus to do something about it.

This is going to become one of the most protected areas in the world. Seriously. Not only are we in a country that's built on war, we live somewhere that the government will have to protect. However much the world might change, the Bay is going to remain a lifeline.

We're lucky to have a very wealthy population with a lot of corporate interests invested here. As nebulous and malevolent as the tech giants are, the people working there happen to call this area home.

Honestly, I can't think of anywhere else I'd want to be. There's a lot that the government gets wrong, but they do their jobs; it's in their best interest. What's actually dangerous are the things people do when they're afraid. I'm far more worried about overreactions and overreaches of power, not its collapse. Or seeing a zombie from Indonesia running around downtown. Come on, it's ridiculous, right?

He's set for something more than yes.

— I guess, but we don't know what's going to happen.

— I know, Imogen. And I wish we didn't have to face this. It's all just horrible. That's why I want us to focus on what's positive. Dire as it is, everything here is promising. What do you guys think?

Our plates sit there, and I need more water. Jake stops fingering at the metal tab and unslouches himself back together.

— I think we need guns.

— Yes, well, there's a lot more that we can get first. What about you, Imogen?

Our eyes only meet partway. Shifting doesn't get us closer.

— I mean, I guess we're okay, but I don't even know what the best case scenario really is. No matter what, it's out there.

— Imogen, none of this is best. It will all just take time, and time is one thing that we have.

He reaches out to get a hand on my shoulder, his mouth lined flat. It starts to warm me just before it's gone.

— Well, thanks. I just thought we should plan out what we need. And Mom's not even here.

— If you want to write out a list, I'll be happy to look at it. But I'm confident in you, Imogen. You can do this. And your mother and I really appreciate it.

— I know.

— Great. Be sure to thank her later for dinner. It's hitting everyone in their own way right now.

NORTH

It's backed up. Way up. Nothing but a steel snake ahead creeping along the empty lane right next to us. And past that is being fought an ongoing battle over pavement.

— Maybe we should try somewhere else.

Behind us more are coming in. The windshields of parked cars flicker dimly back from the shoulder, the reflective lenses of crumpled forms still on their way to the top. No climb or Everest. Craned over at you, saying nothing. Up.

— There's room.

— What?

— There's room right there.

I put it in reverse and cut backwards. The car behind me is close, but the driver just watches as I pull forward and back again, forward and back out of the line until we drop squarely into the gap.

— You're going to hit!

— Am not.

Cutting the wheel brings me half in line, but it's too tight to fit and I tap the bumper that's there. I go again, but this time gun it right into the curb. A sharp bump before I can stop, and the rear cradles partway into the cyclone fence. Nose is still fighting the traffic that's not letting me back in anyhow.

— You totally scratched it!

— Yeah, well, we're here.

— You could have killed someone.

— Are you coming?

The grey damp tackles us, keeping the store from sight. Jake catches up from checking the back, but he only keeps pace behind. Hands in pockets. It's a place for passing through. Maybe some too-serious runners, but that'd be it. There's no biking under the colossus of Golden Gate, no tourists zooming by in yellow little Disneyland cars blasting tour guide blather on open air. No one's out walking but us.

— So camping supplies, right?

We duck in on dirt before reaching the deadlock. Cold metal keeps heavy ahead, lined to park, lined to get in. People pushing with their faces stacked.

The warehouse is bustling frame-to-frame from its oversized entrance. Each rack of outerwear has its own crowd trying things on and testing the quality. Only the sports gear sits untouched. Jake's back abreast with me.

— Man, it's not like any of these jackets are zombieproof.

I push through, sidestepping the rocks of people in the way. Jake catches in the counterflow as I break to the camping and mountaineering. It's stripped. What's scattered on the shelves doesn't hint at what was there. I bounce between. A torn open box for a lantern that must be missing something. No more pocketknives. A few waterproof travel sacks. People are struggling to pull down the last of the sleeping bags that are pinioned to a rack that's fighting them. Too many for it. The only canteens left are flasks.

— Imogen, come on, what are we going to do with any of this?

— We might have to run.

— And what here is going to make a difference? Man, there aren't even bats.

— I don't know, just stuff.

— What we need is a real stockpile and a better way to fight. Everyone here is just trying to look good for the apocalypse.

There's something on the floor half hidden under the shelf. It's a compass complete with signaling mirror. I hold on to it and keep looking.

— You actually want to make us wait in line for that?

— We don't have one.

— And we can order it online. If the zombies showed up right now, the last thing we'd need to know is where's north.

I hold it. Someone is grabbing every rain jacket, ready to corner the market on Gortex, outfit a small army against bad weather.

— We need to get food and weapons, that's it.

— I'm not leaving with nothing, Jake.

My hands are full on the plastic.

— Fine, come on.

We're headed towards a man who's slowed so that we don't meet. He has something heavy and goes another way into the racks.

The line curves into the main walkway. Jake and I wait, untalking. I look and look at the thing that could save my life a dozen times from now. Not one version takes form.

AIDAN

— HEY BABE.

— Hey, what's up? How are things going over there?

— Um, okay. I just needed to go for a walk. Figured I'd call and make you keep me company.

— Well, I'm happy to do that.

— Good. I miss you.

— And I'm glad to be missed.

I grip the phone snug to my cheek. The hard edge presses back.

— So did you get what we were talking about?

— Yeah, as best as we could.

— Anything cool? Ready to start bashing some heads?

— Uh, well, nothing like that yet. I think there's a hatchet somewhere and our old bat from little league.

An arterial tumble fights loud on the other side.

— Oh man, no, you have to do something. We're at least tripling what we have. Wish I could just send you some. I mean, maybe I can.

— No, don't worry. It's only a couple of months here anyway.

Aidan stops, stepped away.

— I looked it up for you earlier. You know there's an archery store in your neighborhood? Just go there tomorrow. Or now.

— Yeah, maybe. Archery could be fun.

— It's definitely sustainable. Reach is the first thing, right?

My phone vibrates and I stop to move it and maybe drop the call. The headline slips.

Breaking news: UND Virus confirmed in Java. City evacuates.

— Imogen?

THE SALON

— So MY DAD wants me to start making a zombie death machine with him.

Wes's hair is flung mail across his forehead. Around us, the coffee-house is spurred buzzing into the afternoon. The acidity of my sip has to move suddenly down or out of my mouth.

— Well, don't laugh.

— Sorry, I just pictured you in coveralls and grease.

— Whatever. You're just jealous of my sweet ride.

— I will be when you pull it off.

He cocks his eye.

— Don't worry, it'll happen. And then I'll just drive over a horde of zombies and come by your house. Toot toot! And you'll come running down, and we'll go out and kick all kinds of butt.

— Your zombie death machine goes toot toot?

— Yup, toot toot! What, yours doesn't?

We aren't the only ones laughing. A guy by the café window is making an ass of himself on the phone, loud and cackling dull over nothing. No one minds. The couple on the other couch continues their cuddle in front of us like we're their TV. The constant pounding of coffee in or out of metal has each of us riveted to this same spot on the street. Here, not elsewhere. Hot liquid spews and spurts in geological shifts. Beans find themselves caught up in a torrent that obliterates them and lays them back into silence. And people go for more.

— Well, that'd be pretty cool. I think you can do it.

— Yeah, I hope so. It's what he talks about now. He keeps drawing up different plans, looking into all the precautions to make something that moves mow through actual tons of rotting human flesh. There are actually some really great forums where people are figuring it out. Some site even says they're going to make a show out of it. Zombiedome. Original, right?

— Well, I'm glad that your dad is being proactive.

A smile ghosts across that he chases down, kills.

— Yeah, it'll be awesome. Plow up front. Some really good ventilation to keep the engine from getting clogged. Reinforced bars over all the windows. I just hope he doesn't blow the rest of my college fund.

— Well, it's not like you're not going back or anything.

— You aren't going to finish that?

— Uh, no.

He dives bird-out-of-nest for the plate.

— You sure? There are starving zombie children in Southeast Asia. They could really use you fattening yourself up a bit.

— Something tells me they won't mind me looking like this, either.

— Your loss. Or theirs.

Wes crams the whole end of the chocolate croissant down in one bite. Flakes stick to his lips that he emolliently slides back in with his thumb, grinning. I meet it but break.

— God, it's so stupid, though.

Wes looks up like I've just pointed out that he has food on his face, which he does.

— What?

— That the thing it all comes down to is us becoming food.

— Well, yeah, sure, it sucks.

His shoes rise to the table.

— No, really, it's stupid. People are coming back to life again. That should be amazing. Even if it's not really that, it's at least proof that we can survive all sorts of things. But what do they do? What's the one thing that it's for? Eating people. Hmm, I wonder what that person tastes like? Oh, and that person over there, better try him too.

— Yeah, you'd think if anything it'd be about sex.

— It just doesn't make any sense. A reanimated corpse should be a vegetable, right? Not a bunch of cannibals all dogpiled together. Where do the ingredients for something like that even come from?

Metal slapsslapsslaps onto the counter.

— You mean besides bad horror movies?

— Yeah, at least ours could try to make sense. I mean, why go and eat people? What part about us coming back makes that our one thing to do? Are they really just mindless predators? Sure, I guess it wouldn't make for a very good movie if you could just throw donuts at them, but people are, like, the hardest thing in the world to eat.

Wes deals out a lazy stretch, jaw and brow.

— Apparently not?

— Compared to everything else we are. We're faster, smarter. We outgun them. I mean, sure, if you turned into a zombie right now, going after me would be easier than jumping on pigeons. But we're terrible food. So why? Why does the one part of us that comes back have to be so stupid?

— Who says zombies are predators, though? Or even really being stupid?

— Well, I'd love to see video of them doing anything else.

— Yeah, but predators aren't all that eat living things, right? They're in groups, not hunting packs. They just go after what's in front of them.

The body-bent damask leans into his backside, hues fleshed with age. And touching.

— Hunting as a predator is a lot different. It takes cunning. It's dangerous and risky. But it's a risk that animals have to take. Zombies don't eat for survival. I mean, they must need it somehow, but it's not to live.

He notices the last flake and gets it with his tongue.

My head shakes small, rolling onto more.

— But I don't get why if you were to take people and strip them down to their most barely alive point they would only want to eat us. I mean, look at our own development. Babies put everything into their mouths. It's all the same. So maybe one really would just eat someone whole if they were suddenly made capable of it. Like, a giant-sized, unstoppable killer baby. But if a dead person came back with that same kind of blank slate, some stripped down point of being human, what's actually going to make them so laser focused on us?

They're to their phones across from us.

— I don't know, Imogen. They could be eating other stuff too. It's not like zombies chewing rocks is going to get a bunch of views. Or maybe it is, but half that country's gone dark.

I have to suppress a small, acetic burp; I don't bring my eyes back up, and the bearings keep with me.

— I just don't get them.

The gone coffee was Indonesian. Your proceeds will help. When'd it get out?

— Look, don't think of this in terms of Kubrick. Get back to being all Romero with me. It's a virus, not regular people with messed up wiring. There's something clearly making them do all this once they've died.

— But a virus should just be wreaking its little havoc and leaving us for dead, right? Did whatever microbe it is just look one day at the person it killed and go, "You know, I really should start recycling?"

Wes laughs diaphragmed into the conversation nearby. It keeps going.

— Well, viruses are pretty simple things. They're sort of the most primitive form of life, or not even that.

— What, they're undead too?

—Just robots.

— Because they go beep boop and have flashing red lights?

He looks back-in-love at me.

— Because they're basically machines that carry genetic information. Cells live and grow. The most lifelike thing a virus can do is repurpose a cell's life systems.

— Like parasites.

— Well, maybe from our perspective, but a parasite is a life-form that gets its food and environment in a certain way. Viruses don't eat or grow or live in any meaningful sense. They infiltrate a cell, hijack its systems into making more and more viruses, and then the cell dies and sends out all the new copies of the virus to more cells.

— So then UND or whatever it is does the same thing, but now with our entire bodies? Taking us over, killing us, and using us to spread more?

The page of Wes's face flips back hard.

— No, maybe it looks like that, but that's something way out of their purview. They have their parts to target, but death's just collateral to them.

Someone's leaving behind us, leaning in too close.

— So there has to be something else if a virus is going to change our behavior.

— Yeah, or you know, bring people back to life. Maybe something hits our cognition, but it's silly watching anyone try to explain it. I found some guy who claimed UND eliminates the death gene and we should find a way to use it. I mean, what is that? I kind of wish it was a parasite from outer space, at least that would make some sense.

I'm flared back to the empty coffee. The words come one by one in stones.

— Or asteroids. Then the end would be certain, and we'd all go out together at once.

Wes sours as I keep going.

— I guess climate change would have been less helpful, fighting over water or drowning in it, whatever. But even if that apocalypse isn't the quick cause of our demise, ultimately we'd all be swallowed back up by the Earth that we've ruined anyway. Fits. Nuclear holocaust is pretty retro, but hey, can never count out the urge to go kill each other. We'd all realize that we're insects, and then squashed we are. But this way we don't even get the dignity of having our souls crushed. No collective "Well, this is it!" party. Instead, we get the fantasy. What we've wanted the shit out of, right? Zombies, freedom from society's burden, a new world where we can do anything. Really live. And it's killing us while we sit around and do nothing. It's like some sort of hokey curse.

My voice has changed somewhere close, more outside than me. The grease still shines on Wes's lips as they purse out, something to be thrust out of the way.

— Well, I'm making a car.

— Yeah, you are.

He looks somewhere distant and not at all here. The door swings, shuts.

— But you're right. I keep getting this sick feeling that all those people over there are being picked up one by one and bashed into each other like Barbie dolls. All for a bunch of broken plastic.

The flakes are stuck hard to the plate.

— Didn't you use to do that as a kid?

— Yeah, that's probably why.

— Death by Wes. Hadn't considered that apocalypse.

— I'm a strict but fair deity. Apparently I'm a bit racially focused too, but I'm sure I'll be getting around to some other countries soon enough.

— I'd like to think of it as getting to know the best vacation spots.

— Good, wouldn't want to offend you.

— Travel never offends me.

The people around us have shifted. They're older, more put together, but they're still the same ridiculous coffee grabbers from before. As ridiculous as us.

GOT A GUN

SOMETHING IS AT MY DOOR, pushing its way through in dim nudges. Near a knock as it creeps, there's no inviting and it doesn't ask. I move to get up at whoever's in on my nighttime privacy.

— Imogen.

— Why are you whispering?

— Mom and Dad. Can you come here?

I bound light across the carpet. It's colder out in the hallway. Jake takes us past their door. There's no gesture for me to stay quiet, but I do. We go to his room, where the only light in the house is still on. He looks pained at the gap behind me, which I shut. He's still hushed.

He looks to the door again. Without looking back, he crouches for the clutter of his bed. A flag wave of loose dark navy flaunts the sloppy boyishness that's left with his butt up in the air.

What he finds is a hard case that slides out like it needs dusting. After laying it flat on the clear part of his desk, he flips the heavy latches. He pulls out a gun.

— What are you doing with that?

— What do you think?

— I, I mean, how did you get that?

— Dave.

— So he just gave you a gun?

— No, I paid for it.

— Is that even legal?

— Yes, it's legit. I mean, it's not legal that I have it now, but Dave's dad is cool. He was hooking us up.

What's there sucks in the still-bright light around us. His fingers grip, already certain and there.

— What is it?

— It's a 9mm. He tried to talk me into getting a .38 caliber, but I wanted a little more stopping power.

The foam has room for a lone magazine with a bullet lunar on top.

— Can I hold it?

— Yeah, sure, but it's mine, remember.

He hands me the black thing. It's more plastic than metal, which has it too light.

— This way the ammo will be easy to find.

— Do you even know how to use it?

— He showed me, sorta. I don't know, we can sneak out to a range or something later. I still need to look up some stuff.

— Okay.

I bend the wand of it low. The sights are a plane I can't come to without putting it somewhere I won't.

— You can't tell Mom and Dad.

— Well, you can't just hide it.

— They'll take it away.

— They wouldn't do that.

— Are you kidding?

He's a worn coin back at me.

— Dad said it was okay.

— No, he was okay with me wasting time on the internet. He still wanted to be in charge, even if he'd never do anything to actually make it happen. If he finds out, he'll take it away and say it was for our own good.

— Well, maybe before.

— Things haven't changed that much.

— So you're just going to keep it under your bed?

— Why not? What if it's an emergency? What then?

Our ping-pong keeps going, factory puffed to an air-cut gap.

— But it's not like he said that.

— Well, we can't just let him. It's mine.

He's stolid with the thing unseen below.

— Which you bought with Mom and Dad's money.

— That they gave for us to use. Look, it's not that big of a deal. We have to get used to it; I just want to give them more time. That's all.

The gun has gotten damp in the palm of my hand, still there. Jake's downward glances finally stop once I put it back in the case.

— Fine, but you have to figure out the best way to tell them. They'll really freak out if Mom finds it while cleaning your room or something.

— When's the last time she did that?

— Jake.

The fire poker corners of him force flat, earnest. It doesn't stay.

— Yeah, when they're ready.

— Right.

We both drift a small step back, triangled to the case.

— But yeah, pretty cool, huh?

— Yeah, cool. Thanks, Jake.

— Sure. Feels good, right?

His eyes are cocktail-party-conversation-bright. He holds it down as it latches awkwardly, no longer quiet.

— Yeah, it does.

LAMELLA

— Well, they've always been after us.

Dad leans against the burgundy of his work chair until it finally hugs him. It grinds sharp underneath. I fold a leg in, cramped immediately to movement that I don't give.

— I guess there's monsters everywhere.

He regards me again.

— I'm not talking about having enemies, Imogen. They're our structure.

I don't know what to say next. Nor does he. He puts the mug down and looks at me.

— What I mean is they lay out the way in which we exceed ourselves, chase things past what's good for us.

— So, what, you think they'd like to go shopping?

I'm too soon into his buoyancy as it sea-rolls past.

— In a way, yes. Overcharging our cards isn't all that different from dying for a cause or mumbling, "Brains." But it's about how we're stuck to it. Not masochism, just the way in which we exceed ourselves. It's us at our most human.

He wants to smile.

— But how are zombies human? I mean, all it'd do is make you want to kill me.

He searches my look through what hurts, sets his path.

— It is a betrayal, precisely. Everything that we call human is stripped down to its inhuman element. They're our fundamental fantasy, to put it simply.

— You know, it's not actually simple if you have to explain it.

— Fundamental fantasy?

I keep blank at him.

— It's our coordinates. How we fill in the world around us. Powys called them life-illusions; I always thought that touched on something nice.

I try to talk through his thousands of pages.

— They're that, now, because they're real?

— No, they've been our fundamental fantasy. Fantasy's not an escape from reality; it's how we apprehend it, the very way that it's built. Often it's a defense formation to fill the yawing gap of whatever doesn't fit the normal run of things.

— Yawning?

— That too. It's how we manage to get some distance from the traumatic thing. Which is now much too close.

My coffee's downstairs and he's holding on to his. It moves.

— What do you think's the real reservoir when it comes to psychic trauma?

He waits as though there's something on the other side of what he's said. Like I have to find it, that it's mine, right in front of us.

— How's it a reservoir? I thought the real point about bad things is that they're dumb and horrible and we have to stop them any way we can. If there's a reservoir, we should destroy it.

— Because what trauma amounts to, Imogen, is psychic injury. It occurs unknowingly. It's not evil, it's not stress. We find things traumatic for structural reasons, and we're who we are because of it.

— But bad things happen.

— They do. And they shouldn't.

— So, you mean being scared to die?

— No, death is nothing. Psychically we've no room for it, and it's not the fear of us dying, now, that really bothers us.

— It bothers me.

— Yes, well, vale of tears. I'm not saying it can't happen. It can.

Water comes to the edge of his lids. He smiles.

— But death, scarcity, that's not what's new, Imogen. What lurks within the traumatic, down in its most fundamental, is simply ourselves, the way we're ill at ease with ourselves, how our wheels spin. So we push it off onto others, onto these living dead most of all. But that's not all there is to it. They're a pure screen for us, but they also touch the point at which we're open, the way in which we really do connect with one another.

Take the problem of desire. Since we can't properly account for what we want, we ask what it is they want. Just look at every drama and romance; it's the supreme difficulty of being loved. But zombies put this question back at us most of all. They're all surface, the what-do-you-want of other people shown in its horrible utmost. Really, it frenzies us, but that figure of someone else who knows is the one thing that brings consistency to the world. It's a fiction, sure, but knowing that only gets us so far. But now this doesn't fit the mold. We can't keep pretending that they know. They put it right back at us. I think. I think they really have done something. Overloaded what's been at the basis of all fantasy, all our constructed reality.

His eyes sink into the salamander layer of coffee. He swirls what's left, making it do something. Mom yells to Jake downstairs, and Dad waits for its meaning to pass through.

— So this is all just about someone who knows what they want? Like, more than us?

He puts the mug down and looks at me.

— Yes.

— I'm pretty sure they want to eat us.

— And how does that make you feel?

He bounces back, throws one leg up, and starts to grope the knee. There's no room for me to do the same.

— Oh, great. Best I've ever been.

I try to breathe out whatever's been put in my chest. Something solid and crammed in. I shift back.

— Are you trying to make a joke, Dad?

He ends what he's doing.

— Obviously they're undoing. Anything's undoing, it's not about what the object is; it's where it is, where it shouldn't be. And what a corpse is is precisely all object, object in its too-muchness. The fantasy, the means by which we function, can't hold it back. I mean, think of the news, how you find it so intolerable; its role is to keep psychic threats at bay, establish the space where the horrors are not. The real sign of its failure is your no longer turning to it.

A duty, still, for it sticks to his words. Our thread droops from what's further.

— What the corpse does, I think more than anything else, is put too much into reality. What they are, zombies, corpses, is the nonsensical support structure of making sense. We have meaning and language precisely because of this excess that can't be properly signified.

— So you really think we are who we are because of zombies.

— Yes! They're our support structure, exactly. But it's only supportive right on the outside. If they get too close, we're gone. In their stomach, turned into one of them, gone. But again, it's not simply about danger, it's their presence.

He runs his fingers slowly from beard to hair.

— They clear the field. Confront us with something we're not built to see. And this presents us both with risk and a radical opportunity.

— To all come together, just like you said we would?

— No.

The negation of any kind of bitterness holds hirsute.

— I mean, I want that, I do. But it's a complete clearing of who we are. Not the kind you get with all the fantasies about apocalypse. That's like pretending to wash away your own hands. You don't save the world by breaking everything down and living off the grid. That doesn't fix who we are. What the blockbusters are really after is the world without us, purified of our own antagonisms. Whatever's left afterwards is pure ideology. That's precisely the step to be avoided. What I mean instead is something radical, just different. We have to embrace ourselves, while the coordinates are changing out from under us most of all.

Lightness comes as though I can finally go. Although I stay.

— So what you really mean is now that they're here, we're actually no longer part of their human monsteryness.

He smiles.

— It won't be part of us. But yeah, it's more than just normalizing them. It's the way that we desire, how we all live and find meaning that's underway. Wherever it's headed, it's not all going to be walls and constant danger. What we'll do is work on it. It's not too bad, right?

The earth of his beard betrays depth, masking a forest in brief diorama.

I don't know what I'm doing with my lips.

SINGAPORE

It's been in my head all week. Snuck in without a name. Should be dancing. Take it somewhere dark and loud. Doing something that's leading to something, even when it's not. Or make an anthem of it. Sing until our throats hurt and people come looking. Out drinking and covered in just as much sweat as I am now. Next morning, find I'm number smudged and skinned on my knee.

The quiet, sexual graze roams across my body as I run straight past with the cars. Not looking and he's gone. Struggle with a few thumb swipes to kill what's next and bounce back to the beginning.

I push hard with the energy that I should have spent. The smacks echo before being swallowed back up by the estuary that comes churning from the bay. Heat and pressure's swelling in my chest, but I'm home already before it's finished. I'm slick all over. My phone spasms to congratulate me as my fill-in friend and personal trainer. Four and a half. Okay, now try it with zombies.

My legs wobble me back up on pool toys. Something's still aching there from yesterday. Shut down one pain by piling on another. Let it pick what shows.

— Imogen!

— I'm getting into the shower.

I stop and listen through the box of rainfall behind me. Whatever else Mom says must be more to herself than to me. The droning goes on until I finally shut the door and start to strip each spandex bit. Plainly there in the mirror, the slopes of my shoulders, breasts, and hips stand still as the terrain that only ever shows from highways or in the air. And around my navel, a soft little oasis that won't dry out, not really her hardened clay.

Nice that I'm getting a little sun. The brown on my shoulders reflects the mauve-and-toffee eggshells of my nipples. My chest looks right back, those eyes punctuated by the pale yellow absence of my sports bra yolk. Aidan still hasn't seen me this tan. Next week and it'll be him doing the staring.

After finishing with the fresh haze of heat and moisture, I go back downstairs, hair cold already. Mom stays still at the couch with her back to me.

— Imogen, your grandmother.

— What?

— Your grandmother. She is in trouble.

— I thought you said things would be fine with her staying.

We're hearing conflicting reports on the evacuation. All regions are now confirmed. Swells of infected have taken over city streets, swarming entire blocks. Singapore's prime minister has issued a state of emergency, asking people to seek out safe zones across the city however they can.

The wood-burnt sheen of fleas tumbles over each other, too far from the panic to keep their limbs from falling in invisible knots.

UND has broken containment. The blockades that have proven effective in Jakarta are yet to be seen here. Zones are overrun as people flee for their lives.

— Did you know?

— I wasn't really on my phone.

Is this confirmed?

The space tingles off camera.

I have just been handed a report that missiles have landed in parts of the city. Where from?

It changes. Stopped.

Again, the outbreak began less than an hour ago. We still do not know the extent of this attack, whether this is part of a targeted strike or more. Well, get some footage!

Eyes come back to us.

I cannot stress enough that this is an initial report.

— Your grandmother is fucked, isn't she?

— God, Mom. No, she's going to be fine. Hong Kong is still far away.

— Look how easy it is. It's just an hour, and the city is gone, just like that.

Where's our video?

— I think we should put her on a flight. She can come stay with us. We'll have to find her some assistance. But it'd be better than what anyone else would do for her.

— But they aren't going to let it reach Hong Kong.

— Sure they are. They can't do anything!

Courtney? Courtney, can you hear me?

— Well, I don't know, Mom. Maybe it is good that they're bombing it so soon. It's horrible, but at least they're doing everything that they can.

— It better work. I just want it to work. I'm glad that they are doing it.

A drop shoots down her cheek and onto her blouse before her eyes have a chance to well up. Her lips are clammed tight. I lean over to hug her shoulders. My chin hits her collarbone hard, and we keep the shock of it secret to ourselves.

AIDAN

— How have you been, Imy?

— Fine. Busy, I guess. Getting ready to go camping with Wes and Jake tomorrow.

— Really? I didn't know the three of you were a thing.

His smile reaches midway.

— Well, I promised they could laugh at me trying to start a fire. Maybe we can even forage. I still couldn't get into one of those classes where someone tells you what you can and can't eat, but I found this really cool visual guide of all the edible plants in Northern California. I figure we start slow and avoid the mushrooms. Get them to eat a dandelion, at least, maybe some bugs. There's some of it here too. Chickweed is supposed to be pretty good. Or wild rosemary. And there's Hottentot fig all over the beach. It's beautiful but super invasive, so bonus!

— Heh, well I wouldn't go picking through the gutter just yet. Don't want to end up poked by that other kind of needle.

The dumb intimation lingers on the screen and hangs there.

— I don't live in a bad part of town, Aidan.

— Yeah, but still.

His eyes and teeth glint blue from the black around him that's my evening to come.

— You know that if you really do end up nomad, hunting is the only way to get the calories you need. Otherwise your body'll be a wreck.

He glances offscreen. The end of it is dead black and right on top of him.

— Don't worry, we're bringing food too. I just wanted to see what I could find. Get the palate past the supermarket, right?

— Arugula not bitter enough for you?

He holds the smile low.

— I don't think it's all bitter.

— Oh, right. Ah, yes, this dirt crumble has such rich mineral overtones.

— Okay, Aidan.

— Well, come on! You can't expect to actually live off of grass, right? You're going to have to be willing to fight and kill at that point. Not just hide chewing on sticks.

The guidebook's at hand, close and dense in its plastic.

— God, Aidan, these are real survival skills.

— Yeah, for way down the line when the whole world is dead and it's just you. How are you going to make it there first, huh? Are you even thinking about what to do when they get here?

— Well, sure.

— Okay, so how do you get out of the city when people all around you are turning? How are you going to get away? What are you leaving with? Where do you even have to go?

— It depends.

— Oh right, plenty of time to sit back and ruminate about it.

There's heat left in the day, coming in.

— Well, there is! It's not like I can run drills. Who knows where it'll spread or even if it will in the first place?

— Oh, like it's not coming.

— It is and it isn't.

— Okay, so a ship of refugees is on course to San Francisco. One of them's pregnant and sweating. People think it's the stress, but really, she's hiding a cut that she got on the edge of a fence that was holding back a mob of them before it got cleared. She falls asleep and gets back up later, turned, and the entire ship goes up like kindling. Some fall off, but most are stuck in the hold as the ship keeps pushing until it's crashed right into Fisherman's Wharf.

My lids are locked from rolling.

— I don't think that's how navigating's supposed to work. And the virus doesn't live that long outside the body.

— Well, then, whatever. What are you going to do if you're the next Singapore?

— I don't know, run?

— Run, that's it?

— Or stay and wait it out, I don't know.

— So you stay. Watch everyone die from your window. Then what? Get bombed by your own government? Wait until you have no more food or water and get grabbed once you finally do something?

— So I'd be screwed just like anybody else, okay? Happy, Aidan? I just have to not be the person who has a ship full of zombies headed right to her. So what? Woo, then nuclear missiles wipe out every-thing between New York and DC! You're dead too. What a great game this is.

He bites and moves back, all of him in and unframed.

— No, I'm not happy. You don't get it. We're the lucky ones. They aren't. We are. We're lucky to have just a ship coming for us. We get to plan for it. Manage the risk. But if you aren't ready to fight not just them, but people too, what is sleeping out under the stars going to do for you? You need to stop having fun with it, Imogen. It's not fun. This is life or death. Yours, no one else's.

The air plant pulses as my fingernails hit the desk together in fours. Bright and quivering, its grey-white skin lustrous behind the screen's dark.

— I'm just doing what I can, Aidan.

— It's not enough! You should see that. Do you know how crowded the range is over here? Or how busy it is in MMA?

— Everything's not survival of the fittest. It's just not.

— That's easy to say now.

— No, really. It is more about luck.

His wince takes him drifted, and he almost goes to whatever's there. Something better.

— You can't just give up.

— I'm not. I'm willing to do it, but it's not all bullets and bunkers. You just have to be good at something.

His drive's cut. What's left coasts closer without me.

— Teamwork breaks down the moment it starts to cost something. You can't get hurt, Imy. But you're the one who has to actually stop it. I'm trying to help you.

We're parsed together. And nothing happens.

— Well, there's no helping this.

— I'm sorry. I wish that I could still visit.

— It's not your fault. They didn't cancel school yet, at least.

— Yeah, like that matters.

— At least it's still an option for you.

— Yeah, okay.

He looks away again.

— What is it?

— Nothing, just the dog wants to go out. Sorry, I should get going. Talk to you tomorrow?

— Yeah, sure.

— Okay, sorry, bye.

The window cuts fully black and then closes itself. The plant is gone to yellow in the setting sun, just like the ones that dried out. But even dead they're mostly the same, just the reminders of what you didn't do.

TOILET PAPER

— I was in the grocery store yesterday. And there was this woman buying up as much toilet paper as she could carry. I mean, the shelves were light, but she wanted it all. She already had one cart full and was working on a second while, I don't know, trying to hold on to more of it with her hands. It was weird. And this other lady comes up to her and starts yelling that it's not all hers to buy and that she has to let others have some too. And the toilet paper lady just tells her, "You don't know! You don't know!" again and again, like that was it. So an employee comes over and says that she can only check out with one shopping cart, which I don't think is a thing, but anyway. The toilet paper lady just shakes her head and tries to carry off both carts, but the other lady reaches in and stops her. So the two women start fighting and tugging over the cart, and the guy working there jumps in to make the first lady let go. But she squirms back with some pepper spray and lets him have it. His scream was so angry. Like, he went from being a nice, forgettable, blue vest store clerk to a bony MMA fighter. So the guy grabs hold of the cart and rams it into her. Right in the chest. She was short and wiry too, maybe fifty. The lady falls down and starts crying that her ankle's broken and that she's going to sue him and the store until they're both ruined. She kept cursing like something animal, making no sense. It just flowed out of her. All that weird toilet paper hoarding energy funneled into screaming at the whole store. All because we're going to have to keep on shitting or something.

— Well, that we are.

— Yeah, but they weren't even running out. Not really. The other woman just took one of her carts and ran. Left behind her own with, like, salmon and stuff still in it.

— And no one did anything?

— Like what?

— I don't know. Just, no one got involved?

— I was only there for the train wreck, hon. Not looking for a ride. Got my things and moseyed on out of there.

Wes's eyes narrow on a far-off plane of his own.

— Paramedics come?

— I don't know. I don't think so. The clerk just walked away and washed his eyes out in the dairy section, left the mess right there. The crazy lady kept moaning until she decided to hobble herself out of the store. She crawled on her back, mostly, like all of her bones had broken. Weird thing to see. She didn't want help. She was doing it all for the attention. Off hoarding toilet paper somewhere else right now, I'm sure. All for clean butts, right?

— All for clean butts.

— It is quite the luxury.

The same not-here spot comes back to him.

— Might be something more to it, Wes, like maybe the zombies can smell us by how dirty we are. Showers could be our ultimate weapon.

— Never know.

The sound of a bus whizzing by at regular bus pace goes thick with bodies standing inside. Wes sighs, and he continues to exhale through it.

— So my dad's been talking about getting out of the city. Like, soon.

— Uh, what? Just because of what could happen?

He cocks an eyebrow, though the teeth are filed down.

— What could happen is pretty fucked up. We're just trying to get away from crowds. At least until it stops spreading.

— Wait, you want to go too?

— Doll, it's not like I'm really saying goodbye to our lovely little waterlocked city. It'll be more of a long vacation, you know I'll be back.

He runs the pads of his fingers over amber stubble and listens to it.

— It's not like I can argue with him. Things are going to change. And if it's all hard power from here on out, that's not good. We just got to have a closer hand in it, you know? On your own, meeting your problems face-to-face isn't easy either. I'm not looking forward to it. But crowds mean all you are is a number, and it's clearly easy to fudge those numbers.

He pinches the nob of his chin, taking the whole of his head up by that point.

— Yeah, maybe. Or maybe it's only the cities that can be protected while everywhere else turns into a no-man's-land.

— That's what you think?

— I don't think anything. It's just a possibility.

Wes bites down.

— Well, either way, it'll be safer to go it alone. You should think about it. Singapore didn't just disappear. It's going to keep happening. It's really not that big of a deal. Like I said, it's just a long vacation. Your parents like to travel, right? Or you could come with us! Come with us.

His eyes gleam flat underwater. The hand that he's taken mine in is a thawing pork chop.

— I really don't think.

— Oh please, no, seriously. Come with us.

— It's not that easy.

— No, but we could make it doable. We'll prepare the way, and you can make it happen for your family too.

— Yeah, I don't know if my dad thinks the same way as yours.

— Oh? Well, there are other ways to look at it, like you said. But he's not stupid. Everyone is going to figure out that sooner or later this will be the last place you want to be. Why wait around for it?

— He's already said that we're staying.

Wes looks at me again.

— Really? But why?

— He doesn't think things will get that bad for one. He hates the panic, and he pretty much trusts that things are still fine. Just because the walls can fall doesn't mean that they will, basically.

Something like a sneeze crawls into Wes's nose and stays there.

— Huh. Well, I'm going to miss you, Imogen.

Another bus zooms by, as filled as the one before. He puts his lips in a thrust and rises to leave.

— Wow, so that's it?

— We're heading for Oregon in two days. No time like the present, right?

He sighs into his jacket, arms up at the elbows to hug me. The weak grip turns tight and we grab each other fierce, his ungainly body pressed into mine.

— I'll tell you where we are and how to get there. If you decide to come.

— Tell me when you're coming back, too.

— Of course.

— It's been a, uh, memorable summer.

We toss the cold vestiges of our time here as we leave.

— Have fun being a frontiersman, Wes. You'll make a good one.

— Be seeing you too, city girl.

TOWARDS THE SKY

My joke bounces back on the table.

— You're still going to school.

— I am? How?

— You can drive. I don't think they'll end up shutting down the highways too, even if the isolationists would love seeing every bridge burned.

I put a forkful of fukujinzuke in my mouth, just a few grains of rice and hardly any of the curry to accompany it. They're crunched like a puddle after frost. Mom's eyes meet mine, up from her plate, while she chews full and slowly. Jake's are there too, watching.

— What's the matter? I thought you'd be happy that we aren't keeping you here.

— I just didn't think it was a possibility.

— Of course it is. It's just an ill-timed measure that is making it awkward for you to go back. Very temporary. You read the articles I sent you, right?

— I looked at them.

— Good. Then you know that the airlines aren't going to be put out of business or anything. Even if everyone is scared right now, people still have to get where they need to go. Domestic will open back up soon, probably once you're already east. The government is only using this time to get their procedures in place. We'll be seeing a lot of guns and such, most of it symbolic, but things will be pretty much the same.

His elbow comes to the table, fork bobbing in hand.

— Just think about it. The fear of infection coming in by plane is simply ridiculous. The flight would have to take off with some sleeper agent on board before infecting everyone. Then how is a plane full of those things going to fly itself perfectly over from just where, exactly? And only to crash here? I don't care how resilient they are, they aren't going to survive falling from a plane any better than we are. We might as well be trying to run from aerial sharks.

I smile but no one laughs.

— The pilot could still be okay behind the door, and then he makes an emergency landing.

— If that were the case, Jake, he'd communicate with the ground and they'd arrange for a secure spot to land. And there's always just crashing the plane himself or getting shot out of the sky. There are too many fail-safes for that to be a serious possibility.

— But it could happen.

— Um, but should I really be going?

His eyes grow wide, then they sharpen onto me.

— Well, why not?

— Because of everything that's happening.

— Brunswick is about as removed from these world events as it gets. If anything, you'll be much safer there than here.

— So you're sending me back to what, a convent?

— That's not what I'm saying. We're not doing this to hide you away, Imogen. We're doing everything we can to help you go back because you're a college student at a very good school. Isn't that where you'd rather be?

— You mean alone with nothing but a dorm room and campus security for protection?

— It's more than you have here. We'll load the car, but what more do you want us to guarantee? The world is not safe anymore. Accepting that fact doesn't mean that it's over.

Mom's stopped eating. All of her is up to her eyes.

— It sure is for some people.

He's unfazed.

— Yes, for many poor souls on the other side of the world. But we aren't dealing with what they're dealing with.

— Because we don't even know what we're dealing with. Each day something is different. And you want to put the whole country between us? It's not just gouging on gas. What if they stop the supply next month or block the highways or we can't communicate? How do you expect me to be that far away when all anyone really knows is that today things are sort of okay?

He takes his time rubbing after he's put his glasses onto the table. Mom stays still.

— I reconcile it with the fact that I don't want you to stop going to school. And I know that this is scary. If you don't want to go, then tell me what you'd rather be doing instead. You want to intern somewhere for this semester and then transfer to Berkeley, okay. But you have to make it happen.

You do still have a life back at Bowdoin, though, and it's a lot better than what you get when you sit around here all day. So your mom and I are willing to suffer a lot of sleepless nights for you to continue that. Yes, it's different. You get to go back to school while the world keeps tearing itself apart. Our normalcy is a terrible thing to bear, but please, open yourself up to it.

She still hasn't changed.

— What do I even do if they come here, Dad?

— You do what your school or the government says. You'll always have us, but no matter what, you're ready to act on your own. You're strong and resourceful. I wouldn't push you if I didn't think that you could do this.

Jake takes his plate over to the sink, where he washes it off. From plate to phone he leaves, feigning apathy.

— But what good is it anyway?

— What do you mean?

Bad air lets tumbling out. What's next is no different.

— What's the point of even going to school anymore? Everything I was studying is going to be useless now. If things work out like you say, the best I can hope for is three more years so I can what? Get a somewhat interesting job? Or I stay for even more, like you guys. We have no idea what the world will look like by then. How am I supposed to keep preparing myself like it's the old one that'll be there for me when I'm done? I mean, how can you honestly expect me to continue to act like things will even get that far?

Clamps at the corner of my cheeks I'm near to throwing off. Dad smiles.

— You have to remember, we're losing China, not the entire world. Time and infrastructure are on our side, Imogen. Not to mention a whole lot of distance for something that shambles. And that's all if the entire human race bungles its job of staying alive. You do still have a future to prepare for, even if it is an uncertain one.

— But this isn't my future anymore. Or anyone's.

— Our culture will adapt. It will be different, sure. But you'll figure it out. So will everyone else.

He shows bright at me, and I go to the stony, downturned mouth of Mom. A rumble crawls into his voice, pulling me back.

— Look, this epidemic isn't summer vacation on life. People continue to work. Every day, we work. Even the horrors of Asia aren't bringing that to a halt. We'll just be buying less stuff because of it; its fine. If you're really giving up on the humanities, change your classes to something more practical. I certainly wouldn't blame you for it, and I'm sure the world will be happy to have another bright architect or scientist. But you have to keep doing something.

— I've been preparing.

— You've been moping.

— I have not.

— You sit around, Imogen. You exercise too much and you talk about getting all these different things like they're the secret weapon for the living dead.

Mom reaches for a knee under the table, and he shifts free.

— She's been working hard, dear.

He looks at her in unfurled pages, a leaf caught before turning back to me.

— Yes, and we appreciate that, Imogen. You're very thoughtful. But now it's time to focus on yourself.

I sit with it, a cold rock into me.

— I just didn't think it was even possible.

— Well, it is.

— Can I think about it?

— Do you need to?

Our eyes lock and it's good there and I slip. He puts his glasses back on.

— Okay, take your time, then.

— I mean, it's not about what-ifs. It's the how and the when that matter.

— And you can't control either of those.

— So you prepare.

— You are prepared.

— Hardly.

— Just try not to think in extremes. You can't live that way.

Mom starts but doesn't speak. Dad continues for her.

— Isn't this what you want?

— I don't know. I haven't thought about it.

— Well, try to. I don't think any of this has been good for you. Go back to where your friends are, where your life is. You have to stay smart and cautious, especially with the drive ahead. But we'll book you some good hotels so you can be safe and get your energy back each night.

— Wait, you're not driving me?

— No, we thought that this was something you could do on your own. We're giving you the Volvo. What, do you think you're not up for it?

He's soft, open on no.

— No, I probably am.

— Well, like I said, think about it some more. It's a lot to digest. But don't let the fearmongers tell you what your life should or shouldn't be. This global fuckup didn't take that away from you.

A sway stalls him. He stands up to clean his plate and leaves me with Mom.

— You really think I should go?

— Your father is right. You'll be safer there, and there's no reason for you to stop going to school.

— Yeah, but should I still go?

— You have to decide. We only want to make whatever you want happen.

— Maybe transferring's not that hard.

Something underneath smiling comes to her.

— Yeah, maybe. If that's what you want, good. I think that'd be smart. Just do it.

MARSH WATER

ALREADY THE WORDS ARE GONE. The dried glue sticks where it's rubbed. Mine, Mom's. Dad's earthen warmth is still on me, straight from a patch of sun.

The blue line puts a seam into my driving. Two boxed GPSs, separate brands, separate satellites that will never come down. A clutch of paper maps crowding where there's everything except the zombies, blocked roads, carjackings, no gas. Destinations.

The thermos locked hot and I'm off. Facing it doesn't make it a journey. All the packing desperate to keep this seat from being another nowhere. It's got to be safe and prepared and mine. Right up against the nowhere it's aching to become once it's rid of me.

But Aidan. Parties will get stupid. Classes will probably not care after enough lip service has been burnt away. It's all on strings ahead, the driving too.

It's an exchange. People and the soil. No space taken, now, but my own.

The sun hammers the water down to pewter. The glow vibrates, pierced by the hair-fronds of cattails and other grasses close and droning as they rip past. Occasional cranes unaware of the undead quagmire this could become.

A call puts the line away. Aidan. I swipe blind at the screen, and it falls down. Debris, and it's in my hand through the dark. Back up again and a wall of stopped cars is there, too close to stop. Slamming on the brakes puts me slow where everything is happening to me and around me like a ride at Disneyland. I just have hitting the car or seeing what happens if I turn. Instead of going, the car trips over its own wheels and starts to wobble. I pull all the way against it and keep the brake to the floor. My hand's on the horn, but I'm over, slumped where the water passes in a passenger line. The diorama's waiting for something to run across. Don't die. Don't die. Don't die.

My side's empty, and I slip forward off of the road and dive straight into the ditch. There's nothing left or right, just forward. The airbag blows and I'm cradled and suspended like a child being tossed about. But then I hit and part of me slips and my head hits something and that is it.

PART II

KEEPING HER

— W‍HAT IS SHE DOING NOW?

— I don't know. I think she's still looking for something in your guys' room.

— Okay, you and your sister keep at it. It doesn't have to be perfect. Just, please try to not hurt the wainscoting?

Dad's baleful intentionlessness stops in my shoulder as I keep hammering. The nail slides in like it's flesh once I'm through. After two more and with no one looking, I pull up onto the upper edge of the panel by the pads of my fingers. I stay long enough to lift my feet from the ground, then I tease the claw back in at the edge between wood and wall. It's soft there, but I don't crank back. I shout to Jake.

— So we're double paneling?

— Might as well use it all.

— Why are we starting from the inside, then? Aren't we trying to protect the windows?

Jake scoops the hammer from me.

— Yes, but you know what from.

— Yeah, everything.

He screeches the bookcase in front of his piece of plywood before I can check. It's more art than shuttered window, roomed over completely in the dark. His pivoting keeps on between the waiting stacks of journals in boots that still need their crease. He's right on the rug.

— So, what if someone gets in while we're gone?

— I don't know. Hopefully no one does. But if someone stays behind and ends up here. Well, they don't need to be assholes about it.

— Come on, give it.

The hammer slips awkwardly back into my pocket. He's quiet and quieter in tide shifts from me.

— But we'll still be coming back. I mean, eventually. Don't you think?

— That is why we're doing all this. So we can.

— Yeah, so long as they let us.

I help him put all of the books back. The wooden frame stands shelves above me. I'd be crushed if a tangled mass of arms were to burst through right now. Anyone would. Too much all at once to actually feel it, probably. I'd at least be trapped and unable to move while parts of me got chewed apart. And then if enough were left, I'd be animated there in my own crushed hell until the rotting finally let me blow away. And that'd be home.

I break out through the front door. The sun is pressing against our cement sepulcher. It'd be warm a few steps down, but here it's all chill. Other houses are already looking back with plywood eyes, even a gap-toothed grin of a crossbar to make at least one clear statement of no one home. Just two in the entryway and be done with it. Get her ready for this silent tea party.

When I go back inside through the garage, Jake is lost in the spandrel closet. He and the boxes are making noise with each other.

— Having fun in there?

— Yeah, lots.

— You should stop and go check outside. I did what I could.

— In a bit.

A few cupboards are left gawking in the kitchen. Gravity pulls hard without the contents to justify them, outraged to bring the doors back to their natural state, down to what might as well be a forest floor.

— Didn't Mom want to do that?

— Dad came back and asked me to get working on the food. Just making it all fit.

— Well, good job.

— I guess.

— Okay. Bad job, then?

— No, I mean.

He stops to come out. The charred wood of his hair is pushed over into a pile where the embers won't settle.

— I don't know. Doesn't feel right.

— What doesn't?

— Hiding all of this.

— It's ours. If we do nothing about it now, it's going to become someone else's.

— Yeah, but what good is that going to do us? If someone does come by, they could really need it.

My palm digs down on the head of the hammer.

— We might need it. It's ours, we can't just throw it away. Besides, it's not like these locks are really going to stop anyone.

— I'm not happy about it. It's just whoever comes searching for food later will need it either way.

Jake's hips shift looking into me.

— What, you really don't care that we could be saving someone's life?

His stare turns arid for me.

— We'll just be giving it all up to the first person who wanders in here. Whoever they are, they'll be someone who dodged the evacuation to run through other people's homes. You really want someone like that tearing apart everything we have and leaving the rest to those things?

Jake looks down at the same bars he's had over and over for breakfast.

— I mean, maybe that'll happen. But we can't help it. The only way we're really coming back is if they let us.

— That's not the only way.

He doesn't look back up at me. I squat for one of the boxes in the hallway.

— We just can't think about the ghosts of people who might come by.

— They're not ghosts, Imogen.

The hammer drops hard on the floor and leaves a mark.

— Yeah, you don't have to board up against ghosts.

Stepping over what will be someone else's jackpot, I go to my room. Hollow at the foot of my bed lies my one suitcase. ANYTHING MORE WILL BE CONFISCATED. Fashion's devoured now too. Survival means becoming comic book characters. Predictable, mechanical, eager to just be alive. Washroom confusion would bring it all crashing down. Maybe it'll be orange jumpsuits.

At least we have somewhere to go.

After running my hand over the denseness of dresses, I stop on the garment bag that's been out and waiting. My white warrior dress ripples clean where there could still be a someday.

Through the closet's dark is a murmur. The verberation pulses, pauses, reaches out again. The only thing that I get out of it is sorry. I can't hear the reply, and Dad seems to have stopped.

I sit down at my desk with the laptop that I can't bring and the window.

EXODUS

The street is full. Every bumper is knifed in for the intersection as all their geometry falls out of view.

— They haven't moved.

— No way.

— Yeah, that car's been in front of our driveway for a while now.

The floor shakes again upstairs.

— Dad, traffic's still stuck!

It settles in place for the pressing of words back down.

— We'll have to keep waiting it out. Just make sure that we aren't missing anything. Your mom and I still have to work on the car.

The driver's arm is stretched out of the window and pointed on nothing. The limb is overly exposed, Marat's. His eyes loll in isolation.

— Want to go see how bad it is?

Jake is all phone from me.

— Maps has the entire grid red.

— So, you want to go check it out?

— Why? We're going to be stuck in it soon enough.

— Then we'll need the walk first.

Jake looks back at it.

— Fine, okay.

The electric car driver rolls his eyes to us, and our descent knocks them back again. We get more half looks on the street that leave only their packed-in proximity.

— We should have told Dad.

— I'll text him.

The siren is louder outside. The warning system wailing is too worn and close to mean anything. It folds through my too-ready steps as a garbled underwater voice churns out from its own echo and stays too long. The old sound goes back again from its eidolon points over the city.

We come to the next gridlock, where everything is water frozen up a faucet. The few cars that have right-of-way are meekly barnacled to the flow, and the rest of California is stitched up the same way throughout. All of its fissures might as well be sidewalk. Nothing moves. Cars only twitch with the rustling of cattle. The glass of them is pointed plaintively towards escape. People begin to pay more attention to us, and we turn back without finding the head of anything.

Someone is at our front door. Both arms are bent, reading it for weakness.

— Hey!

The hand slips and drops what it had.

— Geez, Imogen. What are you two doing out?

— We wanted to see the traffic.

— Yeah, well, it's bad.

Mom is standing at the uncovered window upstairs.

— Do you need a hand?

— Sure, I don't think this will be enough. Could you hold it up? It's pretty hard wood, actually.

I hold the board in place and wait. Each blow passes terrible into my fingers and chest. The house cries back, into me, with flat, metallic shrieks. Our only pet, and we're putting her down, healthy.

— And wedges inside, right?

— I took care of it.

I push into the door, the bar. All there is to tell is that it's hard.

— Well, seeing as it meets your approval, I guess that is that. Ready?

We open the garage and Mom is in the back fussing at the side yard door, which is sealed too. The bag at her feet could be filled with cans and bottles by the way she fingers at things.

— Mom, I think it's fine.

— This is where they'll try to get in.

—Jake, could you help me?

I stay with her.

— So, I guess we're ready.

Her eyes are wide when she sees me.

— To what? Give up everything so we won't be left to die from inconvenience? They've already shown us that they're complete losers. And still, we are following their stupid orders.

She looks back again at the door. In a twist she kicks the corner of it with her toe, and it shakes. She stops to look it over again.

— Well, it's what we've got. At least we see it coming.

She turns back.

— Yes, it's what we've got.

Mom picks up the bag and drops it to the floor of the passenger seat while Dad and Jake start to pound away at something. She sits and looks straight ahead at the street. The electric car has moved a few feet.

— We aren't going to wedge that door shut too?

— This is the best we can do. Come on, let's go.

Only Jake puts his seat belt on.

— Ready, family?

We drive straight towards the gap between the electric car and the sedan that's behind it. The sedan clams up at our approach, taking a few inches.

— Wait here.

Dad puts it in park and kills the engine too. With the keys, he gets back out and walks down where the man inside tries to look forward.

— Hi, sorry. I know this is really crazy, but would you let us in?

He looks back wordlessly.

— Sir? Sorry, but could you please let us in?

He gets the window cracked. What comes out is lumped and needs clearing.

— I've been here for almost an hour.

— I know. I know it's terrible. But this is the only way I can get in. It's not like I'll be arriving any sooner than you. Please?

He sits back up in his seat and looks again at the car. His hands shuffle and stick to the wheel as the siren tones back up away from us. Then he nods, barely.

— Oh great, thank you so much. We really appreciate it. Thank you.

Dad walks back and gets in but doesn't turn the car back on. We all sit in silence.

— Well, this is great.

The key only rotates enough for the radio. Placid NPR voices continue their discussion of the crisis in Maryland, which he's quick to smother under the twists of gnarled messages until we land on the emergency broadcast signal. We wait through the garble that pitches a horrible up and down until a monotone, prerecorded voice takes the cabin.

The following is an alert for the residents of San Francisco County. The City of San Francisco has been declared a dark zone by order of the governor. All area Containment Centers are entering lockdown. All residents must evacuate

immediately and arrive at their designated relocation site. Due to the spread of UND,

all previously scheduled Center integration has been canceled. At this time, there is no

known present threat. Repeat: At this time, there is no known present threat. The United States remains in a state of emergency under martial law.

If you suspect someone of having contracted UND, isolate the individual, confirm their condition, and exterminate. If unable, seek out someone who can assist you through this process.

— Okay, enough of that.

— I think I've found it.

Jake passes a picture forward.

— Some cars are abandoned on the bridge.

Dad looks at it closely.

— Goddamnit. Why would people do that? It's not like there's anything to actually run from. And where are they going, anyway?

He pushes back into his seat with his chin smashed in hand. He looks again.

— Well, someone should be out there opening a lane up right now.

The emergency broadcast alarm garbles against the near mute volume, and we wait for its avian calling over water.

— What if they're not?

Dad breathes down against my question.

— No, they want this to be smooth and orderly. They'll do it right.

It's longer before anything moves. With something like a cheer, we start back up and watch each one edge forward. The electric car lurks along, and it's continuous head nodding and hand hailing that keeps the sedan back as we lumber into the street. A tortured turn throws us hippoed in line, where we take up the entire bout of progress. The sedan inches too close, but it's not enough to keep going.

— I guess this is finally goodbye.

Dad turns around after putting it in park, and we're slow to look back at him.

— Well, a long goodbye.

— Sid.

— Yes?

— Please don't make this into a game.

His mouth twitches on something that can't be spat or swallowed.

— I'm not mocking anything.

— Just don't, please.

— But I'm not.

After Mom doesn't respond, doesn't move, he looks forward and breathes out through his nostrils. Jake's eyes are in his lap, and I scan the street and settle back at our home. I keep to its features, the steps that descend at a right angle, the reason I thought all stairs were made of Legos as a kid. But the plywood keeps covered all of what makes the flat-faced Edwardian feel like home. We start to move, and a van blocks my view.

I've already done all the idle phone work that I can when we get to the Presidio. The pace has almost been just another packed weekend commute. But the sun has everything gripped in yellow. We'll be lucky if we can see it set over the ocean a few hundred feet ahead.

I wake up and it's dark. There's indigo over the ocean with no way of seeing what's there. A part of Golden Gate is lit in the distance, and the car is off with Jake asleep next to me. Mom and Dad are both gone.

—Jake, get up.

I'd have to shove him and I don't. The phone says that it's almost nine, and there's no knowing how we'll get beds.

A person brushes past my window and leaves a chill across my neck. I'm stuck close as they hurry with torn gravel to the lookout ahead. A gathering of some kind is huddled there to watch something or nothing, right where we waited for the fireworks to start last year.

I nudge him.

—Jake, where did Mom and Dad go?

A dead sound comes out first.

—I don't know.

—Come on, we have to go find them.

—They probably just went to see what's going on.

We get out together. I stop but leave the door unlocked, and Jake's gone before I see what he did. My feet hit hard into the cliffside path that the shadow slipped through. I'm stiff from shivering and hugging against the chill. Jake's form takes the lead through the blinding light and dark of the car beams.

The siren drone falls apart and apart just over the cliff.

There's a group standing at the edge, face to the bay. More appear, sitting down or leaning with their backs against a barrier. Jake goes straight to the ones who are looking out, and Mom and Dad are there, talking.

— Oh, look who's up. Tom and Linda, these are our children, Jake and Imogen.

— Nice to meet you.

There's no seeing their faces.

— So you're sure that's what your son saw?

— Yes, two jumped off. There was a crowd. Maybe they were trying to bring them back in.

— That's horrible.

— He saw all that from here?

— Binoculars.

— And now he's been traumatized.

— I'm not traumatized.

— Yes you are.

The boy crouched on a cement slab could be eight or twelve, the utility vest he has on is too big for him either way. No binoculars. Over the water hang lights and a layer of vehicles in brick beams of red. It's solid and I don't catch movement. A gust from the bay bullies me back a small step.

— Any word on what's happening out there?

— From who? There was a couple earlier that said they'd walk ahead, but they just went back to their car. Don't blame them. We can't either. Not with Samuel shaken up like this.

— But someone should.

The pair is still too close together for their features to come through.

— I could go ahead.

Jake steps right in.

— That's kind, but I think we can wait a little longer.

— I can text, Mom; it'll be fine.

— I'm sure there's someone else.

— It's not that big a deal.

The sound of a car driving by has us meerkatting back at the road. A second rumbles away, and Dad, then the rest of us, starts back.

Two pairs of taillights carry off towards the bridge in the wrong lane, the calcified cars bright as they go. The figures of others are caught down in their red gorgon gaze. What's just ten or fifteen miles per hour feels like speeding, desperate to shatter the day and us with it.

A third comes, and we watch the headlights as they get closer. Dad steps turgid into the road and raises a hand for them to stop. The light hits his body fuller and fuller. He's locked in their indecision until brakes scream back in protest.

Dad stays firm near the hood with his hand still raised. There's movement and the driver comes back with a gun. It's pointing right at him. Dad's palms go slowly higher in silhouette, and his voice presses through.

— Where do you think you're going?

— You want to get shot and run the fuck over?

Dad backs up and slides blind between the cars. We're there to catch him as the barrel holds, stares, then goes to the wheel to jump away.

— Sid!

— It's alright.

Dad's eyes fall between Mom and me; they're unfocused and set still from moving. A shot rings out, then three more. The car accelerates suddenly and crashes into the side of a station wagon farther down. One of them is stuck on the horn, which bellows melancholically back up at us to break with the siren in the air. The man from before, Tom, is standing just a car length away with his legs squared and gun now lowered, watching the wreck ahead with campfire warmth. He starts off towards it with the weapon limp at his side. Someone screams.

There's a shape already over both hoods, reaching for something through the driver's side window, but it's wedged tight against the car that's pushed half off of the road. Whoever's there in the hit car moves like they're panicking, as afraid of the hand as she is of the could-be corpse, could-be mass shooter right beside her. The man named Tom keeps going and others are rising in his wake. Jake starts walking.

— Jake, don't.

— We have to go help.

— Help what?

— I don't know. Help.

— Jake, stop.

He's going, but he holds on the strain of my look. He slowly comes back.

— We're fine. Let's just get to the car and stay put.

— Dad, no one's coming.

A snarl of murky red roils his mustache over beard.

— Well, why shouldn't they? You can't leave a city to evacuate itself. What did they think was going to happen?

— I don't know, but we can't stay.

— Someone had to stop him.

— He's not a knight in shining armor, Mei.

Mom cuts into Dad's look. More are at the car, hurrying away from the car.

— If we don't go now, we'll be stuck here too.

— But we have to be at San Rafael.

Jake's voice is clouded into the automated message, and I shout back at him.

— How can we, even? We'll have to try tomorrow.

— We'll just take another bridge.

The car we're in front of moves slightly into us.

— Hey! Come on!

There's yelling inside and Dad yells back as we move. Jake's hand is hilted right behind, and I pull at him more.

— How is it going to be any different? Let's just wait this out and leave tomorrow.

— They're closing.

Our faces are together.

— Someone just shot a guy. We're trapped either way.

Dad flinches at a pop in the distance that could have been fireworks. When Mom grabs his arm, he talks.

— There's no reason; it should be simple, clockwork. We're not the East Coast. They shouldn't be leaving us here like this.

A car pulls out of the line, clipping another. People shout but it veers around the wreck and turns down to whatever lies in the next curve. Something of a glare comes from Dad; it's on me but suddenly turns and leaves the wet damp of melting ice.

— This isn't safe. We have to go.

Mom tackles Dad with a hug that takes us buckled back into the car. With some delicate turning, we work our way out and drive. My eyes burn peering forward. We pass people standing about aimlessly, a campfire at the corner of the road with beers and loud voices. Another car tries to take our lane, and we stare it down until it drops steep into the gutter. Each intersection takes constant work to leave. Dad has to speak with the lone woman who is waiting at our driveway to get her to move, mace in hand. It's a seesaw in and out. She gets just the corner of her nose back in as we break our way into the garage again in the dark. Walking through the house feels cold, and we go straight to bed, all on phones for what happened.

THE AMERICAN WAY

MY PAJAMAS ARE dense with the condensation as I'm stuck down both sides. Just a cold morning on a quiet street. There's trash in the gutter but nothing else outside. No more siren drone. No gunshots or cries of vague urgency. No real way of telling what happened.

I put my phone down where the clunk sounds generations old and out of juice. The screen's all weight and naked looking up. More than black. I'm there right back again, clinging for its light.

A garish mugshot under Crissy's smiling. Crissy 2, Zombies 0. Eighteen likes, no talk about that zero. The box on the ruined face wants me to say who it is.

A smiling dog is luminescent with the grease of Tegan's hair. The sky is clear behind them. So what is everyone doing for post-consumerist pet care? Two days ago. Stock up.

If you come, bring something good. It's ours and it's staying that way.

We are in Hartford, Connecticut. Today is October 13. We are in a basement. We have twenty people here. Children, elderly. There is not food here, no necessities.

Mama.

The screen's black but for bodies fading out to the edges. Clam eyes of kids no higher than shoulders. Some held. Skin washed featureless with the empty room. There are candles, but only three and the camera's light.

It's closed liminal right behind them.

Pharmacies smashed. Stores smashed. We have no water, no gas.

Her voice is hard and rushing.

Crying.

Planes are flying around, dropping bombs. The children are very scared.

Crying. It's the one short up front, teal next to her crouched mother. Maybe two.

Please, organize a route of passage for us. Help us. Help us evacuate our children.

It stops. Another girl up front is holding a doll.

My thumb stays, flicks.

The noise is too loud, hitting, just hitting as I bring it down. Trapezoids of greyed brown shoot from black and are now a face. There are eyes but no focus. I need help. The noise takes over and she stops with the pieces jarring in movement. If anyone gets this, I need help. There's no crying.

Hang in there!

·_·

A streak of chin and the button to play again.

The phone's a lump in my hand until I bring it back to its spot. The cord is there and I plug it together.

They're hands-to-phones around the table. Someone's been talking. The boarding has things dark enough for everyone to glow. What's outside now could be different.

— Imogen.

Mom hands me hers. The picture is too zoomed on charcoal that's not a pant leg and its foot. Flesh comes through from the center as I pinch it away, making more appear. A door stops them from spreading further, and they're on it like flies, dried to nothing, still. The charred layer stays past the frame, past where it was taken.

— It's a Center in New Jersey. Someone got in and found it like that.

— Overrun.

The faces all have open mouths. Jake's voice is heavy to me.

— You can't tell.

A plastic clunk hits the table before Dad looks up.

— This is all we're going to get.

The illumination ends on a smeared scratch.

Mom steps away to do laundry. When she's back, she goes to the freezer and pulls out something. Cars pass but it's hard to tell. It's dark enough to need the light, but only for the kitchen.

Oil begins to crack and Mom fills the rest with scolding. Of course they'd do something like this. They stopped after New York. We're nothing to them. They'd see us all dead before letting us get by without them. Everything went to holding up Europe; nothing for us or for Asia. And there are no consequences because they're already gone.

Jake and Dad look down into their plates, eyes pooling like lentils. I'm full too soon, but what's left makes me go further.

— It'll just be for a few days. Then we'll see what happens.

SCOUTING

THE GARAGE DOOR jumps at a screech. Something's holding down, choking the bellowing that won't stop. It's lashing and we're caught in each other. Cracks of daylight cut through, and the few beams dance and dart and scurry across the concrete. Jake pushes me and gets the button slammed.

— Whoops.

— You're burning it out!

— Sorry.

I get in front, where the side door's waiting to burst in on us if it wants. Light breaks to show how nice the day is, and I groundhog out for its emptiness.

— Anything?

— No.

— Well, good, I guess.

The air is grey and quiet. And too bright. I don't face it; only the back of my jacket takes in the street warmth. My hands fumble on the hard outdoor coldness and the lock slips easily enough. I tap and wait. The street glare stays right behind, but I end up winning. The door rises and I come swaying the lock. Jake doesn't look, and Mom and Dad are there to see separately themselves.

— Let's go.

The SUV starts up, the garage door latches, and the street keeps like it always has. There's talk about weather that could be accurate, but Dad stops it and makes us the only people left in the world.

Turning the first corner and my throat seizes in on the plastic wrap of itself. Suddenly my mouth waters and suddenly that slips somewhere down the wrong way. Wet and slick, I cough it off and stifle it down together. Something remains, won't go away, but I can breathe again with the ouroboros out of my mouth.

— You alright?

And it's the same. There's no terrible scene. Nothing's wrecked, not cars not houses not bodies. Everything online didn't mushroom around us overnight. The boarding keeps on, but it's the same quiet air that's been sitting there from us this whole time.

The sun is too bright through the mist that hasn't moved. It should have burned away. The intersection was crammed full, and now it's hollow down the corridors. The laundromat greets us as lit up and glassy as ever, street bus for no one. Corner stores are still blocked.

The sun is hanging in the white. I wait with it and keep hold of the orb until the white put inside of my eyes begins to ache. The rays come all the way down, and all they do is make me squint and turn away. Losing, I still have them with my arm, fully canvased as it takes them lightly in. My fingers rouse up in the something that's arrived from elsewhere. But they don't get the way back that no one's found how to take. There's glass to break and no emergency. And they touch nothing.

The quiet hits us. We wait and look for anything at all, but there's just what's paved over. The car whirs into the barrel of the six-lane boulevard, one giant creak on the floorboard that gets us where we aren't. Dad crawls us to the center and we look hard down both full stretches. There's only the silence of a few left-in-place cars to look back. We move again on to what could eventually be downtown. We turn.

Stout buildings with nothing to tie them together continue sentinel over us. We're exposed to their soot.

Red flashes keep aimless down the row until they're gaunt out of view. We keep driving to something hanged. The words are clear in campaign yard sign lettering with a code no one can scan.

DON'T GO
We Will Survive
11th Avenue Jack in the Box Parking Lot
WeWillSurvive.com

— Should we?

He looks back as a pigeon drifts downy in front.

— It says they're here for anyone who's staying in the dark zones.

— That's it?

Jake's soft between mirror and screen, mouth parted.

— Anything could help us, Sid.

— Yeah, if they're there.

He stops cupped at the door, lip to chin.

— We just have to be careful. We don't give away anything, okay?

He looks to Jake, to me.

— I mean, they sound fun.

He's caught, and he exhales.

Red flashes blink and blink until they're stopped in the street that should go all the way to the sea. The road doesn't let us out and we're driving.

The mostly bare shoulders shrug into a cluster of parked cars. The food grab on the corner looks empty, and curved to the small parking behind is a tent with WWS printed white on black in type-writer font. Someone with an assault rifle is earnest in place.

Dad just parks. We approach the gunman like it's nothing, and he barely moves. On some hidden cue, a woman comes out from the tent, arm greeting. Jacket canvas hangs loose in the length of her untied brown hair.

— Welcome. Hello. Thank you for stopping by, I'm Moira.

She steps forward with her hand in front until Dad does the same and there's a grasp.

— Sid. This is my wife, Mei, and our children, Imogen and Jake.

— Welcome, welcome. Come on in, family. We're happy that you've come.

The guy keeps looking past us to the street.

— We saw your sign. Trying to figure out what's actually going on.

She narrows on the nothing more that's left between us.

— Good. Well, you're here where we can help, that's the important part. Come on in.

Laptops are peopled at the back, sitting gone from the parking lot grime around them. The only thing to see us is the basic conference table that's doing nothing in the middle. Paired metal desks wait for clients and no one else.

— Would any of you like coffee? Water? Tea?

We hand over headshakes and pursed lips as Dad breaks in nodding. Her hair walls and turns back with a filled paper cup. The char of it stays in passing.

— You all sure? I've done away with a lot so far, but coffee? Something's got to keep us who we are.

— More than ever.

She looks at Dad and takes her own that's gone cold. It goes to all but her eyes.

— Not like anything else sleeps.

The space is concrete between us. We've sat, and the chairs leave no room.

— Could we start with a survey?

A pen is quick in her hand and waiting.

— I was hoping that you could give us a better idea of what's going on. We've broken the order, obviously, and it doesn't look like there's many of us.

— Oh, don't worry, you made the right decision for your family. You're safe. But a few minutes of this would really help. A quick icebreaker; part of the coffee, right?

There's a clack behind of something being moved. Only Mom turns.

— Okay.

— Great, thank you. Maybe it's a bit silly, but the data really does mean a lot.

Her fingers clasp along with the pen and unhook.

— So to start, how do you feel about the government's resorting to Centers to build survivorships across the country? You can answer with strongly disagree, disagree, indifferent, agree, strongly agree, or I don't know.

— Uh, well, it's not quite as simple as that.

— Yes, I know. This is just to get us going.

There's just the air in his nostrils staying back. He settles and keeps tight with it, measures, doles it out.

— Well, it's certainly not gone well. So disagree?

— I strongly disagree.

She turns straight down from Mom.

— Okay, good. Great that you're both giving me input. I'll put down disagree. Next, how much do you agree with the statement "I worry often that I will contract UND"?

— Agree.

— Why? Death is death.

— Okay, indifferent?

— Indifferent it is. How about for the phrase "If I see the military, I will either run or hide"?

Dad pushes the air right out.

— I don't know.

She makes something of her non-reaction. Mom too.

— And, "I am open to trusting people"?

Dad pulls the air back through his mouth.

— Agree.

— What? Who are we trusting? No.

Dad's reaction hides in the outcrop of his beard.

— We're trusting these people right now.

— This isn't trust. Using each other, maybe, or wasting our time. Do you even know anything?

Hues blare between her and Mom.

— It's the last one. How much do you agree with the statement "We can survive and build a new society if we come through in love and support of each other"?

— Agree.

— Eh, indifferent.

Mom's voice stays swollen after Dad's. A pen scratch flicks into it.

— Agree it is. Okay, great, I hear where you are both coming from.

She writes more into the grey white with the laptop framed between us. Mom leans gently in to look.

— How many of these have you done?

She's neutral back at me. A drawer opens and comes with a stack half as high as the mug. The edges flutter in her hand and send her back to me.

— You're not alone, if that's what you're thinking. Things are only quiet right now.

— I'm sorry, can you just tell us what all this is about?

Dad's voice is under glass and gelled with Mom. Her smile and then her smile comes back.

— Yes, thank you. That was all I wanted.

She stops short on some pain and talks through it.

— Now from us. We're We Will Survive or WWS. We're a national grassroots organization whose mission is to enable individuals to adapt to post-societal life. The landscape is changing, but there's one thing throughout that everyone needs: community.

The screeching of a printer wafts behind us.

— What happens when your neighbor runs short on food or water or they don't have any way to cook? How can you help them if they've already broken into your home? Or someone tries their luck on you in the middle of the night? Or kills you in the street just to get what's on your back?

She stops.

— Community. That's what saves us. So we're doing everything that we can to achieve that. What it takes is a network of communication. Otherwise, everyone you do or don't see, yourselves included, is going to die here very quickly. Days once they've arrived, weeks if they haven't.

There's walking outside the tent. No one comes in.

— It doesn't matter how well stocked or defended you think you are. People have already tried to get by like rats. They scurry off, lie low, but by the time they're forced to rear their heads back up again there's nothing waiting for them, just death. But if we stand together now, we won't have to hide. Not like that. We can really prevent it from happening in the first place. Nip it in the bud, right? Actually keep the corruption from taking control.

Dad's hand drops and he puts his knees into the gleam of her.

— And that works?

She curls in parts, unsmiling.

— Where it's been given a chance, yes. The Centers are no alternative. I dread to think of whatever's happening there.

— We backed out last minute.

Dad speaks down from the surface of her, words into his lap.

— They're a junta; you'd be lucky if they only saw you as cattle. Because why? You're another mouth to feed? A mouth that's been weaponized against everyone?

She comes short in the silence. Back again.

— We're giving them a wide berth; you should too. But that's going to change at some point. It won't last.

They look at each other without looking.

— You can relax. No one is going to come to your door to kick you out any more than they are to help. That's your prize for cold feet. What's here looking you in the face is all opportunity. And it'll be gone unless you're willing to work with us. United we stand.

She makes a smile that Dad's still bent stiff for. She goes to Mom. She's still. And the stillness we're all weighed in is laid close.

Dad's voice is his own from his lap.

— I'm afraid that we aren't fighters.

— Yet. You aren't fighters yet. But you will be. Surely you know that, right?

She looks alternating. There's no response.

— You don't have to worry, training would be to your ability, and there's plenty of ways to help. It's not a charity; you have to be willing to give to receive. Fair's fair.

The rings of brown in green and black of her are flat.

— Keep thinking about it. Right now, we just need to be able to reach you. Where you live. What supplies you're flush or light on.

Dad sits warm in the words, their parts still growing.

— This really is your best hope. There's no running at the first sign of trouble anymore. Nowhere to go.

His hands lift and fold where he still doesn't look up.

— Yes, well, be that as it may, I don't think we can.

She breathes slow and deep.

— If all you are is passive, then there's nothing we can do for you.

She bites lightly, turns to Mom and back down.

— Do you think you're impervious, sitting where you are right now?

Someone starts looking, and we're looking back at each other. Mom is off somewhere she's no longer listening.

— Every day sees more of us dead. With them. You either do something now or you're waiting for it.

Dad gets ready, glinting hard back.

— So that's it, then?

She doesn't move.

— If any of you change your minds, hopefully you find us. You look like a great family, and I don't want to lose you in the next few weeks.

She's up for the coffee.

— Weeks?

— When things change. Don't worry, you'll see. Just, good luck keeping your head down.

We're stiff away from her, the others, into the flap.

— The future has to be fought for. And not everyone will share it with you.

— Thanks.

— It's been a pleasure. Hopefully I see you again.

She makes a show of waving when anything else is too late. The people in the back don't look up, the guard stands still, and I'm given a fistful of pamphlets. WHAT YOU CAN DO FOR A NEW TOMORROW. I start flipping through PROVEN EFFECTIVE ZOMBIE FIGHTING TECHNIQUES when we're back.

— Hey, Dad. There's a car.

— What?

The mirror has his eyes.

— They're following us?

No one answers.

It's a block away when we turn right instead of the left that's home. We're floored and I'm forced back to the seat. Dad twists Argused through a four-way stop and brakes wide into one of the culs-de-sac. A slight squeal and he U turns to stop behind the only car that's there. He shuts off, and we're nothing together. It doesn't come.

A resting click ticks the engine.

— What do we do?

— Let's just get back another way, Sid.

— They could be waiting for us.

— They don't know, and you were driving so fast!

— They weren't turning off.

Limbs drag Jake closer.

— You guys are being so paranoid right now. Why would anyone care? There's hundreds of houses to break into.

— It's just a precaution, Jake.

— They're just people, and we need the help. They already could have screwed us over.

— Really, it's fine. We're just playing it safe.

Jake moves back like he smells a fart. His mouth is tight to keep it out.

— We could walk home. We aren't that far.

— That'd be just as obvious as driving. Worse, if anyone's actually there.

— We wouldn't stand out. What if we took the back way?

He blocks the view of it.

— What back way? You mean that?

— The dune trail's right behind us. We just have to climb the fence and follow it back in.

— That's a cliff back there, that's why it's all locked up.

— We could figure it out.

What shines back isn't me. Mom and Dad are half turned.

— Well, it's that or people's backyards.

There's nothing that passes between them. Dad talks into the steering wheel.

— We were just playing it safe. It's fine. If we see someone, we either run, or we confront them.

— Or maybe just wave and pass by?

— Or that. Everyone just keep a close watch.

The car starts up before there's a way to protest. We edge and peer unseeing back to the right. It's quiet, long, and empty. Home's there and gone. We cross, and nothing's roused.

— Were those cars there before?

It's next to normal the long way back. Nothing is any different. We overshoot our turn, still nothing new to the nothing. We hook along another block and pull up to our driveway.

I'm the one with the keys to get out. It's stillness on the movement as the car whirs inside.

GRAND LARCENY

— So you really don't think we're doing this too soon?

— Not after yesterday. It'll be fine. We'll knock and make sure that we don't, uh, intrude.

— So they have the jump on us.

Dad's eyes go to the line and pick it back up.

— Everyone will have to do their best not to let that happen.

— I thought you'd be game, Imogen.

Jake passes by with the good crowbar and a hammer loose in his hands.

— I was just asking, Dad.

— There's no need to worry. We're going to do this the right way; not let anything go to waste. If anyone is still around, now's the time to say hi.

— Except this isn't just saying hi.

Dad makes room for Mom. I plant my foot with a twist that's more of a stamp.

— Why aren't we making this easier on ourselves? Go door-to-door first. Canvass the neighborhood before we start robbing it.

He stays at his hands.

— I still want to draw as little attention as possible. People will understand.

— Yeah, they'll take one look at us and realize that we aren't handing out Apocalypse Day gift baskets.

— So maybe you should go join WWS and make a difference.

The smirk on Jake's face begs for me to stop it.

— I'm not saying that we should do nothing. But we still don't know anything. If people come back and find their stash gone, then why wouldn't they come after us? Or we make them starve. You guys are acting like we're ready for that.

The smirk only wanders off in boredom.

— Like we've had anything other than time to get ready.

— What, now you aren't even willing to think about things?

Jake tightens his grip on the crowbar that's never been used.

— What I'm thinking about is what happens every day we do nothing. No one else is lining up to protect us. We stayed, so this is what staying is.

— Well, again, all I'm saying is that we could do a bit more to make sure that we aren't threats or targets to whoever's still out there.

Dad puts his hand on my shoulder. It's birdlike and emptied out of the arm behind it.

— Anyone who spots us will see valuable allies, that's it.

— But.

— Imogen, I don't want to be out there any longer than we have to. We can talk about this after we're done. Okay?

— Imogen, come here.

Mom's frame points in elbows to me, nearly doubled by the weight of her shawl. It's draped for dinner, a life on the street. It's something more to come to.

— You keep using that head of yours. This is the easy stuff. It's only going to get harder. Just think of everything we do today as practice.

— Yeah, I know.

— Do your planning so when the time comes you won't have to think at all. This is what you're getting your degree in now, right?

— Right, Mom.

— Okay, good.

She hugs and pushes me back before anyone turns.

— Oh, that thing's still so dark. Are you using my cream?

— Mom.

— Keep using it.

The boarding's no different. Plywood glistens in a scar that's hard against Dad's pounding. No way for anyone to let us in, but we're all terse to it. The board sucks in the sound, and still the hits are buzzing beneath. He puts his mouth almost on it, tender and right there.

— Hello? It's Sid and Mei, next door. Are you home? Rachael? Eric?

He pounds singly again with the side of his fist.

— Hello?

Nothing comes back from inside. Dad looks at us, the street. The mixed up, musty smell makes the ghosting its own waiting thing. The tools come kindling forward. With a nod to Jake, they both start working at the panel. Hammers clink spiked into the claw heels. Dad's pops with a twist, Jake's only a little. Jake cranks and hammers and cranks again and gets it mostly free.

— No, try pulling it downward, not out. Let the tool do the work for you. This.

Dad repeats the process almost seamlessly. The flat tooth bites deeper as it reaches in with its side instead of the point. Mom stays facing the street. With another bout of clinks, Jake gets a nail to fall, and together the last few come untoothed.

— Let's put it right there.

The door itself is normal underneath, maybe clammy.

— So again, it's leverage, not force.

Dad widens his stance and peers over as though he's about to drill a hole. He pops into the base of the wedged claw and alternates with cranks that pull him deeper each time. The door rattles but stays. It's the thick wooden frame that gives way to quicksand. The work is hard on his hands, but he rocks fully into it until he's made a way past the deadbolt. The door tries to open but the inside is held at the chain. His smile sighs through the gap as it pops away.

— And there you have it. Grand Larceny 101.

— Don't listen to your father. That's just breaking and entering.

— Oh, just you wait, love. We're only getting started.

The air inside is thick with jade mustiness. We make their way in, the last of the hellos stumbling into walls. Mom stays stiff on lookout as I follow. The forgotten nighttime tries to overwhelm me in an aching sort of nothing. It has my insides down to syrup with the thump of my heart all effort. The tension strains till it's dashed on what's ahead.

It's colder within. There's the stairs, the console table in the entry-way, the square of kitchen farther down. The details are dead, and I leave them.

Neither hides their steps, and there's no more answer than the creak of the floor. A drawer opens, a closet, but they keep moving.

I'm standing on something, papers bleeding from the study. I walk carefully to where they used to be. A stonecarved duck is on the floor too, on its side. I pick it up and the marks are rough. Back on the desk, I pull the drawer open and shut it back on things unused and useless.

The den joins to a dining room that's stayed static, but the kitchen's another mess. Food's out that shouldn't be. I stay back from the basket of grey mush and get to the boxes. Only one is open, and there's a smashed bag of prunes on the floor that Mom might keep.

Box by box, the day-of disappears. I jump snackward to the fridge, where the opened air gags me. The shut only blows it into me and I'm stuck, stinging and getting it spat back out onto the dishes in the sink.

— You alright?

— Fridge.

— What was in it?

— I'm not opening that again.

— What, you don't want to dig? We could read when they left on a milk carton.

— Right.

— Or maybe they had to put down their dog with no time for a burial.

— Jake!

— Well, they sure left behind a lot of dog stuff.

He begins to look through my pile.

— Shouldn't you be upstairs with Dad or something?

— Nothing there. He's just tripping down their memory lane right now.

— What?

— I don't know. A bunch of photos and old kids' stuff is left out up there. So that's what he's doing.

The house is quiet.

— Okay, fine, I'll get him. Can you start loading things?

— What is this? It's all the fancy stuff no one actually eats.

— Might as well.

— Oh yeah, are you going to make us a tapenade?

Jake dances a jar at me.

— Not if you keep doing that. Anyway, there's still the pantry.

He checks the label as I leave. Mom's shape is still in the doorway. The sheen of her holds on to the light as she's statued away.

My hand catches on the rail. It's thick with the grease of an old range hood. I look around for something dead, a rat or something bigger. But the floor is empty and my nose is just cold. There are long white bristles of hair coated across the entire glistening length. I fold my arms and abrade the residue that won't go as I hurry up to the top.

The air is stagnant and dim enough to make me stop. Only one of the rooms has a candlelight glow. The others are inky. A shift of something comes beneath the clamor of a stormy afternoon.

Dad's at the edge of a guest bed with a lamp bright on what's in his hands. Shining squares of glare show green and dirt brown with grinning faces all over. The poses are all set in the same sky-blue T-shirts. Dad shifts them to the foot of the bed and looks up.

— Imogen, hi. How is everything?

— Fine. Jake is starting to move some of the food to the car.

— Good, good. I just found the Parkers' old photos. They must have pulled some before they left.

— Yeah, we should probably help, though.

— Right.

Dad doesn't get up from the snow pile of school papers and art projects around him. The flurrying's as far as the forging. His hand goes back and he suddenly recoils at the crinkling.

— It's just, sorry, Imogen. Realized we didn't stop to develop anything more of you and Jake. We just let it all sit where it is.

— There's still some stuff.

— Of you two growing up, yes; and we were about to lose that. I just can't believe I didn't think about it.

He waits.

— Well, we all need to live lighter now, right?

— Lighter, yes, maybe that's what it is.

It's still quiet.

— We got to keep going. Is the upstairs clear?

He moves without getting up.

— Jake left that. I think there's rubbing alcohol.

— Okay, well, just need to find the garage.

Dad closes the smiles in on each other with a plastic clap. We go, him holding on to the disinfectant, me with my hands close. Jake strides through and stops before the kitchen.

— Are you guys ready to help?

— Have you found the garage?

Dad walks past me and then Jake to leave.

— I think it's there.

Two doors; the first pulls back hollow on the paleness of a hot water heater. Dry floorboards only leave room to hide, and I close loud on it. The next is steps down to concrete before fluorescent brightness pops on stacks of plastic and cardboard. Not much is premade; it's dried, canned. Beans and grains and veggies that could feed the block. Gallons of water snake along the bottom in no real direction. Packages for batteries, coffee filters, hand sanitizer all make little mountains for the taking. I lean in close to grab hold of a dog toy that's still zip-tied, and a hole opens under and shifts. It's been drilled into at other spots too, touched and discarded. I leave it too.

Canisters of gas huddle to the side, four of them.

Two carloads go by. Two trips to clear a legacy. We don't talk about their better furniture or the liquor cabinet. Dad has a couple of bottles and the rest stays cellared.

The pile builds quick back home. There's lunch waiting with Mom after, and I have a small cut that Dad makes me clean. My bowl is full of fried rice with rich globules of lap cheong. She says we earned the green onion, a sheared gap now at the windowsill. Dad reads the label of one of the bottles, and Jake and I split a can of soda that we can't finish. We drink more water, and Mom has hers hot.

We start back again down the street, emptied of what's behind and ahead. The panel is the same again with the broken door and what's inside.

We pantomime excitement as Mom pulls up from behind.

The next is naked. Nothing but the curtains keeps us from looking in. The window's there to break, but Dad knocks.

— Hello? Anyone home in there? It's your neighbors.

— And we're here to take all of your stuff.

Dad turns with his eyebrows in an eye roll. He tries the handle and it doesn't move.

— Can I break the window?

— No, I don't want you getting cut. Here, let's try this. Pay attention to how I ground my myself. It's all in the back leg. That's your power. Then it's fully forward with the foot. Hit flat and near the lock.

Dad hones his focus; he even balls his fists down. The kick isn't flashy; it's just loud. He tries again, then once more. The door reverberates and is made thick. He shakes his foot out, and Mom starts to move, but he raises his hand. Fiery, he puffs out and kicks the door loose and loose and once more through. Our clapping and the turgid rocking of the door wafts over his still-bent back.

There's no calling the names of who used to live here. Blond with surfaces for a face. Wife in grey cardigans and hair always up. A point of nose and cheekbones to match, her turn from acknowledgement always down and to the side. Nothing else from their geometry. The catalogue furnishing doesn't hold them either.

It's clean, hardly any smell to it. The air is diminished but that's it. They could have run off to a boat or a weekend home right at the first word.

The couch and TV take up an entire room with only a tablet and a remote for the rest. No dust, just black plastic. A sharply cut mirror catches me across the way, where I'm such a street kid.

Jake plops down on the couch, arms wide, legs extended.

— You think it has more streaming?

— Not now.

He turns it on.

— I just want to see what works. Not like this place is going to be any good.

— I'm sure there's something. Come on.

— Fine.

The screen opens to a menu of apps that don't start. It's as clear and plastic as it ever was before they're sent back to darkness. Jake mocks disappointment and Dad pretends that he cares.

Mom's still huddled in the entryway. The kitchen has no more than a few boxes. Light meals, light on the calories. I hold my breath and swing out the fridge, where there's only beer and some condiments. A bilious bag of takeout keeps them right where they are.

— You like to roll the dice, don't you?

The bathrooms have a lot of medicine, which Dad sorts through. Some drops into the trash. My same deodorant is on the counter, and I take it.

The bed is still made. Two clocks, two mirrors. Inside a box is an array of stone and metal, everything polished down to hole punches. I shut it and leave as Jake comes in ready for something, and he flops full onto the bed.

There's detergent at the laundry machine, a bundle of bottled water that's good enough. The few that are missing make the plastic move as I lug it past the his and his and hers bikes that are capsized to hooks.

The eggshell surfaces hug tense to a highway rumble. Pressure starts in my ears, pushes me out, and weakens my grip till I'm through.

Dad takes the car to the last house. Everything's stuffed with some blankets that he thinks Mom will like. There's a breeze, and the road is still quiet. Dad comes out with the bounce of an adventurer, and we're up the stairs with the same trick-or-treat go. He's ready but stops.

— Aren't you going to knock first?

His turn puts the crowbar and hammer to me.

— Oh, yes. Well, go on, take it.

My arms flex to hold both at once. Dad raps on the exposed part of the door and barks a weak warning before stepping back out of the way.

Jake joins me at the other side while I scratch the black crow's beak in. It slips once it's hit. I balance the rod back in place and swing again. With more taps, it's stuck. I try to tug the handle down and it shifts the stone weight of it. The beam is bowed, and I try again and again. Jake takes a step back.

— You look like you're ringing a bell.

— Is that a good thing?

— Um.

My fingers are rough on the pads and aching to bone. I squat to jab the bar in below, where I start bobbing back and forth. Jake picks into the top piece.

— Jake, don't do that while your sister's there.

— Sorry.

He joins me. The tectonic shifts try for a good jump until they're off. I linger back up and arc for the final beam. Jake finds a way in at the corner, but I barely keep it there.

— Okay, you can do this one.

— No, I want to see how you'd do without your mom and me here.

— Really?

— Yes, what would the two of you do?

Jake sighs with his arms ready.

— I guess we'd just let the piece fall.

— You would make that much noise? Not to mention the risk. It could easily hobble either of you.

— I guess.

— Don't guess. Just think about it. How are you going to get this thing off?

A twist of my foot doesn't take the dust from the cement.

I could find something to stand on. Or maybe just catch it.

— You don't want to break that thing's fall. What would you stand on, then?

I go for the one option that's not the car. The pieces come together the only way that works, on their backs and crisscrossed. The long nails gleam dead and it's paralyzed at my feet, an alleyway attempt at a spider.

— Sid, that's not safe.

— Do you think it's safe, Imogen?

I press the toe of my shoe on the center. It's firm.

— I won't fall.

— Sid.

— So that's you solution?

— That or let it drop.

— Guys, it's not that big of a deal. I can just pry it with one hand.

We both stop over the dead wooden bug. His arms are ready.

— It's probably best if you do it yourself then, Jake.

— Hey, you're hurting the spider stool's feelings.

— That's not a spider, it's a self-inflicted accident waiting to happen. And an insect.

— See? Hurt feelings. He's definitely a big, scary spider.

— What? Why? There are plenty of predators to choose from in the insect kingdom.

— Like what?

Dad's winced as I look back.

— Jake, would you please?

He finishes and I slide my spider out of the way, letting it keep its shape. Dad's eyes follow me to Mom. She's loud enough for everyone to hear.

— Don't get yourself hurt.

We're penguins together on ice that's as much leviathan as land.

— I wasn't going to.

— I mean it.

— So do I.

She looks close.

— You can't get hurt now. Nothing's worth you getting hurt.

— Well, then I won't get hurt.

— Good. You do that for me.

— Okay.

The door swings open, and Jake looks back.

— Good job, Jake. And you too, Imogen. Let's try and match the pace of the last one.

Stepping inside sets us marbled adrift. It's a while before we speak across our distances.

— What happened here?

— Maybe they moved.

— The bed is gone.

— Well, I can think of worse things to take with you.

— Are you finding food?

— Not really. Even the spice rack is cleared out.

— Maybe there's something in the closets.

A chill's behind me. I turn around and place my hand over the back door. A tug on the handle and something keeps it stuck that's not the lock. I yank it mostly free from the plywood.

— Someone got in through the back.

— Are you sure?

— Yeah, the lock's busted. They shut it back up again after.

Everyone's drawn to see.

— Well, this sucks.

Dad looks back at the broken lock.

— No, no this is great.

— Great?

— Someone else is here. Nearby. They have to be.

— Yeah, but we don't know when this was.

— It doesn't matter. Whoever did this locked the place back up, just like we are.

His teeth glint free.

— So?

— So they care about the neighborhood, how it looks. They don't want anyone else in here.

Dad steps out into the backyard and shrugs. There's no gate, only planter boxes and pots full of soil.

— We might as well take some of these back.

Neat stacks of boxes line the garage. A few are out and open, but there's nothing to do with them. Old books, old technology, old clothes. Scraps of home projects with nothing in the tangle. The only thing that says there was something real here is the lack of anything at all.

— So we're not alone.

— Technically we already knew that.

— Yes, but this is close. Almost certainly someones.

— So should we keep going?

Dad stares at nothing.

— Not yet. We can wait a day or two and see if they show themselves.

— Like we have?

Mom's eyes are on him, and she doesn't speak the rest of the way home.

KNOCK

Something slams downstairs. Thud thud thud. A chill crawls thighs-to-back on me as my tailbone slips into free fall. I don't get up. The pounding happens again. Mom and Dad are mollusked to the back of the house, and their words lose shape as urgency carries them up.

It's back to quiet and Jake lopes by. Coming out and down, it'd carry me straight to the vestibule too, to the door. The frame shudders under the return, making the door pulse and quiver in place, all of its small windows chattering against the barricade. I won't stay. As good as that would feel, I'm not going to.

— Imogen, just wait!

Jake's stage whisper stands the bombardment, cast and giving me cover. The door's in the dark and there's no way to see past. The clouded space is bound tight. There's pacing now, and I could have already done it. But then I'm suddenly nimble and passing by without anything changing behind me.

Jake's joined to Mom and Dad, whose eyes are blind past me. I circle in with them through the din and start to look off the same way. Mom prods at him, almost coming in where he's already braced.

— We need it!

— No one's getting through like that.

I break off for the light, hushing them in the banging as Jake's voice crawls into the gap.

— They'll have to move on, right? They don't know that anyone's here.

— Pretty sure those are knocks. Sort of.

Something close to disgust towards me gets blocked by Mom's back.

— Jake, where is it?

It's low and rising in his hand. Dad exhales and twists into indistinct movement until he presses it back down.

— Just, wait; be very careful. We're not going to shoot through anything or go brandishing it.

I step in and get partway.

— Actually, my window could work. We'd have the full view.

He doesn't look back.

— No, no, I just have to go there. I'll talk to him.

Mom moves in front.

— Sid, you take the gun.

A rumble eats into the floorboards as Dad shifts from her to the extended thing.

— I still have no idea how to use that. You'll be fine, right, Jake?

— Yeah, I mean, I watched some videos.

The hits turn to kicks.

— Just keep a good grip and do not use it. Even if you think you need to, don't. I mean it. We're going to deescalate, okay?

Their eyes are locked close, bringing Jake's broken facial hair to Dad's. Shoulders turn slowly for the door and leave a gash of night behind. I fill it with a rush to the drawer where a paring knife drives rubbered into my palm and wristbones. I come after.

The knocking plays on in dreadful staccato, irritated but not done. Pacing or nothing comes back in between, and there's no other with it, though I'm stopped, searching the darkness beyond.

They're at the stairs and the piercing kicks have stopped. I'm the only one crouched and ready to hug whatever crashes in and jab until it stops, until it's quiet again.

Dad bats the air for him to wait, and Jake shifts with me there too. He goes without turning back, examining the door for anything. Breathing, a shuffle, a brush that passes through. Nothing comes. Dad stops short of it and steadies into the glass-paned black, into the barrier.

— What do you want?

His voice isn't loud or stern. It's just normal, uncertain.

Behind, responding, there's only the shifting of an animal in his pen. Dad speaks at the same level.

— Are you there?

He's a step closer, another and he could lean into it.

The door slams hard. Harder than it has. Everything earthshakes and the plywood outside somehow moves. A pane is cracked, and Dad falls back with something mumbled free. I go and Jake has the gun with a shriek behind us already swallowed.

I go for the knob and take the deadbolt with my knife hand; Dad comes in the way. He's locked and leaves me to untangle myself. I get back and no one speaks. There's something, the weight of wind outside. Steps or something else, but nothing comes. I can scream and the words don't form, only the pressure. He stays and turns stony away as Jake runs upstairs for the window. It's still quiet.

— What were you doing, Imogen?

There's a gap at the edge that wasn't there.

— Nothing.

Neither reacts. Mom drifts another step.

— You shouldn't have said anything.

The silence brings them to a burnt up mass.

— We don't know what that was. Anyone could have spotted us out there today.

— We should have just gone like everyone else. Just kept going. What would have really happened if they got in?

Dad pushes against his contrapposto and squeezes his eyes from their glasses. Each sentence takes a breath.

— We're safe. A little worse for wear, but that's it. I'll seal it up better tomorrow.

— Whoever that was is still out there. And they'll come back now that they know we're here! What's there to stop them? There's only one thing.

She holds the thing of it tight to herself.

— They knew either way, Mei. I know what it means, but we'll tighten up; it's okay. Having bigger walls hasn't kept the whole world from falling apart.

Mom's eyes come to rocks.

— Hiding isn't going to make us any stronger. We have to show them what we'll do and be able to do it. Strong, that's what we are now. It's that or nothing.

— I wasn't going to let us fall into the hands of whoever that was. We aren't going to be scared by it, not into action or inaction.

He glances as the lithic point tumbles down her cheek, where it's lost in darkness. Mom speaks to herself.

— We're trapped.

— Mei, it's okay. It's okay. We're all shaken up. All we can do right now is make ourselves lie down.

— I'm not going to sleep after that!

— Then we'll do something. Work or keep watch if that's what you want.

Dad's arm rises, but it doesn't give so much that she has to accept or refuse. She looks down at the knife and moves back upstairs alone. He's still and framed by the door, and then he faces me.

— Help me make sure it's secure. You can put that back.

I keep it with me. Eyes on the unlit surfaces, tight grip on the knob and the lock with the weight still in the right place. The living room windows are above the stairs and untouched, but we go over them too. Last is the garage, undisturbed beyond the shock of us walking in. We don't go outside. Back upstairs, Jake confirms that there's been nothing, and Dad tells us to call it a night. I stay up doing nothing until there's no more to sit through.

WHO'S THERE?

I ONLY LET Jake know that I'm going. I'm stepping out and that's it. He doesn't pause or say much with his fingers fighting on the controller plastic.

I swipe Dad's pocketknife, no wallet, and sling over a sash of a backpack with nothing but a couple bars. The door wedges make snow angels across the floor, and they could be lying murdered when I'm back. I blink away the stinging and keep stepping forward. It's lighter out on the sidewalk.

Each of the passed through doors looks the same with what's inside still in the way.

I turn the corner and two people see me from across the way. Both their noses perk, almost sniffing at me. He's leaning against an apartment, and she's hands in pockets, legs wide into the kind of antsy split that's waiting for a table to clear. My coming over to their side slowly brings them neutral until they're drawn ghostlike back at me. I talk first, and the apparition melts between us.

— Good morning.

— It's still morning?

— Maybe.

The sun's lost back in the shapeless white of the sky.

— You guys live here?

He eyes me and doesn't hide it. His face is long but a thick, auburn beard completes a button rim around it. The girl looks at him and answers.

— Sure. So does that make us neighbors?

I check back briefly where there's no one.

— It might.

He relaxes his shoulders a bit and she smiles. I throw my hands into my jacket pockets. The knife is right there too.

— Was there anything strange that you saw last night?

Her face twists to apprehension, then concern through the long sienna wisps that drift out from her ponytail. I come light on what glows in her and stay there. The rest lies behind a beige Giants cap and faded denim jacket that says she does and doesn't care.

— Strange?

— Yeah, someone started banging on our door around ten or so. Ran without saying anything.

An eyebrow rises into his hair.

— Our door?

— Yes.

He touches her shoulder, thumb pushing tender to muscle.

— Did you get a look?

— No.

— Well, we're with others here. We could ask them. But everything seemed normal enough to me, right?

She turns perturbed in small doses. He tries looking at me the same way again, the blue-grey warmth of a proffered blade.

— Sorry.

— You can come upstairs with us if you like.

I grip the handle to hardness till it remembers bone. I shake free before they look. He only waits.

— It's alright if you want to stay.

— No, I'll come up.

— You sure?

— Yeah, sorry. Just, you know.

— You can call your parents first.

— My parents?

His eyes shoot awkward to her, who's caught him there.

— Sorry, just a joke. Come on, you should meet our group.

— Don't worry, we don't bite.

She starts with the urge to take my hand. He and then she turns to lead me in. I could jump on them screaming, and there's someone looking down from the fire escape. There's a rifle on his shoulder and a beer in hand, and he does nothing to show that he sees me seeing him see me.

Someone is already at the door when it swings back.

— What are you guys doing?

— We have a guest.

— A guest?

— Yeah, I mean, what fun's hanging around here all day if we can't be hospitable?

— Jesus, really?

— Yeah, really. It's our home too, Eshan.

His hair and skin shine dark as he's puffed. It's not the boyish luster that brightens when he finally looks at me in a seamfree change of tune.

— Sorry, we're just used to being a bit more democratic with our decisions around here. Of course you're welcome. Not unless you're here to rob us or anything!

I snort away a smile, softening my eyes down so they don't roll.

— I'm kidding.

— Right, so I just came to see if you know about any assholes out last night.

— Last night?

— Someone banged on her door and then took off. That's it, right?

— Messed it up, yeah. It was pretty scary, actually.

He gives a spark of recognition and leans in, still from inside and us out.

— And where would that be?

— Just down the street a couple of blocks.

— Really? Where, about?

I stop, and they already have enough to find us. Then we'd be on even footing.

— There.

— Oh, so we are neighbors?

He extends his hand for me to shake, his gaze matching the firmness of his small, fervent grip.

— I'm Eshan.

— Imogen.

— Imogen, huh? I like your name. Please, come inside.

He turns his back, leaving a red-faded designer T-shirt for us to follow.

— My name is James, by the way.

— Hi.

— Alyssa.

— Hi.

My hand falls easily into hers. It's pale and cold and smooth everywhere but the fingertips. James only nods tender for things to move on.

The apartment is a dingy mess. There's a desk and an uprooted radiator sitting where packages belong. There's also a baseball bat and some shoes. Doors linger back along the wall, but the daylight hitting in from upstairs promises something. Eshan leads the way.

— So welcome to our home. Our little fortress.

— It's a nice apartment.

— Yeah, it's fine. We think she'll hold up alright.

— How many of you are there?

There's more stair climbing, and the others stay quiet between us. Eshan reaches out for the rail that's about to end.

— We're a decent sized group. Once things went the way they did, I got a few of my work buddies to come over, and now we're family. It's what we were thinking about for a while, anyway. James and Alyssa were here too, and the other apartments, well, opened up.

He pauses for them to add something and only smiles pass.

— It's cool to find someone else.

The stairs carry on but Eshan goes straight to a door and opens it, no knocking or unlocking.

— We have a guest, everyone.

We go enmeshed with boxes to a room half vacant with dorm room essentials. A guy and a girl get up from opposite ends of the couch. Like everyone, they're in that older-than-me grey zone that happens past the mattering of birthdays.

— Well, hello! Told you there'd be recruits, Alyssa.

She chews out a smile of raspberry-mauve lips. Hues of fresh roasted hazelnuts curve around her cheeks and dance across the ribbing of her turtleneck. And to carry whatever point it is forward, round Asian eyes like mine beam fire from ice.

— Hey, I'm Chloe.

— Imogen. Nice to meet you.

— And you!

She looks me up and down, still chewing on her smile after a needled handshake.

— So what's your deal? Are you on your own? Heard about Eshan and his troublemakers?

— Troublemakers?

James steps closer as though to get a hand on me.

— She's just kidding. We dodge evac, start taking a few things here and there, and suddenly she thinks we're outlaws.

— What, you think the army's going to give a warm hello if they decide that there's something they left behind?

— You mean besides us?

The smiling swings free of them, and Eshan comes to her side.

— Which makes it run or be gunned for all of us so-called illegals. But really, Imogen, how are you set up?

Their seeing blankets around me, some sides soft. Eshan is close, the still-silent goatee man a pebble kicking back in the sheets. Shades of friendship from the others that I shift to meet.

— I have my family. Brother, parents. We were going to go, but, well, we got stuck and figured it was safer here.

— It is, but for how long, right?

— Don't scare her off, Eshan.

— I'm not going to. Although maybe I should.

Chloe buckles into laughing that's strong in its pitch.

— Sorry, my boyfriend isn't always this much of an ass.

He inhales sharply on a thin-lipped smile.

— If you want it that way, fine. We can hang out while you take on liabilities that we aren't at all ready for.

Worn gesticulations keep their movement.

— Um, I just wanted to see if you knew anything about the guy who almost attacked us last night.

— Sorry, not everyone appreciates leadership.

He wanders back towards the door without looking at me or his girlfriend, who's still smiling.

— I don't remember anything, do you guys? We were all here hanging out, mostly watching stuff.

James and Alyssa exchange glances, silent in front of their parents.

— Mason stepped out for a smoke, I think.

— Hey Cameron, why don't you make yourself useful and go get your buddy?

The thin, quiet one with a hook of a face looks at Chloe with a sudden wave of offense. Assent's whispered and he goes. I keep low to Alyssa and James.

— What's the matter?

— Oh, he's just trying to cut his meds. He's more fun on them. Well, fun's a strong word. Come on, you guys know I'm right.

James purses free his lips.

— It's a tough thing he's trying to do.

— Oh, you're just making nice in front of her. Come on, he's on edge all the time. You can't make everything life or death.

— Right.

Alyssa's arm wraps around James's waist where she hangs slothed into him.

— So, um, Imogen, what were you doing before all of this?

Chloe mirrors them by herself with one arm akimbo while they wait on me.

— I, uh, was going to college.

— Nearby?

— No. East Coast.

— Ah, well, sorry about your friends.

— Um, thanks.

Our eyes drift away. Then James tries.

— I'm a barista, by the way. Used to be at Incantation Coffee. I don't know what your setup is, but we have plenty of green beans that we still roast fresh at home. Would love to get you a bag or two.

— Oh, you don't have to.

— No, really, I want to.

— Hey, that's our stash!

— No, no, it's mine.

Alyssa hugs his waist tighter.

— He's got his own hothouse plantation too.

— Oh, really?

— It's a few trees. They don't take up much room or anything. They just need humidity and a few years.

Chloe butts back in.

— Yeah, we can all wait, right?

She languorously recedes to the couch and lies more than sits. Her limbs manage to take up most of it.

The door opens again without knocking and a beefy set of shoulders comes through. He's all pale flesh in a tank top with gym shorts and black compression socks below, giving Eshan a nod. He's not tall, but the gel in his hair tries to make up the difference. And he still has the rifle strapped to his back.

— Hey, Mason. Meet the new girl.

— I'm just stopping by.

— Yeah, I saw you.

— Right, yeah, do you have a good view up there?

— Could be better.

James leans into the moist, sleeveless slab and eyes what's propped there.

— Come on, dude. We're just hanging out here.

— I guess. Cameron made it seem like something was wrong.

— Yeah, well, that's Cameron for you.

— I just don't see the part where this helps us.

With his arms tight across, Cameron watches the effect of his words with a waver that's either beaten-stray or a fissure ready to give. A voice comes lazy from the couch.

— What about the part where you help us, Cameron?

Eshan springs back out of the kitchen with a boyish, ameliorating grin and half a laugh.

— Oh, we like to have a lot of fun here. That's us! So our, uh, neighbor here wanted to know if you saw anything strange from the tower last night.

— No, nothing's here yet.

— Just a person. Someone tried to, I don't know, bang on our door to get in or something. Was there anyone at all that you saw last night?

His eyes shoot to the jet point of his hair.

— Oh, well, yeah. There was someone, but all he did was cross the street.

— Wait, really? What'd you see?

— I don't know. Not much. He was only there for a moment.

— Okay, but what else do you remember? What time was it? What'd he look like? Was he carrying anything or with anyone?

— Um, it was before midnight. I don't know what he looked like. White, I guess. But it's not like I can see faces from up there. He was mostly just a jacket.

— Where'd he go?

— That way.

Mason points a blunt finger towards home.

— And you didn't hear anything after that?

— Sorry, I was only really there to smoke.

His eyes loosen away from me.

— Do you think you'd recognize him?

— What? No, sorry. I just saw a guy walking. It seemed normal. I thought he lived here or something.

— So was he young? Big? Skinny? Anything?

Beads of sweat sit on his puckered forehead, and he prods into the maybe hot, maybe cold flesh.

— He was a guy. I don't know. He wasn't too much of anything.

I'm where a gritty private eye would threaten to beat out a confession if there was one. Or at least flick out the simple thing that would turn the stool pigeon's spiteful life upside down with all kinds of legal or not so legal problems.

— Okay, well, thanks. I'm glad it was just a guy.

— Yeah, sorry.

Eshan approaches with eyes intent for mine, eyebrows undefined spots of night on polished agate.

— I wouldn't worry about it. Dude's going to be long gone. Just an asshole, right?

I'm gritting my teeth as he keeps talking.

— So maybe we can work something out. A bit of a collaboration, perhaps?

There are soft and hard looks waiting for my response.

— I'll have to see what my family thinks about anything first.

— Right, of course. But don't you think they'd want to do something like that?

Alyssa's are the eyes that I stay on. James does and doesn't want to look. Chloe is watching for sport. The thin one still doesn't want me here and the large one is off in space. But Alyssa's are just fresh-cut whole wheat bagels looking back from a plate.

— And we helped you out with the thing.

— Well, you saw someone.

— Right, so maybe we could try trading sometime. Or even pool some resources.

Alyssa shoulders forward.

— Or work together for scavenge. Hold our territory if we ever have to. Make sure that all of us are safe.

Her fingers pulse over the air at her side. The sea anemone bits hover there longer until they grip in bony excitement over my mostly genuine yes.

— Right. Well, I think that'd be great, really. I mean, it'd be stupid if we didn't try to help each other out some, right?

Eshan waits and then gestures to the door. I go with him, but our feet don't match pace and I'm looking around the room to register some sort of goodbye.

— Well, think it over. Talk about it with your family, but I look forward to meeting them.

James comes in.

— Hey, we can walk you back. That is, if you want.

Alyssa's behind.

— Maybe. Yeah, you can come.

Chloe jumps up from the couch, all limbs.

— Ugh, well, I could use a walk! You boys enjoy the quality time together.

They don't look. Eshan calls out as we leave.

— It was nice meeting you, Imogen! Tell your family we all say hi.

BOBA

THE NEXT KNOCK is crisp and sure of itself. I drop the book that I'm not reading while the house magnets to the front without Mom. Only daylight is there through the cracks.

— Can you guys hear me? Hello?

His eyebrows plop in front of me. Dad's brow settles in with the pelts, and they jolt right back up again for me to answer. I nod and they follow as I come to where the door with too much shallow glass will still be a shield if it swings in.

— We hear you.

— Oh, hi. It's Alyssa.

Jake stands a little straighter.

— Hey, what's going on?

— Nothing, really. We were just going to go out for a bit and wondering if you wanted to come.

A squint steps into Dad's furrow. Jake's arched to meet it, but he only shrugs back blank as paper.

— It's okay if you're busy or something. Just an offer.

— Yeah, I mean, maybe. What were you thinking?

Plywood silence sits on the other side.

— Um, can we maybe talk face-to-face?

— Okay, yeah. Come down to the side door.

Dad's lips curl and crest. We each unmoor and go in some kind of motility. Dad keeps in front.

— Just stay on your guard, always. Learn everything you can. Figure them out.

— So we can go?

— Yes, of course. You aren't prisoners here. You don't have to break out.

The line is hard between us.

— But everything we're running from is out there. I trust you both to be careful, always.

Jake nods.

— Cool.

— Being in the same boat is one thing, but working together is very different. When things go bad, it's different. Okay?

His look is close and plain at me.

— I know.

He puzzles the meaning to himself and ends it with a sudden smile and hug that leaves us at the steps of the garage.

— If anything starts to feel wrong, you both come home immediately.

Shuffle. Thwack. Skid. Plink. Clank. And the door swings easily free.

— Ah, there you guys are.

— Hey, thanks for coming over!

— Yeah, of course. No reason for us all not to hang out, right?

The question hangs in the air. Chloe picks it up.

— So, we were going to go look for boba. Want to come?

— Seriously?

— Yeah. What? I had a craving. And then I gave Alyssa that craving. Now we're here to give you the boba craving.

— Sounds dangerous. Maybe we better lock back up.

— Yeah, you guys sort of jumped the gun there.

— The gun jumped itself.

— Oh, so you speak in cryptic badass now that the world is over?

Chloe watches my eyes, a smile skulking underneath. I burst into laughter and she leaps on it. James and Alyssa warm the space around us with theirs. Jake smiles.

— At least there's still boba, probably.

— I mean, I guess we should be able to find some.

— It's just powder and tapioca balls, right? How hard can it be?

The brown of her catches on something red and fall colored within that's being drawn out by the distance. It stays.

— Well, I haven't had taro in a while.

Jake shrugs out a nod.

— Sounds good to me.

— Aw, look at you. You know you want it!

Chloe pushes him, making an inflatable clown that holds tight. He smiles downward and doesn't come up with anything to say.

The five of us cram into the orange-black hatchback. I'm wedged in between Chloe and Jake while James rocks into the front. The meat of it is different on both sides. Indifference looking away but still too close on my right. A childish lack of boundary moving forward or into me on the left. Chloe puts her hand plain on my knee in excitement. I stay still and feel it with the tingle of cryogenic sleep. I wait for a message, any kind of rub or squeeze or departure to say what she means. There's nothing other than that thing to decipher. It's there in a way the world hasn't been, and then it's not.

The stop isn't far, back on Geary. A horde could be tumbling its way across, but there's only air to greet us. James parks into a clean U-turn that leaves the nose facing home. A jerk on the brake sets gears crying underneath and we're out.

Alyssa draws a pair of bolt cutters from her pack. She passes James's open hand and rests the teeth into a link that begins to lose its shape, and the rest clatters to cement. The mismatched cluster of couches and high-tops is over to the side, unclear what for.

— Aw, man, I've missed this place.

— It's not that packed up.

— Well, it's not like they were going to start up anywhere else.

Alyssa and James hop over the counter together and Whac-A-Mole back up. Her low, two-handed grip on the bolt cutters keeps it ready to spring into someone's throat. She steps sideways, forward to the kitchen, before letting go. Chloe pouts but bounces up catlike until her other boot is caught on the ledge.

— What's it like back there?

— Just empty.

James lifts a box upside down and nothing happens until he flips it into a corner, where it also does nothing.

— They've been closed for a while, right?

— Yeah, but come on, we're here. There's got to be something.

Aluminum tops sit in rows over blenders. Cups and dome caps are still wrapped. The first few cabinets are empty until a stack of hospital-white boxes pulls down with a stretch. James jabs his thumb into one and plunges for the nondescript, machine printed label.

— There we go!

— Really?

— Do we know what to do?

— Sure, you boil this, mix in that. Then it's just milk, ice, and sugar.

— Milk?

— Yeah, anything you have. Whatever you want, I got it.

James points a bag at Chloe.

— So now you're sharing?

— Well, yeah. It's not like I was going to swipe all the pearls for myself and make one every night while you're asleep. Yeah, I totally wasn't going to do that.

At their place, Chloe serves up mugs filled to the brim in white slosh. They're dark with the brown from coming back through snow.

— Do you have any straws?

Her eyes stop.

— No.

— Then how are we supposed to get to the boba?

— I don't know, just drink it!

Chloe makes the couch jump underneath me, and the rest of her curls into the splash to nurse two-handed in thrust lips. A smile presses out of Alyssa.

— So is this it for you guys? Come what may?

— Come what may?

— Yeah. Is that the plan, just being here?

Her eyes and lashes and lips carry out a flat line to us.

— Well, it's been working so far. Who knows what's next.

Jake sits up straight.

— Of course we have plans. They've just changed is all.

Alyssa smiles down.

— I'm not trying to grill you guys. I just want to know what you're doing.

— They're here for the great boba, obviously.

Chloe's voice is deep on the slush.

— Right, keep it up and we'll get a line out the door.

— Not a problem if they're paying.

Our laugh is forced. Neither of us is quick to answer.

— I don't think we've really been doing anything. I mean, what's there to do, right? No actual news. Fortressing's not nearly as good as running.

— Well, it's not like you're waiting to lie down and die.

An ember glows in her, and she leans forward, ready to smash hard from soft. I talk with cold teeth.

— Are you?

She's bashed between reactions and I'm already past.

— I don't know, everything's jerked us around so far. I'm just glad that part's stopped.

Chloe's leaf-pounced to me.

— Oh, because things are going to be great now.

— Maybe.

Something shines, and James squeezes hard at the crest of Alyssa's knee.

— Hey, we're glad we met up. Stick with us and we'll all be better off for it. Numbers matter, right?

Alyssa stares straight back.

— Numbers are what got this whole thing started in the first place.

— I'm not talking about them.

The door opens with Eshan and the others loud with the rush of a hunt.

— Oh boy, bubble tea!

— Hey babe!

— You guys actually did it. Wow, that looks great!

— And you're our first customers.

We're all smiling except the guys behind him, who are just tired. Jake lifts his cup.

— Best I've had in months.

— It's okay. I mushed up the balls too much. But you can't mess with the power of milk and sugar, right?

— Oh no, this is great!

Eshan grabs a mug and has to tilt it back for the center to move. It hits snowballed in his face without falling. He tries to swipe parts of himself dry, not looking at any of us.

— Aw, let me get you a spoon. Messy baby.

Chloe bounds up, breezing past his glare. The other two take cups and stay there.

— You guys want to go out?

— What? You just got here.

— Yeah, but we found something.

— You found something.

— Yeah, come on. It's a surprise. Might lose the opportunity if we're too late.

James and Alyssa look at each other but stand, glasses too. Eshan eyes just us with dessert counter glee.

— So are you two up for it? It'll be close, you'll see.

We let slip our assent and go.

GROCERY SHOPPING

WE'RE TIGHT AGAIN in the back. An inch over, Chloe claws at her pants in bouts. Light speckles of tan grapple across her cheeks while her lips let free a quiet, restless burst. My glance drops to the canvas of my lap, where the surface is calm and waiting to leap back up again and flail. Her breath continues its tingle on my skin, arriving through networks of lithological layers. Cold and damp and distant, but right here. And now what will it do?

Eshan speeds on in an unabashed lacework of soot on white. We chase after through the rolled stop signs, but the distance still grows between us.

— He's right, though. We are going to have to keep on looking.

The hill up then down takes us to a spot where Eshan suddenly makes a turn that sets us back the way we came. Chloe smacks her knee and makes mine smart with it.

— Not this shit again!

Jake bends past me.

— What is it?

— Just these assholes that Eshan is convinced are still somehow getting shipments.

— What, at the grocery store?

— Yeah.

The city blocks give way to green, and we're at the coastal cypresses that are encrusted along the golf course. What spreads of grass I get are bare, no different from the playground that's right below where Jake and I used to play. The piece of me that was there is caught up in the cold, stagnant metal that forgets me as I can't reach it.

The sudden outdoor emptiness is stopped by clusters of fencing down below. The cement is defiant where razor wire clings in patches. There's no gate, only a pinch of fences closed in on itself with zigzag switchbacks. It'd take pivoting just to make a way forward, and that's if you don't end up somehow trapped. There's too much cyclone mass to try and run it all over.

No one's about.

Eshan parks at the playground. James does the same with the clog of metal down ahead. The guys are straight to the trunk as we're pulling up, and Eshan comes arms wide with the stark white of a smile.

— What the hell do you think is going to happen here, Eshan?

— Relax! We're just going to make some friends, babe.

— With guns?

— That's how we make these kinds of friends. They aren't going to like us if they think we're deadweight.

— They aren't going to like anyone stupid enough to posse walk right up to them.

He passes a sidelong glance back to James and holds his response. Chloe stops to look at him too, not showing what she thinks.

— Buddy, they know who I am. It's fine. I just need everyone here to put their tough guy faces on for a while. I'll do the talking.

— Why do you have to be such a little shit about this, babe?

A maritime gust works its way at my nose and mouth.

— Little? Oh, why'd you have to hit me where it hurts?

Eshan's pantomimed arrow to the side is more undead than he could have meant. My smirk encourages him, if only because it takes a stupefied look off of one of our faces.

Chloe has her arms folded in full pout, and Eshan rushes over to take each shoulder up close. The fingers slide without taking root.

— Chloe, you know I'm doing this all for us. We just need to prove ourselves. Show them we're good friends to have. They have something we want, and we gotta have something they want.

Glances pass, and Chloe leans out of his grasp to find something to stare at in the houses across the way. Eshan comes puppied back to the rest of us.

— Okay, we're going to hold them, but keep low and unthreatening. Don't do the whole direct eye contact thing either. We're just here to show that we have the numbers, right?

Alyssa leans into James's neck.

— Because that's a great idea.

— Jake and Imogen, what are you carrying?

Jake sees my immobility and sighs. The thing he's kept hidden doesn't come easily.

— I'm not going to shoot anyone for you.

— Of course you're not. We're here to make friends. It'll be a huge help to you guys too, for sure. I'm talking fresh produce. Just be cool and follow our lead.

Mason thrusts an old hunting rifle to me. I slowly grab at the stock that he has right at my chest, and I let it sink in.

— Don't give her that. Come on.

— It'll be fine.

— What?

— We don't have ammo for that one.

— What? Why?

— We found it.

— You found it?

— In a house. There just wasn't any ammo.

— How hard did you look?

— Hard enough. Geez, keep it if you like. It's just a prop anyway. Unless you were planning on using it.

— Dude, that's not cool.

— Relax.

— No, take mine.

James extends his own on two pinched fingers. The barrel swings scythed right out of a poster about how it's only a piece of hard black plastic that will keep you living. The wag slows to disapproval.

— That's not yours to give, man.

— It absolutely is.

— It's alright. I'll be fine with this.

Everyone looks at me except Chloe, who's pained.

— Let's just do it.

Eshan laughs a little and pats me on the back. His fingers grip at the bone and jerk me lightly before they fly back off.

— Alright, you heard her! Let's do this!

— Yes, go show the tough people how tough we are.

Eshan looks past Alyssa's undaunted harrowing.

— Yes, let's.

We plod in pairs down the sidewalk. Bit by bit the fortress reveals itself. An empty driveway for roof parking where they can see down the street, but there's no spotting us from this side until we're here.

— You know Dad and Mom are going to kill us.

— If all else fails, play cute and innocent?

— Maybe you do that one.

We come pooled down at the start of Guernica. One of its corners creaks on its own, and the weight of this many bodies in the street is something suddenly thick with warmth. There's no wait or reaction for our beast with too many heads.

We stand facing nothing. No doorbell to push. Eshan looks over to the dark storefront. He almost waves but stops himself. His air frets in and releases with a smile as three forms step out, all of them thicker than the rest of us and built differently from Mason. His is shaped and theirs just grew. Loose jackets and military style rifles make themselves out before the faces.

— Gentlemen, good to see you again. Thanks for coming out.

— What do you think you're doing?

— I just wanted to show you I wasn't lying. Here we are for a friendly introduction. So how can we work together to help each other out?

The man in the middle is disappointed with limp blond hair waiting to turn grey. He's fat, but even in the day's stagnation, all the mass does is insulate the abandon of snuffing someone's life out.

— No thanks.

— We're not asking for anything. We're here to work hard with you.

All of the man's wrinkles roil around the bulb of his nose.

— Ah, how considerate. We'll be fine.

The sour spit of his words makes the others laugh quietly. One relishes the sneer, the other, actually handsome, keeps his pleasure at a remove.

— Okay, okay, play it like that. But we all know the truth is there is no fine anymore. If we're here, we might as well help each other out. I mean, why not?

— We don't have to do anything. You either get that soon or you die.

— Okay.

— And stop coming here. God, don't you realize how annoying you are? What makes you think we're sitting around, waiting to be called out by someone looking to weasel his way into our shit? The only reason we're not shooting your pathetic little group down right now is because, well, I don't even know why, myself. Do you have a reason?

The pause tenses hot to the top of my chest. Eshan mouths out nothing, but the man turns to listen to the whispers of the guard, who's now excited as the other waits by uneasy. James interrupts.

— You're not looking for a fight any more than we are.

— You don't know what we're looking for.

— Yes, well, that doesn't really matter, does it? We're all fighting them, like it or not.

His mouth cracks at the corner.

— They aren't here. And that's a fight no one wins. You're stupid if you think otherwise.

— You sure have a funny way of looking at things for a businessman.

He pauses. Something brings his eyes downward and alone.

— I'm a man with a target on my back, and you're not touching it.

The other two keep looking at us. The handsome one's on the guys, the other, larger, prying, only looks at us girls. I glare back and he smiles.

— Just get the hell out of here and don't come back. That's as much help as you'll get.

The fat man shuffles away, shambling more penguin than the bear that he was. We're eyed over one last time before the others turn. Eshan rouses back up at them for something to say, but they're gone.

— Let's just go.

END OF THE WORLD

We don't have anything to burn, only the stretches of scrub and sand and the long shearing of the water. James turns us back before anyone tries naming what might be buried behind the seawall.

Bone white wavers over the emptiness of the Great Highway. Stripes of it drift back and forth in a current, tiptoeing their way out of here. It's blocked somewhere ahead, he says. I'm the only one that he's telling this to, but whatever I have to say is hurried away by the beach houses that receive us.

The damp alleyways of beaten apartments go in catacombs that have the sun straining in above. They're all clammed tight and mussel black, indifferent when we get out to tear apart someone's picket fence. Each post clings to the rail to stop what we're doing to it. The crushed bugs add up until we get into the bushes and give up on the rest. Throughout the effacing, the sunken home that we chose stays shuttered with the others, hiding from its own spot on the street. But the broken concrete and shapeless junipers still stand uncollared in fresh dirt. Awake. Alyssa stomps through it.

— You know none of this is going to burn.

James hooks a dirty thumb into his pocket.

— It will if we make it.

I slice myself against a board. The cross-section on my finger is all white except for the pooling of red. It hurts, first the surprise and then the ache. Chloe steps me back and holds my hand up with a soft touch. Giving eye contact, she bounds a kiss onto the finger and falls back to the space in front of me.

— Hurts less now, right?

— Right.

The four of us head back again onto open pavement with the smell of the ground still in the air. The boards are chapped and exhausted right behind us. James drives to the coastal Safeway that's still shelled with the same half-homeless look from before. The parking lot is cleared out, and someone could be there in the dark. We pull in by the dumpsters, where it's too quiet to know what comes next.

— You really think they'll have it?

— What?

— Lighter fluid?

— Oh no, there's nothing in there. It's shelved out.

— Then what are we here for?

James reaches into the trunk, where the boards look back startled, snakes in a can. They siss to tug out a plastic canister and a hose.

— That truck's been there for a while. We already checked; the trailer's empty, but it should run on diesel.

— Why does that matter?

— Burns slow and strong. Gas could work too, but it flares up on you more.

He talks while looking ahead.

— How do you know?

— Just, you know, research.

Alyssa torques off the cap of the tank that's a spookhouse skeleton at the cabin stair, trapped. Their choreography forces through the lack of practice. Each move is double-checked until my bladder is wincing at the sound of the canister. Chloe leaves me to dart around to the other side, where she climbs up, not quite looking at us in the darkened haze.

— There's gum!

— Oh boy.

— You guys don't want to know what kind?

— Is it mint?

— Maybe.

— Nobody needs mint.

— Tell that to your girlfriend.

Alyssa stifles a laugh and looks at James.

— I brush my teeth, thank you.

— Well, I'm still getting it. You want some, Imogen?

— Uh, sure.

She's squirreled somehow in and rocking as they raise the syphoning can for the hose.

— Man, I like this guy.

She's down and smiling to smack over a crinkled fistful of condoms to Alyssa, and she turns bodied red.

— Don't say no. They're going to expire anyway, and then what are you going to do?

James takes them from her, his movements stressing their normalcy.

— Thanks, Chloe. You sure?

She's already chewing when she hands me a piece from the tin, and she makes James and Alyssa have some too. She also makes us turn up the music, and she smiles massaged by the volume. Back again, we carry out the cooler and blankets and armfuls of fence. The sand makes us linger more than it slows us down, and I go alone by the concrete with the city there to see me. The lowered sun is still the only shape on the ocean and beach around us. We watch it blare against its own weight. Chloe takes it in fully, smacking out more flavor from the gum than I am.

James starts to break the fence parts with his shoe, and he keeps at it when Alyssa goes to help. Buried pieces come free against my hands while scooping a disk into the sand. Charred and air-soaked bits, something plastic, something glass, something kelp, shell. Chloe calls out and we go to see where anemones of ashen paper wave from an old fire pit. The area around them is still worn. We look at the circle longer in the noise before sitting. It starts to smell with the diesel over the boards, James crouched for a child.

With a stand-in torch, he lights up the stack of what was the way in and out of a person's life.

— Woo!

— Yeah!

I join their throaty vibrato. She gets louder, then I get louder, then she gets louder too. I look up into the darkening sky and shout again and try to grab hold of the corner of a first constellation that's stuck now with a dead-bright satellite. I'm tackled by a laughing Chloe, and we dance and laugh tonelessly. Something tribal comes out and I bare my teeth in a faux movement. She giggles wildly, and we tumble back onto the blankets and crawl over for the beers.

— There it is.

The sun glows a bright explosion. The colors are simplified between yellow and wet slate as the darkness keeps pressing down on the world around us. Chloe rocks cross-legged into me, and I puff out a grin to push her back.

— This is not a bad place to be right now.

— Not at all.

The first beer disappears by the time I see the sun has left. The glow on the water turns on every expanse of nothing around us. I check the car but drop back to my empty bottle, which I lean in to replace. James jumps up from us and spreads his arms wide against the ocean.

— We have the world ahead, all the dead behind, and us here in the middle. We're right at the end of the world!

Alyssa throws sand at him and we laugh.

— Maybe Hawaii's the real end.

— Yeah, Hawaii would be great.

— We could start looking for a boat.

— It's not.

— You sure?

Alyssa begins to play with her empty shoes, and I poke at mine.

— Yeah. Too many people had the same idea before they stopped them. No infrastructure for it. Things stop coming. It can't be going well there.

A gull drops to the sand and looks at us. Its head cocks and bobs, and it flies off again before anyone does anything.

— Well, thanks for taking the fun out of that one, babe.

— Sorry, just something I looked into.

Chloe fingers at her phone until music comes without the bass that it's there for. The noise we make builds up again until the two of us have bumbled our way into sharing a blanket and the gyroscope in my head starts to drift. James and Alyssa have already settled into theirs, and the knit blobs spasm with limbs that can't be kept track of. James smiles at me for smiling and tosses a question.

— So what's the one thing you'd bring back?

— One thing?

— Yeah, just one.

The minty beer is in my face as Chloe interjects.

— You can't make us play that game if we already know yours.

— And what do I want?

— Uh, coffee.

— Coffee's not gone. We have coffee. That's not the first thing I'd bring back, anyway.

She's digging her toes pert into the sand. Purple nail polish.

— Really?

— Yeah, roasting has taken a huge blow along with everything else. But any kind of craft, any kind of art is just a thing that we share with each other, right? So what if we only share in smaller ways now? All that matters is that the thing we give still feels like us, but more. Maybe all art has ever done was evoke the feeling of giving someone your food, offering them a place to stay, goofing off. It spread it out past that person-to-person moment to where the good feeling took on a life of its own. The world's already gone. It can't handle that kind of connection anymore, not for our lives, at least. So maybe we're less now, but maybe we're more us. And at least the plants seem to be taking it just fine. Good coffee will always be there waiting for us.

James looks at everyone yearnful and avoiding the dark.

— Well, damn, you just had that one sitting in your pocket, didn't you?

He smirks at Chloe and takes a drink. Alyssa kisses him lightly on the cheek.

— Yeah, we'll see how you are about it on the day we actually run out, babe.

— Well, we're all headed for some bucolic fortress with a farm and a bunch of dogs eventually, right? It's coming.

— Yup, a place where we can work the ground all day to give it away. For the feels.

James only nods at Chloe, who clams back up too. I make him talk again.

— Then what would you bring back if it's not about that?

James laughs silent.

— George R. R. Martin.

— Oh God.

— Well, there's no other way we're getting the end of Game of Thrones!

— You don't even know if he's dead!

— Do you think a postapocalyptic society has built up around him to keep him writing?

— Probably?

Alyssa bearhugs him from behind.

— Eh, you're blowing a wish on a few hundred pages.

— Maybe I'm blowing my wish on a few thousand, hm?

— And what are you going to do when you realize that it's not as good as you'd hoped?

— I don't know. Does it matter? We need the real end. See how it all falls apart and what climbs out from the rubble.

— Wow, what an escapist!

— No, he's looking for a guidebook.

— They had dragons.

— Does there really need to be an end, though?

James's face clears crystal to me.

— Well, yeah.

— But we have our own stories too, right? Just like anyone else. And we all have to live our lives out without knowing how they end. So what does it matter if another story goes unfinished? It'd just be like meeting someone you'll never see again.

He leans back like I've said something funny that he won't laugh at.

— I think it's actually the other way around. We're all stuck living with finished stories.

Alyssa loosens her grip on his shoulder where he stays smiling at me. There's sand that glitters from his beard in flecks of teeth.

— But we don't know anything. We're sitting here with hardly any idea of what's happening in the Mission, let alone the rest of the world.

He smiles doubled again.

— It's not the how that I'm talking about, it's the what.

— What?

— I mean, does it really matter if we end up bit or in a ditch or so alone in a bunker that we blow our own brains out? The point is that that's all we expect from life now. No matter who we were before, that's what everyone is ultimately waiting for.

A gust rushes past me and over the fire on its way back out.

— No one here's given up.

— No, we haven't. And that's the point, right? What makes us human? Pressing on with the end there in plain sight.

— That or we're really just as stupid as the rest of them.

James regards me again. He takes a drink, which makes me take a drink.

— Who are you, Imogen? What are you? Come on, who's the you that's here with us right now?

James builds exuberant and waits. Nothing shapes into an answer.

— I can tell you, I was trying to get all I could out of Incantation so that I could break off on my own. Patch over all the parts of me that weren't ready to run a business. And even if I was never going to be in the right place and the right time to hit it big with just something, I knew how to make myself useful to the people who were. For six years, that was me. Maybe all I was ever going to get out of that job was the wait, or they'd expand somewhere and need me to take over, and I'd feel like I did something. But that was who I was, good to go. Reliable and aching to stand out. Is that the guy you see sitting before you?

Some sort of yeah shrugs into the circle. Alyssa comes around to look at him better.

— Well, I'm not. A lot of the parts are the same, sure, but the story, my reason for being, it's not in the same place. Look, maybe I'm not saying it that well, but you know what I mean.

Alyssa steps in front of him, her hips in his face.

— Aren't I a reason for being?

— Of course you are, you know that. But we're up in the air together too. We're all books with our ends ripped clean from the spine. Nothing left to look at but the blank cover. You don't just adapt to that and move on. You bury all of the old you or you just stay with it.

She slowly straddles his legs, which he accepts, begrudging as she crouches low to him.

— What else you want to bury?

Chloe whoops as his shoes shift underneath. Alyssa stares down into him, cheeks burning bright with thin, plastic movements closer.

— You should put another log on, babe.

— Yeah, he better!

James rolls his eyes at Chloe and comes free. He stays basked in the spotlight, bringing all of the boards, boyish and javelined at once.

— Well, what about you?

— What about me?

There's something sharp in Chloe's voice.

— What would you want back?

James gleams obsidian in the fire. She squirms up straight and takes some of the heat with her.

— Amazon.

The boos raise the circle to the ocean's intoning disembodiment.

— It's not like you guys don't miss it. Getting everything now is way too much work.

— Yeah, but look at how sustainable and free it all is.

— Not that free. And what's sustainable about us living off the city like bacteria?

— We're hunter-gathering!

James grips a board, spear in hand, only to toss it back when no one else laughs.

— Hunter-gathering isn't so great when you want more than just berries. Dried ones, I guess. I mean, it's not even like we need anything right now. We're just taking things. Aren't you guys tired yet of all the useless shit that people ditched? There's too much of them left on it. Come on, you know you want your two-day shipping back.

I stifle a burp, and Alyssa's the only one to notice. She smirks and moves close.

— You're so bad, Chloe.

— What?

— The world ends and you just want to shop.

Alyssa curls back again in surplus laughter.

— No, I don't want to shop. That's the point. I want to have the things I need right when I need them.

— And what more do you actually need?

She stops and looks over to me.

— I'll know it when I see it.

Alyssa falls forehead first into James's chest, who's ready to catch her.

— I bet even you can't guess what I'd bring back, Jamesy.

— Hm, your followers.

— Hey, they're still there, technically.

Her ponytail lashes at the space behind her.

— No, you ass. It's all the old people homes.

We wait on James's expression, which won't move. She turns back to us.

— My, uh, grandmother. She was being taken care of back in Virginia.

— Oh.

— But she's been gone for a while. You know, up there.

The words are simple through the hush.

— It's not like there was anything more you could do about it.

— No, and my parents and brother couldn't do anything either. But they still stayed.

— You're here, babe. Nothing good would have happened if you went back.

— Yeah, I know. I'm only wondering what it was like. To be there through it. Drown with someone who doesn't even know what's happening.

The sea roar blankets over us for a moment. The only one who's smiling still is her.

— You know, I have dreams of being chased out there. Everything a corner to escape. I don't ever really wake up with the details, but each time it feels like it's her who's been after me.

— Alyssa.

— I just think it's a funny way to remember someone.

— Well, shit.

The roar comes in again for the space between us.

— Imogen and I are going to go on a walk.

— We are?

— Yes, we are.

The chill at the edge of the fire welcomes me awake. James keeps Alyssa tight but calls back.

— Hey, what's your thing?

— My thing?

— That you'd bring back if you could. Can't go without telling us.

— Well, I miss getting to do this.

I raise my bottle and chug down the rest. Everyone cheers and he toasts back at me, off balance with her weight.

— I knew I liked you.

Alyssa stares with cat eyes as Chloe carries me off and flails what's left of hers into the shadows.

I keep my grip on her tight past letting go. We're headed for the cliff face, where the lookouts are modest overhead. Our legs are heavy together at first, but soon we're just walking on cool sand with an unpeopled dark. Chloe glances back and I don't. The pen-ink surface of the ocean continues to swallow as much of the world around us as we allow.

— Okay, enough with things we like. How about you tell me one thing you hate?

— Oh God.

— It doesn't have to be big! Or, you know, about anything. It just doesn't have to be so positive either.

— So you're taking this from show-and-tell to angsty teenage years?

Her laugh carries out alone with the self-sure warmth of mahogany.

— Are you going to give me an answer or not?

— Fine. I hate toasted sandwiches.

— What!

— All it does is cut up the roof of my mouth!

— But warm and gooey makes anything better.

— It's not worth hurting myself for it!

My grip relaxes in her histrionics, but she doesn't let go.

— Man, we should go on a deli run.

— Yeah, I don't think that's going to happen.

— Aw, you're no fun.

She has on a necklace that glimmers despite itself. Just a teardrop of something. The sort of thing they said to get rid of or die from.

— So what do you hate?

Her steps turn viscous, archival with the air damp around us.

— I hate. I hate. I hate cilantro since it tastes like soap to me. The only reason I think it exists is because of a plot to ruin perfectly fine Mexican food. I hate the way people act like they can meditate away the guy on the bus that smells like piss and smoke, or he's leaning too close or playing bad music. Just yell or find a way to really be nice about it, I guess, but accept the world that's around you, right? I hate waiting anywhere for a table. I hate the cold. I hate anyone who thinks they can tell me what to do. And I hate getting red when I drink, mostly because that's nobody else's business either.

— Oh God, right. Am I red too?

— Eh, you're blotchy. See? There on your chest. But I know I'm a beet right now.

Her finger is icy at the tip and burning in the palm.

— Shut up, you're beautiful.

— Yeah, beautiful enough to be served up with some goat cheese, walnuts, and arugula.

We laugh, and I can't feel mine from hers.

— Oh no, you're much too pretty for that. You're just the full beet salad, none of that green filler.

— Well, only if you'll be the golden beets with me.

— Maybe I will.

Our laughter dies down to nothing and I push forward and kiss her. The feeling of it disappears from anything but shock. Shock of doing something with no sense of what it is. Gravity keeps us glued, hands and everything else uncertain of what more to do. Chloe breaks downward first.

— The beet thing was corny, wasn't it?

— Careful, you'll make it worse.

— Maybe we're just hungry.

— Yeah, well.

Her eyes rest, doused now of their ongoing fervor. What shows through is tempered metal looking to be put in its right place. Alien and sentient and serene. When I feel her lips on mine again, rough, chapped surfaces bar the way. And I stand there waiting, giving. A little movement lets me in, a tectonic shift from another horizon felt nowhere but here. We both fall lightly into the opening between us. The chafed parts moisten away.

Our lips dance together, fit into each other's lack, show the other how they move. Give things that can't be seen. We don't taste the same, despite the beer and the gum. She's mostly green apples. My hand starting to feel hers like an object I can play with, my other reaches up to where I can ripple my fingers over the lake surfaces of her side. We kiss harder now and let it hurt, but something invisible gives way and makes her pull back from me.

— What?

She's not looking at me. A strand of hair is still stamped to her lip, her breath pounding with the waves.

— We should stop.

Everything, the way she's standing, craters right into my gut. Her expressions are changing again from me.

— You want to stop?

— Imogen, can't we.

She says it too fast. She begins to hold her arms together, and my chest tenses in a hot burst of pain.

— Can't we just say we had some fun and head back?

— That's what you wanted me out here for?

— I don't know, blame the alcohol! Or blame all this damn end of the world talk. It doesn't matter. If you don't want to forget it, we can tell them that we kissed and make the guys all jealous they missed out. Is that better?

I take a step towards her and she sinks slowly back. The taste of copper spreads out from under my lip.

— I don't like you for that.

— Well, I think you're great too, Imogen. But come on.

— Come on what?

— You're going to make me say it?

Her face is fuller as we continue until maybe she really is like a beet. The ball bearings of her eyes are hard and still in the dark.

— I'm not gay.

The same teeth that I was just getting to know come out with ultra-violet ease.

— Well, neither am I.

— Great, then let's get back already.

— But that's not what I mean.

— Well, whatever you mean.

— Just, what does it matter anymore?

— It matters to my boyfriend.

— Does it?

She stops to shout but the atavism drops. Something in my chest is taking over.

— Why are you even with Eshan?

Her jaw juts out and grinds over air as the fire billows back to her stare. She has me there where she can do anything, where we're both new and unwritten.

— Because I don't want to be alone.

Her limbs are hard, to ice.

— Well, why would I?

— Why would you what, Imogen? Why would you what? What are you going to do? What is it you can do, huh? Take me into your parents' home? Get them to start feeding me? Treat me like your pet? Just don't even try!

My throat drops to only letting one thing out.

— Why does it have to be the way that it was?

She starts to back from me sideways, crabbed and with arms eaten.

— Better to stay with Eshan till he gets himself killed than die somewhere together with you.

She leaves as quickly as the sand will let her, and with the heat up in my head, behind my eyes, I turn around and move farther into the black beach. My cheeks are dry and crusted with salt by the time I trudge up barefoot on the jogger's ramp to the empty cliff house. I'm back to the streets of homes on cold storage, keeping an eye for broken glass and hobbled by the asphalt. A light is on in one but I just take the avenue and move on. My lips tingle in their own burning. There's no number for me to text a new explanation to. But in its absence, the all of her that I have now is fully with me, green appled and poison.

MOUTHWASH

The alarm brings me aching back. I stop it above my head, nothing notified, the bars gone. It is still getting power, and I leave it there.

Long shower, outdoor clothes, I start to put a bag together. Mom has a cup of thawed berries and cold, naked toast in front of her.

— You can pour yourself coffee. This is for you. Pick out whatever you want for the toast.

I fill a mug until it's black, then a glass that catches the light.

— Was there anything you wanted to do today?

The pushing breaks and breaks the bread back to cloth beneath the peanut butter glob. I don't quite watch as the factory edges shrink and I bite with the fruit on top.

— I'm going out. Did you want anything?

— With your friends?

— They're not friends.

Her eyebrow moves, astray.

— Well, get your brother to come too. He'll keep playing all day if you let him.

— Okay.

I leave brown dust with no more performance.

— But is there anything you want?

— Just be safe.

I get up and tell Dad that we almost joined a gang.

— People only see each other as tools. And for what, insurance? Incremental little advantages to feed fantasies of having any kind of power right now? As though life's all a zero-sum game. Like it's that simple.

The book and pen are cudgeled tight to his robe.

— It's why we didn't rise to the challenge; it's structural. Every one of our wounds is self-inflicted. And what's the real goal of it?

Jake continues to read me as we're both unmoved.

— To use you like pawns, and you let them. What were you guys even thinking? How could you just stand there ready to die for absolutely nothing? I know you're better than this. Do you really not care what happens to you? To us?

I'm empty on the response he's put onto me as something still builds into words.

— We were just surprised. It seemed safer to play along.

Dad swallows and waits for the next thing to say. When it comes, the uncertainty is all force.

— Well, stay away from them. If you have to interact, it needs to be with me. I have to be the one. And don't go to that grocery store, for God's sake.

Jake has me through pinholes that I don't stop for.

— Is it still okay if we go out?

Jake breaks to me.

— We?

— Well, Mom and Dad are working.

— There's no more service.

— So should we wait until it comes back?

Dad puckers to himself on clenched teeth, the corner of the paperback rising with his thumb.

— Bring that gun with you. But talk to no one.

Perched and full of sand, my shoes wait to be used again on the porch.

My feet keep on, inside, gritting ready for forever. Jake is at once too close and too far back.

— Why'd you tell him about that?

We're across from where the light was on last night. There's just a cloth covering, beige and thin.

— Because he needed to know.

We're quiet as we walk out of view to the entryway I choose. Circling reveals a waist-height window over grass. Something tingles in me as it drops in thick pieces, easily shed. Enough clears and I get boosted in.

It's stale and acrid with the crushed carpet. I help Jake up in sugary crunches and leave the figurines.

— What happened last night?

— Nothing.

— Why are you lying to me?

— I'm not. There's just nothing that happened.

He eyes the mouthpiece of an old pipe before throwing it in. Then the boxes and matches.

— Well, I thought things were good. I mean, that was dumb, but we still need them. And it's not like they're going anywhere.

— Who knows what we need.

— Imogen, come on. We have one gun and no one to help us.

I carry dietary fiber in for the mouthwash too.

— Maybe we should just try. Nothing's stopping us from being better at it.

I swig and gargle in song, moving to spit onto the bed behind him. Jake jumps to the dresser as I mist it high in his wake. It's loud and sticky between us with dense mint sterility, and we laugh something weird.

— What? Now it smells better. Come on, this is fun.

We start back where that window is grey dark above us.

— There's someone there.

— Okay, so?

— We could leave them something.

— Why would we do that?

— I don't know, why not?

— Because that's weird.

— I don't know. You want to say hi?

He lets the house or apartment come to him.

— No.

— I'm going to knock.

I've already done it by the time Jake has something to say. There's no sound as I lean in.

It keeps cool with the clouds caught in the glass.

— Maybe they're out.

He doesn't do much to meet me as he keeps looking at the place, and the word that comes barely makes its way out.

— Probably.

TIGER EYE

The door's already busted through.

— I told you.

— Well, we're here.

The bare platforms still have the streetside lustre of hyper-genera-tional produce. All around, it's a snack-stomped circus floor. Some wilted edges. There's a mass on the shelves but it's all surface cleaner. Pale dust sits where the survival proteins and powders were, in front, where the bread used to be.

— Guess they had time to clear out.

— Yeah, who though?

I sigh at him.

— We're just a couple blocks from home.

— Yeah, well, you got me here, so let's find something good.

There's only an old yardstick behind the register. Different kinds of trapped milk are still in the fridge.

Concrete tarred with use brings us to a back room that's piled over with crates. I push the cardboard with my toe, and a dark spot shoots past me.

— Shit!

Jake holds laughing in the doorway. There's a tight ceiling on his volume that I hit him to stop.

— Geez.

— Are rats a good or bad sign?

Jake's lip floats back at me, and I get into it. The petrichor wafts in pockets, some of them poop, and I come up with a bag of snack mix. Jake looks and hands it back.

— Man, why can't there be something good? You realize we don't have anything desserty anymore. Like, at all.

— We have actual sugar. And chocolate.

— Yeah, how am I going to make an Oreo?

— I don't know, by trying?

His smirk fades with the darkness.

— Let's go somewhere else.

We start back and there's a clatter in the street. It lingers slowly over to us across the asphalt, keeping its bell pitch until the noise gradually stops, distracted. Jake rushes tight to the counter, where the window is stopped up between raw shelves.

— What is it?

— I don't know. Someone's digging through trash.

It's an old man bobbing near a bike basket. He's going through bus stop garbage; piles around him fall into the street.

— What's he going to find?

— Hopefully not food.

His foot leaves the ground.

— What if it's Oreos?

Jake pulls back unsmiling.

— He looks like he needs help.

— So now you want to say hi? We're lying low, remember?

His breath comes in a stream.

— He's old.

A far off shout shears over us. The man looks up with his arms buried out in front of him. The words are gummed, but it comes again, closer, and he looks out more clearly. His hair is short and tight with wrinkles on the bulb of his skull. Mouth sunken, eyes rheumy. Another shout makes him wince. There's no source and I'm too low for another angle. He gradually raises the flattened paws of his hands where they hover without the strength to keep still.

The voice speaks again calm, pleased with itself. The shape is there but there's nothing to see. It meanders and the man smiles, gradually lowering his hands to come forward. A crack shakes into the boarded glass, and I'm jarred from the spot. He's low behind the concrete trunk. It comes again and the side of his arm tears open. His private moan slips in outrage laid bare on the sidewalk. Someone shouts hey. Bootsteps put the streak of a raised arm into view. The cry, bellowed, tries to form words, take the right shape to stop it. They meet the air and the crack comes again and the form falls back hard. Cringing gives way to convulsions as the impact of bullets begins to rain down, each one wondering if it's the last. The legs stand right in front of him, and they go to the bike basket. There's something wrapped around the handle.

Jake faces me full. He's boiled red where a lump has his throat.

— We need to go.

He fights from faltering, and I reach out and miss before I grab him.

— We will. It's okay.

He comes still with the store.

— Hey, give me it.

Severed gestures break across his face, and I stay until he hands the gun eyes down. It's light.

— You have to push here first.

— Okay.

— Don't use it.

— Yeah.

The word comes hard, turned to something.

Someone's bag of supplies clanks outside; it's muffled but there. Boots clack into the street, coming closer through the intersection, where they stop, hold, and gently parade away.

Jake's looking sinks me to the same spot, anchored together until the heat stays and I come back up.

— Fucking shit.

Jake shoots up, eyes wide and halting as I keep through the noiselessness.

— You realize what he's doing? He's glutting himself on it. Like that makes him the king of the jungle. Tiger. They're the ones that are mean about it, right?

Something plunges through.

— Imogen, don't.

— What?

— We need to find an opening and go.

He keeps at the window, put between me and it.

— He just killed someone over garbage. I mean, garbage!

My voice is lathed to air. Jake bends back to the shelves, watching. His words grow deliberate.

— We have to wait for him to come back. I don't think he can see if we go quiet out the front.

The market keeps grey around us. I step-crunch to the door and wait in the glass. The back is still open where we can hide in the cardboard, wait for night.

— Now. Now.

Without looking, I push it slow enough to stop on the pieces in the way. My heart thuds and thuds to keep going. Jake gets past me, looking right. He starts running and I follow. There's someone coming from across the way.

— Hey!

We're in a deluge with nothing but foot slams that can't keep quiet. I start to look back but the running carries me. The air is Jelloed and fighting to stay stagnant as the scrape of our start lingers, chasing us down.

Shots ring out, twin pieces of cinder block taken by lava, imploding their fury. It's too far. Jake goes straight to an alcove and pulls me in. We're stopped, lungs gnashing, backs fighting whole for the cement.

The shock of the volley has pittered to dogs down the street. Jake jams away at a shop where he's more exposed. The boots are silent but coming.

— Hello?

The word is long and playful behind us.

Careening in place, coin already flipped and buzzing from the landing, deafening. Same coin no matter what.

Jake's stopped. Breathing that can't go deep enough steps in as my chest takes the new shape. Swollen, twisted, then gone.

The turn to fire back; I hold the strength of it like a thing. Killing the bit-back twist of prey. All there in the turn. Nothing matters except that I shoot.

He's down in the stumble, suddenly definite and clutching the side of his thigh. The scream doesn't get anywhere with something dark on his face, ski mask, and we're too far apart to keep looking at each other.

— Did you really?

— I got him.

Jake is close to smiling as he darts for the muffled screaming. There's nothing directed, no words, just the shock and fear of something suddenly broken. Jake grabs my wrist and tugs as though that's all.

— No.

His shoulder is out of cover.

— What?

Jake's lips wrest against his smattered black. The sounds keep coming frustrated against a new limit, grunts not fitting anywhere until the man falls back to his elbows.

— I can't.

There's no removing the tactical lump. The rifle sits out of his lap, hand away, leg pooled under. He catches back onto me, neither of us moving to fire when we should. What sees me stays unbound and penetrating. The only other thing in the black is teeth.

— Push the gun away!

It comes out like the right thing for someone else to say.

— I'm not going to do that, girl.

The mask catches his nose on the way up and stays, cutting in. He pulls again. What's stuck is in layers, flesh and combat boots twisted for a sinuous, ongoing peeling back.

— Yes, you are.

— What, are you going to take it from me? Come on, let's see what happens.

The wall keeps pushing.

— Okay.

— Oh, good.

Light movement inches him back. A hand yanks me. Again. I don't turn away.

— If I'm going to be killed by a little girl, at least it'll be one who can aim. Or is very lucky.

He's not far from the storefront and is using his arms.

— Stay where you are!

— So it is just demands! You disappoint me.

Jake pulls me away.

— What are you doing?

— It's alright.

— No, it's not.

I push him off.

— Imogen, please.

— Just hold on!

I look, gun ready down the sidewalk. He's stuck, only smiling. Something grabs pincered around my waist, close and dragging me back. I try to slip free and can dig my fingernails right to wrists, but it's only when I start to go with him that Jake loosens his hold enough for me to move, forcing our escape from the one who's bleeding and now laughing on the cement.

We make it to the end of the street, and I've run right into Jake, who's stopped short and trying not to move. He's in the way, and there's another of them with his gun at us. The other grocery store storm trooper. The readiness comes blind and killing more.

— Drop it.

And this is how we die. In the street or piled in the dark.

— Do it.

Because we wanted to have something different for dessert.

The cut of his eyebrows moves.

There's nothing to do. It clatters in front, and Jake screams fuck in a way that hurts to be next to. The mercenary glare shuts him up into a quiet, fuming knot. He comes quick, khaki legs pumping, and has hit Jake across the face with the barrel. I throw myself over him and pull back.

— What the fuck?

He's pointing eager back at me. I slowly come straight and leave Jake to get back up. He doesn't.

— Shut up. Bag.

He rips it from my hands and tosses in the gun, safety on. He also checks the snack label.

— Now walk.

Jake's hand covers a thick pool of red rising over his cheekbone. He tries to swallow and stops but turns to go anyway. I nod through his breathing that still won't come.

— Okay.

Each step makes it worse. The worn shops are basement stiff, corners waiting to be left alone. Jake's head is down but he's not looking anywhere or back at me. The Tiger chortles, and it's him from before, too. The creep.

— Ah, what a friend. I guess we lost our opportunity, little one.

— It's not like you gave me much choice.

He shrugs with his shoulders still fighting to keep him up. The blood is piss-damp around him.

— No? I thought I did. I thought that's exactly what I did.

He stops to find a better position, but there's nothing.

— And you and your skin and bones friend there thank me with a bullet.

Up close the yellow parts of his eyes glow amber. There's the heat of something ancient welling from within. Buried and climbing out, its onetime life still frozen, preserved, and continuing on today despite having lived past its flesh. And it looks up, demersal from below. Eyes migrating upwards.

— You're the one who shot at us.

— Yes, yes I did.

He basks reptilian in it, untouched by the mire around him. My hand is locked and tight from clenching.

— He was just an old man; there was no need. He wasn't doing anything.

I swallow past sandpaper and grit before he can respond.

— You're a freak.

The wind picks up in the street ahead. Towards home, city topiaries bend from their confines. He picks back up, struggling but getting bigger from his spot.

— There's no such thing as needing to kill. It's not a chore. It's what makes us.

He looks high at the eyes behind and presses something there before coming back. He regards me, my expression, my shape, my clothes. There's no effort to make me shrink or shudder. His ochred eyes say nothing, leaving just a face in a different mirror.

— Come. You will come with us.

— What?

— I said come. I do not like lingering, and we have our own hospitality for you.

He starts to lift himself up but doesn't go anywhere.

— We're not your prisoners.

I make him laugh, no voice.

— Then call yourselves guests.

— What do you even want with us?

— Him? I'll see. You? We'll see.

Tension sweeps under me. Caught in a free fall, seized under by a shapeless tingle. Familiar and strange, on the outside pushing in. Always in, where you can't get it out. Jake shoulders forward. The spot on his cheek has him harlequined. It's so bright and firm.

— Bring us to the owner. That man from before.

The upturned captor's eyes roll to the one with a gun at our backs. He laughs alone in puffs.

— I want to speak to the manager!

His voice is impossibly small. He brings it back up without getting to the same place.

— Oh, you stupid sheep. That bag of bile is not going to help you. But maybe we could still give you a look.

There's complete silence behind me.

— We're sorry. Okay? We're just really sorry. My sister and I were only scavenging. We didn't even find anything. Just take it; it's yours. We won't come back.

His laugh rolls to a stop.

— Oh, you're right about that. Now shut up unless you want me to decide what to do with you right here and now.

Jake only swallows, and that's enough for the sagging tiger to scoff at us.

— Help me back, brother. This one's still stuck in the meat.

He makes a show of wiping blood from his hand and raises it up.

— You two stand over there.

We do what they say and nothing more. There'll still be time to get away. Scarred, maybe, but forward. The street is too open to do anything other than get shot. Feet lie still across the way and say not yet too. The wind picks back up and a gust of it billows through the intersection. It breaks against my face and forces its coolness down my nostrils, making me breathe. Forcing me. It takes the warmth of the sun with it.

— Come on, help me up.

Pop of the gun driving itself in, all one blow. My gasp and Jake's jump happen senseless to the wind and sunlight and blood that's around us. I turn back slowly to see a new thing slumped to a puddle in the street. The head and limbs are swallowed in on themselves. The man who hit Jake stares down at nothing, spits, and he's still. Just there. Ready to scratch his neck and fart if he has to.

— What do you want us to do?

— Hm? Just go.

We move slowly, carefully, a Scylla with one head choking on the other, the bright, wide Charybdis swirling behind me for something else to swallow up. I gesture and he kicks back the bag.

— Fucking asshole.

I go after Jake and the statue doesn't look. He keeps away from me the rest of the way.

We hide from Mom and Dad together until we're alone in our rooms, the doors shut, the childhood plush lying still.

Dad comes to Jake and the voices buzz, wait. When he comes to me, he's quick with his own thoughts, drawn here despite himself.

— Why didn't you guys start icing it?

He watches the gun come unchambered, meeting the magazine without checking the difference.

— You both have to be more careful out there. I can't just take you to an emergency room.

The room's ritual flat as he leaves.

THE SCREAM

The scream has to be coming from somewhere on the block. It's close behind us, tied up in the weight of the neighborhood, where it's being pulled out against itself.

No one says anything. We wait short of it, what's happening. But it doesn't end. Male shock, anger fuels it against what's being fought off. Burst after defensive burst flies word-stripped, nothing but the push of diaphragm past vocal cords.

Heavy swings are buried in the cadence, empty spaces with the breathing. We stay still and it continues strong, brave, then something slips. The sound starts to drift and sink, trying now to tread water. The yelp that follows begs for something more than our silence. It swells, but what it's left with is more surprise than anything, experiencing itself just as vicariously as we are.

No words, not even their shape; only the life that keeps pushing them out on the cold of the night air. And to what?

The scream cracks into a high pitch. At least it doesn't stay before collapsing, still with nothing to say. It's past desperation to what's turned into the will-be last movements of diaphragm, vocal cords, and blood. Something tries at the end to change it, but it's just wet.

My ears ring adrift with the swell of nothing. Our food glistens dully and Dad looks away as he rises with the chair screeched. Jake darts with him to the curtain, leaving Mom set blank on another spoonful in. I get up too, slowly from her wrist that's almost in front of me.

Each glassy square outside is hollow over the held in greenery. Our tree has the dark deep inside against the far-off streetlight glow, all of it unanswering. We're the only sound.

— Anything?

Dad's voice is above a whisper, too quick to pin down. What sounds out is more to myself.

— There's nothing.

— What do you think that was?

The silence comes in again around us.

— Well, murder.

— Yeah, but it could have.

Dad's voice is wooden.

— No, no, I don't think it's that.

— But that was just one person. It didn't stop.

Jake waits, still holding back where the closed sky is more dawn than dusk.

— If it wasn't a group, then it probably wasn't premeditated, at least.

— At least?

He checks me before also checking the door.

— We're safe here, that's what matters. Let's keep the lights off.

Mom sighs but hasn't moved. Jake narrows to me, the bruise in front lopsiding his features.

— It was towards them, wasn't it?

— Yeah.

The word is painless. I look again until the whole nightscape writhes in tiny tentacles of itself.

— They would have been louder.

Mom lets the dish clatter in the sink, and she begins washing.

— Mei.

She keeps shouldered away and Dad turns.

— We can check in the morning; they might know something. We have to.

In my room, the rosewood glow spreads yellowed pages across its square of ceiling. Dark at the edge, the brightness breaks through the antique fogging in cut nouveau squiggles and bladed leaves of vinery hot as the sun. Inside the glass gut, a dance of dead gnats stays suspended in the wreckage of their own making, all of their frail and indefinite bodies unthinkable overhead. One structure rubbed out by another.

Mom's form presses into the doorway and kills the show.

— What are you doing?

I roll towards her, nowhere to look.

— Nothing.

— Well, don't keep yourself up thinking about it. We're fine, and whatever is done is done.

— I'm not.

— I know that look. Just remember that only you matters. Only us matters.

— Okay, Mom.

Her hand stays before closing the door. And the outset night stays silent.

— Well, looks like it wasn't them!

They're antlike in front of the apartment with gear that's changed their shape. By the time we're close enough to talk, Dad's put himself in the way with James smiling free of eye contact.

— Appreciate the concern.

— We might have come, but you made it pretty clear you didn't want to see us ever again.

— I don't.

— And yet, here you are.

The rifle bobs faintly in Eshan's hands while Dad stands with the crowbar tied to the side of his pack, somehow ready. Eshan's eyebrows arc free of him.

— So what is this, now you're back? Realized you can't just do nothing?

Dad brings up a hand, fingers raised.

— Save the cockiness; it's not impressive. All that matters is that someone was killed here last night. If we do nothing about it and tell each other to buzz off, then we'll be clueless to the danger we're in.

Eshan's features lose their mirth.

— Well, the danger's been there. Talking tough now isn't going to help.

He leaves Dad sidelong and faces the street. Cameron is steely beside him but the others are tired. Alyssa builds a bridge to me across the sidewalk, and my smile is soft to her. There's no Chloe.

— We have some friends to check on, and if everyone is accounted for, we're going to keep looking around until we've found something. It won't be long till we find what happened.

Dad keeps still as Eshan keeps talking.

— If you can play nice and not get in the way, then come. Otherwise, you can go back and do whatever it is you do. And maybe we'll let you know how it goes.

Dad looks the rest of them over. He sighs lightly.

— We're coming.

— Great, I'm sure it's going to be a lot of fun.

Eshan is quick to look back at the street as I push almost in front.

— Where's Chloe?

His lychee eyes strain back at me, light impurities on something cored.

— She, uh, isn't here. She left.

The words stay locked outside where I can only look at them. James and Alyssa's reaction is incomplete; indefinite directions.

— She's gone?

— Yeah.

— Where?

Eshan purses his lips and waits for it to arrange his thoughts.

— I don't think she wanted anyone to know.

— Yeah, because she went off loaded with our stuff.

Cameron moves closer, holster protruding.

— It doesn't matter.

A sour jut seals the problem shut with shoulders gargoyled, then sloped. The flow of grabbing cement and smashing it into that goatee until it's a mark on the sidewalk fills me quick with warmth. Dad shifts.

— Right. Well, lead the way.

A lock of Eshan's grown out hair stays branched to the side with his stonecarved hue more grease than glow in the crossing of the street.

Everyone follows, and Alyssa and James are the glue. They look at my parents before coming closer.

— So, how are you guys? It feels like it's been a while.

— Has it?

Alyssa watches me. Before either of us can say more, we're on the other side in front of a house that's overgrown by apartments. The door is narrow and bare.

Eshan hands Cameron his rifle and climbs the steps, his knock empty on the wait. Something moves within until there comes a slow scuffling of separate locks.

— Oh, so many of you!

— Yes, we have a few friends with us today. How are you and your wife doing this morning, Mr. Lau?

The old man smiles squinting, almost flattered.

— Oh, okay. Okay. And you?

— I'm fine, we're all fine. Thank you for asking. There was a bit of a commotion last night, though. Did you hear it?

He searches out an answer.

— No, I don't think we heard anything.

— You didn't hear anything? Nothing strange, no fighting?

— Oh no, I don't think so. Bed before nine!

The old man's eyes light up.

— Have you already been around your house today? Do you know for certain that everything is sealed tight?

— Well, I suppose.

— Would you mind if some of us came in just for a moment to make sure? Something happened, and we want to know that you and Mrs. Lau are safe.

— Uh, I'll have to ask. Just wait here.

The thinned figure leaves the door open. Dad is softened as Eshan keeps the smile to himself.

— She says it's okay, please.

— Thank you, Mr. Lau. We promise to only be a minute.

— Oh, you can stay as long as you like.

Mason and James go up. What's inside matches the home across the way with the always open back window. Sparse grey heads reading actual newspapers by daylight. An old TV, old furniture. The Chinese print with its uniform bland boldness and the same urban image printed over and over each time. Just a chair now.

Cameron sees Dad coming and turns away.

— It's good that you guys are doing this.

— I guess.

— It is. Let us know if you need help.

Alyssa puts her hand to her face and is stopped by the baseball cap.

— We saw them out one day. They were walking their dog; she's really sweet. They asked where we were still getting food. It's not like they need much, so we've been doing this.

— Everyone's not ready to watch people starve, yet.

— Come on, Cameron.

The rifles clack into each other.

— What, it's fine now. But you know it's going to hurt us down the line.

He scoffs lightly at Mom's glare. She whispers something to Dad, who holds it in.

— What happened to your face, Jake?

Alyssa comes close to him. He turns both towards and away.

— Nothing, a pipe just fell on me while I was reaching for something.

— Hit you pretty good.

— Yeah, it still hurts.

Jake doesn't look anywhere. The door bursts back open when he finds something else to say.

— Hey, how are they?

— Fine. Was given a nice rundown of all the best dried mushrooms and seafood to look out for. It might turn into a free cooking lesson if we play our cards right. Do you guys use that kind of stuff?

— Of course.

Mom's voice is graveled down in what Eshan grins through.

— Well, there's somebody else who, uh, we kinda think it is. I mean, it sounded like you'd imagine he'd sound. If you had to. It's a little ways down.

The street is split open and taken back by the wind. It makes noise in the trees bigger than the rest of us, and it keeps our walk from claiming back anything at all.

The hollowness hasn't changed, but however much it's aching to be filled up by the flow of cars, people, it's untouched by us. Something's not there, thrashing in hunger, ready to gnash what comes.

The ringing in my ears is back and louder. Different squares of apartments and condos corridor both sides with heavy hooded portals. The day's bright brings their menace low each time over the sidewalk.

— It's the one who tried to kick down our door.

A blink tears at my dryness with the blinding refocus on something close. I nod back to Mom.

We stop at a house that's out of place with shingles all the way down around the teal of a garage door. The stoop shoots up and no one goes to it. Every other window is wide, these are tall. It looks back at us. There's a side door below the front.

No one moves.

— You want me to go up?

— Sure, if you want.

Mason climbs the brick and bangs right on the door, checking the covered windows idly after. Either side of the street is too clear on us for yards.

We wait. James tries the side door below and it opens dark inside.

— Hello?

The sound doesn't go far. He steps in and Alyssa is alongside with the rest of us huddled. The coolness of concrete crowds the garage and outdoor scrap. Catacomb stillness doesn't break as someone hits the light, showing a small car and room just for trash cans.

The door inside cracks open in James's hand and catches on something.

— Hello, Mark? You alright, buddy?

He turns back on a grimace and pushes again as though there's a person on the other side. It begins to shake against him, trying to get at us, and each shudder wants us to know it. Whatever breaks free screeches sharply inside. He stays there, waiting to be tackled by what's within before he takes the step forward.

— Anyone here?

We climb one by one until it's me. My veins tense and fight themselves with nothing to look for until I'm up where the walls are seafoam. Most have gone straight to the living room cacophony of furniture.

The original layout is gone. A knocked over lamp is in the way where an end table is on its side, all its contents spilled. Legs jut like logs in socks. The furniture forms its wake but the rest of him stays hidden from view until I get past everyone.

The blood has a thick pool around him, glistening flat into egg tempera. Framed by the wall and the couch, his eyes are skyward, mouth still open for breathing. Something's caught in horrific wonder, the words stuck on the sunken tip of his tongue. Pinned. The smell of unwashed socks wafts right up as I get a look.

Eshan holds himself in the hallway.

— Yeah, that's Mark.

A SWAT team rush for the stairs goes behind and he hurries right after.

— There are kids in the pictures; they could be hiding!

Dad sighs and breaks away.

— Don't, uh, touch him.

— Thanks, Dad.

Stillness takes back the room around us. There are bookcases with different sized boxes throughout. The TV has been drug over into the corner to face the wall in some sort of punishment.

— Poor guy.

— Maybe someone should check him for bites.

Cameron goes heel-toe into the mess of it and stops in the would-be kids' toys. He gives him a swift kick in the ankle. The black boot against sweatpants and shinbone sends the wet whole of him riling, some parts Jello, others stiff. Mom almost wails and Alyssa steps in with the body stopping her.

— What is the matter with you?

He shrugs away.

— That guy doesn't care.

— Thanks, man. We really needed to see that.

— That was so stupid. He's obviously not bit.

Her hand goes balled from her forehead as Cameron glares effacing.

— He asked.

Cameron leaves us there with it. By his feet, a broken frame shows a tall, middle-aged man with two dark-haired children. Big toothy grins. Activewear out on the beach, somewhere in trees. The wooden handle of a baseball bat sticks out from under the couch.

— He was a person!

The house sucks in her shout. She starts back again and puts something lively together that's close to shuddering.

— So, what do you guys think happened here?

Mom keeps in front despite herself. James and Jake look at each other. Neither starts, but the smile under Alyssa's cap keeps the question right here.

— There's a bat. Guess he got cornered with it.

The socks are loose on one end and darkened at the heels. Batteries, old remotes, nail clippers, playing cards, plastic figures. A cup spilled over onto the carpet and something dark with it.

I take a step but still can't get the full of his face. The peak of a nose keeps over the rest. Alyssa draws it out high on display.

— One good hit with this and you're done. It's scary going against all that reach, but if you know what you're doing, you can get in close midswing.

What's there are tide pools of red. The mess sprawls on as I look. Alyssa keeps talking.

— At least he wasn't left to die.

James is unpupilled to nowhere, so is Jake. Mom is up close to the body, electric and in the space of some duty where whatever the kick was, it wasn't enough. I push back.

— Maybe we should search him.

Her eyebrows course behind Alyssa.

— You really want to?

— I guess.

Alyssa nods with Mom still caught between me and the corpse. I start backwards before she can tell me no.

— Yeah, okay, wait a sec.

The house is long like ours, pulling me away until I'm looking at weeds through a kitchen window. There's a plastic basketball hoop down on its face with the wrong balls scattered about. A tee is set.

Two plates are out on a table not big enough for more. Prepackaged Indian. Chickpeas and some sort of grain. They're stagnated, but someone could finish them.

Nothing's been moved under the sink. A folded wad of dishwashing gloves is stuffed at the bottom and they're crumbly inside. I swipe a box of baking mix that's out on the counter too.

— Surprise.

The Giants cap looks down and up at me. Everyone else is gone.

— That's awesome. James took your mom and brother down to check the garage.

I hand it to her and she stops short.

— Well, Chloe would have loved it. Made us cupcakes or something.

I can't feel what sort of face I'm giving.

— She left, uh, these sprinkles she got really excited over that looked like stationery. Metallic little things. They probably taste like plastic.

Only her lips smile.

— So she really just left, like that?

Alyssa bites on air.

— I guess she got tired of waiting. Out there alone must have seemed better than this. Anyway, it's not like everyone was going to just part with everything. We're fine, but she definitely didn't pack light.

Something shifts upstairs, the sudden sound coming from those cracked lips and nose too.

— Any idea where she went?

— We never talked about family, but alone like that? Hopefully somewhere quiet or in need of extra hands.

Mine are jestered in yellow. A practiced sigh bursts between us.

— But I didn't think it'd be her. You know Chloe. She's not the loner type.

— Who knows anyone, now.

Her eyes change on me.

— We'd better.

— Yeah, I guess I'll go dig after that matchbook.

— The what?

— You know, some clue to let us know where he went the night he got killed. It'd put us right on the trail of some local starlet with a story too dangerous to tell.

Her cheek cocks, eyebrows still doubting.

— Ah, well have at it, then, gumshoe.

I get in first by the end table and edge it aside. Two stretched steps and I'm there with nowhere to go but squatting at the guy's face. This is where the girl always gets it in horror movies. Wasn't cautious enough, thought it was a normal day, and bam! First to go.

— Don't ask me to get you.

Uneven patches of scruff are up close within the hue of forgotten banana, mouth the natural bursting of the peel. Half caught saying something or belching gasses. Stained, uneven lower teeth. Jagged, even. I'm begging to be bitten. I reach into the first pocket. Cotton scrunched up on itself. Unfurl it from inside. Aaand no underwear. He starts to sway thick and fleshy under the coarse sweater, oatmeal damp with red. Feel for it through the rubber lining. Nothing. Pull out gently. Don't get it caught. Have to reach over him now. Practically snapping up at me. I grip the pants by the hip and pull them closer, straining to keep steady, countered only by the weight of him that I have in hand. Angling and prying at the puckered cloth isn't working. At least they aren't soaked. I have to wriggle out a spot. In, and there's the limp weight of something pressing dead against my fingers.

— Oh, yuck.

Downward and away from that, seeking out the end.

— Nothing.

— Well, they are just pajamas. But thanks for doing all that.

I'm up with my feet still planted where it's dry.

— Well, I guess that's that.

The middle of his pinky is almost severed into a little wave. Alyssa calls out at the base of the stairs.

— Are you guys done yet?

Silence continues there and here. She puts her hand back on her hip.

— Yeah, I'm getting hungry.

Eshan makes his way down wearing a toothy brown dinosaur mask.

— That's not funny.

— What, why? You don't like it?

— He's lying right there.

— Well, it's probably his kids', and I don't think they're around.

Must have gone off with their mom. Come on, maybe this is just what we need to blend in with the horde.

Each word moves the jaw, making his mouth an esophagus.

— Yeah, they couldn't get it right in the lab, but a cheap bit of plastic will do the trick. And what would you actually do, anyway, hanging out with them?

Mason gets past Eshan with a sealed box and Dad waits to come.

— You learn anything?

He stays there for an answer. I call up.

— No. Someone ate dinner with him last night.

Dad holds the idea of it.

— Well, it's pretty much a crypt up there. The beds are totally unslept in.

Alyssa starts to go up and he puts out a hand.

— Don't bother.

They look at each other, suddenly close, and they come back apart. Eshan is in the far part of the living room, facing only the shelves.

— Why would anyone leave all of this behind?

— Maybe they didn't care.

— Or they weren't thinking that a bunch of people would be dumb enough to come here right afterwards.

Alyssa doesn't acknowledge Cameron, who's leaving everything he touches open. Mom's back and holding something.

— Maybe the ex-wife really did have motive. Why not have your revenge?

— That's a pretty vicious why not.

— Maybe. But the why not's pretty big now too.

Something shifts underneath.

— It was the kids.

We turn back to Mom. She's looking down at what she has.

— They got worried and ran off to find their momma.

She tosses it back on a box and goes after something else.

— And then Momma came back and found that Dadda had lost the kiddies. And then she got mad.

Her singsong voice has everyone stopped.

— So then what's there to stay for? The kids would still be out there, somewhere.

— Or it's just someone random.

She shrugs from Eshan.

— Or that. Who cares? This is ours now, right?

The question slowly sets everyone free. Each move unravels what's been sitting flat with the stillness of spiders. Three Maglites against too many packs of different sized batteries. Five or six car batteries laid out as well. Cameron and Eshan grab a pair of hiking boots without saying whom they're for. Trash bags take the loose household goods that matter. Armfuls of paper towels and toilet paper. Cotton balls, bulk aspirin. Matches, lighters, unscented candles, a camping grill, lanterns. Fishing gear, water purification tablets, a whistle. Different sized knives for unclear jobs. Three life jackets, one of them adult sized. Surgical masks. Dust masks. Knee pads. Drain cleaner. An opened six pack of scouring sponges. Another unopened. Laundry detergent, both for the machine and handwashing. The bowl he had kept his keys in, which are still there. His crushed sneakers that he treated like slippers. Another ball.

The house stays too quiet. Even in the parts that we're in, something never leaves. Cameron and Mason drag the body out in blankets. Later I come past a pile of trash and the taped down plastic lid with the words **DEAD BODY INSIDE** scrawled in black. I touch it and it's heavy with the density of yard waste. Dad goes looking for mail and carves in with ballpoint

Here Lies Mark Graham

Father, San Franciscan.

Set behind clothing in the bedroom is a locker. Mason is quick to drag it out and stab right into it. The leaded belly shudders as he throws himself into each jab, prying at the metal suture until its sphincters tear loose and lose the air that's inside. At the crack of the door into the dresser, polished and matte textures glisten black within. Three handguns and a semi-automatic rifle factory fresh alongside a single-barrel shotgun that looks inherited. Boxes as well.

Two handguns are hard plastic, no more complicated than holding a drill. The other is metal with a girl's name written in cursive on the side. The glow of silver hatching along the barrel is anchored with a rosewood grip. It starts to sink into my hand. Eshan asks to see it as the rifle gets passed around.

— What, you have to have the pretty one, Eshan?

James is holding the rifle now.

— It's not that pretty.

He hands it back. Kimber. Dad lets them give us it and the old shotgun along with their ammo. Alyssa smooths things over with hints about seriousness and safety along with a promise to take us out tomorrow. He says thank you.

That night, we have dinner surrounded by the boxes that need a place. Mom and Dad speak in their room. And now enough guns for most of us are in the closet along with our coats and shoes and umbrellas.

LANDS END

THE FIRST POP volleys back and forth at our faces before it's deflated in the net. Cement puffs and nothing else. My breath falls, gaining back space as I let the palm press me to more of an angle. I look hard at the bottle and into it, right through to where all that's there is ringing. It's only me when I squeeze, squeeze until the next thing happens. The shock sinks in with nothing different besides the air behind the wall.

— Come on, I'm sure you can hit something.

Jake's mouth cracks at the start of a grin.

— You know I can.

It shuts. He raises his up in jerks, attention splitting between me, the target, the gun. Alyssa says something beyond my earplugs, and he's steadied in ice melt. The torrent cracks and whizzes again between us, a meteor shower of our own making. Only the box falls flat to the court. We cheer and he focuses again. Two shots and the coconut water bottle bounds away. He smiles more to himself than us.

I take back the spot and stare at what's left until it's only me and it. The squeeze makes me hold the recoil after. Again against it, and I keep tighter. Again, and the shot falls out of me. The can tips from the top and rolls away.

— That might have been the wind.

Jake jogs in.

— It's so streaky for me. It's like bowling; I'll get lucky, then do nothing but miss.

— Don't think like that. There's certainty in it. You hit or you don't. Just keep chasing it until you're done.

Alyssa's voice is closed in around me. James pushes too.

— You hit things, that's what matters. It's all practice.

— I know, I just can't tell when I do something right and when it's wrong. Things feel right, and I miss, then off, and it hits.

He shrugs.

— Then try not to hit. I mean really, try less.

Jake brings them back with their wounds showing. Mine you have to look for.

— I think we killed them.

Through the street, the blue of the bay is close to the blue of the sky. No clouds or boats to mark it. Only the green and brown mix of Marin keeps them apart, heavy where the horizon would be. Alyssa turns from it.

— Hey, when's the last time you guys were out there?

— What, around the bay? Not since summer, I guess.

— Really? But it's right there. We still go, sometimes. It's a nice day. Why don't we just walk out to the water?

— Yeah, we can do Lands End.

The sky's warmth penetrates my jacket, searching my limbs and waking them.

— We said we'd help unpack after this.

— Yesterday wasn't that bad, and it'll still be there later. Come on, call it a mental health day.

They have us in smiles, and Jake is already nodding. The street is filled both sides with sunlight.

— Well, it'll make up for the last time you guys ditched me.

James's laughing is cased in cedar, and I let mine fade before Jake looks.

— Okay, then let's go.

Every house is another body to rob; but in Seacliff they still hold to their fantasy. Most neighborhoods chase the Painted Ladies if they didn't just give up like ours. All over a gallery of peacocks, same artist, same style over and over again. Carefully chosen gradients or reckless discount rack paint, daring prime or soft Easter pastel, though most turn away in beige. Monet and his cathedrals brought down to your home. There's always something jagged left disruptive there too. It's textures, no feeling the person inside. They come out and they're visitors themselves. It's staged. Well maintained and manicured, but it's all priesthood for something that's never seemed to live.

But Seacliff has the whole world. Quizzes on walks about Doric and Ionic. Places to sketch later with questions to push out just what it was I liked. Dad wincing at the word nice. Neighborhood shape and form exploded to something new and dried again for me in art history. Now it's just this.

The first rows of homes are still dress shirts. Their grey-brown squares of lawn kick up into bits that I'm winced at as we go.

Liberties get taken the more space they have. Homes begin to recline along the street and forgo the second story. Otherwise drab houses adopt columned entrances. Oversized windows throw large parts of rooms out onto the street, enough space to cull what's private for more sunlight.

The grid opens where the street curves and slopes for the eye to have everything at once. The top sets high apart and makes the rest give itself cadavered over. Style is choice instead of happenstance. Live in a redbrick Jeffersonian! Take up with Tuscany and sunbathe on the finest of balconies! Or gird yourself in crisscrossing Bavarian timber! Modern, mega-sized box windows. A Spanish hacienda where someone's always having a drink. And what would complete the tour better than a stonemason castle with a tree swing out back?

It's a Small World is left in the air from across the way, each posed in greeting. The authority crystalizes as we get close, flat and probably unlived in; still doing something. And the barricade that's crammed in at the mouth of the street has the grandeur stifled.

The blockage is omnivorous. Gleaming barriers stand at chest height where the undead would be caught in wild-stretched staple remover barbs. Concertina coiling says we aren't welcome much either. Someone even splurged for some downtown-looking anti-ram bollards. There's no clear fortress or sniper's nest, only the viscount view looking back at us too far ahead. Nothing moves. The words Keep Out or Be Shot stare back.

— Um, should we be here?

— Well, we're following the sign.

Jake gapes at her hand on the edge.

— Relax, they left.

— You sure?

She slides back part of the coiling, slinky fresh and already cut. The weight of something held in swells past the opening.

— Someone else did this, but we haven't looked. I mean, forget what's inside, the houses themselves could be worth moving into, right?

Her eyes shine from the cap, and Jake and I are close to smiling as James pushes the walk along. The coiling jolts back into place.

— We'll need to wait for the guys, anyway. Let's just take El Camino.

She stops light on a grin.

— You're so uncomfortable with change. But fine, no sneak peek today.

Windows leave the next street. What's alongside us is low and tight with the feeling of passing someone by. No footsteps or voices, only pressure.

The last of the houses line the coast, where they shirk from being seen. They lie with the ground, most at a modern cut, another broader and Spanish, and they quietly reach out and grab their piece of the bay. Each one's an outpost against the world, just a length of building and sky greasing you along. The first view that comes through the trees is as much of them as it is blue. Glimpses slip into the descent of yet more courtyards and balconies layered down to the water below.

The trailhead for Lands End emerges with the same simplicity. Cypresses break into the skyline higher than apartments. The light goes between and glares on black trunks. Diffused, white moves where the foliage has it capped. The dirt smell comes before the ocean, and the damp already sinks in to give me something to warm against.

— Well, the bridge is still standing.

— Okay, it's not been that long, James.

— Still full of cars, though.

— You thought they'd rust through?

The stretch of blue comes slowly, deliberately, crest after moving crest.

The way's traced onto a slope that climbs up and then down to a thicket that's secret below. Thorned vines are close until it's only branches and a bit of fern creeping along. The sun's caught back in the trees, and wherever the growth has the bay it's pleased.

Next is a tangle. The texture of roots and branches bursts and brings us straight to a model lung. Yellow nylon is furled up where a tree grows into the path. We slow. Alyssa mouths that it's okay but she takes out her handgun. James shakes his head as we do the same. Paper lies bright in its dampness. Anyone there would have to be crouching right behind the base of the trunk. Or gremlined into the thicket above.

She clears the other side as James arcs behind.

— Pretty gross.

— They don't know what they're doing.

— It's wet wood.

— Why would you camp when there're hundreds of houses you could stay in?

She comes moonshoed back to us.

—Just moving, maybe? I don't know.

— We should get going.

There's another pocket, but the darkness is only dirt. We lose the shapeless congestion and come to an opening where the path is snaked before climbing its way up again, sun the only thing waiting for us. I just leave glimpses back at the water.

— There you go.

— It's so clear.

Powdered dirt swallows the steps and the scenery's tossed aside. I fight gravity to keep pace. Plop plop plop on each buried spot. The fresh green stubble of the half valley scampers after.

The first way out twists down in stairs that go straight to water. Parts sheer and drop out of sight.

— You know, there are supposed to be sunken ships out here that you can still see when the tide is really low.

The stairway cuts into branches like junipers that finger and grip the path against the sun. The water bears its weight up through the growth, all of it there. Someone's in the shadows, already looking from a hammock, book in hand. His mouth stays open under a slope of whiskers; no words come out. We're already stopped, and his leg hangs where skin shows.

— Good afternoon.

— Hello.

— Nice weather.

He stays in place; we're not close.

— It is.

— We were just stopping by to see the water. Do you mind?

The question passes from us, his face flat.

— Well, it's there.

— Yes. Do you mind?

The black shape of him is faded past its wear, still thick and crumpled. He's been smoking up.

— No, I don't mind. Enjoy.

— Great. Just had to get some fresh air.

— Uh huh.

James stands aside, getting one step closer to him as we start down. The fine dirt swallows all but the edges. Uneven lumps keep the movement uncertain while branches knot and tangle at either side. A trunk veers in, all weight as we go under.

The plaintive tumble of an animal whine comes at us from behind, maybe scuffling. The man watches us descend, nothing but a hiking pack there with him. Sticks are stuck between his seeing and mine. There's a view and a drop, and I have to leave it.

The smell is dug down to earth around us. The sides are dark while gravity keeps us on padded steps. Nothing happens. The crashing of the waves resounds and the whimper-cry comes crawling back from under its sheets.

I'm blind in the monochrome spectacle. Air wet with cold presses right into my eyes so I only have the dancing of the water. It's all black navy layered with white.

There's enough driftwood on the rocks to be James's eighteenth-century shipwreck. He starts the way to them, where we hop unthinking on.

— Well, that was fun. Can't wait to see him again.

— He's got a dog.

— Yeah.

— Why would you tie up a dog like that?

We're forked tight and unable to turn as the crashes come barreling between us. The water's close.

— I don't think it's his pet.

It strikes over rocks nearby.

— Oh.

The words are swallowed as I push them out.

— He's probably just waiting.

Jake wrenches at it. His features are part of the coast and hard to see.

— Really? Why? It's not like there's nothing left.

— Maybe he's been living off the land or whatever.

— Then catch a seagull.

— A dog might come to you.

He screws tight. They've been looking at each other.

— That's sick.

— It's that or dried and canned.

— Well, we still have frozen.

— Really?

— Technically.

Alyssa has her arms crossed.

— She's got to be someone's pet.

— But so what? What can we do?

He touches her brief past her welcome.

— I'm just not okay with it.

— Yeah, I mean, I don't like it either, but things are different.

Their eyes are locked. My lips break back into the cold.

— It wouldn't hurt to just ask.

— Are you guys kidding? There's no good result from us asking about that guy's dog.

James ends on Jake as Alyssa glows with more.

— It'd just be a question. And besides, we have him outnumbered.

— That's not going to help.

— What, we can't talk with the guy? It's just talk.

Jake opens his mouth and almost stops himself.

— Nothing's just talk. But we can stay in control, not let him try anything.

James kicks back his head.

— Oh man, really? Well, what do you guys want to actually do about it? It's ugly, but this is where meat comes from. It's always been them or us. And you do realize what's happened everywhere, right? How close we actually are to doing the same thing? Worse?

His mouth is pinned into a smile.

— If that's how it is now, then it won't hurt to talk about it.

My small line in the sand gets spoken right over.

— We aren't going to try to rob this guy of his dog. It's his whether we like it or not.

— James.

— Look, it sucks, but things are more important than this.

Alyssa steps in. Their fingers fan apart from each other.

— We're just going to ask.

He stops and the water rolls closer. Slipshod movements burst through, neck and shoulders, until he's facing us.

— If we're going to do it, let me do the talking.

— We don't need you to handle it.

Air brindles between them.

— It's not that. He'll be at ease.

Her eyebrows cock up and mine are low. Jake's holding at his breath.

— Just, please follow my lead on this.

There are piles of rock and stripped branches that someone's brought together. All it's left is a tearing back down again.

The base of the stairs hangs from its foundation and the less-than-green side of trees has nowhere to go but in. The same branches that graze us will have the dead scratched too.

The flat of his face is there, waiting. We keep on, children to a bus, and James holds pace for the top.

— It's great out there.

— Yeah, I bet.

— You picked a good day to come out too.

— Yeah.

The word is wary and drawn. His eyes dart back and up again from the pages as we come closer than before.

— So, what's going on?

— What's. Going on?

— Yeah, just wondering, you know, what's your story.

He looks above reading glasses. Something's lost past his stare, soiled and red. A braid.

— I have no story.

James raises back his fingers but stays.

— You don't need to concern yourself with me.

He turns down, passes his look to the rest of us.

— So if all of you would be on your way, I'd be having a much better day. If you care about that so much.

The wire frame droops from pointing chestward at James.

— We aren't here to mess with you, man. I was only wondering about you and your dog.

— My dog?

— Yeah, your dog.

He lightens back to his book.

— The dog is fine.

— Sure, sure. It's just, some of us were hoping to say hi, maybe pet it, if that's alright.

— It's not.

The book closes. He's younger than his dry-tinder beard. Alyssa warms in.

— Oh, come on, we just want to pet her.

— The dog is dangerous.

He's gone back to hard and she smiles bigger.

— Really?

— That's why it's tied up.

Light whines weave into the ocean hum. No one else speaks, though James is still the one who's closest.

— That's funny.

— Really?

— I mean, what, it's your guard dog then? What's it protecting you from, cliff zombies?

— I didn't say it was my guard dog.

— So what kind of dog is it?

He bolts uncaught from the hammock. We stay in place.

— What it is is mine.

— Easy.

He's shifted in place with something stretched wide at his eyes. James takes a step back but doesn't complete it, watching that Alyssa does too.

— You all should go.

The words have their air from the ocean. It comes back and the pressure looks for a way out, and I'm roused to speaking.

— No, we're people. We talk. So answer her question.

Fire swells in the way as he bites deep.

— You want to talk? You don't get. To talk. Talking. Is what ruined the world in the first place.

His voice cuts out of his throat with the heat of it washed over me, and I fight to keep over the swell.

— So go.

It stays twisting in pointed tendrils.

— That doesn't give you the excuse to what, butcher neighborhood dogs? What kind of sad, perverted shit is that?

His eyes set low.

— You can call it whatever you like. Now go.

My fingers are gripped on dry strength. James sighs clear to everyone, and the voice breaks it.

— Leave!

Our eyes are locked. James is closest. He's cheek-clenched and takes a step back, facing him. Nothing. He takes another, and the guy keeps watching. Palms slightly raised as panting builds steady back into something pitched. He's with me, moving back, and I go forward.

The man with the braid puts himself right in the path, bent, hands ready. There's nothing drawn. His teeth show between breaths with the saliva welled in him, ready to spill.

It's forward or back. He starts to smile.

A crack cuts through the trees, leaving it to verberate there hurting with us. He stumbles, almost comes back, and falls sitting. His hand goes to his chest below the shoulder, legs not finding their spot. The grey-brown dirt just moves.

— Jake!

A groan is thrown into his breathing.

— Jesus Christ!

— Jake, it's okay. Just put it down.

James steps in, still facing him.

— You made me.

— What?

— Why did you fucking make me?

He struggles to keep himself upright. Something gives up, but his heels continue to dig troughs that inch backwards. Jake and I are both slow to turn and look at each other.

— Make you?

— Guys, don't.

His eyes keep me where I am.

— Alright, listen.

The voice comes up from the sand. It continues.

— There're still people who can fix me. Just get me to the Kaiser, I'll show you.

He looks at how his hand is glazed over and he pats it flat back onto the spot.

— If you want my stuff, fine. You get me there, they'll give you more too. No hard feelings. It happens.

He tries to smile until his head hangs back, eyes shut and upwards.

— What do we do?

James has his gun out, close. Our focus turns in.

— It was an accident.

— It wasn't a damn accident. But you can still undo it.

He struggles to look back at us.

— I'm sorry.

— Don't be sorry. Just get me there. Or leave me. Whatever. I can do it myself.

His good shoulder lurches forward but the rest is locked.

— I. We can carry him. Right?

Her straight sigh turns him back to Jake.

— It'll be okay.

— Please.

Alyssa walks right up to him and raises her gun. The braided man stays there, refusing to look up. Ocean air cracks hollow on itself and she fires into the bent part of his head. Something flies into the brush and makes sounds while the rest of him crumples.

— Jesus! Really?

Jake's mouth hangs open. There's no splatter.

— We weren't going to take him anywhere. Especially not wherever he wanted.

— Alyssa, you didn't have to. I was willing to do it.

— Well, it's done.

They're close, arms touching. Their breathing broaches on something hugged quiet and away. The laid out hand doesn't move.

— He didn't give anyone a choice.

The toes of his boots are up. Mud's crusted onto the soles with the sand.

— We should be quick. Someone may be coming for all we know.

Alyssa moves right in as James gets to Jake. He's flinched against him.

— Hey, it's okay. You did the right thing.

Jake steps back and James lets him. He joins Alyssa.

I'm caught on something to come. It doesn't. The ocean continues and the barks from the trees have stopped. I turn.

James has him rolled on his side with blood still coming from the ruined face. Mouth cracked apart, one eye looking out, the other mostly closed and bled on, all of it sinking straight to the soil and making roots. I move alongside and lower through to the clearing.

She lunges forward and is choked by the rope. Her tail wags with eyes too desperate to see, mouth snapping air. She's a wiry mixed breed terrier. I offer my hand and she knocks it with her skull. I put it right back and her teeth hit me hard, but she doesn't bite. I bend down for her side, and her head throws back fetched. Her body is thin with mats underneath and twigs. She is a girl.

The dog-wet cold keeps me, and there's the edge.

Alyssa comes into the overlook, and the dog bounds back up again. I press against her with my face out of reach.

— Well, she's sweet.

— Yeah. Nothing looks wrong with her. She's just really excited.

— Guess she's ours now.

The cliff has a view of all the other coastal rises to stand on.

— How are you doing?

— Um, fine, I guess. I didn't think that was going to happen.

The dog tries to go to both of us at once, two short legs rocking in place until Alyssa squats for her.

— Didn't think what would happen?

Her fingers crawl into the white fur and scrape at segments of skin. They lock in like ticks.

— That he would try and stop you? Or that we would try and stop him?

The dog begins to bounce back out, but Alyssa keeps her there until she starts to play fight with her.

— I mean, neither should actually surprise you, right?

Her face tries to escape its own tautness, at the brow, by the ears, lashing back into her ponytail. But all that softens are her lips in two plump lines.

— You made a call. Jake backed you up. I backed you both up. That's what matters. Right?

She looks at me closely as though a leaf is stuck in my hair.

— I didn't think anyone was going to shoot.

Dread gives way to shock gives way to anger in street poles gone by.

— What, you think I like this? Killing someone I don't even know?

There's no response and she doesn't allow one.

— Because this is all of us. Okay? You do not get to put this on me.

Teardrops leap into the sand. She gets up and turns away before coming back.

— It was your brother who jumped first. And I don't blame him. But you put the knife in and you have to follow through. You hesitate and that's it.

— Alyssa.

Her eyes don't come to mine with hair that's dense and moving.

— What?

— I don't know what to say. Okay? I went in and everything went to shit. I just did it. And then you guys just did it.

She looks at me as though I've just said nothing.

— Let's keep going so we can get out of here.

The dog is wagging her tail at us, looking up. Alyssa makes us hug or try to. We stay separate in each other's space, where her abdomen's exposed. She whispers into me.

— We're killers; it's fine. This is what keeps us here.

Calm makes her look at me with something that she likes. The knot keeping the dog will take some work, but we go back to James.

She goes to the backpack. Nothing interesting comes out except a cereal-box-sized bag of weed. A pocketknife drops too. She picks it up, flicks the end ready. It's two-tone and dense for stabbing with letters laser cut at the clip. She closes it, looks at James and where Jake is bent, and she slaps it into my hand. It's easy into my pocket.

Out to the side of the body, James already has little white packets and a pair of keys up against a tattered wallet. The license is taken out and laid on the man's chest with his glasses, leaving him his name and face. The rest is thrown in the bag.

I help Alyssa take down the hammock while James kicks needles into the space. We get him wrapped, and Jake comes back and makes himself watch. A few sticks have to keep the thing pinned together. James drags the bundle and Alyssa eases the weight behind. The dog eventually stops trying to tackle us. They perch the lump at the edge and look down where there's more land before there's water. They check it once again and push him over. The body stays caught together as it bounds into the rocks and comes to a heavy, uneven stop at the shore. We look as it begins to get wet with the incoming waves. James goes back and returns with the book. He gestures to everyone who stares, and I shake my head. He tosses it out. It unfurls wildly and stops in another grouping of trees down below. Alyssa puts on the pack and the four of us start back home. We take turns leading the dog, who comes along with constant yanks. We settle on Ella.

PLAY

Flesh breaks into firework chunks of red and yellowed grey. Undead thrall after thrall throws itself to the conversion. Splat, crack, pivot. Forward, crush, snipe. The whole of it inflames with one that's behind, and it's tapped back to oblivion too.

The back of the couch pushes on my stomach. He doesn't look. My arms fall over so I'm hanging at his side. He's blank. I slink over so he has to shift up, looking at me now that I'm down with him. He turns straight back to it.

— Having fun?

His fingers keep moving, eyes loose for just a moment.

— So this is what you want to do.

His shoulders are fused over the stilting of his arms and legs from me.

— Okay, I'll play with you.

He drops the controller onto the coffee table, and the screen is surrounded by thrashing that turns everything red and rocking until the arm blender breaches the camera upright from a dark, falling form. It's in a fetal position as the monsters stand around and slash at random into the air that we just were.

— You want to play. Play.

He's still looking at the screen.

— Wow. Okay, well, come on, let's talk.

He pushes hard to his forehead where the grease ripples at a swollen blemish.

— What do you want?

Moans, growls, a hiss. The controller hasn't stopped rattling.

— To talk about what happened.

— Why?

The word clenches after me.

— I want to know that you're okay and not. Stuck on it.

He sees me, looking for nothing.

— It just happened, Imogen. We just killed a man because he had a dog that wasn't his.

— He didn't give us a choice.

— No, you didn't give me the choice.

The words are all hard and dropped on the table.

— Why do you keep saying that? It's. It's not true.

He shakes his head, letting the weight move. The rattling is pushed into something louder.

— All I saw was what would happen if he grabbed hold of you. That's it. And it hurt. It hurt to feel that about to happen to you.

— I could have taken him.

— Really? And you were going to, what, make us watch that? We were supposed to let you tackle a guy who weighs half as much more than you? You think he wasn't going to do anything? That you were just going to get your way? No one's out giving credit for trying, Imogen.

I hit the button to kill the console and the noise stops.

— I wasn't going to fall right into his arms.

— Then what were you going to do?

Dry ice stays on it.

— I was going to pass by.

Something painful and flat comes laughed out.

— So you really were going to get yourself killed. It's like you think that everything has to work out for you. And all I do is keep covering. You make things so much worse. You just tear things apart and leave me stuck like nothing's happened.

His shoulders drop towered and he exhales with the same seared-to-bone urgency.

— That's not fair.

— Fair? What, you had to get us caught? Where we'd be lucky if they were ever going to let us go? And this guy today, we were just going to see if we could talk him out of it. And I'm the one who did it! I mean, what, because of a dog?

He lingers, mouth open.

— It's not about that.

— No, you made the situation about him or you. So we went there. For you. I went there because of you.

Teeth have the bottom of my lip as Jake stares horribly back. Breathing's closed in, and it's hard to talk.

— So that's what you think?

A puzzled squint shoots briefly between us.

— You're a fighter, Imogen. I'm not; I don't want to be. What I am is a survivor, that's it. That's all we have to do.

What's left breaks on a kind of seeing, and it leaves me bottomed out to something crushed and trapped over asphalt. I stand still with him.

— Well, we need balance, right? One part fighter, one part survivor?

— I don't know.

He sees our black reflection.

— There's taking risks, and then there's something else.

— Something else.

— Yeah, I don't know. I'm tired. And I killed someone today. So whatever.

He waits, looking still at nothing before just sitting down. I come too, more into the couch than a body trying to fit back into me. But my head gets to a part of his shoulder that's soft enough to stop. Different movements scooch me awkward, and we wait.

FIRST WORD

A slash of raindrops hits the window. The water is stretched on impact, broke to pieces. A gust brings it back together as they all slip down. The tree branches lift and shake furious in the wind. Buffeting, tapping, waiting.

Laughter swells through the room. Dad is caught bobbing in place, jutting his neck out, twitching his feet in a tumble.

— Is that a giraffe?

— No, I think he's dancing.

— Really? Uh, Dirty Dancing! Or, ah, man having a seizure!

Dad stops, slams down his hands in place over and over, and starts again, his lips leading the way.

— Piano. Beethoven!

— Rachmaninoff!

Cameron leans back, giggling at himself with his eyes tight. Dad flails surrender. His fingers pinch into pieces that he starts popping to his mouth.

— Popcorn!

— Crackerjack!

He eagerly points and waves his hands for more.

— Peanuts.

That's the one. He bends low and starts sniffing the ground in lines.

— Dog? Peanut dog?

— Time!

— Oh, Snoopy!

— Come on!

Noise erupts in bittersweet textures.

— The dance! You guys don't remember the dance?

James and Eshan shrug blank at each other. Cameron too.

— Jake, you should know it.

— I thought you were a mop.

We laugh, some putting their drinks down or picking them up.

— It's what it looked like!

— Okay, okay, next round.

Dad looks pleading at Mom and me before sitting down at the end of the couch, where only whisky is there for him. A mischievous grin darts across his face, nose-in-cup as Alyssa nudges me.

— It's you, Imogen.

Jake claps hard as I get up.

— Yeah, and this can tie it!

I get a smack on the back from Alyssa as I'm rising; it puts me forward. Mom is grinning and red, neat in her chair. My card has President of the United States.

My eyes roll. I start marching.

— Soldier. Military.

— Parade.

I throw my hands swinging, mouth jabbering with eyes that go nowhere.

— Speech.

— Dictator.

I signal for more and place my hand over my heart.

— Pledge. Flag.

— President! US President!

I rush for the next.

— Should have led off with genocide.

— Hey, no interrupting!

The next card reads bookworm.

— Two words. First word.

I reach for a piece of air and teeter.

— Book.

I start wiggling in place. My feet are locked at the coffee table with the rest of me liquid.

— Worm! Bookworm!

Alyssa smiles wolfish. Next card is candy.

I frolic and lick the air.

— Lollipop! Candy!

Jake pushes forward. Great Wall of China.

— Good God.

There's something loud outside. It's painful through the distance, a car crash too fast for these streets. As it breaks pitch, the rupture slips into a heavy, guttural revving down.

We're crowded in total darkness. Woahs go out but grow quickly still. No one speaks.

Someone hits something on the way to the kitchen and curses. Dad points light from there, giving us eyes.

— Jake, here. Go fill the tubs.

Limbs spider over the back of the couch and stumble away with a light upstairs.

— I thought they rigged the grid.

— Probably the storm.

Most get up between the leaving blades of light. Mom and Cameron are still in place as another shines on them.

— We can drive around in the morning. I think the nearest substation is in Sunset. We go there, maybe we can figure this out.

— Wait, you actually think you can fix it?

— Well, we're hardly technicians, but it couldn't hurt, right guys? Maybe it's a simple fix.

— I can think of a few ways it'd hurt.

Cameron still isn't up from the couch, but Mason is already jacketed.

— It's probably a downed line. We can't fix a downed line.

— Well, if that's the case, maybe we can find where there's still power. We'll figure it out either way.

— That or it's to medieval times we go.

He's suddenly behind me. The tingle of Cameron's jeer sits moist and alien on my shoulder. I step too close into the others but keep my elbows as sharp back as I can.

— One step at a time, fellas. Let's just get through tonight. Here, take this.

Dad hands Eshan his flashlight.

— No, we'll be fine. Our eyes just need to adjust.

— You sure?

— Yeah, don't worry.

Mason has stepped out. I can't tell where Cameron has gone.

— We'll walkie back to let you know if we have power. You guys are good for tonight, right?

— Yeah, we'll be fine.

— We have to be.

BATHROOM

Dark already. I grip the frame with my fingertips as I turn inside, clinging to where I won't hit anything. Stuck in place, I feel for the door behind me until I'm shut in on the darkness. I reach down, blindly fumbling over ridges that give nothing in return. Clicking and tapping makes the piece turn warm and clammy, close to flesh. There's a burst of light that sets the corner of the shower in an electric glow of washed-out white. The pierced perspective is dampened by the bucket that's sitting inside, the flat black circle on top drawing the focus and setting it ajar. The spot twists me right down to it, getting me with both hands tight behind the ears. I'm quick to drop the light where the toilet huddles next to me.

I sigh. The button resists, and my pants come down in dry bursts until each part tears lampreyed from my ankles. I remove the socks too before dropping my underwear into the pile and setting the light on the counter, where its spotlight ricochets multidimensionally across the room, rolling slightly. I stretch one leg slowly in until I can get the other one up, perching on the rim of the tub, thighs strong, the balls of my feet strained.

I'm almost full in the spotlight with only the bucket here to see me.

It starts to come out, falling a few inches from the drain. Bits fly off in welding sparks below, but they don't go anywhere they shouldn't. The pressure leaves the place it's taken inside me.

When it stops, I keep the rest uncomfortably tight, losing the relief.

I clamber back out, still damp, and pull out the bucket where it smacks down without a bath mat. My fingers keep at the plastic lid like there's treasure with its yellow tent label. It's slow to come off and it hurts until the cover pries back abruptly enough to make me stop. The weight of the contents stays together but they shift. Choked, I wait, half looking until I let my air breathe back out again, then shallow back in. With a spin, I seal it shut again with my butt. The rim cuts in, and I still have to drill my feet to keep place.

The half-used roll by the toilet sags across from the swollen one on the counter.

What comes is not pleasant. The supplements get things compact but without bringing them together.

I get as clean as I can and seal back up. I crank the tub anyway but there's not even a rumble. Letting out the pitcher of old dishwater gets a full coat down the porcelain, and the drain rings full of air.

Fwoaheeeeeee.

DRAINAGE

The hose hits hard into the container without losing much in the switch. James lets go, smiling.

— You can look around if you want to. I got this.

The water forms a line on the bottom.

— I'm good.

Mason comes back. Boxes and cans pelt down into cardboard, mostly out of courtesy. Alyssa comes close.

— How's it going?

— Good. I think we might have three.

— That's more than I thought. Wish we knew where to get more jugs. Maybe we could take it to market.

James smiles.

— Water heater runners.

The level has slowed to the less-than-half, more-than-half that says nothing more. Mason walks by and touches the tank.

— Don't, you'll stir it up.

He pokes around like something's there before slowly backing out.

— Anything good?

— Not that I found.

Alyssa frowns down into the container.

— We really should see if we can trade someone for more. We aren't going to just find them waiting for us out here.

— Look at you. We catch the glimpse of a market downtown and now you need a ledger.

It drains even slower as Mason has the first container capped and up in one movement. The water leaves a shallow, clouded lake in ours, making a flatness that could be waded into for miles.

The hair at my neck shoots needled to the sound of talking. Alyssa heads to it. The only voice out there is male with the texture of soot. It's tangled in a thread of intent, coming in bursts. James breaks ahead to be the first to step out as we go slow, sun in our eyes.

— I just wanna know how you guys got that.

The man's hands are open at his pockets, fingers stretching with fish scales at the ends, the skin taut and glistening dryly.

— I'm not trying to get up in your guys' business. I'm just asking.

Mason still has the water tight to his belly, phantoms of strain at the edges.

— What, you won't talk to me?

James takes one more step forward.

— Hello.

— Hello. And how do you do?

Each word is deliberate and jestered to the ground.

— Look, man, I need to get hooked up like all you. Where'd that water come from? This one work?

— We worked for it.

He exhales loudly, the direction haphazard and sharp.

— What, you think I ain't looking to work? There's nothing to do around here, man. Nothing's work; it's just living.

He cradles back a step into his sweatshirt, unclear what he does and doesn't have.

— I just want that water, man.

— Sorry, you can't drink it.

— Man, it's wet, right?

— It still has to be boiled.

— Great, so you'll give it to me for cheap?

— I didn't say that.

— Then what are you saying?

James is grimaced. The man's stubble curls unevenly around his lips, the acrid smell of him coming now.

— I'm saying give us a minute, alright?

The man exhales but stands his ground. Mason slowly sets the container down on the step, his head damp all over. A forced quiet comes from Alyssa.

— Container!

— Yeah, I know.

— What's going on? Why hello, sir!

Eshan moves in from behind as though for a handshake, high now at the steps.

— Sup, man? What you want for the water?

— Oh. Yeah, we're definitely good to trade. What are you offering?

— Offering.

The man blows again out the side of his mouth.

— I can get you a car.

— We'll take gas. Don't need a car.

— Car comes with gas, idiot.

Eshan smiles darkly.

— Just the gas. How much of it?

— Man, I don't know.

— What else, then?

He looks up.

— I got some beer.

— What kind?

— Man, it's beer, ain't it?

— Next.

He pauses. His teeth begin to draw out of his mouth where they stay Swiss-Army-knifed.

— I got a woman. Everybody needs that.

Alyssa's eyes go to James. Eshan's go to Mason.

— No, I think we're good on that.

— What, you want me to do it?

He only looks at the guys.

— No, we don't want you to do it. I think we're okay today. Sorry to waste your time.

The grin drops and he starts to shift in place ready to pee.

— Man, I need that water.

His lips curl back in dismay that could almost be a smile.

— Come on, man, it don't get more basic than that.

— Even if we wanted to trade, you still can't have the container.

He looks up wide at Alyssa.

— What, I can't borrow it?

— No, you can't.

— Anyway, we really are good here. So thanks.

Eshan steps forward as though to sweep him away. The man thrusts his hands into his pockets and rocks backwards, looking up again. Mason is behind the newel and puts his hand to the small of his back, where he draws unseen, legs grounded. The doorframe is close and sturdy behind me, rough and somewhere to hide if the upright certitude doesn't send me forward.

— It's the water heaters.

Looks turn on me.

— You just need a hose and something to put it in, okay? Drain the tank.

He shrugs as though he's just found some change.

— Alright, I can do that. Thank you, miss. Sirs.

Jogging off, his hands stay glued in his pockets, clothes loose and obfuscating.

— Goddamnit, Imogen.

Bright amber is looking back too from Eshan.

— What, you'd rather have Mason shoot him? Or do you really think that he's going to run out and get all of the good water before we do?

— I'd rather be badass enough that people don't come up to us with that weak shit. If some guy like that thinks he can beg his way through all our stuff, what do you think someone who's willing to take it will do?

Eshan's arms come free, moving in front of him, to the side, and back to rest on his new-holstered hip.

— Oh, so we should have shot him.

— Damnit, what you told him is worth something. And he did nothing for it but waste our time. You basically encouraged him.

— Hey, you were happy to make a deal with the guy.

He scoffs at Alyssa as Mason throws the water in with the others and moves back past me inside.

— I was happy to see what he had.

— Oh, I'm sorry. I didn't realize that was a big mystery.

He exhales, the ghost of a smile gone across his face.

— Man, whatever.

— Ah, see? Now you're doing it.

— Very funny.

— Man.

Alyssa and Eshan look off towards the corner where the man has disappeared. James hesitates and turns back, pursing his lips and looking at me for a moment.

— Good job.

A response doesn't come now that he's gone. Eshan and Alyssa say something else that I don't catch. And we have one more house to go before we run out.

BOILING

THE SURFACES ARE flat but coming alive with pots crowded furious at launch.

— You sure that all these houses are empty?

— Yeah.

— You check?

— Yes, Mom. We check.

She picks up a wooden spoon and dips it in.

— The bigger risk is being seen from the street.

— Who's seeing you from the street?

She listens with her whole body, doing nothing to look up.

— Oh, just people.

— People?

— Random people.

— What random people? I don't see any random people.

— Nobody. Just anyone who's still here like us.

Mom looks again into the pots. Her finger dips briefly inside for the heat to come, and the wetness rubs immediately away after.

— People. You need how many more containers?

— As many as we can find, I guess.

— But how many? We're already fine. All we need to do is keep going to Mountain Lake.

— I don't know, but we shouldn't just leave everything there.

Her eyes cut to somewhere on my cheek, where they stay focused.

— Our bottles, our boiling. Don't know what makes them think that it's theirs to say what to do with.

— Oh come on, you just said I shouldn't be doing this alone.

— And you want to turn all of this excess into what?

She grips the stove corners and the surfaces shimmer back in front of her.

— I don't know. Collateral?

— Collateral.

The word comes out small.

— And what are you going to do with all of this collateral? Find more to have?

She comes close for something hanging behind me, a strand.

— Money's already done what it could. It's not going to help us. And now you're letting them get you caught up in nonsense. All of us.

— Things run out, Mom. We haven't eaten anything fresh in forever already.

Bogwater stumps on the windowsill are still waiting to be thrown out.

— And what's going to improve that? We have food.

— Well, not enough for the rest of our lives.

— For as long as we need.

— Oh, right, because once the zombies have been kind enough to kill most everyone, we'll wander back in where everything will be ripe for the taking.

She glares hot. The sunlight behind shines with her.

— You know that's the best plan that we have.

— It's not a plan. It's just doing nothing.

— What, you like crap? We have more crap here than you could ever have out there.

A lock of hair has frizzed out from her scalp, floating astral at me.

— I don't know, Mom. It's something to do. And it helps us.

— Help.

She spits the word.

— If you could just stay at home like the rest of us, you and your brother, that'd be help.

She turns where the buckets of soil have the patio. Her shoulders shudder on themselves, and she rubs hard at her face.

— I don't speak out a lot. Not about all that you have to do. All I have to do. But Imogen, people are dangerous now. And they aren't worth it.

She doesn't move from the spot. I come close and touch her.

— Yeah, Mom.

The water rises in oily bubbles.

I DO NOT SLIP

— We got it from here.

— I'll ride with you guys.

— Actually, that's alright.

James is looking down but Alyssa stares at me flat and forward, watching as I turn back to Eshan.

— What?

— Don't worry, we got this! You guys did all the work, so have some time off. Take a family day or something.

His movements keep pained with normalcy.

— Um, thanks, but I wanted to check out the market too.

— Yeah, but you've already done so much today. Relax, you deserve it! We'll come back with your share. What, are you worried about that?

The wall of Eshan's smile builds out across his face. Dad is quiet behind me and unfolds his arms.

— That's fine, just come back before dark, if you can.

He looks out at everyone and grips my shoulder broadly. Eshan stops him as he turns.

— Hey, how's Jake been? Haven't seen him around as much lately.

— He's fine. He's shown some real vision with that water still.

— Well, we look forward to the results!

Dad nods slightly and catches my eye before shutting the door behind him. Pressed flower smiles are there when I turn back.

— What are you guys doing?

— It's fine.

— What, so I'm not allowed to go, like I'm some kid or something?

Eshan raises his shoulders.

— Look, Imogen, let us handle the negotiations. After we figure things out and build some relationships, then you can come spend all the time you want over there.

— Okay, you don't get to tell me where I can and can't be. And what difference does it make whether I'm there or not?

Eshan stops himself, and the darkness of his eyes settles back on me, the gloss gone.

— Imogen, you can't make nice out there when things get tense. If it's time to be hard, you have to stay hard. Harder, actually. A group is only going to be as strong as its weakest link.

Mason and Cameron stand indifferent between the white doors of the street-soiled car. Alyssa is still plain at me with something uncomfortably sincere painted across James's face.

— You guys think I'm the weak link?

He tries to smile.

— It's not what I think, it's what you do. You crack when you're under pressure, and that's a huge danger to the rest of us.

— I crack?

— Both with that man yesterday and the guy at Lands End. You make calls on your own that no one can see coming. You slip up, and frankly, I don't see a way that we can change that.

He looks down onto me and my throat is hot and tight, perspective closed on everyone.

— I. Do not. Slip.

He shrugs airy away.

— I don't care what you want to call it, Imogen. You have to stay with the group no matter what. You know it's life and death out there for everyone. And this has just been the easy part.

I swallow and only have the hardness. It makes a clear, open space with nothing that moves. Nothing.

— Hey, things are still good. Alright? We'll tell you all about it later. Just, take the day off and think it over, huh? We're all learning how to get by out there. We make mistakes, we just have to learn from them quick.

Eshan holds the hesitation of a hug until he backs away to the car, which is loaded with our water. I turn to Alyssa, who calls out without a smile.

— It's just until we figure things out over there. It's no big deal.

James picks up what's left.

— Hey, I told everyone that they're being paranoid, but give them this one, huh? Just think of it as division of labor. I mean, you guys get that still working, and we might get something good going. Even have enough water for real showers again. Just think of it, each of us with a whole bag of hot water maybe every other day. Life-changing.

Alyssa opens the door.

— Anyway, don't let it get to you. Walkie if you need us! The range should be good enough.

It's not long until they've driven off too and I'm alone in the driveway.

NO

Mom calls to me, but I shout that I'm going out without hearing what she's saying. The bowl has the keys and the closet has the gun lying on the shelf. No one comes after me in the garage as I back out, close it, and go.

On the stretch downtown, glimpses of what's far ahead get pasted over in swaths of hills. I press harder to the floor, feeling everything work, proving that it can, that it will.

The sound of something in the distance gets thrown in. I ease off to hear it again, but nothing. The street stays stagnant. No signs yet of a vibrant communal anything between the boards and the broken windows that no one's bothered with.

Up over the hill reveals Eshan's dirty-white car in the street. It's stopped and surrounded by angles of gun-black metal with people still standing next to it. My gut drops as I brake and they look this way.

The broad armored cap of the closest truck almost has the rear swallowed whole. Wedged in front, another raised truck is cut bullish in the way, their beetle-black swarm on moldy white tearing at the car. They're pulled out to the side, down to their knees with hands to heads. Something is laid sticklike in front of them, and the figures cage in.

I can't see everyone.

Faces look and say something to me. Go. They might shoot, but I could turn right around.

Nothing left to help. We can clean up whatever's left, find out what happened, but they're already gone in it.

I'm accelerating forward. The others start to move to receive me. What am I going to do? Shots break the stillness from the air but stay pillowed and distant. Nothing changes around me as they're only now starting to aim my way. I lower my face close, eyes tanklike behind the wheel. Bullets smack now into the metal around me. The glass breaks and I can't see where I'm going the same way. Nearer. It's going to hurt.

I clip their truck and whip hard into something else that's on and suddenly under the passenger door. A thud and a crack and a soul-swallowing crunch rip over me, rocking up onto the sidewalk until the other side of the car is filled in with a protruding wall. I move back from its broken teeth, but my side is stiff and doesn't move right.

Volleys pelt into the car. I flatten myself again but searing hot pain erupts in the center of my shoulder. A sound comes out of my mouth that I didn't put there, but I don't listen to it. I pull at my hip, the whole left side of me seizing up already, and I shift weight while trying to stay low. More gunfire sends a cascade of glass falling into me from the back seat, but I can still move, pressing and pinching until the gun slides out. I pop the safety but my seat belt won't open until I tug it again and again. The car is stopped in drive. Shouts and someone screaming terribly fog over the crumbling space around me. Bullets come in again, leaving me nowhere to crawl to. It's either out or over the door. There's a pause. I swing my wrists against the broken glass to shoot and see that I'm seeing double. Or there's too many bodies. People I can't distinguish wrestling brutally. No one's there to stop them. A hunting-camo-clad head is bobbing blurred at the clipped truck, and I shoot twice into the area before I stop to refocus. The shooting's stopped.

Someone screams the way they do when people are opening up in all the ways that they're not supposed to. I push at the door and have to push it again before tumbling out. My feet shuffle me across the battlefield, hoping my silhouette is hard to actually hit. The only thing I have is a weight that keeps my gaze down and forward, blind on who's here and who's left. There's no more capped head of tied orange hair. I almost fall onto the crumpled back end of the truck and look over to see it looking up, a face now. She's going to say something and I swing over the thing in my hand and squeeze it until her perforated chest starts to pull her down to the asphalt.

Cracks fill the air again, so close that they're already breaking apart in me. But it's Mason's chest that bursts outwards in red over the cord-twisted form of one of theirs. He topples over the body, hands darkened and managing to keep the rest propped. The shooter lowers his gun and tries to keep himself behind a column. He shifts back again to see what's left between us and is silent about it. I bend over for the shot girl's rifle and get it over the hood without my bloody arm to hold the sights. He tries to hide but nothing happens when I pull the trigger. I check it one-handed, reading nothing in its contours, and let it drop back to the ground.

Nothing moves. All those bodies laid out. What looks like Cameron is lying face-first on the ground. The back of the head is open, but it's still his messy cut brown hair that's wet. Eshan is the set of legs from earlier, the mahogany of him glistening in the sun, mouth mid-sentence. Mason's still stopped.

The man across the way is just looking at me. He turns to the other truck and back down to his assault rifle. His eyes land right on mine, the rest of me hidden in metal. We're somewhere cold and stark together, caught across a blue-black landscape of flat and jagged stone. I fumble for my other magazine, but it's not there. Still staring, I stretch the toe of my shoe out to the girl and put it into her side. I struggle to shift her without turning away, almost hopping to stay forward. She shakes willingly, but nothing seems to be hidden there. Her gear is light and scattered up close. No sidearm, just the bulge of a tactical looking fanny pack. He's watching without seeing any of it.

I dart down to the pack, yanking with one hand until it starts to gape apart. Fistfuls come out onto her stomach, parts and papers scattering to the ground. Inside is a cold, metal jawbreaker. The jump back up with it takes out my vision in the rush. But the truck is there to hold me.

He's moved. On the way to here, rifle dropped, a long knife hangs out in his hand. My fingers fumble to pocket the grenade for my gun, touching where it's still hot. One or zero. One or zero. He's at the other end of the truck, full in sight. I have it glued down in my hands as his blade drifts up, waiting. Sweat beads on his thin mustache, and he makes no effort to smile or grimace or communicate anything at all. We just breathe. I throw the gun up one-handed and he lunges forward. It tenses hard in my hand just once. The outside of my limp wrist catches the blade and it slides down through to jar somewhere against bone. My stomach turns to the core. He takes hold of me with his other hand and begins forcing me down, keeping his leverage against me. I fall back and step on one of the limbs but I keep tumbling out of his full reach. He pulls at me and yanks the knife free and back up again; I twist my good arm as he mushes into her wrong and he lands on his chin in front of me.

He tries to swipe from there but a piece is taken out, leaving the motion to come slow through water. He tries to right himself, pulling forward, and I step hard down on the inner hook of his arm. The joint crunches into the pavement, grinding and grinding in his trying to break free. He scrapes at my ankle, unable to pull me down or him up, and I hold it until there's just batting. At its distance, the pinned hand keeps the knife afloat and at sea. The quiet of red drips onto it. My jacket sleeve is soaked inside. With a hot turn of my wrist, I find something glistening underneath. He only looks down now and breathes. Pinned; I use my heel to stomp and dig at his fingers until they begin to open. He groans with me against him until I can slide the knife away and stop. I step off and forward and kick him hard with my toe into his head. He rolls back, mouth begging open with baby urgency, but no sound comes out. He's bleeding. I'm slow and tense with my unmoving arm as I use the other, fingers arcade-claw-firm down and up. He tries to lock eyes with me as I tighten on the wet handle. The oiled and dusted parts of the all-black road steel me before looking back. They're round and dark against swelling red. Something flat lies in them, but still on a base level they're sympathetic. One scraped hand reaches out in some sort of plea as the other hides at his stomach. In jagged movements, I drop right to my knees almost on top of him and bring it down overhead. His mouth hangs as I cut into his neck area. The point enters above his clavicle, pinning him from reaching up to stop me. I lean back to pull it out and come in again, down, more into the neck this time. A mouthful of red comes out angrily, and he thrusts both hands down towards his crotch. I tug out, reposition the blade low with numb fingers, and fall chest-forward, driving the stake of it down to the base of his skull. The metal slips off of his spine and plunges straight through the whole of his neck, slowing with me behind it. My arm tears but it's there, digging and putting my bleeding on top. I throw myself back as soon as it's set, watching as he tenses in unclear movements; falling and shuffling backwards, rough across asphalt. A wheeze tries to keep air coming in but gags on the flow. I push for my feet but my shoulder fires in pain that's over and under me and I stay hard on my butt, watching for him to die in stillness or one final explosion.

The blood is flowing peacefully from the gorge in my arm. Down here it's comfortable, somewhere I can do nothing. My head falls to my chest, and I can almost see both of their faces flattening into angles up and down. She's stony pale and street-washed, and his mouth is tight apart. I rock back onto my elbow and start pulling up my arm to see. The fingers are locked and trying to move them only brings in new pain. Blood keeps sliding from the fingertips. I need pressure. Something. Their faces look cardlike back in their up and down. Faces I put that way. I'm the one who can walk away. So do it. If I can just keep from losing any more of me.

Rocking forward doesn't pick me up. I bend my knees, and one of them is caught stiff. I do it again, pushing hard against my working hand, and I raise my butt strained from the ground. Crabbed, I throw the weight forward, putting it all back onto my legs. My hip flexor cries out locked. I lean on the other while keeping it straight and bend the leg slow back to shape. My vision goes dark with nothing to lean on, and I hold myself without vomiting or falling. Pole in the storm. Just stay up.

Mason is compact to the ground with his arms close, whole and broad, a hog. His forearms have stopped holding him up, but they're still in place, forehead now with them.

— Mason.

My throat is tight and desiccated. The sound doesn't fall far, and I move my lips again. He's all dark.

I step, step again back to the SUV. Away from the truck, the coming breeze crashes shored onto the all-over brimstone air, churning apart the layers.

There's something close to movement. A shape is underneath, stuffed into the crevice against the wall. It's pinned but almost shifting against it. I pull at the door, which is weighed down with dings and tears through the metal. I lean with my whole body to keep the rest of me from falling out of place. Something tumbles that I'm too stiff to look at. I push myself lower to see the magazine sitting under the seat. Phantomed pains cry out in the stretch to get hold of it. Before I reach, a moan comes from the other side, soft and indistinct. I toss it onto the seat and then the gun. The sound comes again, but it could also be air leaking from a tire. The magazine slips neatly in place, and I get it racked against the seat belt.

There's almost a gasp when I pull myself into the seat. It's the surprise of something caught on diaphragm. I wait with the windshield spidered cocoon white around me. Twisting the keys out of the ignition lets the engine quiet too. I stop myself from returning them to my jacket and force the clump into the top of my front pocket instead. With another stretch, hot waves of electric pain pull me into a sweat, one wetness taking over where another leaves off. There's an actual cry now that I'm leaning in. Ant fighting the shoe. The movement that I'm in stays nauseating in its dense stupidity. The glove box drops open, and I tear out papers for the plastic capsule box. It falls, but I wedge it tight back into the corner, where I get a full grip on it.

Band-aids go flittering on my lap as I grab on to pads of gauze and the bandage roll. After smearing their packaging, I set them back on top of and off me. Contorting, dog lashed at the hand on her haunch, I lean with my right hand at the top of my jacket, shedding it from the drowning ache of my shoulder until my forearm scurries free with it. The back peels slowly away from me, leaving the rest of it a shriveled appendage. The olive green is gone and turned to a near black pomegranate. Just pulling my arm from my chest shows how much more I have to feel. Sat still before the pages of a freshly opened book, I raise my hand to the shoulder. My thumb hooks under the collar, reaching in to throat the permanently gaped maw of some ancient bottom-dwelling fish. The first separation from skin is more unsettling than painful, the piece moving elsewhere. I reposition the rest of the jacket forward so that the weight can help me. Thumbnail scrapes the skin above the hole, stopping me with my own throat sound. I'm still there, though, right above the spot. The spot that's there in me. I hook the sleeve all the way through, down to the elbow, the canvas peeling damp and sticky in someone else's flaying. But I still let myself yelp as the core of my shoulder is rocked and rumbled seismic. Something singsong and familiar sticks to my voice in the reverberations of my breathing that almost carries me through. Something packed away and feminine. I groan once more in that tone just to finish it. My hand is there at the elbow, one last step to go. The image of my forearm being torn off with the jacket, already rotting with the rest of them, sits there, right underneath, hiding in a birthday surprise. What am I going to lose, because I'm going to lose something. I go to the wrist instead and pull from there. There's pain with it, but the rest sloughs off, showing a rich separation between the top and bottom of my forearm.

More blood flows over onto my lap as I drop the jacket and try to peel back the gauze and throw it on. The pieces turn immediately red, and there's the feeling of something falling far into a pit beneath me. Blood flows over. I open back up my eyes. Little pads of rubbing alcohol sit in impossible pieces at the box. One clears some of the edges, showing yellowed and browned skin underneath against the serrated and smoothly cut lines. I can't make myself put more inside and shove down gauze instead until only two are left for the gunshot. The top one comes back off, spotted red, and I wrap the rest in tight.

Cleaning my shoulder is easier in the skewed perspective, and I swab gently at the hole on a burning sting that aches deep underneath me. The bandage gets wet and doesn't take under my armpit until I keep it clenched with the pressure of a loose tank top strap. My eyes go dark, and I force in more air, nose and mouth.

Tumbling back out onto my feet, gun half in hand, the open street is still logged over with bodies. There's nothing else that I need in the cab as I put one foot back in front of the other. My heels meet bones-to-pavement with the flesh of me pumped full of air. The boys are still there. Nearer, past the others, I approach Mason, a planet finally up close.

His back is pierced over but without much blood anywhere. At his stomach, he's on someone who's almost not there save for the shoulders. Deep fingernail scrapes are dug across the man's face, and his eyes pop open through the gouges along with the end of his tongue. The crushed foundation of throat is too far away.

The flat of Mason's back rises lightly in fine movements. I step closer and rest my hand on him, feeling for the rise, which is there in warmth.

— Mason.

The word is fuller now. I try pushing him, but the small bit of weight that I displace quickly sinks back. His eyes are closed flat.

— Mason. Mason.

I stand in place looking at him, looking for change. My heel takes me back a step, and in another I've turned away. Cameron's glasses are bent out from under his face, the downward look penetrating.

Only Eshan stares out at me as I draw near, the words said and unsaid spilled between the both of us. Nothing now. I lower slowly down to one knee, painfully as straight as I can with already too much pressure. I touch his face and bring his eyelids down, rubbered and tactile against the pads of my fingers. My palm rests on the top of his chest before I slide down to search his pockets. Keys in hand, I go bent until I'm in their car. Puffing comes hard and wavered, and there's just a walkie-talkie with me.

— Hello.

The static hums.

— This is Starfield. Hello.

The stale smell of body odor is leaden inside. The engine turns over normally, and I start to back in and out one-handed from the trucks, both hollow with menace, rear-ending my way through and maybe rolling over something else too.

As I pull away, the walkie sits silent between my legs.

The car slips between too fast and too slow on roads that have lost their familiarity. The pedal is sensitive, and the seat and mirrors throw my view childishly low. I brake hard for my first turn and lurch forward to keep going again. There's a parked car that I clip with a screech, and I press harder to go through and avoid all the other things to hit.

I see less and less of everything. There's road ahead but the streets and buildings are greying in around me. Somewhere I'm drawn to. If I just don't have to say it.

There was someone on the sidewalk. I'm pretty sure. Density all around. I'm driving into it. The curb hits me somewhere and throws my shoulder into the door. I slow and straighten without being hit again anywhere else. Less to feel now.

Cars fill the street ahead. Things and people on the grass. The brakes stop me before I pass it all. Park and keys stuffed in over the others. Open the door and throw myself out of it.

Cars and trees and the sun puts blotches in my eyes that I can feel right there. I press into it. Some come to me. They shout, at me or themselves. I try to stand still in front of them and slowly extend the gun with it swinging upside down. It slips free and clatters, and I come down after it.

IN THE HUM

THE RUMBLING HUM OF METAL. Something coming through, big and right on path. All around me the noise is thick and growing. There's movement, a knocking and rustling. The time there was an animal in the wall and facilities did nothing. Right there, in the same white spot. Days of it. Coming closer, thalassic pressure approaching from underneath. There's no cresting through. Covered, it's already on me. I can't see or move or feel, but it's there, working its way to me.

A merging clicks in as though from elsewhere, leaving a vacuum of questions, of questioning. No longer grounded with an under, I float in the nothing that grows to mercury around me.

Something is at my arm, here. I feel nothing, but it's there, pulling. The rest of me rocks in the waves, tethered, but to nothing. Breath falls on me, soured and stripped of its heat and moisture. I rock and get breathed on. And on.

A yellow glow keeps my eyes fixed, shaping from a smear into dandelion brilliance till it's hardened down to a lantern. Someone is at a table, face in front of it, reading or in thought. Or maybe staring. My neck breaks free from a clammy connection, but the rest stays, cocoon tight. An ache rushes in from behind, and I press my eyes shut again until it passes.

The form is up blocking the light, turned cyclopean towards me with a tangle where the features should be.

— Relax.

He comes closer and presses his palm rough near a smack onto my forehead. I twist to the side and he persists before letting go.

— Don't worry, you're out of the woods now.

His hands drop to something out of view, shoulders high without bulk. My mouth is dry and tumbles polygoned on just the one word.

— What.

I try to hold my eyes open, but my head drifts to the side where it feels right in place.

— Save your strength.

I keep them apart and turn for his, grabbing at their points. He stays looking at me.

— Don't do anything. Just rest. You're safe.

My next words don't come. A new weight falls that I can't stop.

Prismatic beams of light stand in cathedral angels above me. One kneeling, one stretching up and down at once, one angling sharply earthward in fury. Hints of green and yellow divide them further, setting imperfect allegiances in place that leave them and their followers doomed. A ripple upsets the balance as the glowing world suddenly becomes rigid and plastic in response, so diminished that I have to turn away.

A woman's here now too, her hair locked tight to the side in braids, one leg up on something, and his extends back to her, casually interlocking. She's holding toast to her mouth, and they've been talking but their words are gone. Their seesawed legs jiggle them up and apart, towards me in steps that I can't see.

— How do you feel?

She presses into the side of the bed. Her coat is still very white.

— I'm here.

The hint of a smile passes the expanse of her lips.

— That you are. And do you know where here is?

I look but mostly see the wild-haired man from last night and his forehead shining youthful with deep, changing lines.

— Are we still at the trading post?

— Yes, we are.

— Okay.

She's young too but fully looks it. Hard-framed, though the beveling in her features and the teased puff at the back break out of it.

— Hugh, could you get her something?

He's there and then a burst of light flies through the flap with just her eyeing me.

— I'm Queenie, by the way.

— Imogen.

She comes closer. Her eyes travel to different parts of me, picking up what I can't see.

— You are lucky.

The man called Hugh comes in with a bowl, which he puts on a tray that comes in front of me. Then the spoon comes down. He steps to the side of the bed and lifts it upright and me with it, and the restraint keeps me snug to each shift. He sits back down and looks oaken over me. The spoon comes up and I bite it blind. Swallowing is an internal stretch. The heater-hot oatmeal comes again, evenly, and again with intermittent chunks of walnut and dried apricot.

— Can I have some coffee?

He shuffles to the table and picks up a mug, swigging down the rest before swirling it with water. He drinks that too and pours in dregs from a simple coffee maker. He pauses before handing me the cup.

— This all goes on your tab, by the way. We're fair here, but we aren't free.

He looks down, wearied of either the cheerfulness or the warning. I nod, and he puts the rough ceramic lip in front for us to ease part of the contents into my mouth. It's both weak and sooty, but the heat and grit are exciting to have trapped. He shoves more before I can speak.

— Thanks.

— Hugh and I stitched you up well. But you still lost a lot of blood that we can't replace unless you give us your type.

I'm tied to the bed. The binding on my chest is what secures crates for transit. It's worn too.

— I think my parents know it.

— You should know your blood type. But we got you on an IV, at least. Keep eating and drinking as much as you can. Nutrition is a big part of healing.

He takes that as cue to scrape up the last spoonful.

— So you guys got the bullet out?

She frowns downward and looks back at my arm, which I still need to see.

— No, it's there inside you. Can you do me a favor, though, and bend your fingers?

Queenie crouches down before ants, and I'm able to make an open fist. It's small over the covers but I can feel it.

— That's good. Now, I want you to bend your wrist back as far as you can, like this.

The fingers extend like hers, but my palm doesn't lift. The pain puts up a wall that I can't see past.

— Okay, so you have some impaired motor function. We'll put you in a sling, and sorry, those stitches will need to come out later.

— Is that going to get any better?

She drops her head to the side.

— It won't be the same as before; no reason to expect that. But you're young, you still have the best odds of bouncing back at least pretty okay. Keep taking a double dose of whatever over-the-counter pain medication you have until you can get by without it. Two weeks max. Write it down if you're not keeping track.

— Well, I'm in pain now.

They both just stare.

— So are you guys going to let me out?

An interval passes before the man sits back down in front like he was.

— So here's what's up. When you came in like you did on death's door, Queenie and I laid claim on everything that you had by deciding to work on you. You don't make it, we get everything. It's ours, next of kin or not. You do make it, we take our share and give the rest back to you. Makes sense?

His fingertips club into each other.

— I suppose.

— Good, then you can have your car back but that's it.

The white strands shoot solitary pathways into his beard, long without aim or direction. Some sideways.

— Well, I need my gun, at least.

— And we need more than just water. But you didn't bring anything else, and we're not driving anywhere.

He winces for me, like that's it.

— You can have all of the stuff from those people. The ones I killed. That's two trucks, some guns, I don't know.

— That's already been taken care of. This is just about our share. For our work.

He looks like he wants to stand up and walk away.

— That wouldn't be there if not for me.

— True, but how does that make it yours?

The strap starts to cut at each small movement.

— Come on, you guys are out, what, some IV fluid and the thread?

Queenie steps back in against the bed.

— Well, if you want to bring us the lidocaine that we spent on you, be my guest.

— Not to mention the know-how.

Stonefaced, they angle high and low against me.

— That's my gun.

— Not right now, it isn't.

— It really is a fair trade. Your life, the water, the gun.

— And how long is that life going be with no gun?

Queenie's mouth turns turtle shell.

— Longer than at most places.

The heat of talking dulls the unmoving ache at my side, which continues to find new ways to cry out. But I'm out of words. Only my feet can move where the blanket has them bound.

— Okay, just return in about ten days and bring something valuable. We can trade it back to you then, one for one.

— What, you mean a gun for a gun?

— He means at value, so maybe, yeah. He's being nice. You should thank him.

She steps back and he comes at me before I can react. Bilious layers of smoke, whisky, body odor, and the weak coffee wash around as he brutalizes the buckle, setting it tighter before releasing it and me from it. And the odor sticks.

— You kind of stink.

He shrugs.

— Yup, I do.

He comes in close to pull the IV, fit me for a sling. I restrict my breath.

— Friends of yours were here yesterday but they didn't stay long.

He hands me the keys.

— Am I the only one?

— Only one?

— Did anyone else get brought back?

He shrugs, looking closely at my shoulders.

— We just burn, usually.

They return to whatever business remains in their stacks and folders lying in more stacks on the floor and across the desk. Back to two feet, I'm more up than I should be.

— Don't you guys want to hear what happened?

Queenie hesitates before looking up at me.

— You were attacked; you got out. Right?

All of her is plain and fresh on me.

— Basically.

She returns to her work.

— Yeah, it happens.

HERE

THERE ARE MORE people here than I can look at. I didn't hear them in the tent or even feel their weight passing by. The movement crashes and flows with parts that don't have to be decided. Someone starts to drag an oversized bag past me through the dried grass and dirt.

Tables stocked and sparse stand with gaps in each other's way. What's closest has someone looking at a toothbrush. A supplier of lamp oil and candle wax tries to catch my eye. A flaneuring couple eyes a random collection of alcohol without stopping. But what's nearly a line, two of them, leads both times to crates of fruit and vegetables. What's there is half hidden and only touched by the vendors. Another watches. Next to bell peppers, spinach, and tomatoes lie different hues of citrus and apples, even persimmons. What's handed about is parts dusty and small and turns my mouth wet at their sized-down fullness. Someone steps in front of me, and a stuffed pack pushes me back.

— Hey.

A wrinkled face with white hairs in it turns back unsmiling.

— Sorry, dear.

She returns to getting their attention, pack in the way again, and the guard is looking at me. I move on.

A man sits surrounded by photos of people on display with Have You Seen Me? and Last Seen written boldly by hand. A lot are printed on paper. His grin stays still at my approach.

— Photos, huh?

— Information.

— How do you know where all these people are?

— I don't. I know what people tell me.

He smiles up, busking.

— Anyone familiar?

The selfies and over-arm poses buzz in a cacophony of cele-bration.

— Can you check? To see if someone's in there?

— Of course. And if not, I'll put out feelers. You don't get guaran-tees in this line of work, but oftentimes the nothing found is a find too.

He smiles again, softer and intimating nothing.

— I don't have a picture on me, but he's nineteen, blond. And there's maybe someone else.

— Hold on, hold on. Details starts at two.

— Two?

— Chips. What, they didn't cash you in at the tent?

He slyly cracks his mouth open as I take a small step back, his chin perking upwards until the look sours. I turn away.

— We all need to find someone!

A group stacked with guns pushes through. The weight of their equipment lashes at the air around them, shackling it with each step.

They draw close without really looking at me, WWS stitched high at their shoulders in white-on-black patches.

Someone calls to me, a hawker with mismatched electronic equipment piled onto his table. But I'm sling-forward, as much dog as leash. There's a checkpoint ahead with people sitting about, and I step behind another pair of guards to plant myself in front of the table.

— I don't know where my car is.

Faces pass around confusion until the scruffiest breaks the silence.

— Go to the end. You're on the hill.

My lips grind a smile together and I pivot free of the place, eyes still on me.

— Are you sure you're okay to go?

Looking out on the street, the fingers of my free hand splay back wide at my side, and I shuffle on.

The red corners of low income apartments process me down the street. Nothing's changed. Concrete and tarped up cyclone fencing hold the ongoing din of the seized baseball green as my shoelace whips and rambles across the sidewalk. The intersection opens to the fortified hollow of a credit union, which at one corner tells me

IF YOU FIND IN YOUR HEART TO CARE FOR

SOMEBODY ELSE, YOU WILL HAVE SUCCEEDED

— MAYA ANGELOU

and something else I can't read without stopping. It's there, parked in a red and curbed. The street-stained panel is sideswiped in black but not bent past using. I keep my arm weightless to get in. Something in my forearm stretches, which I have to stop for and the world is gone. I'm still leaning with the door shut, boxed air around me. I reach in a finger to graze the surface of the stitches, and they hum electric. I see if it's wet, but the skin is only swollen together, its lips tied.

One hand to turn the key and again to put it in gear. My grip is weak and trusting at the base of the wheel. I ease back to a stop just to crack the window and give my stomach the time to do something. The breaths begin to clear it. Back again, I pass a couple working together behind a shopping cart tarped over with a frying pan.

It hurts. It hurts, but I can do this.

Another is headed towards the trading park too, but she has nothing on her. Her arms hang stiff and open at the side, the spaces between carried tight. I brake as I'm past and stop to watch her in the rearview. She continues on, long brown murk to her hair. She's clothed heavily with the whole of her somehow dimmed, and each step's delayed and staggered and snaps.

There's nothing ahead for her to have walked out from. But she's there, moving. I back up slowly, all mirrors to keep just straight enough. Her face is down when I get to her, covered by that hair as though she sees all she wants to. Her reaction is dull to my full stop, and she's bleeding at the top of her head. Her hand looks hurt too. But she steps, steps again towards me. For me.

Her parts liven without any other reaction. Eyes show flat in tumble-dried brown as peaked lips curl and writhe. My heart pushes at all of me with my breathing pan deep. My hand on the wheel is useless and she comes closer, an etiolated turn at her cheek and brow.

The palm hits heavy into the window. Her face is right there, looking in for me. Fingers worm up to the top of the glass and press in ready to pop. One is gashed at the side, and split nails come in and strain hard against the crack. She's too fleshy to be from anywhere else. And too young. One hand slips back out and comes again in a loose fist, loud and causing the window to shudder raucous at me. I make some sound and it excites her. Red drool falls from her lip and she presses her face into the glass, smearing it, teeth together in a click.

— No, no. No!

I stomp on the gas and she flings out of view. I don't look back and continue on straight, crying. There's the translucent smudge with tinges of yellow muddled with red, and the tears come harder. The weight of seawater forces its way through me, poured out.

— Mom? Dad?

The garage is cavernous behind me. Metal parts lie scattered over cloth at the kitchen table, and the rooms keep static, same as all the others.

—Jake?

The silence stretches taut to the stairs' fibers; they end in dark. Pulling up a step with my arm, foot, foot, then another, arm, foot, foot, my shoulder's an egg.

Mom and Dad's room is still too empty. A TV that's only ever played the news and old movies holds the space from the bed. Too much clear white carpet. The furniture has its invisible spikes that stop piles from accumulating.

I step in with the crunch of shoes where they shouldn't be. On top, dried paint drops of blood splotch and ride down. There's only shadow when I pull my foot back to see. Blood rushes on the look up and twists my stomach. I step into the jamb on the wrong side and hit the back of my arm. My scream grates slipping over the pain. It tears for the ceiling, and what comes is metal and tense, a bird shrieking about something that won't stop. I cut it off before it's done, and more is coming, if just to come.

I push myself back to the hallway, where there's Jake's open door as I'm plodding back to my room and landed sideways in bed. Keeping my arm still, I kick and fidget at my shoes. The bow's so tight, lost in strata, and my ankles wait swollen. I slip, scuffing off things that I shouldn't. I hit my ankle. I knock one free. I do nothing. And nothing.

It's dark and I can't move. My arm is locked and the other's dead asleep beneath me and far from touching. I flop myself up, trout, unable to feel if I've been lying on my thumb or my wrist wrong. If I was anywhere else but here right now. Up with a tingle taking over my side and a lingering mix of pain and stiffness and void across it,

I plant both feet down, shoe sock, and go. The hip-bruised steps come out in sand.

— Mom? Dad?

Complete emptiness eats my voice and waits for more.

— Anyone?

The stillness pushes hard against the one thing alive in the house. I keep listening in place, feeling for any difference. The still-warm bed could bring them right to me if I crawl back in. But they would expect me to be here if I could.

I've no light, and each movement is more feel than go. Downstairs to the corner until I'm facing the open door to the garage.

My breath comes in slow, stretching the webbing of my insides. I get myself a glass of water against the glint of the mostly covered windows. The pour fills me back in, rushing through a river of stone. I leave the rest of it pooled.

To the side, two of the four walkies sit in their charging stations. I tug one out and check the frequency.

— Hello?

Slim, lingering static.

— Hello? This is.

A hiss breaks in.

— This is Starfield. Over.

Twenty-five miles. The entire city, at least on paper. Anywhere they could be right now.

The drone stays flat and unvaried until it begins to swell in my ears. I start flipping through the channels. The pitches pull up and down to make different kinds of silence. I toss it to the couch and refill the glass, which I bring to put myself carefully into the plush.

Feet up, I click through again, five seconds, click through, maybe seven, each layer of static different and unresolved. Nothing to hear.

I return to our channel and prop the walkie to face me like a doll and try to hold my arm safely in.

Bam, bam. Bam. The sound pulls me up, dazed from nowhere. Past friendly, the last hit was confident. I swing too hard and steady myself back on the cushion. The room regains its shape around me as it bangs again. I'm firm on my feet and plunge stiff-as-poles through the kitchen. The would-be parts of the distiller lie toppled into themselves, catching what light there is. I feel for a screwdriver. Another knock, bam bam, and I go down to the side door.

— Fucking what?

My voice is cracked leather; it's chewed up instead of grizzled. The banging stops.

— Imogen, is that you?

James's words smile against the wood that's between us. Alyssa joins.

— Oh my God, Imogen. What are you doing back already?

— Hold on.

I awkwardly pocket the screwdriver and kick free the supports. The lock's slow and heavy, and I keep hold of the door, gripped tight on sea legs. A light throws their smiles into scarehouse grins, and James's wedges into the full of his beard. He comes forward ready to grab me but only steps in. Alyssa surges close, and there's the wisp of something satisfied.

— Wow, I knew you were tough.

A dry fissure cracks down the laugh of my throat.

— Tough is the last thing I feel right now.

James is already up and has the kettle on the stove like I'm the visitor.

— Let me make you some tea. Come, you shouldn't be on your feet.

Alyssa peels the door from me and shuts it, turning the lock.

— Where is everyone? They aren't asleep, are they?

Her cap is gone and hairs float in the absence.

— I thought you'd know.

James calls from the kitchen.

— Wait, your parents aren't here?

— No.

That's all I can get out as I keep moving stiff-legged. Alyssa takes my good hand to steady me as James mulls over his words. It leaves something swallowed in between.

— Well, don't worry. They're probably on their way back.

Alyssa gets me to the table in a hard grip, and I pull out the screwdriver to sit. She looks down at me before joining, face close.

— Things are different out there. You sure you're feeling alright?

— Where were you guys?

Alyssa looks flat back at me, and James leans against the counter, where his light beams into the ceiling. The glare blinds me from his face.

— We were checking out the trading post, waiting for Eshan. I think we heard the gunshots but didn't think anything of them until you came crashing in.

His hands float like paper for a place to rest, the counter, his hip.

— You're. Looking better.

Alyssa nods, unlooking.

— We made sure someone would take care of you and drove off with the others to find what had happened.

Her throat catches on itself, but she still takes hold of my gaze.

— Why were you even there, Imogen?

I cup my bad hand with the good, hot wrapped over their stony tips.

— Why weren't you?

The spare lines of her face glow hot white in the light.

— Eshan split off from us, if you remember. We still don't know what he was doing.

I pinch numb pads hard onto fingernails, slipping and grabbing back at their shell edges.

— Well, I found them no problem.

Her eyebrows lose their arch and gather darkened together.

— And you think it goes down any differently if we're there with you? What happens to all of us when Eshan stops ahead for their ambush, guns drawn?

— I just know what happened when I was there.

James is loud at us.

— Hey, no one's to blame on this. Okay? Fuck those fuckers who jumped you. We don't ever make the same mistake. We stick together as much as we can, and we keep our weapons up.

He draws out the tea satchel and holds it there dangling. His words drive back to a steely point.

— Imogen, what did you do?

The uncirculated air turns each word into its own fight.

— Gunned it. I think I hit one. Shot another when her gun jammed. Stabbed the last one. He stabbed me back.

— Man, you call that stabbing?

Alyssa's eyes lose their focus, turning to memory.

— There were four.

— Mason.

A line flattens across James's lips.

— Sounds terrible.

Down into the earth, sounds terrible pins me through.

— I don't know. I just kept going. It was physics.

James pours the hot water into two mugs, returning the movement hushed to ceramic. He carries them over with care and extends one that smells like ginger.

— Well, badass or not, I wish you didn't try to save them. It hurts to say, but it looked like they weren't making it either way. Who's to say things still don't take a wrong turn for you too? Are you going to be able to keep all of that clean?

— It's closed; I'll be fine.

— You'll need help.

— Well, I thought I'd have that.

He turns lightly outside of the beam to me, but he can't keep there.

— You didn't tell them.

He swallows.

— That's what we were coming here to do. There wasn't time before.

— It's been over twenty-four hours. It has, hasn't it? And they're still out there.

Alyssa leans in close, hand on my knee. I jerk back without much room.

— We couldn't leave.

— Couldn't. Eshan and the others are dead, almost me with them, and you've been rushing off to, what, find new friends?

A smile seizes her, sighing. Newspaper features crest in front of me. I jump to get up, and she's on me with her hands at my chest and shoulder. Squirming, she slips into the bandage. I scream. And it drives her closer.

— Stop!

I step back to try and kick her in the shin, only grazing. She forces me down, hand fully on my shoulder, and bounces up to keep where she has me dunked.

— Imogen, stop!

James's voice is deep and pleading. Her fist darts balled and leveled in front of my face.

—Just listen for a minute!

Half-gone, she has strange eyes. Down into my face, her breath holds straining in hard streams.

— You know what they were doing when we showed up? Watching you bleed out. We had to plead with them to take you to some sort of doctor.

She checks the back of her hands for my blood, then throws them to her waist.

— Yeah, so they're assholes. But they have something. Do you know what makes people show up to that market? Why it's not abandoned like everything else? There's no leader; their numbers and guns don't mean all that much. It's their rules. They're simple, and they're enforced. They make what you do, what you can offer, actually matter. They aren't constantly flailing.

My teeth are hard against each other, acrid in the crammed in subway car. Alyssa shakes her head and turns to James.

— Fine, I really don't care anymore. Babe, let's just go.

He stays centered where the steam has stopped.

— No, she gets it. Imogen, come on. You know we're sorry about what happened, about how brutal that was. Nobody saw that coming. And I'm always going to wish we were there to stop it. But you know that we can't pretend nothing happened and wait this one out. Look, you don't have to do anything. Recover while Alyssa and I join up with these people and figure out what's really going on out there. You've been through too much. Just focus on you right now. That's all you need to do, and we'll take care of the rest.

I reach over with my right hand to bring myself up from the table, one foot compensating for something.

— Yeah, you going to help me bury my parents too if they wind up shot or bit out there?

— Wait, really? Bit?

He holds in a laugh as I stare back.

— They're here too.

Their eyebrows cock odd angles into each other.

— Do you want to see the mark one left on my window?

My voice slips louder. I shuffle past Alyssa and swipe the light along with me.

— You mean Eshan's?

I rock back into the dust and cardboard air of the still open door. The shape of Eshan's car reflects darkly below.

— We made a trade.

The spotlight sambas ahead as my sock grinds into the pavement. On the other side, I flash a circle through the film, sapping most of its color and throwing the light onto Alyssa's face, then James's, souring them as they come.

— You sure that's not from earlier?

— I was sitting right there when we. Saw. Each other.

— It's yellow.

Fingers graze over the surface, picking up uneven gelatinous bits and rubbing them off into clay.

— It came right at you? Was it fresh?

— Yeah, all very intact.

— Anyone we'd know?

Clarity shines at the corners of his look back at me, me and the slick of the door.

— No.

— Well, I had to ask.

— No, you didn't.

— God, you don't stop, do you?

— Well, what'd be the point of that?

The rumble of tires drawing closer stifles his grin and the start of mine. The sound reaches its point somewhere outside. A door slams and footsteps scuffle out, closer. The garage cracks and crawls heavy into the joists above us, and the slats shudder high after it, revealing us to headlights with everything in silhouette. I put myself silent into the gap.

— Imogen!

The shape starts hunched to a tackle and Jake is with me. I have to brace myself against the car door as he stops just short of grabbing me.

— She's here! They all are.

— Easy, Jake.

Dad lurches into the beam without coming closer, watching.

— Are you alright?

— Um, sorta. What about you guys?

Jake stares into my left side, which I turn back to the car. He leans closer, jutting the ridges of his lip.

— What's with this? We can't even park inside.

— Yeah, well, go ahead and fix it.

— Imogen!

The hard movement of shoes charges into me. Mom grabs my good shoulder to swing the bad out to her.

— Mom, please.

— What did you do? What did she do?

— I'll be fine.

— What happened? What did you do?

Her fingers still claw into me as she looks up at James, lips apart and pointed.

— We didn't do anything. We weren't there.

— You weren't there? You left her?

— No! She fought off an ambush. She tried to save everyone.

— And you let her?

— We weren't there. But she's had real medical care. She'll be fine.

His words are syrup-slow and physical between us.

— For what?

The shock springs back through her as my ruined half becomes a specimen in her arms.

— Mom, stop.

— What happened to you out there?

Tears and spittle come unwelled in front of me, ancient with wrath and suffering. As it comes, her features grow hard behind, already drying up within the burst. Dad's voice breaks out over her from the door.

— Tell us!

The leftover hiss still in his mouth tenses me over. Light and dark writhe around their outlines as he comes closer. His head is a mash of wrapped gauze pierced dark at forehead and chin. Between, the pink line of an eye clams swollen as his mouth almost whispers my name.

— Dad?

He reaches for his side, holding himself in a way I've never seen before. His old jacket is slickened into a cherry-black bib. I shuffle forward and cling, arm raised woodenly to make room for me. A rough kiss and the shock of something cold and wet punctuates my forehead. Mom holds me there from behind.

— We thought you were dead. There was one of them on top of.

His mouth grows still, apart. The split in his lip flowers out at me.

— On top of a girl. She was. Divided. And it was at her, gnawing into what it had. We thought it was you.

The closed eye turns on me.

— I tried to shoot, and it threw me down. It was right on me, and I was just dough. If Jake wasn't there.

He turns the whole of a swollen cheek to look at him.

— He had her by the hair until she turned back. It was a her. If I hadn't kept onto her too, it would have been him instead.

— At least we got away.

The mudflats lower and nod, set again to me.

— We left still not knowing who she was. Whether her clothes were yours or not. Her face was just gone. And here you are.

His grip and mine loosen on each other with Mom still a wall behind me.

— Here I am.

She puts herself between us, burst capillaries breaking apart.

— I thought they were already dead. And you.

She pinches the edge of my bandage into its cotton fiber.

— Yes, you're here.

PAIN

I TRY to sit up and a wave of nausea rides through to break cold over me. I'm stuck to my breathing, the chapped surface of lead. Shallow, bright pockets of stable self that won't slip away from my idle fingering, down to where I'm fastened to curves and thread. Underneath is my weak attempt at breakfast and above, just out of my skin, dangles hyperventilation. Me a pinprick between the two. Just me.

I grab my arm and carry it up into view, slowly between the pain that's there and the spikes that can fissure me at any moment. The shoulder radiates hot, but still with some distance held back. It's there, a manifestation. The small separations of my skin grinning down a black slope, the way back inside right there and waiting.

I lay my arm down but keep a pad on the ridges. The bumps that shouldn't be there begin to pop and scatter like rabbits. I graze one too hard and tug us both forward into nothing. Slipping over that first sear lets me lose track, and the dog leash sits on the other side of my finger, waiting to go again.

Ashen eyes watch me from the door. The filings of white in Dad's beard bring his bottom half to sand.

— Don't pick at it.

— I'm not.

He's slowly in, uneven, coming to me as though looking onto the edges of the night.

— We're all lucky to be here.

He stands and waits, holding the platitude. I push back into the pillow.

— Well, whatever we are, we're still here.

The gap widens on the vestige of a smile, protruding at the crest, the corner, but my words are tacked onto none of it. I can't right myself any further, and the twin anemones of my feet lie trapped in a current. He sits into them.

— Not all of us.

— No, I.

I drop to the glinting of his beard, unable to move from it. Unable to be anything else. My breath comes stable.

— It's weird, knowing they're just gone. It really shouldn't matter. But we're moving on and they don't get to. This is the biggest mark they get to leave behind. It happened; that's it. I don't even get how people can still hold you like that. They shouldn't. I mean, they don't, not the whole world of them. But still, they do.

Dad is silent and all eyes at me, black and slippery.

— And for what? I don't feel special. I'm just here.

They sharpen, showing something writhing underwater.

— I keep feeling myself fall back over you again, Imogen. It's that dreamlike way your body holds on to prolonged sensations and repeats them back to you.

He grabs his knees.

— That wasn't me.

— Parts of it are only now coming out from under my fingernails.

— Dad.

His eyes break back onto me.

— No, you were fighting for your life while we were getting ready for dinner. And when you didn't come home, I told your mom that you're a grown woman free to go and to sleep where you want to. We did nothing until it was almost noon.

My feet are stuck beneath the pull of his weight, which, turned, begins to box me in. He doesn't look away.

— Dad, I'm the one who's responsible.

— You've killed people. You had to; I'm infinitely glad you did. But you never should have been put in that situation.

My throat is clenched through to cracks. He exhales nose down, and the words come slowly with his eyes shut on plunged rocks.

— There isn't any lesson to this, for you or for me. You could be walking down the street and the same thing could happen. I know that. Wait here for the return of any kind of normal, and maybe we just end up like that guy. Graham. We can't fix it.

He holds the shoulders of the mattress, ignoring my toes as they jut back, heels caught. His voice is almost gone.

— I don't even know how to be there for you anymore. The one best thing I can do is to just stop whatever's coming for me from coming for you too.

The siren that's been back on pitches to its peak again.

PATCHWORK

— No, you stop it.

— Come on, let me carry something.

— Don't be stupid. Do you want to hurt yourself again?

Mom shoulders both bags onto herself, but I get the door before she can.

— We walk if we don't get a good price.

— We don't even know what prices are.

The way is quiet. Big trees and clear weather set us alone with something offered and ready to take. The grey stretch keeps empty and tingling to be filled back in. It's a hush on the apartments that's ready to cave.

The grass yellows as we approach. Someone grins at her ant struggle. The items clunk out on the trade table, all of them new, and the man eyes and tests them slowly.

— It's nice stuff.

His lips and fingers fidget a numeric spell at them.

— Thirty-six is what it all comes to.

Mom shrugs silent at me.

— Is that worth a handgun?

He turns back down to what we're giving up.

— Maybe for forty.

— Well, we'll take forty.

— You don't got forty. You got thirty-six.

Mom's downturned sluice parts and seals back up again.

— Is that really the best you can do?

His eyes float wide like butter.

— It's. What it's worth. I don't get a cut or anything. Here, another of these would get you to forty.

He holds up the compass I got, still in its packaging.

— We'll try to get one for thirty-six, I guess.

He flicks through quarter after quarter and slides them across in stacks. Washington's face has been pressed flat with their three letters branded over the outline. The backs are still birds.

— You have until sundown if you want to get any of this back.

I fit my pockets ridiculously full and amble into the stalls. There's a jab in my ribs.

— Look! I think those are ours.

— Mom, it's fine.

— Well, why should they keep them? I want it back, don't you?

The lines of her teeth are cut glass in the sun.

— They aren't going to just give them to you. They're full.

— I'll talk to them. Where is it you're going to be?

I turn to the tent and she nods, touching me before she splits off for a face that's already warming to greet her. The flap is heavy to pull apart.

— Oh, look who's back.

— Yup, still in one piece.

— And it's good that you managed to keep it that way. Come, let me take a look at you.

Queenie clears the morning's breakfast from the gurney and rubs her fingers quick together. They're still sharp with cold when she grabs my wrist.

Her face comes down close, the mauve rim of her mouth delineating the distance from corner to corner. Her breath begins to stick to the surface, pillowing in subway steam. She briefly meets my eyes for assent.

Her thumbs are narrow on my forearm until I'm prodded flat. Queenie unzips a black case, finger rising benedictive to her mouth before returning for a pair of scissors. They come down to me, U hook easing into the connection between stitch and skin, snipping the point free. Cascading down, out, and over, the beak snags up at one, tugging the black tendon neutral. Coarse pads run down my arm when she's finished. She comes up to my side, where she takes in the same warmth of air as me.

— I hear your friends have been around.

I'm patchwork in her hands.

— They're good people.

Something she does leaves me jostled forward.

— Well, that won't get you too far around here. Not unless you mean good at or good with.

The side of her hand presses in and worms something deeper free.

— I thought the WWS was all about hope and helping people.

— Maybe according to their PR department. But the games they play get more people killed than saved or whatever you want to call it.

I turn to her but she doesn't let me.

— Aren't you one of them?

— Me? No, most of us aren't out for lost causes. WWS is just security around here. That doesn't mean as much as they think.

In front of me, she lays down the scissors next to spidered bits of black.

— All those guns and they're not in charge?

Her voice strains at its own volume, elbow staying in my view.

— What, they're going to shackle us to our tents and bring in trade by gunpoint? No, they're more like a clingy boyfriend, always going on about how much you need them and how great you are together. Just keep your head down around them. They're going to do their thing, so let them.

As soon as she's given me her eyes, they leave for the different parts of the room. The fly-points dart and float, and they sink back into my shoulder. The bulge of her lower lip falls open behind. And it stays there.

— Guess their thing isn't keeping the roads safe.

Compressed air hisses through her words.

— No, but that's not anyone's job, is it? I mean, you're not paying them.

One black tangled piece rocks into another.

— I paid you just fine.

— We'll get to that. You know, you have a bit of an emoji on your arm now. I think it's smiling.

I wince from something too tight, and it fades unacknowledged.

— I still don't know why it happened.

— Why? Why not? What's the difference?

She gives a half smile that tilts off balance on my gummed up response. The rest of her is dead still.

— Just. Let go of them. The sooner the better.

— Who killed my friends?

Her frame stretches catlike against the back of the rolling chair, hip caught at an angle.

— They're dead, aren't they? That's more than most get.

She smiles.

— It didn't feel like they just wanted their stuff.

— Well, probably not. They were probably trying to fuck with them first. Find out where home is and all that. They do it all the time.

— Who is they?

— I don't know, just the nobodies who bought into the burnout.

— The what?

Her fingers catch over a pen that she stays short from picking up.

— How do you stop a forest fire that's going to eat everything in its path? One that's too big. All there's left to do is wait to be consumed. Or. Or you decide to start fighting fire with fire, burn your forest down and beat the horde to the punch. That's the burnout.

— What, so we're the fuel?

Hooded lids carry her pleased to the hot white cut of the tent flap.

— Perfect pine.

— Wait, how close are they?

— Just don't cross the bridge, okay? If you want stories, you can find someone else to show you their scars. What's past is past.

Her shine fades as light comes in with the breeze.

— You've dealt with them, so you get it too. Just don't be weak. That's all.

Something else keeps with her.

— Well, speaking of which, my gun?

Queenie settles into the chair and faces me with a slow, quiet pleasure.

— What about it?

— I can buy it back now.

— Oh, you have thirty chips? Water's gone if you were hoping for that too.

I pull up handfuls and divide them into piles on the bed. She watches me finish. The desk drawer sticks into her, and Queenie's back with a manila folder, cradling it doll-like to me.

— It's empty. Consider the ammo tip for all our good work. And that grenade, what were you going to do with that, Rambo?

The gun dances skewered by her finger until she sets it down in my lap. My gut clenches at it, the same name on the side. I can only feel the air move as she takes each quarter next to me and squirrels them over to the drawer.

— Go fishing.

She smiles to herself, then to me.

— So, you want a drink?

— Now?

The last bit of shimmering, clear liquid rocks in on itself under her fist.

— Now.

She holds the word down to her chest, tawny cheek raised. I get up, gun banded, and put myself at the tent flap.

— I don't think I can.

I keep from turning to her sigh.

— Well, you know where to find me.

Mom is standing across the way with jugs between her feet, the sun hitting her full.

— Are you done? Let me see.

She makes me show her on the crushed grass. There are fewer eyes than before to notice.

— How'd you get those?

— Oh, I just met some people who wanted to wish you well. I saw your friends too.

There's a shout far off. No reply. Then another, different. A hard pop. Pop pop. Someone calls out a name.

My wrist is seized and I break the hold unlooking.

— Ow, Imogen!

Faces glance upwards, not on weather coming in. One lands on us and briefly sours.

— Come here!

Mom's quick hobble pushes our way back through the reshaped park. We're alone in our urgency, though there are more at the gate in a dark, curious mass. Far past them, two stand over lumps in the street. A leg stretches to shift one.

— Oh God, come on.

The water jugs pincer ahead, low to the ground. Turned back, one of the figures waves an arm high and loose. A new figure comes into view.

— We're going.

We pass the turned backs at the entrance. One draws a gun as he watches, his motions gradual. No bullets waiting in the car.

Across, the scissor-cut air between the apartments receives our crash to the street. We make ourselves small and quick, turning the other way, two dots stretching from something bright, loud, consuming.

— Hold it. You two stop right there.

The voice grates down on itself, closer than it is. Mom has already halted over its unbreakable suddenness, and I skid to stay with her.

His gun is drawn and leveled right at her. Then it shifts to me.

— Where do you think you're going with those?

— Where?

— You heard me!

The barrel points hard at Mom.

— You stole them. Drop them. Drop them now!

One, then the other hits the concrete along with Mom's foot.

— This is ours.

— Don't lie to me! They said you stole them.

— We didn't.

— Then why are you running?

He steps forward. My jaw is clenched tight, unyielding, even to speak. Feet are glued, eyes wide and drying. Only the next thing can happen.

— Because, that.

— They aren't your concern. I told you not to run.

— We aren't.

— Shut your mouth. You, let me see that arm.

A scream tears out. His eyes only break for a moment, and he looks back at us. His mouth grits down, and new shouts rise behind him.

— Goddamnit. Fuck the two of you.

He leaves us as though we're already gone. He's steps away by the time my voice comes dense and tinny back to me.

— Oh yeah, fuck you, you worthless, post-world fascist!

He doesn't turn back or show that he's heard me. People are running in the distance. Mom bars me aside with a thin arm already holding up the dense plastic. Her step hobbles me on.

— Don't talk to him.

The empty space between buildings buzzes back again, looming from the nothing apartments across the way. I flinch into a stutter as sporadic gunshots continue. Mom drops the water to get me into the car. I sit and stare at what's parked ahead of us with the wrinkles of black trash bags taped to its windows. The floor rocks with each container, and Mom slides next to me.

We breathe, throat used cold. I can only look at the splintering creases that sit behind glass. Mom starts the engine and pulls away without checking. Speed picks up, putting blocks between us and them, and thick tears well and slip out of me. A sound comes out, all too childlike against the tight plastic around us. Hunched, a hand reaches for the clear part of my arm.

— It's alright. Nothing happened.

The road roils beneath us.

— We can't just let this happen.

Something comes right into the street, hidden face dropping forward as though to meet us head-on. Mom accelerates in the final moment, but the engine doesn't respond. It only hesitates, then tries to push too late, opening the pit of where we want to be. The body fills it, bone to dash, limbs to wheels and axle. I'm hard against the seat belt and have nothing to grab on to. The car lists with Mom's foot on either the gas or the brake. We head for the curb, but straighten back out slowly with the broken thing behind. She doesn't stop.

PARKING

SOMEONE IS STANDING by the corner, face into the all-white sky. Her hair hangs auburn over front-slanted shoulders. We pass her, and she turns, a torsion of feet with body coming from behind. Her features are lost between the red-brown sheafs, piercing blank and still through their fullness. Our driveway falls behind us.

— Let's just be quick.

She's gone when we return. We drive straight in, almost too fast to stop. The door pings and pings as Mom jumps out. I go to help, though her hands are already at the garage door.

A suppressed set of shouts thuds avian at what'd be the living room window above. Before I can look, something falls from our stairway and hits Mom. Laid flat, both she and the thing are slow to move. Then it positions itself onto her.

I kick into the tumble. It persists woodenly, and I kick and step onto it again. She's hit too and rocks instead of rolling away. I scream as hands are on her, wrinkled old fruit and thin. Head draws back in, and what I do only gets at the cheek. It keeps coming, face after arms. I fall to my knees and hit it as hard as I can with the heel of the gun. The smack of plastic, metal, and skull puts the face flat into Mom. The seed buried, blood ready to gush forth.

I try again and it turns to the side, lampreying the air. Again. It rises through, nose fragmenting underneath. A hand scrapes impassive into me and there's pain. I hammer back in, but the face stays whole in front of me. My arm is caught underroot, keeping me with it. Stagnated blood has splintered through the features of the old man whom Eshan made us visit. The eyes aren't his anymore.

He turns to my wrist, coming straight into it. Tendons and skin tear to pull me back, old pain and new gulped together in turned milk. Something carries me over the sidewalk, the old man spidering behind into the gap. A tug brings me up, he mirrors my rise, and I'm drug to the stairs. A baseball bat rushes past and Jake brings it down onto his neck. He continues to rise. Cement blocks my view as grunts carry on through. My shin hits a step, and Mom's fist drags me up.

The smack of meat spreads to a pop. And another. Dad's past us with the door broken on its boarding.

— Jake!

He stands heaving between the dented old man and the long-haired woman, who's already come close. Jake turns up to Dad instead of her. The splay of fingers reaches him, jolting him unseeing into the street. Jake's shirt pulls out of its shape behind. Sprinting in slippers, Dad takes the shoulders square from behind and flings the woman off balance. The impact shudders through below with a crack that makes me cringe. She struggles in crab-ticks to upright herself.

The old man is back on his feet.

Jake watches, caught out where a car would crush him legs first, and he circles back wide. Dad makes a wall for him, mechanically raising the gun. He doesn't fire. They near as we huddle up through the door. The slam hits hard.

— Is anyone bit? Are you bit?

Jake holds at his ruined shirt, which Dad flips over to show the raw tracks on woolen skin. He turns back to us and stops at my arm. The length of it is wet in long streaks with rough shoals feeding the flow. The seal's open and drowned. Muscles keep tense over others that have given out, and my elbow doesn't unhinge. Mom is stuck to my side, gazing into the pattern.

— Mom.

Her eyes stay low. She spreads one spot of blood wide and keeps her thumb in it.

— My beautiful girl.

— Mom, you.

— I'll be fine.

A brush of shoulders separates us as Dad goes to the side of her head. His fingertips lightly separate the hair.

— Mei, you're hurt. Let's go sit down. Get you something to drink.

— I'm fine.

Something like a sob spits out as I speak.

— No, no. It went for her. There.

Dad keeps his breath till it's vapor.

— Where?

He reads through Mom's pupils and pulls at her ruddied coat. She waits, bent. The skin is purpled throughout, used up. The kaleido-scoped core twitches, pinned by the ridges of a plain cotton bra. But it's unbroken, all of it only brought terribly up to the surface.

— It's not a bite. It's not a bite. It's not a bite.

— Don't worry, it's not a bite.

He gives a short, careworn laugh before the chair lets him step back. Jake brings water, which she keeps two-handed and barely sips. Dad helps with the medicine box under his arm as the weight of bodies shifting continuously outside presses through in dull fragments.

— We need to clean that now.

— They'll get in.

— We aren't taking chances.

He comes right to me. I stay standing across from Mom, who sits held up by thread. Dad blocks my view to hurriedly douse rubbing alcohol along my arm in heavy gulps. They tingle and bite, and one really digs in. He washes the blood away with cotton and rubs at the gouges that have gathered right above the elbow. Below, my forearm is worse. It feels crushed, but it still looks the same and the bones haven't changed. There's nothing to shake off in the gone-through hurting, and Jake is sitting with Mom.

A packaged thud is left on the stairs, and we're all out of view. The gauze drops as Dad tries again to wrap it tight to me.

— We stayed in the back of the house, waiting for him to go away. I thought if we did anything, it'd draw more.

Something like words rises outside. The sounds tumble out full of vowels with undigested G's and H's, forgotten before they're finished. Dad's teeth close in on each other.

Behind, Jake's gun is with some leftover books, its nose on the edge. Mom's eyes tighten gradually and reopen back on nothing. His hands leave me.

— There.

We try to stay in the moment of quiet until it breaks.

I take the left open box of bullets to the kitchen counter. The gutted magazine slides from my Kimber and stays in the weak pincer of my left. The first bullet needs to be forced. My arm strains back on the pain, but I stop and readjust until it's in. Burying another on top of it, then another, cuts what could have been nausea. One scatters across the floor.

— I can. You can do that later.

I exhale, set it down, align it, click it in.

— Imogen.

I put it back firm in my pants. The noise-swell is cold metal hail, and I go to the window. There's someone else outside.

A woman approaches with a crowbar. The auburn zombie meets her chest forward at our car, and the swing is hard enough to send her stumbling out of the way. The woman jumps right in. The old man turns from pawing for us and begins to shuffle, which sends him over the same edge with a bang below.

— Someone's in the car!

Without turning back I slip the lock free. A hand touches me on the way out, breaking the barrier as the words tense unuttered behind.

A man watching from another car sees me first. His gun stays drooping from the driver's side window across the way while he shouts a name in the street. She's already set in our car and sees me, gun leveled at her from the base of the stairs. She throws it into reverse.

I shoot. The windshield punctures once, twice, the third lands to the side before the soiled white changes gears and barrels away. The man across is aiming at me and shoots back. I fire faster into him and the driver's side door. He shudders at the first shot and crumples onto himself. A hand is up, then slowly down. Dad hurries after me from where he was caught watching, turning with the other handgun when the dead auburn woman interrupts.

Our car screeches to a halt. The black window has captured a gleaming segment of sky.

I level the gun at her. Dad fires.

— Imogen!

He's lost ground and can only move to bar the zombie back. I'm out. Our car waits. Dad takes a step to the side but doesn't manage to get her to fall like before. She's back on him, keeping the gun useless in his fist.

I run across the street and hear my name again, briefly checking to see our car still in place. My elbow burns to yank on the pierced door, empty handgun high and swiftly down onto the head of the man, who looks confused through it. I let mine go and reach for his lap to grip the blood-wet gun imperfectly. He claws for it and my arm, head staying low. He brings me in, pulling until I twist and stumble scraping free, coiled from me. Our car is still in place near the intersection, engine running, as I carry the bloodied gun.

Her hair is drowning Dad in willow boughs that sway with suffocated movement. Dad bites at his own mouth, losing more to her. I measure the angle as I place the gun to her hair and blow a hole in it.

She stays there with the back of her skull chipped free. I fire again, a third time, and thick, lithic blood comes out of her. Dad cries out as she bears down and he buckles beneath.

I fire two more times before it only clicks, the sound sending up a deaf roar of teeth and blood-wet beard beneath, his eyes knit shut against it. The woman slumps, missing something, and Dad throws her to the side, where she still moves, no longer at him. He pries one hand, then the other from her, but only shuffles back.

I rise jarred, seeing our car, the old man, both where they were. Dad stays glazed as I take the gun and leave him the other.

The old man's head doesn't look up anymore. One hand reaches out from his hunch, locked in the classic pose. His feet move over themselves in jolts tied gyroscopically together. Peering from facing down, his sea-deep gaze lies unchanging as I bring the barrel to its side and pull the trigger. I don't stop.

Dad gets back to his feet. The side of his face is torn by asphalt and the pieces still there. He looks to them, to me, to one vehicle and the other. Our car switches gears and drives off.

— Hey!

Dad waves both arms unplugged as it slowly disappears. I stand there with him.

— Come inside.

— No.

— You're still hurt.

— So are you.

He sighs.

— We have to check on your mom.

— Jake's with her.

The furrow of his eyebrows hits me with a weight from somewhere else. He turns and walks away half righted, leaving the bodies in the street, only looking at the man, who's still slumped at the open car door.

The front door shuts.

The street is wide and quiet. I check Jake's magazine and put it back in. It has its own slickness. I near the man slowly again. He looks away, hand to his middle, the other red at the shift. His hair is dark. Older than young. The cab has seen better too, but it is probably salvageable.

His breathing meets a gap that it keeps coming up against. Stopping, starting again. A word falls out between.

— I.

A breeze picks back up.

— Didn't know.

— What?

— Didn't know.

He turns to grab my gaze, blood painting his teeth. Each word is too heavy for him.

— Guess it comes around.

He closes his eyes and presses his forehead forward.

— Do you want it?

He looks up where I hold out the barrel doorlike for him. He returns to his original position.

— Just let me rest a bit.

I nod, and he ceases to acknowledge me. I keep the gun back, left-handed and useless, to slowly reach past him where he stares ahead, unmoving. The keys don't turn easily, but he only breathes. It's canine passivity, still warm. His fingers rise anemonially as I carry them free. I shut the door on him as gently as I am able, locking it and retrieving the scuffed Kimber underneath, leaving the bat.

CLEANUP

THE ELDERLY ZOMBIE is winking in the hole where his eye used to be. The gung gung's teasing vacant with half a jaw dropped and tongue hung wide on display. Jake holds his breath as he takes the wrists. The blanched, never-ripening banana skin wrinkles and goes taut in his grasp as the head bows down and away.

— I'm not going to get used to this.

Both hands drop hard into the laid over recycling bin. Stooping, Jake rises with a handful of halved pills that are quickly brushed back off onto the mute flat of flannel.

The head slumps in first over the feet of the girl, who is already buried to the black bottom. Jake thrusts the sides further in grisly loaves until all that's left is feet.

He rises back up, spitting the air out of his mouth, and he looks at me.

— You don't need to do this.

I shrug eyebrows and maneuver my good hand until I'm steady behind it. We pull hard to bring the plastic fully up, pinching me tight behind where my arm's been bound. The sets of shoes stay out in front of our faces until they sink lower. Jake dumps a dustpan of red bits in after them. The tape rips quickly and gets labeled DEAD INSIDE before the sealed container is kicked back onto its wheels for the Parkers' side yard.

— Not with our garbage! Take it to the alley across the street.

Dad stands with his cleaning gloves glistening, and Jake has already left me with the other, smaller sealed bin. Same label, same destination. Dad turns back into the garage, and I follow, finding him staring at the open car door.

— You should go inside and get the sling back on.

Dad hits a button, and segments of glass spill out of the driver's side door until they lock in their hurry. He stands back to look at it. Towels that are soaked through in places hang over the seat.

— Goddamnit.

He shakes a piece off of his shoe and leans in for the keys.

— It's running on fumes too.

— There's still that car we left in the garage.

His beard caterpillars, and he pulls hard at the end of the glove, where his hand is still locked. The marks on his face strain with him.

— You didn't even give them a chance to stop, Imogen.

His eyes stand elsewhere on me.

— They were stealing our car.

— So what if they did? What does that change for us?

The stare continues to hold something hard inside me.

— Someone had to stop them.

The photo-frame gaze suddenly melts to a plea, only to turn again into something else.

— Yes, so you kill the person, probably have to kill anyone she's with; and we get back something that wasn't even ours to begin with? That's it?

My mouth keeps gummed as breathing becomes a mass inside me.

— Why violence? What's more important than a person's life? Now more than ever. You know how to talk, and you know people. Didn't you see how they looked at you? You caught them like that, and then you killed a man right in front of our house who would have otherwise just run away.

His eyes keep coming bird-winded to my cheek. They come and they rest.

— Imogen, that was just murder. It wasn't either you or them, and it wasn't to save anything. You were in a difficult situation and did something so terrible; just for a car that wasn't even ours.

The muscles tense in my arm, casting a Maglite on its impossibilities. The range cut, any strength uncertain. A glacier clears raw from my throat and I stumble after it.

— If we let them go, they could come back again with others. We'd end up just like that guy we found.

His eyebrows go wide.

— So that's it? That's your advice? We kill everyone we come across? Every minor threat quashed because there'll be no peace but death?

The line decants in its own moment before drilling back down.

— We are not going to live our lives in that kind of fear, Imogen. I don't care how dangerous the world is, we don't live just to be cold-blooded killers

He breaks from me and stops back again at the wrecked open door.

— Is that really what you've become? What you want?

His eyes turn fully onto me, and he continues almost smiling.

— Real strength, Imogen, is knowing how to be vulnerable, especially when that's all people are anymore.

The word tunnels into my gut and retches back out of me.

— Vulnerable? That's what you want?

I fight through the need to swallow.

— I just got finished prying a zombie off of Mom, and she doesn't look right. What's the right kind of vulnerable for that, Dad?

I don't let him answer.

— And some asshole at the camp power tripped all over us at gunpoint. He could have killed us both, and no one would have cared. What should we have done there? Or how about Eshan? Should I have tried using my words before or after he was executed?

His eyes flare and narrow just as quickly, thick finger protruding loamy at me.

— Don't you do that. Do not. You are strong enough to stay on topic.

— Topic? You mean defending what we have; that thing that people have been doing since always? What's there to even say about it?

He steps closer, and I keep half the space he closes.

— What happened with Eshan, with you, is horrible. I should have been there with you. But you didn't tell us. It happened; and it never should have. What you did was what you had to; and you're still here. That's all that matters.

His features pull tight as sheets.

— Imogen, you cannot let that trauma control your life, and you cannot let it drive your actions. You have to own what just happened. And I will hold you to it, always.

— You don't think I own what I do? What's there to even own? He shot at me. The only thing to really say about it is don't end up like him.

Dad's mouth falls ajar, a tarred up thing looking at me from asphalt.

— What, you want me to be haunted by them? See their faces at night? That's bullshit. No one's there. It's just the constant swimming in it. All I get is the movement and the pain and the not knowing if it's all about to end.

He burns it away.

— It was not weakness to stay inside and let them take the car. And it definitely wouldn't have been weakness to try and talk them out of it. If you can't handle that, if another person's life is so cheap to you, then you don't deserve to walk around with that.

A hand extends. My eyes swell dry to globes with nowhere to go.

— No.

He stays static. The word comes out heavy again.

— No. What do you even mean, deserve? What's there to deserve anymore?

Lips tight, he gestures with readied kindness. My wrists go stiff and neither of us moves. A gust comes against the opening behind me.

— What are you even going to do, Dad?

They part with a slight headshake.

— Nothing. Now please give it to me.

Placid lines wait for an answer. Mine tighten and try to make the sound of laughter.

— Dad, this is a zombie apocalypse.

It's hard and segmented. He doesn't meet my laugh.

— You don't understand. I'm not doing this because you're my daughter and I love you. This is what you need to do. You're either a part of this family, or you're part of what's out there. For your sake and ours, it has to be kept separate. The torn up state of the world is not worth brutalizing every part of ourselves. We have to at least try to be better than that.

His fingers extend, still open.

— Please, Imogen.

— Dad, I can't.

His arm slowly lowers, and his lips purse softly back on themselves. He takes a step towards me, and I flinch. He pauses. Gesturing behind me, he passes to grab the garage door shut. The light leaves us in a gust, and slowly he passes again, close, and continues inside.

WAIL

A WAIL BRINGS my eyes open on the dark. It continues and holds them there while a guttural rumble punctures the rise. It instantly falls back to the same low growl, a cat at war, ready to move again. Things grow quiet. The black atmosphere presses in around me and the room goes heavy. The shriek rises back high, wild and crashing. Something is hit outside our house and the cry carries into it.

I kick my legs out of bed and peel back the layers of curtain. A hunch buckles in the street below, coming from the congealed stain. The wail rises again as the head hangs low, intent on what's beneath. Teeth scrape back down into asphalt, more felt than audible. The shape, female and balled, has its arms spread across the spot in unchecked supplication. Her robe billows out, the hidden movements carbuncular and sudden. Her head lifts to search one side of the street, then ours. It's the old woman, at least it would be. She rises to her feet, held together in a way that she shouldn't be capable of. A white thing stands its ground, nearly out of view, and scurries into the avenues. She follows.

HOW'S IT GOING?

A SHARP KNOCK comes to the door, levying each of the spaces between with pillowy satisfaction. I stretch free to find our driveway throbbing with movement, a racked roof. A shoulder passes behind from the study and is already gone when I turn.

— It's Alyssa and James.

I stay rooted to the desk, where the guns are still out in plain sight. The new one and Jake's fit shoved below in their cleaning cloth, but the Kimber I keep. It's a fist from my back waistband and it leers with each step.

— Sid, man, is it good to see you! Sorry it's been so long. How've you been?

Dad's response doesn't make it upstairs as I close the gap.

— There she is!

Alyssa's faded cap still has her ponytail tight. They both clog the doorway in vests.

— You okay? You don't look all that much better.

I dance my shoulder back and smile sunbleached down.

— It's like the world won't stop until it's torn it off me.

Their grins come gently still and stall back to Dad, who hasn't turned.

— You can take off your shoes and those, uh, jackets.

— Oh, thanks, you just get used to them.

They stay close as Dad locks the door behind them, and it's another moment before they unfurl their boots in black segments. They're new.

— Your, uh, face.

— Yeah, it will take a bit to heal.

His hands move for something to do.

— Coffee, I can make us some more coffee.

James's eyes go bright as Dad turns to the kitchen.

— Yeah, that'd be lovely, Sid. Thank you.

They're slow to look back as I call out again like a girl on a balcony.

— How're the trees doing?

— Trees?

— Your apartment plantation?

— Oh, well, they're still alive.

Alyssa narrows to him.

— Are you sure?

— They should be. Honestly, they're just bushes.

The corner of her mouth hooks tight as she pulls to the foot of the stairs.

— Are you really alright?

She's where it's more than a scar.

— Yeah, probably. Maybe I should find a shield for it.

— Looks like it's been that.

She lifts her wrist drawn to mine, but it falls.

— I'm glad to see you're doing well.

We follow James to the dining room, where Dad is pouring hot water into the coffee filter with a nest of owl mugs huddled at the base.

— Where is everyone else?

James sits wide into the chair with Alyssa taking the space in from behind.

— Mei isn't feeling well. Jake's upstairs with her.

His eyes knit close.

— Is she okay?

— She just needs some time.

— Well, we can help bring her in if you want. They'd be happy to take a look at her.

The reflex of Dad's smile lingers as he lifts the dripping filter by its tail to pour the coffee evenly out. The sound caresses the air as we watch. James breathes deeply into the half-filled mug, keeping tight onto his initial sip as Alyssa leans in.

— Out there's worse too. There aren't even that many of them, yet, and still they're flushing everything out.

She stops herself on the mug.

— Thanks.

Dad only nods, waiting. I search for her eyes, which come back ajar onto my face, forcing something out of me.

— Do you know how they got here?

— Besides walking? No. But you kill one and two seem to pop back up.

— If you can kill them.

James's voice strains close to something funny as he watches his fingers lightly dance along the rim until they lie at the bottom, flat.

— Good shot or not, they keep coming until their brain is torn apart. Like, most of it, just gone. Kneecap them and go. Unless you really want to spend your day burying someone.

James smiles to me, and I shift the face of my owl to his. Alyssa paves over it to Dad.

— Have you thought yet about moving to a WWS camp?

He scrunches together a short no as she drinks through, matter-of-fact. James repositions and grins broader now to him.

— Those people, the ones who killed Eshan, Cameron, Mason, they keep coming into the city. What we're doing now, it's like we're avenging them.

— We don't need to upsell it to them.

Alyssa sticks hard to her coffee as James stares down fully into the table, teeth on his lip. His voice stays close.

— I'm just trying to see the positive too. Nothing's wrong with that.

The statement gently hangs until their eyes rise back on us. The cup comes down quiet in front of her.

— There's nothing positive about patrolling.

Her return of the word is picked over and stretched apart. Pad and fingernail play at the rough parts of the handle, and she continues.

— Half of the time we don't even know what it is that started the fight, and usually either they run or us. Otherwise, it's waiting around and letting other people know about the nothing that's happening.

James keeps water-still.

— Well, we aren't playing sheriff. If what we do ever helps anyone, we don't know it. But it is necessary. If we're going to be anything more than wanderers out here, someone has to fight for it.

Dad sits closer, suddenly whetted.

— So the people you're talking about, they're what, bandits now?

— Burners.

Alyssa looks down at the word as James beams back.

— They're just, I don't know, wired for killing. They'll do it most any way they can. Trick you into letting your guard down. Lead you into an ambush; and they change it up too. Sometimes people get taken alive, but whether that's to torture out information or for cannibalism, well, I don't really want to know.

Alyssa lifts back up and lets her words follow dry.

— They will try to take your scalp; we know that. It's supposed to be good for trade. They built themselves up by killing, so I guess it makes sense.

A board creaks upstairs and carries off into nothing as Dad throws his wrists among the wide-eyed ceramic.

— But why? You are just talking about regular people, right?

Tremors of recognition lie boiling; Alyssa stares back at him unchanged.

— Yup.

His mouth hangs from it, waiting as she breaks out from her cap.

— They didn't go through the same nothing that we did, Sid. Centers weren't ever overrun; they were incinerators. Not for undead, for us. That's what's been happening. Except they didn't have the same luxury here.

Dad leans into her words.

— They made people do it themselves.

The corners of her lips keep coiling back at each word. It doesn't stop. A rending pinpoint of torsion grips its way through my chest. It shoots warm and crowds the caffeinated return.

— Thrown into rooms and told only one, maybe two can come out alive.

She keeps the story there, hay-chewed and tasting only of earth. Everything at the table stands still with the edges lost; the cups each their own hole. Blind tunnels lying just there beneath the ink-black surfaces.

Dad watches intent as words begin to crawl back out of me, trying to be something firm in the middle of it all, synapses spiking at my cheeks, aching and laughter-spent.

— No one would just walk into that. They'd come there already armed. Or just run.

His eyes narrow onto me while gathering his jaw back to speak.

— At what point do you run from the guns that are drawn on you?

The bright endocrine warmth screams dense, recoiling tight at my diaphragm into a cornered octopus. I'm glued in place, somehow small. Something of James's comes through.

— That's what they were pushing everyone to. We'd be there if it didn't. Pile up.

The pressure holds underwater.

— I don't. I don't see how people could just let that happen to them.

The words hang useless between us. Dad parts his lips, but only an owl in front of Alyssa gets picked up and drained.

— Whatever really happened to them, to their families, what those people want, now, is just the end. And it's worked.

Dad peers back over to her, an incisor bared.

— No. No, you must have something wrong. If that actually

happened, if people had to do that to survive, they'd just be victims. The trauma wouldn't make them anything more than that.

She carries on in the same Phrygian tone.

— They don't act so traumatized now.

— You don't understand. That kind of violence can't be from some sort of moral lack that's in us. It's not. You can't just tear something out of people to get them to start murdering for its own sake. The Hobbesian push to kill your neighbor for a can of soup, for the possibility of a can of soup, it's miserable and pathetic, but that's only starvation drawn down to its stupid conclusion. It doesn't stretch as far as what you're saying. To actually busy yourself with killing, good God, killing for scalps? Whatever oblivion this is, we still have things. There's no reason to be at each other's throats. We're still us.

His palm slides into the table, taking it all. Alyssa's shoulders build backwatered buttresses over her close-wrapt hands. Only her eyes stand wide against the faded brim.

— Sid, the only kind of trauma that I care about is for the ones who didn't make it. If you want to go check on who's left, drive east.

His mouth shifts open, which James clears with a resined smile.

— Sid, this is it. They'd just rather kill us as people; it's all they need.

His eyes drop for something.

— It wasn't zombies who took their time cutting two up on Polk yesterday with their bags still bound tight. Regular people, just carved into until they didn't have faces anymore.

Neither looks at me.

— That's what happens if you're out on your own. There's no more safety in anonymity, not with them. People and firepower, that's all that matters.

Alyssa puts her hand on the table as though to reach Dad. All of her sharp edges fall back into what's said.

— You won't stay hidden here much longer. Come with us.

James's pelagic smile redoubles, rising in his seat, bigger.

— No one's asking you guys to fight, okay? Not if you don't want to. People earn their place by buying in, scavenging. That's the new world.

The ball of Dad's beard chews at the end, gulping it through.

— New world, huh?

The words are grating.

— And you want us to gather for you. As what, tribute?

Alyssa goes bright, almost relieved.

— Contribution. But what you have will be enough for now.

— Enough for what?

— To keep what's been happening to you from getting any worse.

The weight sinks on perfect display through the table.

— We're doing just fine.

— I definitely don't see that.

She still doesn't look at me. James smiles without looking back as Dad talks.

— I appreciate your concern, but we really are fine here, and we're more than capable of facing our problems head-on. It's tough, but it's been nothing we can't handle. If there's a flood coming, as you say, then we'll deal with it then. With each other's help, I'm sure.

His voice keeps hold of the room, leaving Alyssa and James with only glances to each other. Alyssa's voice is leveled down.

— There's no flood. It all just one day happens. Either you're all killed or maybe just one of you; does it make any difference?

— And you can only fight those odds with us. Just one night. You could lay low there for a while, meet some people. See how you like it.

— Thank you, but no.

His hand is stuck to the table. James turns briefly back to me, only registering my presence and intimating nothing before slouching casually again.

— Imogen can speak to how well things are run; they're why she's alive.

Nothing happens. The stillness breaks on Alyssa.

— Sid, come on, is this an autonomy thing? Fuck it, join leadership. You could do it. I mean, you don't even know what you're turning down, and you're acting like you've already seen the worst of it.

Dad declines the look while I break for the empty mugs, getting to the washbasin as his eyes start to glow back hot as rocks.

— Thank you. For the welcome. But you're fighting other people. I can't bring my family into that.

He casts his brow into a splayed triangle, gazing forward.

— You can chase whatever violence you want. But there's no room for it, not here. Thanks for the offer, but no.

The room's his again, everything pushed. James's lips curl tight together from the half view that I have of him, and I'm washing things more than I should.

— What we're doing matters, Sid.

— I'm glad to hear it.

His hand is hard on the table, everyone staring down. Alyssa looks up with a slap that sends a loud, tabled hitting back at her.

— Damnit!

James is back and waiting.

— This isn't a social call, okay?

She wants to scream.

— Look, I'm really sorry. We want to convince you, but if we can't, we're not walking away. There's no going empty-handed.

She leans in, but the light loses her under the brim.

— Is it the stuff? Really? The stuff? Is that what makes you feel so safe?

— You want to come see what's left in our apartment? It's just furniture.

Alyssa takes the space in front of her.

— We need things now. It'll be no use holding back since we know you guys. There's a lot we helped collect.

— So you think that makes it yours?

James shifts forward, the smile gone.

— It's yours if you're the one holding it.

He speaks as though grinning again.

— You really will make such a difference right now, Sid. It'll all have an immediate impact. And you'd have guards. Community. More resources than you're actually putting in. This, this has no future. Just say for now that you're joining. You can come for that tour or we can give you a list of some things to bring in from time to time. It'll be worth it, you'll see!

Dad's down, face static. His wrists sit back in front of him.

— Let us think about it.

— I'm sorry, but we can't wait.

He stares hard into Dad. Alyssa tries to smile.

— You'll really be much better off.

Dad's breathing holds miniature.

— We aren't coming with you.

— Well, you might want to later. Offer's open.

James looks down into a device.

— It's really no hard feelings. I mean, we obviously like you. We're just going to call some guys here. What's the actual address?

Dad stays looking down harder, stiff-limbed.

— Two four four nine.

James starts to push into the square thing, and Alyssa looks away. The grip from the damp spot in my lower back eases gently free, not quite behind them. My arm hurts, and I bring it together tight in place, right in front of me. The zipping slide, click turns Alyssa sharply to me as I level it at the back of James's head and pull the trigger. Their eyes are unable to shut at the sound. His neck is pierced through, and he falls forward in a sudden deluge of spasms between them, desperate to catch himself on the table with a raw-hewn, wet gasp. Alyssa's eyes tear wide open with blood splashed over them; a shriek gales out from her, rearing from him onto me. Her arms lashing, unable to keep me from firing into her chest, which rips open at her in whorls until she too falls over. She hits the chair and the table, and her limbs float on the floor.

Dad's eyes mirror back wide, brow splattered, lip near trembling over uneven teeth.

— Imogen!

The voice is hard as the gunshots. He leaps up, and the warm barrel's end dips right into him, catching for a moment. A backhand sends it flying against the wall.

— Why! Why did you do that?

He takes me between his hands, and I start to slip. He keeps me there, up close and sluiced. Nothing sticks. James is making sounds like drowning, but he's still trying to watch, his hands starting to drift in spider legs.

— Imogen!

Weight bounds down the stairs, and Jake is here too.

— What happened?

His socks are in blood. Unable to turn to see, James begins to lose leverage over the table as he tries to raise a hand. His eyes catch mine adrift as he slips back from his seat into a fold on the floor. The lump of him is sunken towards Alyssa, who's not moving. They're a mound, flat and amphibious, something pieced together to fill a gap in the fossil record. Their impossible shape weighs black, yanked up and still bleeding on the floor.

James's gaze shoots high into the ceiling, bulged to absorb the light-dark yawing of the room. Nothing moves. The voided sound, the hit-in-the-face smell. Alyssa's nose is in the floor, her arms swallowed. Just a shape and a cap behind him.

Dad pulls me back, too near to see.

— Why on Earth would you do that?

Black tendrils lash hot into my eyes, blurring my vision wet. Whatever words stumble from my mouth aren't mine.

— I had to.

— Had?

His features rear fishlike away, writhed and unable to break free. He tries to look at them and can't. His arms forget what they're still doing at me and come hard to his forehead.

— You killed them. You did that.

The word comes out gut-punched and biting down on itself. A lurid swipe cuts the air over them to coax something out of it that's neither them nor me.

He keeps me in the new-made space, crashed apart. What's me is stuck to something already there, a ghost, and whatever's inside and outside about it is on his eyes against me.

— We could have turned it to our advantage. They. They shouldn't have died.

My chest turns again into a hot, hard knot that I rip through in a sudden shower.

— Fuck them.

The words still aren't mine, and they stay next to me. My stomach twists, and I keep downward on his reaction and the thing that he sees in front of him. The dark shape in the corner blurs chair-hidden at the edge of my vision. White movement comes and merges lineless into it.

— What'd they even do?

— They wanted everything.

Jake comes back up, his hands dark.

— It's in the living room.

— I didn't want them dead.

His words are slow and cold.

— And they knew that.

My throat barely lets anything pass with what still isn't tears.

A shadow draws close, a set of fragments eddying together behind Jake. Fingers and gauze keep in a knot at her center while the rest hangs apart.

She shows yellow in the light, latticed in pain. Her eyes blaze leaden back to take the room in with one strange look that leaves us there like chairs.

Dad moves against her branched out hand.

— Let's sit back down, get you some water.

She turns free, ungripped, and our eyes catch each other on a deep, sea-dark surface. A pool of red has taken hold of her pupil with oily, egg-painted brilliance. My wrist is choked to the bone, yanking me in. Her mouth parts and does nothing more. Waits. Jake breaks from the table.

— We need to find someone for her, Dad.

— She won't.

— Something's been wrong.

A hand rises to my cheek in parts rough and moist until it's ripped scraping from me.

PART III

STINSON

The highway screams empty, clear from the pushed back flow of riderless cars on the bridge. The path carved in sidescrapes choking all the way up to the tunnel, dragging me on over tossed luggage, a broken off door reaching up into the wheel well to gut me from the start. What's already passed, a better car, still-sitting supplies, all drips lethal cold. Just trusting the tunnel to be open at the other end feels tearing. All its weight crushing above and around in the strained-dry artery, moving stuck between cars, where anything could jump in through the cold-blown window and have me mangled.

The handgun is still vised at my thighs now that I'm going sixty. Inertia brings me farther, faster, but I keep cutting it back, snuffing the downhill speed that could crash me through what's next.

Trees on trees with nothing human to fill them in. Flat baywater breaks to the right, and the highway-green-signed choice San Rafael or Mill Valley draws me away until I'm turned under the concrete. An empty streetlight watches as I roll to it and through.

A few clustered trucks make me brake down to an idle at the side-stretched lot of a motel. It's doors and doors long, all of them blank, and curtains holding in nothing but a bit of space; or more. Grass-lime and indefensible, but still some reason to be here. I keep going before there's movement.

The road curves to a series of shops, beige-bland and still waiting. An auto shop to fix the window. Plastic and duct tape could close the hole, but I'm already gone.

The first gas station takes the intersection to a T. EMPTY sits faded over the prices in cardboard. The glass, the garage stay unreacting as I pass.

Driveways creep into the road from the hillside, the rest shrouded in fences too dense to see into. Hedges and ivy tumble after in piles, each segment somewhere to hide, a trap in the nothing. I round another bend on a 7-Eleven and come to a stop as it's gone. An apartment in the rearview and the few houses across the way aren't quite empty. The cars here and there are too casual to be forgotten.

I turn around and thread through the parking lot. Plywood covers the surfaces, and I coast to the side and stop. Someone has hammered away both sets of concrete stairs at the apartment on the other side. Nothing in the windows. Ahead, a sidewalkless jungle carries straight into the hillside, scabbed with houses to hide forever in.

Out, I keep the gun pointed in my hand and stay looking at the apartments, three doors on two floors and twice as many windows. I hold it flat and wave as friendly as I can make waving a gun around to nobody seem. The rubble lies piled between the empty railings.

I get to the front and find a corner where glass shows through. Supermarket sterility reaches me from the outdoor dust, too clean and mothballed at once. The shelves are bare through the dark lotto sign with the refrigerated display left murky behind. I turn back. The sun blares from the houses across the way, and I lurch into a jog and drive.

The tear of the engine through the overgrowth washes me back tight in metal indefatigability. The houses get nicer and begin to take views of the mountains, now that they're there. One built on stilts has a woman watching with binoculars that droop as I pass. A rifle leans broomed by her at the railing.

Switchbacks circle me above their ridges, off again through thicker and thicker trees and slowing for guardrails. They break to yet more houses, above and below, and I speed ahead into the cover of another copse that's waiting thick with littoral fog.

The car wind immediately puts my face to a moist chill. Everything turns room-close and picture-flat. I come down slow as the white takes me on all sides, and it keeps with me. Looming trunks stand in and back out of view. A street cuts sharply in from the road above, mouth gaped at the stop. Fog still has the road buried where more trunks are reedy together, coming out and out from under an endless sheet.

The white-closed forest breaks to an underground expanse of valleyed hills, each cut down in a ceiling of white. The flattops have nothing but green below. The ocean shows in a wedge, then again in full place of the hills. Blue for green under white.

A truck comes too fast at me around a corner and smothered on the middle line. I stay and let it zoom, too close, a dextral wall of earth holding me in. It slings a gale into me that's possessed. No person behind the wheel. Their brakes light up in the rearview, but I keep fast around the next corner with the constant buffeting of wild air behind.

The road pulls into a Martian stretch, flat and finally on top. Scrub bound at the shoulder. All above, the white's narrow and bringing the world down to its point a few hundred feet from the gelled horizon.

The way down lurches heavy into the cliff, listing with amusement park deliberation to carry me through. Postcard fragments of sea-shorn rock crest from the whitecaps below, and I almost hang facing them as I keep curved yet ahead. Ahead.

The cliff rises again only to push free of me when the first town appears.

A sickle of beach coves into the water fit for condos and bodies in hot sand. Resigned to a downward slope, the road curves sinuously for the barren stretch of white, already there.

One sound barrier into another shields the first set of homes as the town rises on the mountainside ahead. My grip's tight on the wheel for a sudden shelling of panels that's the bolting middle of some beast through the street. I slow with no one on the scaffolding there to watch. Someone comes through a crack in the obstruction and raises a hand gently. I'm stopped, the way forward all brush aside from an empty trail. He's waiting, and my hand is low in place. I idle in. He eyes the window, then the door.

— Hi, there.

— Hi.

He holds my smile with his own.

— Passing through or looking for something?

— Both, I guess.

His hand is friendly on his side, half hiding the holster. He breathes in his view of me.

— Well, you're welcome here at Stinson. Come pull on through. You can park here behind me.

The main street continues vacant and hidden, shuttered in its openness.

— You want me to park here?

— A little walk won't hurt you.

He eases the partition out and gestures to a spot on the road ahead of an RV and a brown-aged truck. There, I unclam the gun from thigh to waistband on the way out.

— Leave that in the glove box. You won't have any reason for it.

The man is blond and weathered at the corners.

— You have yours.

He stays silent, hand still at his side. I let the rest come slow and careless.

— And it doesn't exactly lock.

— It's not going to need to. Come on.

He's warm in the wait. I lean over and stow it under a clutch of papers.

— Will you let me pat you?

I glare into his kindness as it holds jellied tight.

— I'm keeping my knife.

— I don't care about that.

He's brisk under my arms and at the hard parts of my hips.

— Have you been here before?

— It's been a while.

His hands come buoyant in front of him.

— Well, bring your trade with you unless you need it dropped off. You're a little early for the market, but you can have breakfast while you wait across the street. You'll find a lot of the newcomers there and whoever else isn't busy.

And if you'd like to get that window fixed, check in with the fire station. They might be able to help you out.

I stay caught in the beaten layers of his shirt and jacket; a translucent tuft of hair stays yawing within the narrow V, spiraling outwards.

— Where you coming from?

He grins flat, his mercury eyes sucking more of me in.

— San Francisco.

— Yeah, I figured. You going somewhere in particular? If you don't mind my asking.

— I, I don't know.

— You don't know?

Away, a pair of fire trucks has been lined at the station.

— Where's there to go?

He pivots back, then in.

— Well, I'd love to say you'd be welcome to stay if you want, but there's only so much to go around. The inns are pretty full up, and most of what we really need is out there, not here.

He looks at me again.

— Just ask around. Say you're looking for work. Maybe you have to wait, but you'll find it. If you really need help, though, just ask.

— Work.

The word buffets in place with the cold-salt air.

— Look, I like to take an early lunch. If you're still there, you and I can talk.

I try to smile, and he gets back to the road as I pull a bag from the trunk. Emptied out, between the clothes, dry food, water, and tools, there's nothing. I put it back and only take the small, strange duffle that I haven't thrown out, which hangs half heavy at my shin.

At the corner, blue-and-gold-painted signs say LODGING and *Valet* PARKING. More cars and work trucks line the dirt, uphill into houses and ahead. A garden shudders with people in wide-brimmed hats, wicker and nylon. One wrinkles a smile and a dirt-rich wave as I pass. Shops are shuttered or have changed their signs. Surf and Survival Shop. FIRE DEPARTMENT AND PUBLIC SAFETY. I move into the middle of the street to go to the bleached-yellow café.

A mishmash of leather and wood seats keeps an almost full room from eyeing me with too much interest. The chalkboard overhead is mostly wiped clean.

My hands ball onto the counter, away from everyone's bright aggregate of fleece and knit caps. An aproned man with a heavy mustache watches me.

— Can I have a menu?

He points a wet thumb to the board.

— What's two eggs and toast cost?

— Not much. Make an offer.

I look down into the bag and he stops wiping. Pushing and pushing the sweat-thick flannel into each corner unfolds a wallet, a hammer, a can of soup.

— This.

— I don't need a hammer.

— Well, how do I know what you need?

— Show me something else.

I try to draw out the flannel and he rolls his eyes.

— No, no, don't do that.

— You could trade the hammer. That's going to last a lot longer than breakfast.

— I'm not running a pawnshop.

His chest is puffed to his height with the canister that still says TIPS.

— Oh, yes you are, Alex. Stop giving the girl a hard time and just put it on my tab, will you? You can keep your things.

His features skew as a thin mane of white leans into the space next to me. He wags a finger away.

— You don't let me have any fun. I got to have some fun. I deserve it.

— I'm plenty of fun for you, Alex.

He laughs voicelessly to himself, his back turned and drifting.

— Welcome. Isaac let me know we had a visitor.

She sits silken into the stool, her spots and wrinkles animate.

— Thanks, but I can.

— Oh, don't worry about Alex, he just likes to haggle when he's bored. Isn't that right, Alex?

He speaks with his back turned.

— What I like is getting paid.

She smiles at me, close.

— The old ways die hard. So, are you lost, dear? You look it a bit, if you don't mind my saying so.

— I'm not lost. I just haven't been out here since.

She nods vigorous into my caesura.

— Since everything else fell apart. Well, we've started to cater to a different sort of tourist. But you're not here for the sand or the supplies. At least, you don't look or move like it.

She has a small golden pendant that's melded into the brown muddle of her neck, bulbous and smoothed over with wear. A thing forgotten.

— How do I move?

She catches splintered on the line and her pale eyes brighten.

— Like someone out of a wreck, dear.

A pang of something throws my gaze down to the floor where my shoes fidget on the stool. She stays quiet until I look back up at her, where she's smiling in wait.

— If you need some sort of help, ask. Otherwise, what good is having all of this?

She looks around at the ceiling and walls decorated with kitschy maritime mounts and bright red and yellow bottles like plastic flowers on every table.

— I don't know where I should go.

— Sweetie, you don't have to go anywhere until you know the answer to that question.

WEEDS

— So WHAT's your mom like, flowers?

— Sure, if you want to piss off my dad.

Grass rolls yellow outside. We twist and keep going.

— Well, if he's helping in the kitchen, they'd be for him too.

— That was special.

The seat shudders hard as the truck metal clangs angry to itself.

— I'm just saying it'd be a lot easier to watch each other's backs on a home-cooked meal. At least sometimes.

— What, you're not getting enough from the mess hall?

He keeps his eyes on the road.

— It's not the same.

The road pinches with countryside barbed wire thin at each side. Leaf-stripped oaks within a rusted cluster of sheds crowd out the hills. Gaps beckon from pens and the feed house as an excoriated FARM FRESH EGGS calls out at the end.

The hills turn to bone, seeds of grass bringing the brown luminescent. There's something more than trees dark in the crack ahead.

— We got one.

We dip to a stop off of the road. From the back bed, Lulu hands Dale a pole, and she tips a bat and an axe both on end to me.

— Lady's choice.

I take the axe under its used head.

— Someone's not afraid to get dirty.

He comes almost grinning to meet us. Dale levels the pole at his waist, artless and familiar while the tongue slides gleeful from its sun-dried face. A thrust lands into his shoulder, putting him off balance. He stumbles back a step, slows, and starts back for more. The pole twists deliberate in Dale's hands to come down heavy across the front part of his chest, cradling him to the grass. Lulu arcs over and hammers the bat into the flat of his head. He drops down against it, and she grunts another blow back in place. His nose is broken and his eyes are bright onto her. The next is louder with a hollow, wet pop, and he crawls anyway towards her. The pole spears into the middle of his back, but the frame holds. I dart into the opening, swinging where he reaches out and putting the hand back tight to the ground, halving it deep. He gapes towards me and tears the mostly severed hand free, thrusting the dead fingers at my face. I scramble back into gravel as he covers the axe. Another bat blow lands at his cheek, and the pole pecks into his limbs, widening him, glass.

— Pick it back up!

The thwacks leave him rolling sightless and centipedal, close. His back turned, I go in, and he twists sharply near. He keeps coming, making me backpedal faster and still there until I plant it into his face, splitting the downcast look to a stump. Air comes gasping up at me where the pressure is still welled tight against my grip.

— It's not dead yet.

Dale's eyebrows are arched into sweat. The hands below extend calmly out and heliotropic to me.

— Go on, you're the one with the axe.

I keep the weight into my right hand, the other only guiding it down again in place. The metal sinks in, sending a convulsion through the dead body that ripples after. Dale and Lulu watch him grow still. My foot squashes onto the shoulder blade and something barrels me back. Dale's glaring me down.

— Don't touch it like that. Not yet.

The pain in me is hit panging. He turns and tugs, leaving the axe head to glisten brown in the grass. He gouges the side deep with the pole, worms it, flips up to something unseeing.

— Treat that mouth like a rattlesnake's, got it? Now you can search him. If you like.

My chest beats wine-thick at the fissure.

— Have him.

The breeze freshens the space around me, and I sink back to the truck. Lulu comes once they're done.

— We're going to bury him since we don't want to risk the fire. You aren't going to help with that?

I break from against the door and breathe deep on the air that's mostly clean. The shovel grip is old, wood cracked more grey than anything else. I go back and stomp it right in the ground next to him.

— You get used to the squirming.

— You do?

Lulu shrugs.

— Or you don't.

The tools are loud again in the back. Sliding. Clanking. No one's turned the radio on. There's a sign and a road.

— Is that a dairy over there?

They don't look.

— Not anymore.

— They just shot everything. Brought it down to jerky.

Tract housing plops low into the hillside. A moving jumble of sheets lies in front of an open door, the fenced stretch of green across from it still bare.

— Is there anyone here?

— Not that we want to see.

Someone is standing with grass up to their waist in a vacant lot. We keep driving. The only thing to mark a long enclosure of dirt is a street sign of a man on horseback.

We pick up speed past a school where part of a person is lying in the dead grass. More fences on fences encase homes, and still the road shoots straight. A long-dead shopping center swells out of place. And then a garden supply where deep brown spillings are slashed out from fertilizer.

Dale eases off the gas for a shuffling line heading to a home against the trees. Lulu lets out her hand in middle finger at the slack faces turned back. We speed back up.

— Locals?

— I think so, it's always a mix.

— It really did make us set aside our differences and come together.

We charge through the wide gash of an intersection, veering desperate to the road. The way cuts through a sudden main street with arbored storefronts as we go. An industrial lot is where it ends, and Dale is quick to jump out, staring down the rest of the way before getting to the gate.

— Still looks good!

They wait for the rattle of the fence to grow still before using a key. A washed-out sign stands billboarded above the roof. There's a padlock on the shop door too that he also unlocks, his movements steady through the rising yard dust. The doorknob itself is busted.

Inside the air is squelched and dim with afternoon light. We're the only ones to move it. A wall of caulking tubes comes first. Pipe segments and other packaged parts stay lined for indecipherable use.

— I can't believe this is all the tape.

— Just take the glue.

Lulu brings a handbasket as Dale checks the last of the aisles. He passes a door with taped up signs for first aid and directions to a portable toilet. I put my ear to it. There's nothing, and I scratch, tap tap tapping. The sonar is tight and muffled, that's it.

Dale steps in and gets it cracked, not showing much inside. He leaves most of what he picks up.

I follow Lulu back to the lot with its neatly laid copses of lumber that leave everything bare. She crunches ahead, keeping from a storage shed as I catch up.

— We could get one of their trucks running and start carting this off for real, but it's not worth that kind of attention, not really. Though it's going to happen anyway if we keep coming like this.

She does a short stutter step, leggy and kicking up dust. Sitting behind cinder block is a trailered cement mixer.

— There it is. Last time we had no hitch. Well, let's get the truck. I want to get the bags loaded before Dale can make a stink.

They're hard to move, and her straight-cut hair lashes into my face. She almost stops me. Dale only sighs to see his truck moved, and he jogs by for the mixer.

THE MAN WITH THE MUSTACHE, Alex, already has a plate for me; a slight nod when he hands it heavy with mashed potatoes on canned vegetables and real salad. It's not a lot, but it's dark green and glistening against the dry, brown sauce beans. A roll dances on top that might be preserved.

Lulu is with her family, fingers long and animated in front of her.

A group bristles at my standing near them. Someone takes me by the arm. The woman from before, as though she's been waiting.

— Don't be shy, no one's going to bite. Come, help me brave it over at the boys' table.

A pattern of creases and rhino cracks leaves them sagacious against the lantern, Dale's unwashed curls laureled tight. There's three around the bench we come into.

— Dale was telling me about how you slew one of the poor and wretched among us.

Glances pass without staying long on me. She laughs and puts it onto my shoulder.

— Sorry, that's just me having fun. Feel like I scared you, making you think you'd come to some sort of end days cult.

Her laugh goes scoriac to Dale and the others, all tied in age and different kinds of hairy. One ruddy and orangelit puts his eyes to me mid-fork-thrust.

— We have other words for them ourselves. Not so kind, but no less colorful.

His hand is chapped and swollen at his plate. I take a bite of the salad. It's wet and tart and cleansing as I talk through the crispness.

— It was a group effort.

— Yes, but you did the deed. That puts you one more than me.

The moon-grey shroud of her mane turns intent across the table, getting Dale to shift arms folded into the pocket himself.

— You found a good one.

The mouthful of potatoes is heater hot and salty. I mix another bite with the beans. The only movement is around us.

— Just doing what needs to.

— That's not exactly true, but it was your deed, and we're thankful. I'm sure whoever the person was would have been thankful too. Their family.

She smiles close and serene with breath like tea. All the food is getting pushed together and goes down easily.

— Well, thanks.

There's laughter nearby as they're swallowed against me. The red one grits over something that moves to get out.

— It's not like they'll ever go away. Not so long as anyone's left.

Her smile carries over to him.

— We weren't going to be here forever anyway. Can't ignore the signs anymore, not when the work's already done.

She looks to me, water turning back over dry stones.

— Not so fair to you, though. We've had most of our lives to try to fight the tide or let it come.

— Not fair to anyone.

They're all trees at me. Dale keeps back as the other waits over something intimated, and she continues.

— Fairness, equity, not something that blows in from the sea. All we can do is make our own and hope the sandcastles stand long enough before they're wiped out by our great equalizer.

— All praise the coast.

The reddish one breaks grinning at his own joke as Dale and the other keep to their drinks. She looks back.

— It more than anything else is the reason we're sitting here, so yes, all praise the coast and the blind inner workings of chance. We've done our work, but let's not puff ourselves up about it.

Her long white hair rocks sea damp as the pushed together tables shift under the weight of an elbow.

— You keep everyone together, Jane, and we'll keep making sure this place doesn't fall into your beloved sea.

— Please do.

They share a sharp smile together. Dale's passivity breaks and makes the other one join.

— The town attracts a poetic sort.

— And then there's us.

I keep making headway and talk mostly into my plate.

— Got to do what matters to you.

The red one catches himself before coming back, something stoked.

— You know what might be the best part about all this? Everything trying to fill in our heads is just gone. The daily outrage, clickbait alerts, vaporized. Not another vapid cry for concern left on the planet. All that's left is beautiful, clear silence. Let it come moaning and groaning too, if it wants. Still won't stand in the way of us having to be who we really are. Free.

His shoulders come around to each of us, ending on Jane, who flows back and forward in the same movement.

— Well, someone can sure give you that earful you're missing if you'd stick around most mornings, Art. Newcomers need more space, more hand-holding. Someone's being a nuisance. Those with the means are on about some belligerent thing that'll expose the rest of the community. And your mind would go numb with the number of times I've had to listen to someone trying to convince me to help retake their home or send us all this direction or that or how you here would have us all on houseboats.

The one who's not done much rouses into place.

— It's the only thing they can't breach!

— And that won't do us much good if we give them the whole town in exchange. There's no way we can get everyone living like pirates.

His neck turtles out.

— It's a good idea!

— Then drive down to Sausalito and bring one up to the bay. I won't stop you.

He looks uneasy at her, and Art bristles back in.

— Don't elevate it. People have done a lot more around here than spout drivel. And if you have a girl like this out prospecting, then she sure as hell has had her hands dirty too. Look at you, pushing her over to Dale.

The texture of outside conversation is diminished. He turns right to me.

— You didn't come here just for the food. Why don't you show us what's going on with that arm you keep favoring? Here, it's fine, I'll show you mine.

I'm rabbit-still, fork in hand as he pulls back beard and hair over a bifurcated bottom half of ear, the top gone.

— This is what safe gets you. Crept in while the guy was going through cars. Maybe just got a bad idea and acted on it, who knows. Once he knew I wasn't letting go, he did that. Pushed him down in the pavement and didn't stop. Jane, here, doesn't like that story, but that's exactly what happened.

Her voice has lost its octave.

— Because you could have stopped.

— Yeah, and so could he.

— You weren't the only one there.

The other one seems only to gulp. Lulu is up alongside her parents, tall with none of their weight. She puts her arm gently on her mother's shoulder to get past the bussing station and crouch to a family and their son.

He starts talking again, and it's longer until my eyes come back from her.

— I take the bad with the good when it comes to it, Jane, same as you. It's the problems you can't deal with. Globalism, that's what killed us. We're not built for it. All it did was line deep pockets and leave the rest of us spinning our wheels at the horror show.

He grumbles down, close to losing his voice. Jane is soft to him.

— You don't really think we've all been helpless thralls to distraction, do you, Art? Most of our real concerns from before were about state violence, systemic racism, sexual harassment and abuse, all very real issues for people here too. The connection between us and the world has never been a fabrication.

The barrel of him crests into the table.

— And what's all that concern actually get but talk? Obligating you at every turn. Damning you for caring, damning you for not. Pitting neighbor against neighbor until people can't even talk without hive mind platitudes. Safe affirmations, nothing the slightest bit challenging. Neither side of it would let people just be. They made their money and their power, terrorized us, and now they've gone down to dirt. So good.

The half bulb of his ear crawls back out, turning slightly against me. I clear my throat with water, and Jane bumps for a moment into me.

— Any sort of call for change is going to be irksome, that's the point. You're upsetting the balance because the balance is unjust and needs to be reset. So maybe those unkind vestiges still inside us shouldn't have us at each other's throats, but words matter. Thought matters. It takes a collective level of concern to actually push those evils out of a community. Otherwise skeletons stay in the closet, people exact their violence on the most vulnerable. Systems are self-perpetuating; they're only true to themselves. You can't just trust the bad guys to be caught or leave it to a fact of life. That's nihilism. If you actually care, the only way to make a lasting difference is to change the logic of abuse itself. Make it unthinkable. Give it no quarter, and it will have no place. You have to do your damnedest to ensure that everyone actually feels safe enough to speak up. Build their place. Otherwise, the world keeps on eating them up. So sure, we can't face it all at once. But even with the way things are now, as horrible as our choices get, we can't just turn away.

I'm caught in the gap over my finished plate as she hangs breathless and hoarse. She makes herself continue.

— The punishment didn't fit the crime, Art. Maybe that man you left crushed could have joined us. We are a better option than most. And maybe then we'd be one set of arms stronger. One mind brighter. And you'd still have your ear.

A tight, metal blow smacks the table, his eyes fire in front of us. Breath carries warm, and Dale's jumped.

— You weren't there. You don't get to cherry-pick the results. You want to celebrate your lack of experience with us? With whoever this is? Keep that ivory tower dream growing off of our backs?

You're the same damn person, Jane. All you really care about is having your precious view and being queen of the socialites.

He gets up, immediately struggling back from his friends, who are lumps against him. Her jaw's a spillway with nothing there.

— Tear your hair out at the old world's problems while this one rips everyone apart. But leave us what's here.

Someone is in his way, and he stops to come back.

— And you know what? They've done more of your kind of good than any of us ever could. Saved what's left of the environment. Broke those class and race barriers right down. The world could be all sadists from here on out and still the bulk of its suffering is done and dusted. It doesn't need you to change it. But please, come save us. Shape us all into something right in your image.

He breaks his lock from her and shoves back the door.

— The next one's all yours!

Her eyes only touch us in glimpses. The pain is taken by something already there. It's weary and unbreakable, rising in the silence that's towards us. She settles on a light grin. Dale meets it and looks straight to me.

— Think it's time for us to call it a night.

I get away into the coastal chill and break off for my cot. Someone is already asleep. In the cabin dim, I dig for my toothbrush and go out to the faucet, where I pace in dirt until I can spit. Mountain-cold water leaves nowhere to dry my face except the shirt from the day. It stays wet.

I change slow and quick between the bunks and undo my bra last inside the new shirt. Someone comes in, and the light is swallowed until I get my feet blindly unsocked and am climbing into the bag. They aren't looking. I tuck the gun tight under my pillow and try to come still. I turn and it keeps digging at the back of me.

SWINBURNE

THE SAME CROWNS and crenellations pass by, coming dark back again at the empty farmstead. The hills are sun-drenched and alone over the spot we dug.

— You both comfortable back there?

— Yes!

Lulu's shout is metal clad. The two of us stay stuck in the space of conversation where our smiles are walled.

— Feel like a chauffeur.

She hugs the back of his seat.

— Heard you guys got dinner and a show last night.

Dale's eyes keep forward, slight movements flowing with the wheel.

— A couple of big personalities.

— Yeah. See? We're not so dull here.

The dark look only catches my missing reaction. We're getting closer.

— If it came to it, and Art got so angry he formed his own group, you'd join him, wouldn't you?

He keeps steady, darting for a moment to see her.

— There'd have to be a bigger reason than that for anything to change. Too stubborn the both of them. A couple of butting rams.

The back creaks with the tools.

— Yeah, but you know, what if?

— I work with you, not them. You too, for the record.

He finds me in the rearview, making me bite back the confirmation. The houses, the left open and billowing one, are ligament stiff, same.

— I bet you can't wait for school to restart.

Lulu's response has dropped somnambulant and small.

— Yeah.

Rounding the corner puts us suddenly beside a forked-in set of cars with someone's legs poled over the pavement. We're slow enough for a face to come blank into view. Farther, and more scatter.

We pick up speed.

— Shit.

One is already coming after us through the lot, choking the desert distance tight across the asphalt.

— They're coming.

— I'll do what I can.

The engine has their voices flat, keeping his low and hers thin. Dale brings his gun to the wheel.

— Maybe they'll back off.

My wrist strains against the seat while I pull out my own, stage-coached and proppy.

Low-grown trees crush the space between us. They keep coming through the lot, the car light and unstoppable. The rust-splashed sign for the shopping center divides us, erasing them before they veer for the exit behind. Shrubbery bursts in the wake as they correct hard onto the street and catch speed.

— They're faster than us.

— I know, I know!

The car rushes in, catching close before taking the lane on Lulu's side.

— Get your window down!

— Shit. Shit.

She presses at the button as they push into view. Pale faces make aquarium shifts in the cab. A long, black thing goes up to the passenger.

Dale shakes his gun at them while trying to get the window out of the way. We're locked straight and straining as his attention is off the road. We dip into another hollow, only sinking closer together.

— What's your fucking problem?

The words are swallowed outside.

They tug in line with us, looking. Dale nocks his gun over his elbow and fires a burst, the pops jolting. Something splinters at their passenger door, but they only half flinch. The one behind aims at him as the other with the shotgun points it outside to the tire. Dale drops into the seat and jerks the wheel, breaking my grip as everything shakes with our fuselages locked together and holding us forward. The air turns humid with glass as everything cracks loudly apart. Lulu shrieks into her lap while a face appears over the door that she frantically shoves the barrel end to. A hand rears with it and she fires, louder, sending loose a wet mist.

We drop into a tight fishtail that Dale wrestles back down. My breath and Lulu's push together, elbow in her thigh. I get up from her cascaded slouch to see their position, and the glass punches through around me. I land hard into the seat belt and Lulu points back over the edge, firing once and two times unlooking. I go to follow, and what's beneath us clangs, which bleeds into a long screeching. I lean against the drift to squeeze a few shots over Lulu to the driver, one making him move. They gain speed into the sidewalk, the shotgunner going for the wheel and the other in the way; faster into the column of a mall-modern office complex that slides him through the windshield and caught onto the hood.

The wool-worn trunk of a pine tree hits us head-on. My clavicle is slammed unbreathing into the seat belt, which leaves me numb once we're still. It won't unbuckle.

Past Lulu's bleeding scalp across the street, the white-fragmented window of the office bends forward, hands pushing it down from inside. A woman, a man, then others burst through the opening, climbing over each other and onto the car. The crashed man wakes up after they're on him.

Pillowed shots come from inside the wreck, continuing as someone falls out the door and hobbles free on a bent ankle. He staggers slow and straight ahead, and two keep with him through the lot. The gunshots continue until there's screaming as more press into windows and the open door.

— Dale, come on.

Blood is locked on his fist.

— I don't think I can.

— No, come on.

Lulu pushes me coming out and hurries to the front. He looks back, eyes lowered at her. She grabs him anyway. He bites in the pain as the rest of him slowly escapes the pinched wheel.

The man is onto the street, waving, the two there with him. The other car comes screeching through, sliding past and spilling out with more shooting. They open fire at the closest, making the man hunker as the others both keep through, their flesh rippling in bits as they continue onto his back. He tries to break away as he is bitten from behind, shot in the shoulder, and shot in the top of the head. One zombie loses its face and the other falls flat from its hip.

The two stop firing and stay quick to the edges of their truck. They wait and gesture something as the ground is still moving behind them. They break free, slow and crouched into the open, pressing evenly to us, pincering, looking at the cab, the sides. The woman bends lower, lower to the bottom, where I'm aimed damp in the grass. I shoot into her hung out form, and she drops hard on top of her gun, crying to get it back out. The tree hums hit, the impact boring through to me as I try again, this time leaving her collapsing over herself, wailing. The truck shudders all over as the man tries to stop me, gunning in fast and denying the angle. I get back but Lulu is already standing and firing. She falls back to the ground, and the deafening swell stops, its space empty and held in with a growing, ethereal shriek.

The breathing coming in, humid in ragged intervals. Lulu's sour and wincing. Dale's duller, flagging. The man Lulu shot back, more of a gasping, reaching. The unbridled frustration of the woman resonating tight against the road. Me. A hard, coursing void churning at my chest.

Then the movement coming around their truck, surging at the sides. The first woman gushed with blood. The man with his head uncapped. The one with no jaw or face, but still there. Another fresh one. A child.

She sees it. Reaching dirt-deep into the concrete, her lower half bends up to inch, inch further to nowhere. She sees me and turns back to them. Her short-cut hair walls her expression from me, silent. Another step closer, the back of her head erupts with a thin, jetting pop. The blood starts pooling.

The closest zombies kneel anyway. A hand pulls me down.

— We need help.

The voice comes from elsewhere, down and up at once. Blood in the same stream continues under Lulu's collar, her eyes reaching me lacustrine, cold.

— Grab him.

Dale looks ahead to the ground as I have him by the shoulder. His limbs reach it like antennae while the weight hurts, taking its place against me. Lulu lays her hand on my back, tying us against the dry shuffle of shoes on concrete, grass breaking, mouths wide and hushed.

The weight carries deeper into my shoulders, closing off my breath on hot-panned thighs. A country house ahead in overgrown grass. Dale sinks to the ground, rooted against my tugging.

— No, come on.

Lulu pushes, pries, and he turns up into her.

— It's alright. It's alright.

He half hugs into her grip, and she stays onto him as he releases. He doesn't turn well, and his voice rises graveled against her.

— Let me go.

A hand comes barked into her face, making her stop turned to the approaching legs.

— Keep dragging him.

She jolts away, close enough for the woman to twist after her. The other with what's left of a forehead lumped into his eyes bumps her along back to us.

— Don't fire at them!

The words cut voicelessly in on themselves, twisting the air with raised arms that loudly shatter the mangled one's skull up free from itself. Lulu grits forward, and something like a warning is stifled before she takes the next shot, close to them. It catches the woman and puts her closer to us.

I scrape Dale back a step, another as Lulu takes more time aiming at the woman's knee, which bolts the wrong way as she continues to come for us. The others circle onto Lulu, ahead and behind. She steps back. One from deep in the street closes her path.

She moves to him in stiff, banded steps. She shoots into his mouth, making it fall apart at the cheek and jaw before the head coils back on itself. He doesn't stop. She aims higher, fountaining the missing mouth skyward, and the feet keep their place in front of her with hands grasping back on nothing.

She stops, stalls while clicking empty down at the knee, and returns to the faceless mass in front of her. Dale drops in my fingers, the crawling coming closer into view. I keep him moving by my nails.

The child tumbles chest first into her, dragging its face through her white-hot cry like summer fruit. It's pushed drenched back from her hip. She has it by the sides of the head, still moving at her abdomen.

Writhing heaves under me, weighted underwater, only physics to pull it back up. I keep going as the woman crawls hands over shirt in front of us.

Lulu's scream thrashes as the child moves higher, together swaying into a fall. The sound she makes lights on fire. It tears wordless into the air. Dale raises the gun, gnarled and fighting to keep balance on the shape that's now three, four. He doesn't fire.

The woman watches his shoes dangle tug, tug over the sidewalk. She's shot with what's left, shredding her face into canvas. The reloading goes slow and rigid as her arm comes forward again and she returns noseless to the shoes. Dale drops in the pull, his fingers suddenly flailing at me and losing their place against the sidewalk. He's back in my hands, but they don't grab. They just hang under their icy water. The breath comes swift and ragged from him.

— Move me!

I put my hands to his jacket again and tug. He tumbles back with wide eyes up at me.

— Go on, move me! Don't leave me here.

I drop hold of him, my arm screaming, lungs scored. He aims the gun back up at me.

— Do it or I'll kill you too.

— I can't anymore.

His eyes wrinkle fierce after something in me. He moves and I slip back, running from the confluence that's centered now just on him. He grits hard and turns away to the opened face of the woman fully at his feet, now with the other man, the child. He fires until her forehead opens up in chunks and she drops flat. The man from before falls into his shoulder, and the barrel jams into the ruin of his mouth and fires and fires. In the fall, the zombie grabs Dale and makes him scream.

I hook onto the dirt driveway to an isolated grandmother cottage padded high with rosebushes. I stomp wooden up the stairs, and there's another gunshot. Nothing moves behind the half-shrubbed privacy wall. The door is cracked ajar and I slam it, lock it, and wait with my back against it for my eyes to adjust.

HOME

THE FLOOR IS CRUNCHING. Powdered clumps of barely illuminated food pointed with wrappers coat the entrance onto the living room. Tiny bones too. The inside air is brought down and still, too taken away to stink. The blackness in the kitchen, in the hallway holds dense and waiting for change.

The deadbolt slides loudly through. The front of my shoe squishes into the mess, slick and crinkling, only it ahead. Another, and I'm through to the foam-frayed corner of the couch, where something is lying in desiccated fur. I get to a part that seems clear and squat quick against it. The burnt matchsticks of my arms taper bent in front of me. The fingers hook apart, locked in spider ticks, and I clasp them quickly back on each other with the nails scraping in. My breath stops on top of diaphragm at the edge of spitting the last bit and what's with it out.

My eyes shut tight, making the darkness grow and come close. My heartbeat comes with it, the current still charging trapped through me. Footsteps, something like footsteps comes too. Soft, gently scratching its way in. Nestled already inside.

The wispy parts of me come back together without regaining their balance, aching back in movement. Up close, the thick plastic edge of the blind holds back a sliver of shirt, a moving shape in the grass.

I swing a chair tight into the doorknob. Still going. The whole house is raised high and out of reach, the porch blank of anything but the door itself. Another joins, small in a persistent counterbeat. They stumble closer together, then magnet apart. One opens its mouth. I thresh into the regolith and find the spot farthest away and wait.

One's still at the door, up with a hard fall that became a slow, heavy sliding upwards until it was already here. Its weight is just there, standing behind with what should be warmth. The air still moving from its mouth is nothing, genderless, neutral. What's in it isn't eager or curious or angry. It's not restless or bored. The quiet is cut off from anything close to wonder. The movement of a rock through a vacuum. It's there with nothing more.

The still-ticking on the wall clicks and clicks and clicks. I'm package-stuffed with air sodden crackers and turned walnuts. The ceramics around me stare white into other spots of the room, over the dust-hardened bed that's at least somewhere to be. A growl rumbles not far below the window. Then a hissing that's more in than out. It walks on.

The popcorn ceiling hums blue black on the dark. Blue black. Blue black.

Something else comes through the grass, and the two sounds meet stony together.

I close my eyes tight enough to press them out.

Two stand dark through the rosebush, their heads a turned mash of hair. I stay crouched to the porch with the old lady purse as steps plod somewhere and stop.

The yard is black stoneware. A tree-pierced fence line keeps the street from the spread of grass that's light with pollen, almost bright enough to show what's lying in it. The woman. Dale.

I slip over the back of the porch with the purse close, hanging exposed and hitting hard on the ground. Their sounds keep on, neither turned. I inch to the side of the house; it's blank of the one that's still there somewhere. Grass hums silent.

I move low into the opening. Unable to look anywhere but ahead, the uninterrupted geometry of the fence line comes closer, nearing in its gravity. Something drones there, a low rumble in the hatching, an engine and more. More.

Looking rough through, the stretch of sidewalk keeps still with a wide, dark spot and something small raised in it. Gone and not nearby.

The bag drops on the other side. Louder, I strain my weight on and over, boots knocking together.

They're around the truck. My stuff, the axe, all the ammunition. Tall forms and short turn right towards me and start coming. More than before. Something rustles at my ankles, and I jolt into the sidewalk, nearing the stain and what's in it. One crawling in a jumble faces me, unlit in front of the bag. The others have the gap already closed. I go the other way, steps bare into the gulped wide continuation of street.

ALONE

A VERRUCOUS NEST is grown pink over the first house, the flower fronds bodied ethereal in front of the rust wire and waist-high grass. A plastic chair sits inside, too close to be used. A faded SLOW CHILDREN AT PLAY has its own spot marked where there's nowhere off of the beaten road to run.

I pedal to a sun-stripped truck, and a dull black sweatshirt with a gardening bin stands inside next to a trellis of overgrown wisteria. The person in it looks up with wrinkles of sweat and brown waves of bed-bent hair.

— Hi.

She stays squinted at me, and I try to smile through. Her voice rises hard between us.

— Do you want something?

She picks off her gloves at me. Around her, the plants are weed choked and inedible.

— Water, if you have it.

— We've got water.

She stops, then picks back up again.

— I can give it to you.

Her face is lined and still. I try to relax off the bike, keeping every-thing slow.

— Thank you.

— You wait right there.

She ambles through to the house, moving older than she looks. Its long row of windows is boarded across the inside, clogging the movement in. Behind's a tin shed where the grass carries on tall below a basketball hoop. New roof.

On ahead, a pair of horses watches from a wide-stretched paddock. The sky and hillside lift around them.

The slam of the porch leaves her firm back in the doorway, stopped with her hands center, the rest dark. Everything goes tense, and I try to keep my hands spaced, shoulders overly sloped. She steps out with a crystalline glass. We come together in the low gated driveway.

— Thanks.

The water is earthen, washing through what's still hotpressed. I finish and offer her the glass, which she takes.

— I don't got much else for you.

— It's okay.

She continues to look me over, disinterested and still staring.

— I just lost my things and the people I was with.

She looks back at me.

— I'm sorry to hear that.

The green and manure come new back to my lungs. I step back in the gravel, smiling without turning.

— Thanks again.

She stays as I pick up the bike and carry slowly on, both of us there too long until I start with the sound of wheels rising under me.

Hanging inkblots catch me in the distance, each of the horses locked with canine passivity. Their chestnut flanks keep muscle and bone bound waiting together. The swollen hillside coats them close in green against the barn towered over with whitebarked oak. Someone has painted the front purple with butterflies and a sunflower.

A burst of objects fills the space between barn and the lone house. A backhoe. Two horse trailers left over from different decades. Rusted tractors. A homebuilt lopsided shed. A smaller barn with a collapsed roof. TV antenna caught inside some sort of tree. A polarized cluster of golden poppies at another deep brown shed. A trailer and a white station wagon, both sinking into the ground.

I stop at a long row of mailboxes on a wagon wheel in front of the house. What's gated is more overgrown than what's outside. Its kennel door is far to the side at a half-hidden pathway marked more by old rain than feet.

The house is shaded dark against the too-bright hillside that's all around. Ahead, the road goes to nowhere. I tap on the newest mailbox and call out hello. The sound of it is crushed in the air.

There's movement and shuffling with the door at the porch. The feet stay facing me through the dull sheen of oak.

— What is it?

— Nothing, I'm just passing through.

— So pass through.

I wince at the tree between us.

— Can we talk?

Something of a sigh comes from her, and she comes down with sandals and a shotgun half raised at me.

— Woah, not necessary!

I put up my hand with the other held low, feeling the space close between us. The barrel stays on me as she calls out.

— Yeah, I'll decide that.

I show more of my face.

— Come on, if I was here to rob you or whatever, I wouldn't be knocking.

— Don't sell yourself short.

She chews on a smile carefully through the grassy mess.

— You don't get to fuck with us just because you said hi first.

— I'm not here to hurt anybody! I'm just trying to not die over here.

Her blonde tangle hides an earthenware glare that keeps the butt cradled close.

— Fuck, will you stop?

— You're the one who wants to talk.

She comes too close for me to fire first. I shrug into something that looks like surrender.

— I'm looking for help. I just lost everything. I only want to get back on my feet.

I keep my face clear and readable. She's not much older, and what softens is still shelled in crags.

— Well, you don't look like you're on death's door.

— Would you rather I be bit or something?

— It'd make this a lot easier, yeah.

She tightens her focus on me, not turning from the affirmation that's there between us.

— Hey, you don't want me here, I'll go.

I can't back up. Each part of her is hard, all outside and skin. A yarned curl of hair is taken in the breeze. I give an earnest smile, and she doesn't see in the static. The porch door creaks and slams in on itself.

— Sara, what's going on?

A large man comes bent from the house. She stays on me.

— It's just a girl, for Christ's sake.

— You know that doesn't change anything.

Her words come rigid, still for herself as she keeps her back to him. The ungiving leg is belted with slats from shin to thigh, and a cane carries most of his weight.

— And if she was one of the girls?

Her face grits, stung.

— She's not.

She keeps anxious on me, eager. I'm unable to turn to him.

— Sara, she hasn't done anything to us. Let her be.

He stands back, stilted shapeless and paper wide.

— She's just looking for whatever she can get. Like we're doing so great.

— We're not destitute.

He sharpens his look from behind, sighing.

— Besides, company's worth something, at least to them.

She breaks, the end of it still on me.

— You think a playmate's what they need?

— Good God, Sara. You gotta let people live.

She narrows.

— Someone has to.

The gun drops to her waist, still ready to gut me.

— Drop whatever you've got on you. Slowly. I'm checking after, so don't try to hold back.

Their faces stay laid out like plates as I slowly pinch into my waistband and drop the Kimber. The woman smirks with the heat gone from her posture.

— Knife okay?

— No.

The same happens with my pocket. She nods for me to come through the gate, and I slowly pick my bike back up. The shotgun is now held low by the man, and she pats me hard enough to see if she'll knock me over.

— Hey, come on.

She only takes my things and nods to the man, and they head back to the house. I come after with the bike and leave it in an overgrown bush. Past is a set of herb planters and some heavily used shoes.

The living room has a smell that keeps stagnant and half vegetal. A kid in a long-worn purple tank top looks up from a pile of toys, her eyes glistening. The woman comes between us poised for a dog.

— Well, fine, we can get you fed up. You need a place for the night, there's a shed out back. You sure you're not hurt or anything?

The words are hasty and bored.

— I'd look it if I were.

— Not necessarily. Come, you want the food, you're going to strip.

The girl stares wordlessly through pasted strands of hair.

— No, I'm not.

— Hey, fine by me.

She glares for me to get out of her brown carpet jumble, arms folded. The hobbled man has his head down in the kitchen.

I push the air hissing through my nose.

Her glare moves to the hallway tight with photographs, where I let her follow close behind and we stop in a room undone with toys and clothing that still doesn't look like a children's room. There are two beds. She doesn't shut the door.

I sigh, still with nothing from her blue-ceramic stare. She only watches as I quickly lift the shirt back over my head, revealing my stomach to the air, where sweat and salt meet. My shoes kick off with the too-worn socks rubbing in. My bra's limp at my chest while I wriggle the pants down too. She stays where the colors ride from chest to forearm. She holds me there before twisting her finger for me to turn.

— Lift the hair.

I roll my eyes and tug up the back, which is getting knotted. She doesn't talk.

— See?

I come back, and the hardness in her eyes has gone clear and private. A twist rides my stomach.

— You fuck with us, and I will feed you to our pigs. I'm not talking about your dead body. I mean you. Cut up and helpless.

The words come out calm, almost soothing, her body somehow naked as mine. Getting at her face, her throat would leave me nowhere. The chopping continues in the kitchen.

— Wow. You already have my gun.

— Yeah, all two bullets.

I search for anything smooth in her eyes.

— Look, you don't need to do this. If you want me to work for a meal or something, I can do it. I'm not going to be any trouble.

She scoffs at my chest and thighs gently bound in cotton.

— Put your tits back up. It's time to eat.

The girls are at the table, one fidgeting at the other, who looks open-mouthed at me.

— I'm not hungry.

— You are, you just don't know it.

— Yes, I do.

The other breaks from her sister to the man bending slowly to place a plate of raw chopped vegetables in front of them.

— Why do we have to eat?

— To keep up your strength.

She talks down into her empty plate.

— I am strong.

— Yes, you are. Because you have a big appetite.

She smiles at how she says you. The girls go quiet when I sit down.

— I'm Nate, by the way.

He extends his palm over the table, which comes rough into mine.

— Imogen.

The woman looks pointedly at her kids.

— Girls, introduce yourselves.

— But we aren't supposed to talk to strangers.

— You're right, she is a stranger. But she's also our guest for now. So let's be polite.

They only look at my side, my clothing.

— Shelley.

— Justine.

The carrots, tomatoes, and onions still smell like dirt and are glazed in pepper and oil. Dry salami is on the other side with a bowl of cold mashed potatoes.

— Hope you like it.

— Yeah, thank you. It's great.

Sara looks at me, chewing.

— How close was the trouble you were in?

— Novato. We got caught out on the road. Then there were zombies, and I was the only one to get away.

Nate makes a grim smile.

— I'm sorry to hear that.

— What were you doing there?

She leaves no room.

— Looking for supplies.

— You come from somewhere?

The word is skeptical and accosting.

— Stinson.

— Stinson?

— Well, you're sure not headed back there.

I fill my mouth again.

— Nope.

After dinner, Nate walks through gravel to the smaller of the sheds. There's nothing to see beyond the light of the lantern.

— Not there?

He turns away from the ramshackle workshop guesthouse that waits for us with screens.

— That one's not safe enough.

The weight of damp wood comes into my nose, bringing iron and manure. Tight stacks of metal panels crush the space inside, leaving just enough room to lay a sleeping bag and some things. The long steel rows are flecked up close with hay and mud, casting zagged shadows that bring their depth staggering to the back. Geometric entrails sect themselves over and over as the pen pieces cramp in on each other. They lean idle and hateful, their purpose only here and right now. An altar with nothing offered.

— I can sleep back inside on the floor. Or maybe in a car?

His face is blacked out past the stubble, nose lit bulbous above. He pauses on me.

— I know it doesn't look like much, but it'll be fine.

The lantern comes down inside, where the ground is uneven with debris.

— I left a pillow and blew up the air mattress. And there's water for you if you get thirsty.

The raw onion on my mouth smacks a mute thank you.

— I appreciate you putting up with this. Things have been hard on Sara. Her girls too.

The air past us takes the murmured sounds of the house for itself.

— It's okay.

His lips lie flat in his hidden gaze. The sleeping bag shines crumpled purple on the floor.

— Okay, well, settle in.

I step spacesuited onto the platform, and the door is closing before I can turn around. A quick slap clangs loud followed by a fast sliding click.

— Hey!

Only movement on the other side.

— You're locking me in here?

— Only for your safety. And ours.

The voice comes into the wood, and I push my palm there as far as it will go.

— This isn't fucking safe.

— Just relax and try to rest. We'll wake you for breakfast in the morning.

— No, no, no, don't leave me here like this.

My breath is wet with the panels.

— You'll be alright; don't shout. You don't want to draw any attention.

He stays partitioned with me.

— What the fuck is wrong with you? I just hung around with your nieces, whoever they are; I'm not going to do anything!

There's nothing. Then the gentle crunch of gravel moving away. The light keeps the boards enflamed around me. I push the door again, and the hinges hold fast as it bends.

— I'm not your fucking prisoner!

I take up the lantern without anywhere for it to go. An astragal growth swallows the gap outside whole and gone. Walls stay skintight to the mangled floor. I crouch and scrape a fingernail into one dark patch of grain, and it keeps. I press against the next board, the next. Boring, chewing my way out if I have to for the bike. Or their house. My gun back or theirs. Someone broken on the floor. The girls.

I come down half balanced into the inflated pad, legging my way off the edge at the gaslit water glass abode. Night-charred wood takes back the space above, bursting in on itself in printer ink shadows. Tarry crevices to the back squid through dirt-swollen poles. The bars are close and uneven, shouldering their way at me, locked in clockwork anticipation.

I raise my palm to one. It's cold, and nothing moves. An iron creak slams heavy inside the mesh and shocks me back.

I close my eyes tight and press them down into nothing. Nothing.

I stop the light and worm into the bag, facing the bars. Their air moves slightly within. I turn pillowed into the door's barometric pressure. A plastic and nylon soup mixes over the stench of the shed. I close my eyes and wait.

Something crunches. It's in the distance, off to the menagerie wreckage. Nothing between here and the house. I stay stiff and shrinking. It stays quiet like a dream gone.

A metal screech slams into the door, ripping it open on the white-blue sky. My eyes ache into the tall, round figure above.

— Come on, it's time for breakfast.

I rise stiff to Nate's bellied silhouette.

— How'd you sleep?

I stop to see his empty hands, the house, each side behind the shed.

— You alright?

I look briefly at his face, then away.

— Come on, don't be like that. We're setting you up right. If you'd rather leave, at least go on a full stomach.

The morning saps most of the green from before. White haze brings the static mess close and at hand. I follow him inside to a breakfast of stale cornbread, juice concentrate, and a pinch of jerky along with a small cup of coffee that's made of more soot than plant. They leave us alone.

— So where do you think you'll go?

— Where would you go?

— I wouldn't.

The surfaces are long without cleaning, and a dry film covers the plates.

— What's in town?

— People. Not like before, but it's not bedlam. We don't go.

It's not much to finish, and I pass the girls wordless and step onto the porch. The sun clashes with the morning chill as they come gradually behind.

— You sure you're looking for people?

I turn back to her, no response for the glint of concern in her voice.

— I don't know. Just seems like maybe luck's better without them.

She hands me back my knife and gun with the magazine separate, her eyes dead on me.

— Well, good luck.

She watches as I waist everything and drag out the bike.

— Thank you, I appreciate it.

Neither responds. I have to kick out a branch from the spokes to walk the bike through and back onto the road. One of the kids watches me from the window as I go. They go inside.

Someone is trudging through the field from the highway. Each step comes hard into mole hills, nearing closer, arms thrown wide. Dry reeds and drooping barbwire are the only barrier. I pedal and pedal, coasting to a faster speed.

RIVERBOAT

A RIVER LIES flat in the distance from on top of the empty highway. White pagoda structures keep tight over a messy dock, storied high against the dust-brown length of marsh that stretches far and running from the farm town.

My breath is chafed cold, bringing the nautical lines and riverboat walkways distinct enough to stop. Boats all the same size, all the same middle-aged pleasure shade of white too dingy to ever get clean.

One is coming out. It drifts free from the dock and doesn't turn, doesn't turn until it crests hard-shelled into the bank down below. Someone crawls from the cabin and starts to run.

Small, dark figures move back on the dock, the long hotel corridors. Constant, slow, ants digging in and out of the contours.

Someone drops from the balcony, hitting shallow water.

I keep on as the light flutters of far-off movement wake around me. Nothing in the narrow gap where the runner was headed. The over-pass dips to the divide between Santa Rosa and Sonoma Napa, the remaining buildings tall and spread off into their surroundings. They aren't quite silent as I pass.

A flesh tone wall rises up, clearing the world again from me. Giving back the feeling of going somewhere. The pedals take my feet.

Plank board homes are left where the division falls to brush and cyclone fencing; something warped and sagging to each. The road constricts, putting its empty stretch far off and still here.

The fence jingles in anticipation. Hands mesh through from sea-thick dead grass brambling all the way back to an open door. A neighbor stands aimless houses down. Cedars and fences paste them back away, hiding houses with better tops and second floors.

A white sheet is caught back on itself with the word AHEAD wavering under a pedestrian crossing chained in tight and empty against suicide. As I come under, a square's been cut free where quiet ripples against it.

A dual section of cyclone and chicken wire spills out with three, four lingering in the aftergrowth. A fresh, rust-hued lacquer coats the face of the closest turned eyeless at me. Together, their long cut, dilapidated cotton repositions on jerky, backwatered gearing. Only the highway divider promises my way past as they begin to follow.

The road binds together in the distance with a rise of metal and concrete standing in the way. It stays dim with movement. The vibrations slowly shift as I get near, drifting into sets of dark clothed torsos that smash together towards me.

I glide to a stop. An off-ramp close to the cluster is the only way around. A body lies in the middle, part of it next to itself. Some of the ones coming are in uniform.

I throw the bike over the barrier and go with it down the grass-tangled slope. The pedal clips me bright with pain on the way. I hurry back up, high-stepped with the bike dragging alongside. A shadow looms above the barrier, and the ones I've passed aren't far behind. I keep going through the slope, and it falls over into my path, sliding, its face going through the vegetation with an arm caught playfully up. Another takes the place above.

I jump into the edge growth that's raised high into the fence, keeping the bike with me like something unwilling until it has to be my shield. The arms grab on easily and pull it out of my hands, where it climbs right on and garbage compactor tight. I fall into the chain link and lose the space to go forward. The skin is soiled but clear with only paling eyes and lockjawed hands to show the difference. Scrambling, I turn back to a pair of feet that's too near to get past. I twist into the fence and climb, the meat of my fingers and shoe tips taking my weight or just giving me an outlet before I'm bit into. I'm over, hard on the ground as the fence sways clinking with the impact of one and then the other. There's no room between the chain link and the property line fence that I'm up against and the poles start to lean in. I crawl sideways, their bodies following, to get to what will have to be an opening. Thorny bits press into me as I go. Another comes crashing down with the momentum to land right into the fence, still thrashing. The metal pushes me with a hand, then a face trying through. I go. Keep going. At the end, the fence is sagging apart, the top pole swayed into nothing. I go with it slapping into me again, again, the prying bits of flesh nipping through. To a forward crawl, my hands push me free into a vacant cul-de-sac lot, where I breathe crushed and panicked, jogging on as the weak spot gets louder behind me.

Everything comes suddenly still with flat houses sitting unused and front yard fencing and matching garages. Three out of the four are variations on the same tan.

The coursing keeps through me, and another one is mannequined houses down. Straightening, I keep on, on, passing as she begins to meet my pace. Trying not to look or see. We're lockstep before she breaks to me and begins to lag.

The variations on picket fences continue. White-capped brick, tight metal rods, classic picket, kennel links. Redwood, black bar, prairie.

Another two stand in desert shrubbery, the gravel losing its manicure around them. No fence. I shuffle to the middle of the road and pick up a trail of now three.

I'm back to the amusement park opening of the pedestrian overpass from earlier, where a squad car walls bullish into the sidewalk. Trying to open it does nothing as the space behind me grows dense with a sort of stride. CHECKPOINT.

I pass a fleshy stain that climbs into the chain link. Steps in and they follow, leaving me caved in if what's ahead is blocked. A narrow gap curves high above and running along with me, if I can get up to it.

A black-padded barstool is behind the highway sign at the cutout, parts faded and new as I go.

On the other side, long concrete barriers cake drowning on top of each other. Their mass plugs off an entire shopping complex with the dull, barbed glint of fencing light at the top.

The way's blacked out behind me, off where the bike is downed and alone at the different colored yards. They watch, almost trying for my gaze. Like they have something that's mine. Shopping center plateaus of sandstone and adobe lie still ahead.

The walkway zags down to a narrow gate that's enclosed in the leviathan concrete. Through it, a barn-framed arcade sends back its welcome among empty seat-height squares and an emaciated tree line. The way in is padlocked in front of a shack, a heavy-stenciled POLICE over a board of legalese.

Jingling rings out behind me boding some sort of treat. Pale hands stay buffeted, simian for my attention as the others keep plodding through the caged switchback. One bend to go.

Nothing left or right. Nothing inside.

I cling to the gate, fingers, toe, fingers, toe, the sound cheering me on. The panel rises partway to the top, where its thick poles pinch against the slabs up to the barbed wire. I stop at the final three lines, flat enough in places for a hand. I grip the side pole one-handed, now two, with my foot wedging into the wall. I'm backed full against it, but I start with some buoyancy, enough to get the next handhold to the wire. Once more again to the top, which puts me close to standing. My feet fit perched on the end, the other side just one more stretch over. My leg rises slow and wide, catching and getting poked on the way, inner thigh, calf. I'm too hard on the line and shaking, shaking, just as they're through and coming tsunami slow to the gate. I try getting down in my convulsions and theirs, and my toe comes against the pressure of a hand, which squeezes me right off, my locked and shaking grip jettisoning me down to my back. Neck tense and the back of my skull still smacks the concrete. I've no breath for the burst flashbulb nimbus of pain. Coiled over, I'm locked, rubbing quick where the sensation is already blurred, hair like flesh. My palm comes back with pale-carved lines and nothing else. I check again.

The noise is violent at the gate, roaring wind and thunder in the day-bright sun, where I'm half blind and still turning insectile on myself. I come to my knees, bent on all fours, and wait to breathe, gravity the one thing I have.

I get up and don't look at them. The checkpoint is empty except for the same barstools and a walkie on the counter that plays static before I turn it back off. I go forward, forward into what's here. The buildings on either side loom and wait to spill themselves out into the bubblegum Middle American austerity.

My head hurts.

I'm in the middle of a huge complex. An empty, grey-form desert stretches on and on at either side with a smaller shopper's lane jutting right ahead. There's a crowd of them at the largest building farther down, lapping lightly in and out of a broken opening.

There's no cover, just the offshoot of cobblestone. Someone is there, face too far to see. He steps in a low, sloping stutter towards me.

I turn and start to walk. The corner suite now marked **TRADE** is also crushed through. It's dark inside past what's left of its pet store fun. Nothing through the mouth, only glass.

I keep going, my shape showing back to me between the trader stalls where shelves would be along with the things I don't see.

My knees are stuck pushing me on but not away; each attempt to pick up pace comes stuttered. Another nothing store ahead where the parking lot lies scattered with vehicles. A zombie is out there, snagged in a maze of trucks between a bulldozer and an RV, all in front of a tight white stack of raised semitrailers. He squeezes free.

The next is crypt-still with no name. At some point it was boarded tight. Next to it, a clothing store is renamed SUPPLIES. The sliding glass doors are forced open with a pile of fluorescent light still going inside. Heads pepper the racks and begin to turn, and something comes out and joins me after I pass.

My legs breadstick on, leaving her crawling in the walkway.

A rise of brick and Tupperware green hangs mammothed ahead, still sending out its economic assurances.

It's destroyed. Tables and shelves have the entire entrance barricaded except where they're pushed over in a single, stretched dyke burst. A body is caught in the breach, and I go gently in to tap it, only rocking. Flat-heeled hips at each pocket and the smell of someone dumping stale pee into compost is all that's left as the cavernous expanse leads on, unbodied. A carpet of mangled blood farther in. What could be a gun.

Something falls and crashes inside, and there's shuffling. I jump back for what's already here, the broken one or the parking lot one. There's nothing. Just a milling nest of more and more at the supermarket ahead and a sea-dark return to silence.

I go off into the parking lot.

Rough. Rough. Rough against the asphalt. My knees bend higher, and the soles come right back down the same too-heavy way again, again. The parking lot zombie, who looks like a Hal, is towards me on a slow, cosmic course. His face doesn't register that he won't make it as his hands keep out, all child.

One of the trailers is locked; and the other.

Next to me, a car is crumpled in at the windows with the inside splattered, forming dark tufaceous clumps on the seats. The rest is gone and the doors are shut and locked.

I check again through the broken gap and drop the glove box. An old bar, but nothing. I leave the wrapper there and eat it on my way before Hal gets on this side.

The same wall of concrete keeps my view myopic on the horizon. There's nothing with the weight of miles on either side until I'm left again with the half-gestured arcade. A mud-red restaurant reaches above it with PETALUMA ANCHOR ONE perched large on top. Hal lags stubborn behind.

My dry grass movements waver through each other in the dark glass. I stick to the wall, where my steps go slow; nothing more audible than shapes within the sun screened windows. The double door opens easily where it's dim with outdoor light. Inside holds a tangle of square seats and tables with exposed ceiling. Blank TVs on TVs angle over every section of every wall with the malevolence of something about to turn on. I crouch, holding the last of the light to see the floor, which is all legs and pedestals around one unnecessary central column. Nothing changes as it closes shut.

Back to the bar, where there's a pile of knives laid out, butter knife dull. Beer bottles pile underneath in tubs with too many caps on the floor. There're a few left unlit in the back of a fridge.

Still no sound past the flux of my breath. I'm armed as I look in the kitchen. Right across, a crumple of towels lies still in the corner with someone's shirt balled in at the head. The body it could have been doesn't show. The range is circled by the cords of an off generator; food packaging piled in and out of a trash can. I'm slow to the other side before I put the gun back in its stretched spot.

A pint glass is in the drying rack, and I watch the water come out clear and easily. It rushes down until the cold is uncomfortable. I fill again and leave it half drunk and wet on the counter.

The grey length of the fridge waits as I hold my breath. I pull on blanched white vegetables. Glass jugs of untouchable milk. Brown bags of what's probably meat stacked for a messroom. I take a block of hard cheese from some eggs and press it crumbling in my hand. The corner snaps and tastes like the fridge, but I let it sit and get moist until it begins to be something human.

I look back around, the gun set close, and roll down my pants. They're sore on the way off. Jumping cold on the counter with my cramped-long toenails to the sink, I get to work. Hand soap makes the scabbing slick and run red until the gashes are miniature in the hair. One's not. I keep going, my face, neck, armpits, wakening to myself underneath. Hard paper towels exfoliate the wetness away and stuff down stiff between the stained pant leg and the spot.

There's a chalkboard that's been drawn on over and over. No message. No real object. Just circular hash marks across the thick lines of what it used to say.

I swing in on the bathroom dark and give myself the time to go.

Ready, the door swings back to a group strolling by. I lunge after the backswing, small as it slowly shuts me out. Two are bulky in uniform, the other stripped naked with flesh grey white and mashed pruny, skinned off, and burnt. A thing wagging underneath. I don't move. They wander closer to the courtyard, the door, and I'm useless in place, crouching as though that will help if the movement draws them in.

I crawl back to the bar and sit against it, letting my eyes come closed and listening, waiting with the caps and binned-high bottles. It's silent but I don't look. Later, I reach in to drink one warm and set it back halfway through.

The courtyard is settled back to a proposal sketch that the concrete has capsuled. Dark air keeps roaring quiet outside. I part the door against me and go low, quick to what's ahead. The final stretch is into lot filled with shining Quonset huts. Hal's in on it, keeping the group distracted with his antics. A light cluster of stores blocks off what must be the main gate.

I start to limp.

The end of a cop car sits burrowed into the fallen gate, where a flypaper zombie slumps over the edge with frizzed down nubs of orange-black hair. A sea flow of mangled bodies lies countless beyond, some of it slick, some of it blackened. What's there stretches through the whole intersection and tails to the on-ramp. The crow's nest at the gate is empty. And the other.

The bodies in front of me are different, strewn instead of mashed apart. Fewer. A gloved hand missing its wrist at the gutter. One zombie is stretched out to a rug. The only zombie. The rest of it is blood and broken doors.

Something shifts. Eyes stare at me from constellated flesh. Most of it is spine with a few ribs. Black, tactical piles are gummed together around it with the fleshy bits sucked out. There are no arms or legs to move. The head's gnawed and stripped jawless at the bottom, the rest of it small. One of the eyes just blinks on me.

A wide machete is scattered to the side. And in the space where a leg used to be, a black military rifle points out. I pick it up from him and have nothing but asphalt to rub it on. It goes to my back anyway, over. The machete fits with some weight in my hand. The eyes are green. I change my footing and bring it down onto the forehead. They briefly buckle, stunned but looking back out again as shellfish. I jiggle the handle to pry it back out, and the pupils drift sideways. Another glancing strike flings a third of the skull free across the street as the wet burst drowns the eyes down.

One of them falls ready to catch through the glassy opening of the mattress store. The routed facade is called BARRACKS, and there's tumbling within. Another comes out from the building, and another.

Between us is a police belt that I pull out, shirking from what drops. It needs another hole. I bring it onto myself, watching them only as my fingers put me strapped with unknown parts.

Beyond at the metal half silos, more come. More bodies than I've seen in one place. One after the other. Shoulders and tilted heads, cop black woven throughout.

I take a step back. And there's more. More ahead, more at either side. I turn around and go to the gate, squeezing between the wall and the orange-black corpse. Something sticks to me as I get through, kicking up wet and dried bits as I run. I leave it there.

HORSE

The gravity of black, iridescent skin calls out from the hillside. Each instance is pulled down, collapsed and kneeling in complete supplication over its tented and sagging parts. It stretches on and on ahead, the far-off sinuations only stopped up in a cluster of pine. Lone houses and other farmland structures stick in place as I go, trudging through the red-dusted off-ramp.

The road carries deep into the new horizon, where grass clears everything human from what's ahead, making me impossibly there with it. Something is lying in wet, shallow mud that could be dead wood.

The asphalt is veined in by old rain.

Islanded behind a dense shower of oak, loose gathered runoff lies through a stressed wire junction. In it, the black eye made white of a cow is impossibly at ease for what happened. The bones of one leg are clocked upwards without much of the meat. Everything soft behind it is gone. Ribs grip the fence where it fell as far through as the metal would let it. Grass keeps the charcoal body stagnant to the water. Anywhere it lashed out, the runoff has it swallowed with the broken fence more shroud than snare, leaving the face half there and empty.

Anchored ahead, a homestead keeps a longhouse of parked cars. It's gated, but a few of them meet me though the gravel. I quicken past the end where they stay behind, back to the green nothing. Cattle repeat strewn in the near flat distance. I mark them on to the juxtaposed lines of two rust-barred feedlots kept apart by asphalt. The locked-in mud has dozens on dozens downed throughout, wrangled back to empty meat. A human shape in it stumbles gently towards me, completely covered but for an upturned hole.

The sign for a nursery hooks me close along the slurry. Black plastic holds plants in long rows that leave everything in sight. The amount is huge. Most are still green but dry and entirely fruitless. I crunch through, pushing on to hooded coverings where the air is moist. The greenery comes lush and transporting, but it's all green on green, nothing human or other-human to it besides the fallen equipment. I drink slagged water from a hose that shoots out cold. A bucket would at least be something, but I drop it. Trees marked apple and avocado have nothing on them besides the tag, and the citrus is picked over except for a small lime that leaves my mouth puckered.

I cut back across until it's gone again to grass, which slowly runs into a long-bordered arena. Trudging quiet past a stable, I keep on to the opening, back and just close enough to see. A hoof stays sideways through the stall.

The rest is a maze of equestrian partitions and tarped trailers. Thin shuffling at the center rears its gravity towards me as I jump the outer fence to the driveway. I let him fight at the gate.

There's a burst of movement in the next arena. A horse keeps far back where it's stopped against the wall, the thing it's running from invisible in front of me. Then it's there, trampled in the stomped-short grass. A grating squeal is pierced into the trees and a rumble of uneven breathing spouts in place. The shape manages to face it from where it's stuck, and the horse stomps its front hooves, ears snaked straight back. The motion crashes on itself, childlike at the small space that it has.

The other keeps showing me where a bite wound is still bright on his arm. The actual gate for the horse is blocked. My hands are deft on the rifle magazine, which pops off completely empty. I drop the whole thing and graze my palm across the hilted edge of the Kimber, and I let it be. The horse is tense in place. On the road, the fence line is doubled up and thick, everywhere except here.

The air stays cloying at my side. Nowhere to go.

I try a post, try another that's not as tight. I push and pull with both hands, push pull again and again where half of me is thrown in pain. It's hard in place but moving, and I'm still just fanning the edge. Hanging on to the railing makes the rest start to buckle as I begin kicking the joints. They resist, and I'm not doing enough, but I keep going, tired and close to the end.

The broken pile inside only looks at me, glue without a shoulder to raise as hands stay mindless in their unpuzzling through.

I wedge the flat of the blade, grabbing where the joint begins to stretch and getting one board free when the gate zombie slips further, chest caught between over and under. Moans and small hisses come at me as I pry. The horse screams.

The top comes back against itself and falls to let me stagger in. Limbs are now a torso that drops over face-first, beginning to right itself behind me. I take up the machete and force myself back.

One swing for the head and it glances off. I step out of its reach and bring the length straight down again into its face, slicing the look unevenly as it keeps walking into me. The point barely gets free. Circling backwards, I make a swipe for its ankle, which jars wooden against the flat of its shin, and my back flares scraped as I shoot back up again, its quick pressure close to locking me down.

The blood stays in my head as our circle loses shape. I fling the weight of the goo into the grass, and it keeps coming, taking my distance. Almost cornered, I charge forward, bringing it down hard and following through with my elbows into it until we're falling. Something pokes me. I try rising free, and it grabs me, the base of the blade locked between my throat and its red-bared teeth. It has us completely tight, its fingers krakened across me, side-shoulders-face. A scream comes out between us, weak and dumb. The top of the blade is blunt inside, but it's still moving to me, jaw working right at my fingers. My skin breaking on sudden bursts, I keep prying, prying against the grip until I get the room to take the handle back up with the end still buried. It doesn't let go of me and the strain between us hooks across my skin and I have to keep pulling, pulling until I give it all of me and crash back flat into it. The machete follows paper-cuttered, and our faces hit hard with it. It still rises through to me, mouth splitting fresh in the effort. I keep pressing with the backs of my arms seared in movement, its wetness all over, and the unfocused eyes coming chameleon with the slow, continuous push that it's helping through, through to the ground. Its grasp stalls, and I lift up enough to come back down, burying all of it back through. The eyes still look but the mouth is stuffed the wrong way. I work a wet hand free to press the top of the blade the rest of the way in, and it watches, still moving but unlocked from me. I stand back up and blindly hold myself together. It's still alive, still there, and I stomp until the outer edge is gone and my foot hurts.

—Just die!

I stumble slow and meteor torn back into the arena. A fistful of grass gets some off of me, but the smell has my nose. A limb hangs dandelioned from what's ahead. The horse is eyes and ears dead on me, its legs lightning stiff beneath. I raise a hand, putting it caught between reactions. I sigh and push closer until it jolts to the side.

The horse keeps at the fence until it traps itself at the end. I close the distance, past the watching puddle that could be its rider, making it choose between me and the opening.

The eyes go wide, breaking free from their helium urge to leave, but I press in again as though I'm doing something, something better than walking away. It side stares at the opening, the body, and eyes me back down, maybe to another puddle. I don't stop and only press into its space, where it has either me or the opening. It holds, holds, finally breaks to the gap, weaving through and surging almost wounded into the road. The nut-brown haunches go and go, turning off at the first opportunity. The mane begins to waft briefly before flying past a dark thicket.

I go back to the body with its eyes not gone. What's left is still something close to seeing; it's unlooking. Underneath, its chest gives like branches in mud while I wrench the handle up and down and free.

I'm far behind but still following until I can see down the crossroad. Nothing to choose, I go where it's thicketed, leaving the path to a ranch house distant behind.

A goat watches me from a backyard lot as though everything around is pillboxed to grass. The solar-paneled garden behind it sits overcast with the same disinterest.

I pass a gated home that's early morning calm. Another that blocks off a whole acred complex of trees and bare vines. I breathe in what could be there, dust-tight nostrils, but keep on to what's next.

An isolated firehouse. It's locked tight but already broken into. I duck under the glass door on through musty office furniture to get to the garage. There are no trucks, and besides using what's there to weigh myself down for a ridiculous biting apart, there's nothing.

Back out through pines, I come to a clearing around a frontier home peacocked by a rotunda porch out of an antebellum film set. A dead dog is in the lawn, but nothing that ate it. Trucks are parked back to the side with the bravado and yard space to go guns blazing. But there's nothing. I pass a hole in the fence that's trampled over and empty. An overgrown graveyard with small flowers is neighbored across, watching, just as still.

A thin, juvenile wood hides one more solar-paneled country mansion, but I stay with the house trailers nearby. I call out at one, then another. The third is dead and close enough to offer some welcome.

Jelly decals block most of the window. I'm suddenly there on the porch, but I keep from breaking anything. Around the side, there's a faded children's truck to stand on. Dark and turned from details, I come back out quickly with a pink kid's pack that needs to be emptied.

The road gets drier, more tangled. A field ends in commercial truck trailers plastered with huge egg cartons that line lupine outside large, metal laying houses.

The rot is so strong I put an elbow over my mouth. Sulfur and vinegar stay slick to my breathing, garlic, all of it putrid and sweet.

Zombies are packed in the parking lot, taken by tourist satisfaction. I go quickly, keeping as far back as I can, but they still begin to flow after me. My feet go pegged.

In a field blanketed by nothing, I come to a red cabin draped in pine cones. The horse is there, nibbling at the ground. It looks up locked at me, the roll of its lips twitching on its own.

My feet keep on, slowly, letting it have the shade. They're still coming. It stares back calm, attentive, gone from what it was. I come onto the grass, and it prances steps back.

— It's okay.

It watches me, making me a conductor, blind or neutral to what's swelling behind. There are scrapes into its shins.

— You got to keep moving. Sorry.

I step forward, and it moves ahead of me, carrying on in a line, watching me with the warmth of its side. The smell of a well-worn coat stays quilted across my face. It just goes, like that's the answer. The trot is loud ahead and slowly takes in my movement, merging under the cover of two large oaks.

— You know I don't actually know what I'm doing.

The road stretches on.

ROBE

ONE IS WORN. The other has a brown fleck in it. Both still have something of their breath. The dark edge of my nail gets the bit out, and the toothbrush comes cool into my mouth. Each rough surface turns suspect as I go too hard where there's no point to stop.

The shower works. I check the door again, then leave to bring in the belt, the machete, a chair from the dining room. I make it secure and perch the rest against the tub.

It's hot, and I choke the noise back down to something urethral. The water hits me dense as sunlight. I don't stop scrubbing. When my skin is all red, I reach out for the machete and scrub it too.

The water keeps going with it in my grip next to the cheap pink razor. I put it back out on the mat to shave anyway and nick the scab that's turned white on my calf.

The towel smells like mold, and I only stop the dripping. My hands, feet take turns bending into the window light.

Clip. Clip. Clip.

Snip. Snip. Snip. Snip.

The clumps fall heavy until it's jagged and boy short. My eyes are dark and round back at me. I don't look at the red-and-purple-gyred hues that have taken hold, each of the edges individually broken and somehow put back together. Or just starting with new spidered growth. I rub where the lines are buckled.

I toss my clothing in the tub and leave it to soak. The dead person's robe is full of doily edges over pale, florid stripes, but it is a robe. I walk past her in the kitchen, where the splatter creeps into view. The chunks of arm are where I left them, and for some reason it's easy to breathe.

Hot cereal. Bad coffee. Loose nuts and some more jerky. Raisins.

The light is warm on what could be a cool day. She is still down where I left her, wood-dark head loped into the grass with the ease of another day. The road below falls to nothing in the simplicity of the hills ahead, as though that's it.

Steps carry me heavy through the house until I have piled the box of malt cereal, a plastic bag of the coffee, stuff from the bathroom, including a roll of toilet paper. Sometimes the wood creeks. My toes sprout in the air, but everywhere else I'm brittle.

I crouch at the sleeping bag in the closet, trying to get it back tight. At the bed is something of a shoebox underneath. I frown and keep rolling, but I check it after. With the care of something personal lies over a dozen seed packets. Squash, tomato, cucumber. Carrot, watermelon, radish. Begonia. I crack open one, and it looks no better to eat than poppy seeds. They're close to empty, and I grab them anyway.

The clothes are lost drifting in their mixed paint pink. I come back with a scouring pad and get to work until there's nothing left but grey. The artwork is restored down to canvas in my hands, but something still remains. I pick at it with my nails and take some of it myself. They look back at me like skins when they're hanging.

With the sun laced cold around me, I go out back. My red feet crunch naked through the needles until the dirt path sticks to me at the gate. The horse is statue-still where she can see me as I plod down to the small stable. The feed is tossed through where I opened it, and the goldfish in the trough barely move.

— Looks like you had an okay night too.

Her ears come back towards me, then she breaks gently away to something else in the dirt. Inside's a saddle with an arcane mass of straps and buckles. I grab a brush. She doesn't move as I come close and place a hand flat on her side, where the hair is oversized and oily. The wall of muscle on Holocene organs holds taut against me, letting me finger my way lightly on. I bring the brush gently in. And in. The dust and dead hair puff into my face.

— I don't know what to do with you. You get that, right?

Her ears twitch back and forward again. Another step and the morning dew begins to wash the sides of my toes. At her neck, she sees me up close before turning back down, stretching paved before me.

The green across from us lulls untouched for miles, enough room to leave the roadside entirely and be almost nowhere. Just a small fence to get her through.

— Better than wherever I go.

The heat of her side mingles into my movements, hanging across my half-exposed chest. I run my hand back over and pick out a last bit of something. The road below is small with disuse.

I toss the brush to the stall and step back to the house, and she turns and gently follows. Her steps are gestures in the grass. Partway, and I stop, looking at her stop too. I clench and stretch up slowly, the robe falling back on me with the tall trees around on all sides. My fingers drop and fidget lightly at my thighs. She's unchanged.

I step back quickly into the stable and look over the saddle. Foot strap, blanket, pommel, the belt that keeps it all on. That seems to be the only moving part. The tangle of leather must be what goes on the head. Two pieces is all. Long metal calipers and scrapers. Hooves. Feed. Even more water. Somewhere to stop where she won't get eaten, stolen, stolen and eaten. Run away when I need her. Freak out at the wrong moment. Fall off or be kicked into another puddle. No hiding at all. Poop.

The pad brings the sweat smell of the place alive in my hands.

— Is this what you want?

The horse noses in and smells it with gentle interest. She keeps going over its sides and contours, tickling my hand.

— Okay, okay.

I come closer and toss the piece to the middle of her back. Her head drifts lower, and I stumble free, looking for something wrong. The saddle is heavy next and pulls tight at the robe. She isn't very tall, but the hard-limbed leather pushes back against me as I hoist it up, nearly losing momentum when it comes over. The robe slips free, and my skin is crisp between us until I close it back up.

The seat is still square to her shoulders and hips. I feel back and forth for the base strap. It doesn't come tight on the first pull; the slack is unwieldy and won't set as I wrap it in one direction, then another. It finally stops in the right position with a knob of it pointing into her side. She only looks forward, but I start again, getting it to what looks okay enough.

I untangle and retangle the leather until it takes shape in front of me, unclear where the ears go. It drops onto her forehead with the top probably right, and there's a hollow pop with the bit against her nose.

— Sorry! I'm sorry!

She shakes her head from me with flecks of dried blood scaled there in dust. But she stays and lets me try again, bottom first. It hangs set for a larger horse, and I bring it in, her nuzzling me in the process. I step back, tense. My mouth doesn't work. She looks, then looks away.

— That's not. This doesn't get to end well. You get that, right?

She stays looking at the hillside or the road.

I head back to the house for my clothes, which are still going to be just as wet and useless.

— Well, what can I set on fire?

GARDENING

A GROWN over sign for USCG Training Cntr is bent with the promise of stockpile or concrete nothing, safety or shoot on sight. Leaving it and the small-steepled tree line, we ride on to where the road was built for emptiness. The silence of cicadas hangs low overhead as the turn proudly says BODEGA BAY.

The tension at her mouth sits balled in my hand as she glides. Clop. Knock. My thighs hug into the barrel of her, putting half of me and half of her all gas pedal. My head is buoyant and even as the roadside nothing passes faint beyond certainty.

The hoodie folds of hills relax into the outstretched line ahead. Ranch homes here and there rise with space colony deliberation, on all sides everything and nothing to see.

Another junk house lies in wait behind a tight copse. Too many vehicles stacked in front, each of them large and dusty. No movement as we go.

Sheds with rusted-out equipment keep their spaces dark and buried inside. Something is tied in the drapery of the next house. It stares featureless on our passing, hand at my hip. I twist behind, and the spot of road grows smaller, telephone wires and a swollen pile of trash. The clopping turns crystalline as we come back to green.

A car would run us down. Almost a mile on either end and hardly the cover of trees to leap into. Nothing comes.

The field isn't empty anymore. Someone is mucking their way through. They stop and change course, but they're gone when I bring the leather up later to stop.

The farmstead off the road is clear all around. The way in is fenced, red shed with a sliding door. Newish RV, truck. The staggered lines of trees are dark-haired behind and there's no seeing into the yard that's sandbagged against the sea of green. What's there is glass-empty to be filled. You're there along with whatever else. No cover, no turning back.

I push my heels and she's reluctant, only taking a step, another for show. I press in, and she goes. I keep watching, and the house and shed melt back to squares on the horizon.

Another family farm looms bonewhite in the distance, couched into a rolling wall of green. Black shapes jackknife across the open dirt, keeping there, sharp within its articulated stretch and far from the road.

A hilltop house and barn watch them with me before dropping on to a dirt-dark feedlot. We keep going, bramble hiding nothing as we come level.

One of them looks up, stops. Something is transient in his hands. Another joins, maybe talks. We keep to our pace as the ant-line lane between us brings us optically together. They stay as we keep on, uncoupled.

Trees scratch them out and turn the clopping back to my hands. What's beyond is mostly roofs and farm trucks. I squeeze her to something faster, and the window of road stays behind, empty.

The valley beyond is iridescent in lime and black-sprouted conifers that reach thin to their mushroom tops. Long roofs shell through, holding the small spaces of industry back from the shire. The green after takes everything, each point on the hill its own possibility. No hiding, no place left except for space itself. Just the getting there.

It comes broken on the flat remnants of a shed. A storied house is dark framed out of something between Redwood and Black Forest. The great home's weight wills the rolling green into something denser than it is, turning the emptiness into somewhere you're lost, rearing sunken behind, rising up. Its heavy trod paddock is clear, the way in winding back and bringing all the hills up close and just as empty, past a barn redone in adobe and lichen.

Anything is inside either one; dark clusters ripple around a line of PVC pipe.

I get off, legs and arms both sore to move over parts turned sharp and dull. Her sigh tumbles onto me.

The gate is chained but only wrapped together, with the lock gelded clean in the grass. It falls right apart, and she follows through with me and the reins.

We pass a horse trailer she wants to sniff, and I stop. The dark forest house windows are clear, some shooting hollow on to the other side.

The slope is narrow and snug for her. Inside, I keep still again and wait for movement, sound, cause and effect. A junkyard pile is wet with dew towards the house, and the nocturnal caging from before is penned tight again next to me.

Mud-broken pools of water pave the way into the field, each step shallow and undoing. Different kinds of squash are dropped ahead like dolls in their vines, some green, some white. They're wrinkled and open with rot, brown coming out of them to bring new growth and dirt together. Nothing alive inside. A zucchini is just greyed at one end, but it pinches soft where I pluck it before dropping it back down.

The shrubs of spinach are thinned out and riddled through, leaving just enough to grab. The dry yellow comes apart at my lips, where my fingers leave something bitter behind. I squat and start taking it apart, throwing in the best mouthfuls before starting a pile of what's both too soft and too dry.

I pass from the nubs to taller sprouts and start tugging. Thick beet skin pries free. I yank it out, hard but whole. Too small carrots, but they're not going back. Radishes. Most of the dirt drops off, and I finally bite into something moist.

The dirt blasts volcanic next to me. I'm stuck out of place as the crack of a rifle grinds tearing over the air. The strings cut late, limbs, torso, dropping me flat to the dirt. She's already running, muscled towards me and hard past into the field, ripping the plants in reach. I'm stuck staring at her coursing shimmer bared with the same malleability, ready to break crashing down and forever at any point.

The gun is useless in my hand, dug in against the beet. Windows are still empty. I force myself from the reeling sky and soil high enough to see someone coming slowly, deliberately down the cattle path that winds in from the road. There's only the half-made row to sink into as I put the barrel out. She stops where she is.

— Hey, I see you!

Her face twists, and she slowly brings the rifle back to her cheek till I can't fall any further. She's far off, but my arms are locked.

— Don't you even think about it! Toss that thing!

— Screw you!

— Oh, you do not want to start like that with me. The next's no warning shot!

Her grip tightens but doesn't come any closer to shooting. I hold ground.

— What's your problem?

— My problem is someone's tearing through my garden.

— This? It's rotten!

My voice comes out like it's been put on paper. Her heavyset thighs clash like pans.

— Well, you're not helping any, are you?

She rolls her eyes.

— What, you think farming got any easier?

I stay rabbited in the open, waiting for her. She doesn't budge.

— Look, we don't got time for a pissing contest. They're coming, so you wanna keep tearing everything up, that's on you. I'll just clean up after. Or you could get your nosy ass out of here like I'm telling you.

The round of her cheeks has the marks of something left in rain. What's growing behind her is waterlogged and melded with the path, snapping with the same rubber-banded effort, the same idle malice. They're wide at the street and coming.

— You scared her off.

— Then go get her, cowgirl. Just get on out of here.

She lowers the rifle for me to decide. Something catches her eye out of view, and she grits before starting back. I come up carefully. Segments of the road are broken all over by the slow, deliberate plodding that's taking her place. Some are already in the way, and she cuts off through the cow pasture. She's not getting ahead, but they're turning now to me.

I shove what I can into the school pack, keeping track of her lumbering to what must be somewhere close. Behind, the horse has stopped on the fence line and is waiting there, watching. I'm slow to her.

— You know, I did just find you a carrot.

She looks at me, expectant.

— Fine, well, it's not like you could have done anything.

The mount comes easily. Fully seen and still standing, the height is new, violent and ready to charge. Any sort of ambush is gone with the doldrum plodding.

We turn back the way we came. The road is milling now, fed by a single street marked **BLOOMFIELD**. There are gaps down between that change with more intent than the faces that fall onto us.

A long, black shoulder lurches in and close ahead. Slack-jawed and lidless to us. I push against the sudden tension that begins to cut us short, crushing it fast like an orange until we slip past its reach, then the others, hurrying faster, faster through the narrowing crowd until they're all back to watching.

Slow behind, the woman carries on sunken through the mud. She puts space between her and them by wandering deeper in, leaving the few that are left to the bramble and barbed wire.

One last ranch house is all that's left before the way out. We ease off, and I find her heading slowly there. We turn and wait. She keeps her rifle shouldered.

— What do you want now?

— Nothing. I just wanted.

My voice drops short in the space between us. We're no closer than before.

— You actually live out here?

She doesn't look up.

— You live anywhere?

Things are quiet all around. The ranch house seems not to care.

— No.

— Well, you're not going to with a friend like that. Not without a group of people as tireless and ornery as they are. Or I don't know, somewhere far.

Her boots are dry with dirt, pack loosely loaded.

— How do you do it?

She gets close enough to stop on the fence.

— I got a place. Places, really. Don't you think about killing me for it; you saw my garden.

She smiles up even though I could get the draw on her.

— I'm not. This all just looks run over.

— It is.

She's lake flat. The pleasure she's taking is earthworn and forgotten, but there.

— How do you do it?

She sighs.

— Well, I don't let them tree me. All it takes is somewhere they can't tell you're there. And a back way out.

Something bubbles oily and reflective out of her.

— If you're here, things can't be much better in town.

My stiffening gets a nod of satisfaction.

— There were people earlier, though. Not sure if they were holed up or tearing through.

She looks at me, uncertain.

— Thirty minutes ago, maybe.

— Goddamned locusts. They're going to fuck up everything. What, you think you're any better? You're the ones who make it impossible for anyone to keep to their goddamned home.

I keep still.

— I'm just passing through.

— Yeah, like a goddamned locust. Don't you know what that is?

She keeps her eyes from the house behind. Someone is far back on the street.

— What, you wanted me to invite you for tea? You going to send off your mare just like we had to? Keep on out of here if you want a friend. I've had my fill.

She bends under the fence with the conversation already dissipated, staying between us and the place with no intention of going further. There's weakness in her lip.

— You sure about it, doing what you're doing?

The lake ripples turn across her.

— Are you?

CHAR

WHAT MY EYES open on is still dark. Stunted shapes crowd in; bedpost, frames, lamps fossilized thick together. The pines are night black from the edge of the window. Nothing moves, but the orange at their sides is electric.

Woodsmoke cuts dry into my nostrils, where it brings campfire nostalgia to a hard, carcinogenic lump. I hurry outside into the gravel, looking through the forest that hides the hillside neighbors. The tree wall glows brown, silent; the wind that's caustic pressing into me from behind is just something there. I turn for the other trees, the road. There is no sky. Only a thick, shapeless egg yolk above.

I tug my shirt over my mouth to find her and she's looking back unfazed. The garage next to the house is just large enough if she'll go in. All the walls are dense with junk. I tug out an old, disposable paint mask that won't dust off. It's a musty conflagration on my face, and I take only the hammer and screwdriver. Back inside turns up sweatpants instead; cutting the leg in the kitchen, getting it to my face.

I come back with the pack loosely set. Her breathing is slow, heavy. The only thing different is the blinking. I lead her to the gate and we go, slow past the garden patch that stopped us here and off to the corner that qualifies as town. A large, fenced pasture with a barn is better, but the buildings are too easily lived in. She snorts, and the analgesic weight of twilight drives us on.

Golden letters read ENDURING COMFORTS with peppermint window frames and garland grey on top. It's smoke dim inside. I start working at the doorjamb anyway until it busts and I come out with a fistful of scarves I can't tell the color of.

Across, a crumbling farmhouse with the words KEEP OUT is the sole witness. The double doors of the bakery that's next are too thick, and I get in by unboarding and shattering a window.

The weight of flour comes hypsomic to me in the dark. I drop the covering and breathe deep with my nostrils straws. Nothing of the bread remains, just its space. I start looking. The feeling is there, of place, of purpose, of morning pleasures, but it's on the surface and not seeping in. What's here is for people. People.

We ride back to the ranch we passed, and I stay in the coarse air looking longer than I have to. It's too much space, a set of houses all sharing the same grass. Cozy neighbors behind a flimsy gate that's still incomplete. They didn't even try.

We're slow inside. The gradual slope up is a killing field if you can see well enough. A skin of white-seeded grass wavers around us. Floating through, the ground is dense with roots that tear at every step.

The first house is a bystander, and I only watch its corners. The fork beyond is where I find them waiting. I watch them. I get down and take a step backwards, another, and turn her trotting away. The school pack drops creamsicled to the grass and I gut the machete out of it. Three.

Their silhouettes broaden in the haze. I breathe deep and still burning. It's the same. The same.

I step in and bring the blade down. Another part comes out, and I swipe. I step back, breathing a little harder. Again on the first part.

It hits into bone that's pushing back, but I follow through only to bounce off.

I can't see. Something comes near, and I swing blind, the resistance, the space between buzzing. Another in the crook and a piece drops heavy, leaving the thing leaning in, all head and nothing else. I pull it stumbling aside and get just enough space for the next. She's thinner, shorter, all the same. Down. Down. The hand bones come apart against me, splinter and sever to roots. I step back and she keeps in. Closer comes a clouded set of teeth that stays there as I swing into her arm. The bone moves and catches hard. The mangled hand comes back up, and I breathe in the burnt flesh, watching its dangling. Circle slowly and back above the bicep, lodging through to her. She leans into it and I rip free, something wet into the sagged face covering.

The first comes charging back, its thick, scruffy head bared alone against me. I can't stop it from crashing me straight down to its shark myopia. I'm caught backwards with it, all of me against the fall as the third comes grabbing too. The weight doubles in front, cratering to a tumbled mass my feet can't keep clear of.

I bury the tip in the brown base of the nearest head. Just a head. It takes it like dirt. The machete stays in as the shoulders rise slowly up like a thing out of the ocean. I run; back enough to turn where my hands continue seismic at the draw.

She comes first, pushing her sharded maw like something for me to see. I stumble and start for the other, who's still caught up in the torso. There's nowhere right. I thrust the muzzle to its nearing mouth until the pop is small and plastic in the ghost-bright flash. It keeps straight to me, and the bottom sluices free. I come back, up at the cheek and pull. The eyes are dark and wide on me as I shrug off a hand at its fall. I'm right back to the handle as the end comes out in spasms from its still-moving whetstone.

Someone else stands in the burnt-orange fog.

The wet end fights against my shoulder while I come down on her head, down until the cap gives out. I shake out my wrist and get back in, working the hole while the stump marks me again and again and what's on me is dark and dampening through. She drops into me, almost pleading, and the other half of me is seized tight, from her as much as me.

The fourth leers over while a furnace tears in me, making me pay attention to it, my hard-stunned wrist. The shark is all slug now, still making its way with the help of the hill, but to where. I switch hands and cradle the beaten one in, moving in my own weird shape far across the grass.

The first house has more coming from it, slowly with the suddenness of black things in a lit log. I go on to the next as they grow in the periphery. What's ahead is empty, the red on red of it pulsing with the woods. The barn's welcoming after I've tried the front door. Or there's a rain barrel at the awning. Up quick, and my fingers dig into the cut roof tiles, the tears at my back already stretched deeper and moving hot with me. My upper body barely follows, but toe walking against the house gets me awkwardly there where I'm in with the mob coming under.

The room is a wreck but not gone through. Quiet into the hallway, slowly. A light, organic creaking verberates around the caught air. Something moves in the next room. The door is closed and padlocked with a novelty plate fixed to the middle. CALEB. A gibber rises, silence, steps and a two-limbed smack into the door. I jump. The hammering comes again, again. Bat bat bat for some sort of attention. It's heavy and doesn't want to stop.

I step slowly, near the stairs, and find a spot where I can breathe in the darkness. The scarf is too limp to get back on.

Plaintive wails keep coming from the room, but the outer drone warms everything in its subterranean movement. I'm dead silent, small. The preserved food and water I've made myself swallow is now an angry lump, and what I've taken won't matter.

They're immediately at me when I drop from the back window. The fire poker is ripped away. My speed stays capped, their reach, their lunge quick as me. There's enough of a path, all by feel but no distance. No way to get free and watch. It's one and then another until I'm back to the open yard, their glaring forms shifted to trees.

She's gone. If she's dead, I missed her. I cough and strain back at the air, which doesn't get better.

CHAR

THE ROAD, the picked through garden patch is gone. Trees hold the darkness close as a white, living haze winds through and over, dipping a small edge of something impossibly huge that nothing, no plane, no bird is able to get out from.

It's coming out, already there and damp underneath when I crawl out of my ball for the bathroom. There's less of everything than there should be. The pain medication is completely swiped, but I swig down an all-in-one cold suppressant.

Out from under an old box, a crisp-faded disc slides into my hands. The spent pills stop a week in. I run my thumb over what's left, getting to the density that's still held tight in capsules launched to nowhere.

I don't get what I need until I'm deep in the back under the sink. Pads, someone's leftovers. The panties stay in the basin as I wash and waddle back on the pad to my pants. My head is blocked out with helium as I go through the overly furnished rooms. It's there whether I look or not. Closing my eyes again so that there's only the sporadic howl or house shudder.

There's still nothing to see. Something has erased the white dark, and now brown has its own life outside. A Martian light breaks close above, heavily diffuse and not going anywhere.

Something falls out there. I go, taking the machete. It's all atmosphere, heavy and choking, swirling over itself and throwing particulate at me. The yard is down to a cavernous torsion of a few sentinel pines, and even their presence is wavering.

I find her leg-locked into a corner. Sloping forward with eyes sharp on the sides, she nods faintly from a nest of boxes and spilled equipment. A shelf behind her bars the way that I hurry to get from her head, then drag it screeching outside. She stays right in place as though there's nowhere to go. I'm slower again around her feet, which are bolted over the mess that's come to a pile with them. Her rear backs into another shelf while gusts of breathing hit me.

— This really became your spot, didn't it? Glad you found something to like.

I go to get a mixing bowl of water under her nose, which the motor of her brings right down. The workbench's been chewed where I emptied out raw oats. She moves closer to eat and watches me as I close her back in.

The air has its own weight. Every small sound is hollow and dense, hanging underwater past its full life. Ripped through the fence, I'd be lost in it.

My lungs are getting hot, and I can't fully catch my breath. The ground is thick with grass roots that make the soil uncertain every step. The space has come completely comatose. An edge in the haze gradually keeps away from me, showing nothing but more of itself. I stop and listen. My breathing stays coarse and muffled, and I try to keep it from getting worse. A branch snaps somewhere, dry in the hidden distance. The darkening wall keeps still on all sides. I step backwards. Again. I go back inside and can't stop the front door from snapping shut on me.

The burnt socket air sticks close to my face. Hazestacks of citron over puce lie under a glassy highway of blue. Showing clear and sapped of color, the chemicals stay together in glass marble twists. The opening is far off and held definite. My finger pads press cold there until they leave a mark on the window. I do it again and the suction bounds thwanging back at me.

Something's coming through, just past seeing. The shape moves from shadow to a pellucid process of step, lunge, twist. It's inside, vagrant passing through in some sort of T-shirt skirt that's been there for too long. The thin chest sags and the hair above has gone to knots. I drop to a set of eyes where it hasn't turned yet and stays looking into the burnt-dry mist, fully intent. Its listening is constant, elsewhere.

Fully alone, the mopped head comes down, shoots back up with vegetative alacrity. It stays on the black cloud edges, closer, dropping back away until it's gone. The arid mist lies still as it flattens and swallows over the spot, and it's only me left straining on bad air.

My eyes are closed when steps stop on the porch. Silence slowly presses back down on the door to a low-toned storm gust. The feet leave and take their time back in the grass, where they come step-by-deliberate-step around. I go carefully after, losing their edges in the walls, the furniture. Each window is high but only glass.

I jump to the machete and stay low as the small sounds carry against the house, drawing me towards the kitchen, where the back is still empty. It comes quiet, certain. Something is raised thick and bobbing on its own, looming forward. I stick to the wall as he looks in, following the countertop with a flashlight. The knob jingles with a key thrust inside, slipping the lock and breaking the seal. It's left cracked in place before it swings the rest of the way in. He stays and doesn't enter as the smell leaches inside. The steps come light, careful with the bat up high. No light; the underground brown keeps the room palpable in its basketweave.

Movement crawls around the island, holding me where I'm stuck close. One hard swing underneath and a sprint upstairs until it's over, a blind thing. The pressure edges in, quiet but there. Only coming.

I grab in breath and switch, putting the gun empty on him before he's close.

— Stop. Stay right there.

The bat shudders electric, priming the pounce. There are no features with it; just a dark square with scruff. He stays in the impenetrable. Then he pushes out words from it.

— How long have you been here for?

The gravel in his words is all outside, approaching with the sound of your own voice.

— You need to go find your own place, somewhere else.

A river rumbles from the dark spot across his face.

— Were they here?

He's locked stiff against the barrel tip, snug into the space.

— They?

— The people who lived here. Old man and woman. Did you see them?

He's poised. I put my footing for the doorway, still facing him.

— No, no one.

His voided features lie still.

— This is my parents' home, okay?

He waits for me while I keep to the elastic distance.

— I got in with the key, alright? I don't want to mess with you. I don't care what you're doing. I'm just here for them. See where they went.

He slowly brings the bat down onto the island between us. It's used and studded with something like bolts at the end.

— It's hell out there and who knows how long we have. Just let me stop here for a bit, please.

His non-question comes right from one way glass. The earthworn impassivity brings its source down to a stark either/or, putting me right there along with it.

I ease a step back.

— You keep your distance.

He eyes me from the dark and nods. With careful, still-deliberate movement, his light comes back on and the door behind shuts, locks.

— Was there a note? Anything?

His side is to me.

— No.

He stops.

— You don't need to keep that on me. You can have your space.

He waits; the glare blurs where he's jacket or girth. He begins to slough free a hiking pack thick as him.

— I know you didn't exactly invite me, but now we're in this together. Maybe I can make it worth your while. You want to go through my things while I search upstairs, will that help?

He lowers the top of the pack, holding back something a snake would nest in. I dip to come up with the arm-length blade awkward until I'm holstered.

— Okay, well, at least that's better.

He steps differently, heavier as the light bobs in front and sometimes onto me. We move in close concert until he's taken my spot.

— Pack's there. Are you coming?

There's a comfort now in his voice; and pleasure. I keep stuck in place, slow after his ascent.

He heads on to the bedroom, out of sight.

— I have stuff in there.

— I won't touch it.

The hallway is tight and easy to charge through. He moves right to the nightstands, the top dresser drawer. Nothing there worth taking. I keep it down for the upswing. He doesn't make too much noise and pockets a few things, not stopping long.

He registers my tension in stride.

— What'd you find?

— Nothing, mementos. What was it like when you got here? Hell, the whole town's gone right now.

He has scratches healing across his face.

— It's empty, just them here.

The crags pass unchanged, emerged and not worn with anything like age.

— Well, come on, let's catch our breath downstairs.

He starts forward.

— Stop.

He sees how I'm holding the blade. I have him in one swing if he doesn't rush in. If he does, the edge will be between us, one central hit before he knocks it away.

— This is not your house, and you're not in charge. You want something you can boss around, get the fuck out and go find a pet with one of them.

That does get a reaction, the brow round then shooting wide in unstoppable, naked pleasure.

— You're right. Sorry, it was just an invitation. I'm still gassed from getting here. Never been much for etiquette.

The deadly seriousness, even regret evaporates on a self-deprecating smile just as the last word tumbles free.

— Is there anything else worth doing, though? I could make us something to eat. They weren't much for spirits, but I do know where they were aging their bottles. Wine country, right?

— No.

He waits for more, cold. I let it dip, just as tense. He laughs small and hoarse.

— Well, I'll have some if you don't try and behead me.

I keep the machete tight down the steps, still facing him. He makes a small gesture.

— Ladies first.

I creep back into the living room, where I'm shelled, waiting for him to follow.

— You and I have really got to work out a common enemy thing. I didn't even know you were here, and your eyes are going to pop with those daggers at me. Any preference?

He stops at a closet and digs into the back, utterly exposed. I can't speak past the tension across my arms and chest.

— Here, this one's good, and this one's even better if it hasn't turned. Get it, turned?

He holds out both, paired twins plucked in attic dust, then enjoys getting them ready without me.

— Come on, give it a shot. They don't have long for the world.

I search his movements for anything secret as the bottles strain uncorked, glasses dance free and cradle full. He gives an obstructed sniff.

— Ah. No time like the present, come on.

He toasts me with a glass in front and fills his mouth.

— Have to clean off those tastebuds.

I take it far back to a tiny gazelle sip. It's biting and full of dark berries. He loses himself on the mouthful until he shifts for the other.

— Oh.

His nose crams the center of the glass.

— That one just gets you ready for it. Here.

I take the other more easily. Cellar must settles across aged vinegar until something baked and spiced crawls forward, finishing on something else that's familiar. I hold on to it again until it's lost back to the long-trapped bite.

— Hazelnuts.

He smiles or at least winces. I take one last sip and leave it to sit on the counter. He fills it back up past where it was and enjoys more himself. The trees behind the house sit jellied in darkness. He nods and raises a finger to me mid-drink.

— I got just the thing for you.

He bends over and dumps out his pack to throw a heavy leather wrap onto the counter for me to take.

— Come on, let's have some fun.

I carry it slowly to the living room. He sits deep into the couch, where all but the top of his head is in shadow. Joining the bat against the coffee table comes a handgun, then a pocketknife.

— Go on, unwrap your present.

A jumble of tools clinks from inside.

— There, that's what you want.

I take the whetstone and give it a small, reluctant glob of spit while he watches me try to keep it fixed to the table.

— That's not going to work. Give it here.

His open hand waits gentle for me. I stay still.

— Look, let me teach you something. If I start to do anything unto-
ward, you have full permission to shoot me, preferably not dead; but
if it comes to it.

He tries to lock eyes, but all I have is the unclear edge of his nose in
front of me. I slowly put the handle end to him. Too far and too
seated to jump forward, and going for the table is a trap waiting to
drop. I scramble back, and he has me before I get past the door.
Can only get space in the dining room, but he has me if he wants, if
he risks it.

He takes it. The point nestles Juliet into him as he places the stone
graceful down the side.

— You're better off holding it still like this. And you need to keep
the angle exact, otherwise, what's the point?

He stares at me, still featureless.

— Another joke. Not a good one, but it might help you remember.

The space fills with scraping.

— It's a good go-to. You can do this all evening if you're giving it a
new edge. Noise will draw them, of course, if you're not careful, but
it beats doing nothing. Or just drinking, if I'm being honest.

He shrugs and stops for a sip.

— Just stay even with it and remember you're making a point, not
grinding it down to death.

He places the machete back down in front of me and watches as I
continue with it. The bat comes up into his lap, and he begins
inspecting it with the light, testing bolt heads one by one and tight-
ening a few with a wrench. The wind pressure picks up outside.

— How far have you come from?

— San Francisco.

— Thought you might be SoCal.

The line comes out somehow folksy.

— 'Cause I'm not old?

He stops himself and stays on me.

— 'Cause I'm kidding. Only fair to take away your home after you almost stole mine.

The house shudders around us, making him talk around it.

— Well, not really. I didn't grow up here. Folks came out five or ten years ago to fix up the place and retire. Thought this kind of work would be good for the body and soul. Not sure what work that really was, but it's what they went on about.

I'm close to a smile. He settles back.

— Anyway, here's as good a place as any.

— Except for the fire.

He files a bolt edge in short, grating bursts.

— Fire's everywhere.

He looks back down to his hands, where his voice is stifled.

— It's good as any for now.

My scraping continues with the sound back to nothing again outside. He has a gash on his knuckle too.

— Pretty late for you to try to meet up with anyone.

He doesn't react.

— Well, I've already accepted it. Doesn't make it pointless, though. And also I met you.

It stays out like a valentine that he's picked up and is still playing with.

— They were probably better off here. I had somewhere that worked for, uh, us. We were pretty well removed, good water. Had a routine that kept things under control. One day, one gets in and. I was in it, just fighting. Friends. Trying to hobble them so you can get to the next one. By the time I knew to run, my wife and son, they didn't make it.

His shoulders are rocks that suddenly break to the living room wall. He runs over its hieroglyphic contours.

— Here, this is them.

He shines the light for me to see past the frame to a couple posed over a baby. She looks out bittersweet, confidence, and the man is mostly clean-shaven and bright with astonishment.

He takes it back and almost keeps from looking down. His face stops, holding both sides tight as his cheek's gripped on to a strained, deep breath. He comes back gently and looks out to the side of me.

— I got back in again to bury them. Couldn't even do that.

He stops, silent, the light looking off nowhere.

— Anyway, it's all that matters, right? Whatever happens, you don't really turn the page after that.

He looks back at me unseeing.

— What about you?

— What about me?

My eyebrows push back against him; he doesn't budge.

— What about you?

— I don't have a story like that.

— But you have a story.

He sits still.

— I left.

— Left what?

— My parents and brother. We didn't relocate, and for a while nothing happened. We were just, there. Things started to get worse, and the people we were with betrayed us. I killed them, right in front of my dad. Couldn't stay after that.

He looks at me like he has something gummed up to say. He sounds different.

— So you left for this?

— I don't know. I just left.

The weapons sit piled between us. He lowers the bat for the pistol, clears and places the mag where I can see the bullet. A cloth comes over the end, wiping and wiping between the intermittent light.

— We should have more.

He comes quickly back with the abandoned glass.

— No, no, here. Just spit it into the fireplace if you don't want to drink it, but have some.

He's quick with the pour and getting it in front of me while his fingers smother the other stem. The hard steel of his arrival crowds the small mouthful that I have, all mineral and metallic and acid.

— Hazelnuts, right? All this time. For this.

There's something moving outside that could be branches. The room pulses with the artificial flicker of the light.

— You know, two means sleeping in shifts.

I stare into his hands, his blackcast face.

A shuddering across the slats pushes me from my wrapping paper sleep. The doors pull at where they're tied.

— Come on, something's happening.

Hot mole scratches crest over me from where I'm a sore, inductile mass. He's sentineled away from me as I stumble up.

— What?

— What's in there?

His voice is pond-still.

— My horse.

The words don't fully land as he turns downstairs. I get what I need to join him. It's still night-dark, but the black is skyless and in front of us.

— What time is it?

His eyes only come wide at me before looking out again. A back is to us from the front of the garage door. Movement continues past it.

— I only see two.

— Showed up maybe a half hour ago. Something fell, and they've been glued to it since.

The inkblot hands trace over and over in place. They catch and drop free, coming back up again. My face wrap and shoes are where I left them.

— Okay, okay, don't go rushing out there.

— They're just going to keep drawing more.

— Wait until it clears.

— Clears?

His chest is broad and close to me but missing some of its original stoutness. I could push him over or at least away.

— You're going to die if you go out there now. And they're still going to eat your horse. Probably you will too.

— You don't know my horse.

He comes close to laughing.

— We can wait for the smoke to pass, or else you'll be blind and winded fighting them. And you won't have my help.

I turn for the door as a hand comes right to my shoulder. It's hot through the overworn jacket.

— There's no telling if there's more. They get caught in weird places or suddenly come around on you.

— She's got to be terrified in there.

— Maybe, maybe not.

His voice comes quiet. It stays liar-calm and neutral, persuasionless, no skin in the game, whether that's been left or ignored.

— Uh, she hates those things.

— Great, so do we.

The contours of his face turn down to bent brass.

— They'll take a bit, just wait.

I look outside.

— Nothing's going to improve, and you aren't the one who put her in there.

He just walks away.

— Looks to me like you saved her life.

The long back is still at the door, praying, prying. There is a hole, more of a mark and nothing within. Heavy arms slip and return back to the same spot, painfully slow and tied to something thought-less. The panel holds against the grip, stuck in place until they come back out, snakes. The other dances behind and I can't see what it's doing.

The sky is the closed inside of an eye, barely showing as the dull, red glow brings everything else to shadow.

The hand comes back to the hole.

I jerk back and trace the perimeter, taking the edge of what's left outside. The bulk weight of the nearest tree. A shape that might be another. Most of it thick, underwater black, the low ceiling narrowing my focus on what's not there.

He has his feet up and head back getting coffin sleep.

A cupboard glass fills cold in my hand and washes the lump in my throat. Taking the sink edge, I put the wetness into my eyes. Again, and into my nose. The window is black inside and out, keeping anything that's there from me.

I sneak quietly back upstairs to change the pad and pee just as there's more wind. A hollow airline roar pierces the upper floor, rearing straight into a howling pitch that braces the walls. I throw my pack together with what's left of the pads along with a few socks and towels.

His boots stick out as I come back down. They're newer and not the ones he came in with. He just ignores me as I put the school bag against the door.

Something is bent now in the hole. The hands stay longer until they begin to slip the inside out with them, slow and playing with it. They put themselves there with quick, unstoppable pleasure, trying to tunnel impossibly through with no face or shoulders up behind, only hands.

He comes like I ask and heads right back to his seat.

— Just keep the watch. You don't need me until they're getting in.

My jaw stays balled as I'm back alone with it. I quickly get food and a chair, putting myself in place like I'm paid. The tension hangs around my temples, and I just watch.

The lower part is bent under its wrists. There's no sound; anything that happens is swallowed on the way here. It looks inside, wire taut, the back of its head, hands, all of it still. The wind picks back up and makes the trees go frantic. A wail hits again into the house, briefly blurring the other, who's been roused into an unstoppable grandfather rage. It joins.

I put my face covering back on and unbolt the door. His eyes stay open on me as I slip out and latch it carefully behind. The wind hits me first, then the dark itself. The dull red skyglow does less to illuminate than to suck the seeing away, a moon that's come too close. All that's left is a blotting out. I stop to adjust but my view is brought down to steps and the garage dim lit ahead, sea creatures risen up against it. Bits of ash and charred needle bite pelting across while the treetops sway free on the arena ahead.

Eyes close on the thin outline of grass, I near the two, both still intent on the hole. I skulk in, ready. I bring it down as hard as I can onto its head, this time kicking the lower back in the same movement. The body stalls and stumbles against the door like some sort of victim. I go straight into the raised forearm of the other with enough force for it to break. The point stumbles somewhere into its abdomen as it comes on to me, making me wrest back from its complete, handless grip. My covering gets caught, and I bend immediately out of it, almost stuck, coughing and wincing with too much of the smoke drift swallowed.

The brained one has come back up and is facing me with a dark line caught in its sheen. Both are too close to each other to do anything; they move in a mass, not one without the other. Sudden steps behind turn into the charging downswing of the bat onto the second, throwing it straight to the ground with a grit crunch. I fill an opening into the other's cheek, and it watches me as it holds against the blade buried halfway in. Its jaw tries to close on itself while it twists me with both hands and pulls at my sockets, my left arm buckling. With all of me, I spin and finish the stroke with enough of an angle to break the hold and send most of the head flinging into the darkness.

He's smashing the other apart. It convulses with the blow, and there's no more shape to the head. He stops himself quickly and only glances at me before looking back around.

— Tell me, what good is this actually going to do? You really need that much peace of mind?

—Just watch my back!

I look through the hole and see nothing. The garage door swings up and biting on itself as the cave space opens. His light comes violently around until it stops on the horse, who's plastic in the corner. The ripples of her coat are stiff with the surroundings, her rear facing us. She doesn't react.

— Don't, she'll kick whatever comes to her.

I speak gently and come into her side view. She takes a small step nowhere, stays. I make another small movement until she melts from the dead end partway to me.

— There's got to be a breach somewhere, and they'll keep coming. We've hardly bought any time here.

An orange-white glow walks slowly behind. A set of shoulders calmly kissed in flame, limbs moving steadily ahead, briefly broken by either a tree or another that's closer. The small slice of skyline behind is the same orange white and moving.

— We have to go.

I tear the wrap from the hands and immediately drop it once there's something wet. With the still-shoed feet of one, then the other, they drag heavy to the side while he stands silent at the passing fire. My lungs are punishing me, and I hurry back inside without him.

The last of the scarves comes tight back around where the burnt air is still with me. I hit furniture noisily to race through one last time, tugging free pillowcases and filling a couple bottles of water, wiping myself down again. He's inside with the wineglass when I'm back.

— You'll probably have to leave her.

He doesn't turn as he unclasps the photo and stows it into a note-book from his pack.

The wind has taken over. Fire on both sides arcs into the red-binding sky with its night-bright white taut in a messy, organic strain. The burning zombie is somehow gone, and the red has filled in everything now with blowing wisps of ash between. Shapes hang towards town that are too far to distinguish or place.

She flinches lightly at my return but lets me touch her and bring the cloth to her face. The craters welcome it in long puffs as I begin to caress their nibbling. She's slow to turn to the kicked through path, and she tries to find the zombies, suddenly pressing sideways into me. I can barely keep her each step ahead while almost getting hugged over.

She stops where the yard now ends, enough for me to get the saddle. It's ready, and the ink dark shows more by the time he comes out, bagged and moving quick. I shout hoarse into the mask and wind.

— Where do we go?

He just eyes the horse, and she steps back.

— Hey, come on, I don't know this area.

— I told you, it's everywhere.

The treetops are careening above us. All the night cold is gone, the smoke thicker. I jump on with the bag tight.

— Come on, there's room. Just grab on to the back.

He starts off for the gate.

— No, you can ride. Hell, go on ahead if you want. She's not gonna be able to take me, not in the dark. And I'm not going empty-handed.

A tree cracks high behind us.

— At least tie that down.

— I'm used to it, it's fine.

He's strapped back again to the intruding geist, head buried, bat a swift appendage from the thickset pack. His voice is far off and muffled in the shout.

— I'll get the gate. You sure you can handle it?

— I'll walk her if I have to.

We move without looking back. The zombie is still lit farther down the road, shrinking into a new looming horizon. I'm gummed quiet as he turns back to where it came from.

— Fire walk with me, eh?

— What?

The wide stretch puts everything around to dark cellophane. Its new, orange-white sun billows far across the skyline. The flames are right there in the unending glow, blaring and massive in their arrival.

Trees glow with their own light at the ranch, which is still held by a wandering figure. We steer clear of the ones who've left but haven't made it onto the road, all of us afloat. He moves on like he's leading us, ready to turn and swing for her head.

— I think Sebastopol's gone. This will at least put us parallel for a while until we hit the next town.

The night-red opening of the bread shop is empty except for our asphalt clop. Branches shudder around us as we come into tall, swaying pines at the first house, then it's on to a day spa and more driveways. A pair of old inhabitants has been roused to watch every-thing from the road. She slows on her own, and he breaks ahead to shove the first from behind and swing into the second. She lets me run her ahead and almost goes too far as he plods back to us. They're left in abyssal torsion.

A two-story hotel is the sprawled site of a last stand. Bodies slumped like cats in the road. Something's flung against the balcony that could have been part of an Old West shootout, set for stuntmen to vault over in slow motion. The door's cracked through. He looks at both bodies as we go and only gives the porch a glance.

The stink still hangs in the burnt air, just a presence.

The way turns warm and bright around the corner. A wall of unstoppably high pines is burning with a few small homes joining them in front, all of it wound together by a long cauldron of grass that's pooling towards the road. A two-truck fire station watches at the end with one left outside. The huge pines stand behind in tight, roaring columns. Oversized growths ride up and down the still-green branches as the grass smoke sweeps into us.

A bright screen of it blares from a roadside storefront that's deep in the same flame, sending her veering as far as she can to the side of the road.

Groundhog tunnels lace across the field, fingering more of it. They've taken another wall of pines right where the road narrows between two homes, one manicured and feeding the flames, the other an unlit thicket. A loud set of pops locks her in place.

— There's no way around!

— What if you go first?

— She doesn't care. Either you're in charge or the fire.

She doesn't respond to my thigh squeeze, and the combustion carries on ahead.

— It's a horse. It'll take care of itself.

Mars red is tight around us and turning to burnt fumes. The bat's ready in his hands, looking up. My heels grind straight to ribs and I lean forward; she starts running. A gust sparks over us as a branch falls without coming down. Hotter, then beyond the heat, the clearing slows us at a set of burning willows sparkling together, the fire swaying with the still-weeping wisps, keeping on. Bright shards hurry across the road by us to nest in the grass. Wild oaks smoking peaceful in the next field.

It gets cool. The fire line is back to a far-off glow, leaving a dim field wide between us. He puts himself readied against the roadside thicket, but it only stays acrid and still with the breeze. I swallow down half a bottle and give the rest to him.

— Give her some too.

With the last bit, he rigidly puts a hand to her face, which she shakes right off. Orchards and more oaks smolder close together, the weight of their woodsmoke hitting us with their bright lit shadow. The contrast turns abruptly harsh, taking grapevines and trees together in a boneless mass of flame. One of the largest has crashed into the road with the top still burning in power lines. He goes down to the ditch and squares there before moving on. A wave and I get off, keeping a tight hold. She plunges straight in with me, careful footing coming face-first into brush. We both move and move until we've pushed scraping underneath.

Something seems human inside, but real or not, moving or not, it's gone.

The fire's suddenly all around us. The unbridled contrast of orange white blinds whatever's ahead as fresh black plumes choke the space down to a furnace, stinging hot and making any movement pain. She's tense under me and runs. I shout but can't look back. Full, hot wafts instantly bake the heat in. A branch hits us and sends sparks into my mouth and throat, making me double over coughing and biting back for damp while doing all I can to keep on. She darts into a turnout to dodge what's looming in. Wind sear lashes as she cries out, coursing like I'm already gone. I stop looking, bent over and straining just to keep my legs with her.

We break out to where the wildfire pulls back on either side. The heat stays pressed on us in the wind, and she won't slow as I come back upright. Space stretches on between us and the burning forest; and the hills we're headed for glow gently in parts. Her coat seems covered in resin, part of her nose scrubbed to a ghostly pink. I can't shake the heat away and go for the last bottle, using it warm on her. She doesn't like it, and it's gone.

We're alone, and the fire is gradually closing behind. The only going back is without her.

She puffs loudly.

We reach prairie with a hill burning towards it. A barn stands at the base, the gravity between the two clear and longing.

Stuck at a cattle gate is a car with people alongside it, arguing maybe. They're small, still caught back on the property. The closest stops to watch us, steam still coming off me.

— Someone's behind me. Friend.

It doesn't sound like me. All my throat flesh is wrung and useless. He responds and raises his hand clear for me to come. She keeps on, creating a breeze that cools around us as he and the others watch, still.

The house is peaceful behind them.

There's nothing behind as I've put too much distance between me and him.

We leave the field for a thicket that occasionally hisses and snaps. The dead night red is in place, time and space its own, here.

The frame of a house on a hill is dark-bright in roaring flame. Ahead, a dense, stories high forest is burning too. The carved sign for CYO CAMP still stands in front of the inferno, utterly vacant with trees and ground cover in different states of combustion behind. She slows to a stop and tries to turn.

— No, no.

The way in starts thick with huge pines at the bend. All of it is on fire, and the road narrows straight into it. The only way forward splinters over and over with sparks raging fireflied in place.

There's the sound of a tree crashing inside.

— It's okay. It's okay.

I stretch to pat her where the hair's unchanged. I barely finish the words.

— I know it's bad, but we both have to do it.

The road turns immediately to darkness white with smoke that blocks the next parts in. Tapestries of fire hang high on either side of us, rising quickly out of sight or drooping into the ground cover, where they spark ashen flurries. Pieces fall indiscriminately down leaving hot showers.

The tree columns keep to their posts as they lose ground. A hot swell of what may have been ferns flowers thick around them, sparks riding into her hooves.

Black cephalopodic arms take almost the entire road through what used to be the camp turnoff, scraping us with nothing inside. Dangling silhouettes lit up where flames reach them. A creek calls out past the wind, hidden in the steep, black nothing of the embankment. A brightly lit arc hangs low and reaching overhead, the trees that fuel it gone in movement. It burns the top of me with an immediate, sea-deep smoke.

A sound barrier holds in whipping flames that come searing for my eyes. We're hit hard and my leg is caught as we're suddenly crashing through bone and flesh. My ankle is ripped out of the stirrup, straining until I snap free. One knocks over, another tackles her face while I try to keep on. She swings her head and snaps into it, flinging the shape thrashing out of her. Another is hot-as-coals at our side and has me; with the machete, I chop down into the parts that are there and not going. She drops sideways, skidding us into asphalt and debris, throwing us into one and knocking me mostly free with it. I try to get up and keep moving, still bent and maybe going the wrong way. The machete is gone somewhere and the school bag fights me. She strains for her footing, each instant waiting for a rabid charge into her or me. She's up before I can get to her and taking a sudden turn off into the forest where the way forks. I'm slow, ankle screaming at any weight. My mouth cracks open to the muffled taste of burnt hair and flesh, but no sound comes out to her, or breathing.

One grabs me by the backpack and swings me over. My forearms hit first and I twist, regaining the plastic through hot brush. I keep moving, rubbing where it hurts. The way she went in is behind, completely intact, a beckoning garden. I keep going.

More cabins come out like hovels, burning close and bright. One with a mossy roof and a lit branch avian on top. Frames glare from above or below, hollowing their contents in complete conflagration. Fire caresses them in parts, beats them in others.

I suck in with nothing but smoke to get through, eyes and throat stuck hot. There's no sound here but the occasional hiss and pop of woodsmoke hung heavy in the road. I'm full of bad air and puffing; I take up a stick and keep forward. Dry scraping again and again.

A sign for pedestrians appears like a thing plunged underwater, nothing around but bright, smoldering needles and fire-stripped bark. A telephone pole banded in metal is still burning within. Then it clears.

Heavy, chalked white has the sky again. It's either morning or it's been made that. The road breaks wide and stretches into the pumice air.

There's nothing but wreckage at the first site, piled between trees still tall with their branches burnt down to skinny human arms. A perfectly intact dumpster and a fire hydrant in black-burnt soil powdered white in parts is all that marks it.

The town is one long road. Trees that would have had leaves are destitute ahead. Nothing stands in the visitor prepared parking. Hard, bushed limbs have burned fully out behind what would have been a lodge.

Burnt bodies are facedown in the road. Otherwise, the asphalt is completely unchanged but for dancing currents of ash. The skull of one is pressed neatly down. They don't have anything interesting to poke at. I'm completely alone.

Everything's dry, chemical vapor pressed down to obscure piles, left in predictable squares. I don't go close to any of it. What was here was something but it's nothing now.

Metal framed ash sits hollow, tires and windows both gone, still smoking at the edges with something mercury crawling out like a hidden alien parasite, finally dead.

A burnt and beaten palm stands at a pile of rubble. Some of it's metal, different kinds of tools. I yank out a two-handed axe. It's heavy and the handle is charred over but firm.

Across, the thin frame of a steeple is sunken to the ground.

A clean stretch of driveway with an unflagged pole. A more official pile of rubble with a steel cabinet standing within. I push everything in the ashes, taking only small, hard steps until I'm there in front of it. It doesn't open. I push it back onto a beam and bring the axe down, again. Again, like plastic. The rising ash hits me, coughing. I've dented it; I stop and keep going until there's a hole. The head sticks, and I pry and reposition until it pops.

There are too many guns inside, shotguns and hunting rifles, mostly 9mm and 5.56, the boxes are warm but fine. I find a scoped rifle with a compact, sage stock. Bolt action. I cough to put things at the limits of the bag and strain away without the stick.

A bird is resting in the center of an untouched tennis court.

The town ends where the trees are still thick and green on a hill and an office-bland building stands with a heavy roof. Early blossoms waft out front.

A sign reads OCCIDENTAL COMMUNITY CENTER COUNTY OF SONOMA. CLOSED, TAKE CARE on the door. It's dim and static within. I break a window and squeeze through after nothing else moves.

The capsuled space is unused with old, oversized chairs, a stale place of small connections and sitting until the day is through. Papers at the desk, nothing even on zombies. Large enough to shelter during an emergency that never came.

After putting my head into the rooms, I prop open the bathroom door for light. I turn the faucet, and it does nothing. The toilet's dry, but the tank is still full. I drop everything and peel back the covering, which is crisp and dusting off of me. The water's cold and stinging on my brow, getting at the corners, where it sticks. Skin grabs back and burns touched. Calcium and cleaner smell stays in my face.

I hobble and drag a console table slowly to the door and into the glass, down and back up to get it on its side. I take the best cushion, my stuff, and find a room with a working lock where I can sit with my leg propped, carefully putting the bullets back in until I stop mummified to sleep.

I open my eyes at the slow screeching of the table. Something heavy forces its way through and is quiet inside. I grab the gun again and go on hands and knees, mindless. The steps are light and hard to trace, and I wait for them to stop at another door. A lock clicks, and I shout through. It's not a shout and sounds just like them.

— Stop.

The form is already turned, its bat raised. He slowly brings a hand to pull off the hood, the mask. It's him; wet, curled hair and a blood-red spot over his eyes that's going to scab over.

— Surprise.

He still stands like he's ready to be shot, and I haven't dropped the gun.

— You made it.

— Mostly, yeah.

He cane strolls the bat to the faux fireplace and sits down, bagless.

— No more horse?

I shake my head, and his features stay plastic in a way that might last.

— Well, sorry about your friend. Bathroom?

— No water. Just in the toilet.

He bares his teeth to himself and kicks out the recliner to close his eyes.

— You knew I was here?

He opens them back up, though his look is unchanged.

— I saw the desk.

I sit slowly across from him.

— Sorry I left you.

He stares, small, tired.

— I told you you could go ahead. No changing it.

He closes his eyes into the burn and blindfolds his wind-seared chin up in their place. The new soles are warped over his feet. A hiss of something outside scrapes the void, and I go stiffly to see. The car from the ranch is parked under a basketball hoop, steaming with a shattered windshield and sagged like it's lost its tires. No one's inside.

I shove the table back in place, and he's passed out. I walk slowly back to the seat, eyes weak until they're finally closed again.

PART IV

MILL

We pass houses built into the mountains on stilts. The angles are steep and wooded against stumbling. Birdsong pierces the air above, holding high in the trees as one wandering sees us in the road ahead. It's stopped, then ambling for a reunion. We go slowly adrift to either side. She chooses him. Her body is worn down and badly burnt on one arm, but some of the skin hasn't turned grey. Her hues move in pastels to Reed. He dances by, and I keep steady ahead as she stops from her falling to change course.

A man comes down from the other side. He bends leering at us, equally, and he jabs a thumb.

— You like Darla?

Reed is hard and keeps on. I stay light.

— You named it?

The man only looks back more intently. Most of the houses have come flat and accessible, but not his.

— Well, that's creepy.

We're close to where he's gashed on a smile. I throw something else at it.

— She looks like a survivor.

The smile grows.

— Yeah, a real survivor.

We're past, and Reed shouts back at him.

— Get it on a leash if you won't put it down.

A call comes skipping after us.

— Keeps you on your toes! Keeps the riffraff out too.

Reed raises a hand without turning back. I come closer.

— And keeps the creepers creeping.

The rock-hewn face grins down at me. We're alone with yards and the mostly empty houses. It's all sun until the end turns back to woods and the railing of a school center platform. The blood is still there up the steps, and we have to wait while Cabe gets to his desk.

— Just saw a friend of yours. Old creep got a kick out of watching one of them take a swipe at us on your street.

— Glad you got a welcome.

He makes a small gesture to the seats, and we pause before dropping our packs with the bat and getting off our feet.

— You really just let them in?

— You still made it in one piece.

His hands are quick to the teacher's desk, grinning where the wood scuffs through.

— It's better this way. Walls are constant work and only bring trouble. Whatever comes here comes.

— Even a horde?

He looks at Reed plain. The stubble he has is sharp and reddened.

— Well, let's see it.

Reed dumps the bag of tinged medical tools, saved bandages, and the jewelry. Cabe starts looking closely through the box with the shine of his scalp.

— No medicine at all? Nothing?

— Wasted, except this. Can do all your cutting or prying, but not too much putting back together.

He lets the bandage drop back in and the stench of smoke returns.

— This is nothing.

— It's what was there.

They lock eyes. Reed doesn't break as he smiles around his words.

— We'd have lugged up some of the cages if we knew how you like to keep entertained. Maybe you could drill it on their shoulders. I bet it'd be endless fun seeing how they chase squirrels. Or dogs.

He doesn't react. Reed keeps it moving.

— Any takers for the jewelry?

The man is baleful back at him.

— Not around here. Unless you want a widow to woo.

Reed glints down from the wrested pleasure that's radiating out to me too. The lines on his cheek hold strong as he drags the chain slowly back across the table and balls it into his glove. Cabe frowns.

— You aren't holding out on me, are you? Keeping a bunch of pet antibiotics isn't worth nearly as much as it is here.

I take his eyes from Reed.

— This is what we got.

They go wider, and I push into the edge, where the pieces shake.

— This is only here because we tossed through it all. Everything's exposed out there; it's just dead silence and the broken building under your feet. All while there're the ones wandering back in and the ones stuck underneath. And it's not like we're the only vultures.

Not to mention the cancer we're probably getting with our bullshit hazmat getup. So yeah, we're calling this one a win. Just go tell your people to hook us up so we can get something to eat already.

The cords of tension break to a laugh that repeats machine cold on its own.

— Cancer? Fine, fine. Go get your food. We'll see what else.

Reed shakes away his smile as we rise and turn.

— Well, who wants cancer?

We're the only ones eating in the next room. Our plates are cooked but cold. The guy who dished out the food comes back to us.

— You like it?

His eyes are bright for response.

— Yeah, thanks.

— Good, good.

He puts his food-greased hands together. Dark, waved hair, maybe the same age.

— Hey, you guys hang around, we got another hen that stopped laying. Cabe wants her smoked. She's already pieced out, but if you got something good, I'm sure you could get in on it too.

Reed pantomimes everything but the whistle.

— Too rich for my blood.

I get his eye, which has been mostly on me.

— This is good enough, thanks.

— Wouldn't want to get too big for our britches.

Reed gives himself a devilish grin that no one reciprocates. The guy stops and starts again on me before breaking back to the trays of food.

— Well, he sure has his eye on you.

— So?

— So if you cared, I could wander off for a bit. Make myself scarce. Maybe go for a nice walk.

He's grinning with wet lips.

— Stop it.

— What?

— You're so stupid.

— See? Told you you made it out okay. It's a better look than mine.

I get the rest of my plate down.

— He's not my type.

— Well, he's breathing, so there's that. Must have some sort of survival skills. Even if not, you've probably got enough for the both of you.

There's the sound outside of something spilling out like logs. It's a long noise and mad. Someone else from the kitchen puts his head out to the slope. Cabe comes slowly back again, deaf to it as the newcomer leaves.

— Good, right?

He sits down between us.

— Well, if you are getting tired of ash, I might have something else for the two of you, if you got what it takes.

Our faces are flat with my cheeks bulged underneath. Reed watches me with him in the way.

— We're listening.

— Good. A family down the road hasn't been back for a while. Name's Cooper. It'd be nice if you checked on them. At least four. Adult brothers with their parents. If they've been killed or overrun, well, then things would take a turn. Do the most you can for yourselves and the community. If they're gone, of course.

Nothing passes between us.

— You just head west down the main road a couple of miles, turn right up the mountain on Cazadero. It's the first trail to the left. Be careful, wouldn't want your intentions to be mistaken for unfriendly. After that's done, go on to the end. There's a mill to check on too.

Reed's a rock in the way.

— A lumber mill. What do you want with a mill?

His sharp-grown intent is untouched.

— It'd just be nice to know how it's doing. Whether anything's been stripped down or nested into.

— Sounds like something you could do yourself.

He turns a slow eye on me.

— It's called delegating. Sort of a thing us leaders like to do. But if you have something better.

He stops there, and we sit silent on each other. Reed grumbles from his food.

— So how do these, uh, Coopers feel about you wanting to kick up a sawmill right in their backyard?

He stays on me.

— Well, I wouldn't presume to speak for them. But I'd have other concerns if I were you.

Reed pauses.

— And if it isn't? Lucrative, as you say?

Cabe sighs soundlessly without breaking his gaze. His eyes are stuck between brown and green.

— Well, you've made it this far. I'm sure you'll find a way to make things turn up.

There's no savor in the words, and a slight nod follows from Reed.

He looks back up with something suddenly close to wonder, horror, on his face.

— If you're not building a wall, what are you building?

The man's unchanged.

— Not everything builds up.

Reed comes close to laughing.

— You're talking about tunnels. That sure as hell is going to be a lot more work than a wall.

— I told you, walls don't work.

— And becoming mole people does? Jesus, everyone with their sure-fire ways to beat the apocalypse. I thought you already had things figured out with your apparently not crazy enough strategy of letting them all in. Can't just let things be.

— We've let things be, and we're doing splendidly. This is something else.

— Yeah, I'll say.

Their words echo against each other, every part shooting desperate out of sight. Cabe stays smiling tight and overdue.

— If there's one thing I've learned about people, it's that they can't stay in place. Otherwise we just break, toys. We're destinations, each of us, not beings. The ones who needed to go out, you two, went out. Scattered to the burning wind. The ones who had to put their foot down and build up, they went up. Far as I know, all that's left of that are some glimmering myths. But for those of us here, well, we have nowhere else but down.

He appraises our silence, Reed's derailed and mine still unreacting. He leaves the table.

— I can give you a tour after you get back, well loaded and with good news, I hope.

— Sure, we'll check on that family for you.

His voice comes tight.

— And the mill. I hope their health is well.

Leaf-dark ivy has the roadside redwood encased. A meadow stands between the clusters, and the sun crashes blinding through before the trees make it black again. They grow closer, rising high out of sight in undergrowth, swallowing what comes. Ahead's a house that's stuck with forest film.

The sun brings everything to celestial lime as we come around the bend. There's a balcony watchtowered above.

— You caught what he was asking, right?

I breathe against the chill, holding it.

— So why even go?

— I don't know. Why are we?

The polished bed of his face keeps me close.

— Destination.

His lines plunge suddenly flat and come back jeering.

— Crock of shit.

We share a smile.

— Was more like he was talking into the wind than us.

The grey-green river valley has a haze glow that weighs over someone and their dog, fishing. We stop to see each other, and he raises a hand from the embankment.

We leave, and Reed eyes a dark-wooded house that has a sequoia rooted through the porch. It's glassy and high at the bend.

— Not a bad place.

A marsh flees to the next ridge, leaving everything vacant.

The river comes back below with the mountainside walled against us. We're quieter, slower until it unbinds.

A truck with a camper is shelled tight at the side of the road. We get close enough to check the cab, which passes empty on to bars fitted across each trailer window. The first is busted out. There's a creak, and a hand shoots from the hole, greyed and clasping until it stops suctioned to the side. Reed laughs. It sucks in, and thudding rushes it against the back on glass. The spidered surface moves under the welding.

— Maybe there's room.

The rocking gets worse as we go with the valley opening bright ahead till we find our turn into the forest.

The hand-painted sign for a place that has live music on Fridays tries to coax us another five miles ahead. The trees are back to redwoods with the grey green of the river brought close, here, around on either side. The air's moist this way, and there's only a rust-strewn convertible at the forest brush that could have died in the sixties. Hood raised, tires long dead, and at some point, its drop-top became a tangle.

— How long until they all look like this?

Reed is slow to look away.

— I was more into Road Warrior.

Another sign talks to us. ONLY SIX MILES TO CAZADERO SUPPLY. And the next near the trail is piled over with red and yellow triangles.

WILDFIRE IS COMING.

IS YOUR HOME READY?

Birdsong starts to run deeper in as the light gets cut out by the trunks and our eyes adjust. Powdered-brown needles take the chunks of pavement forward with nowhere else to go. There are four mailboxes.

— What do you live off of here?

He looks quiet back at me.

The path leads crepuscular to a parked truck. It has clear sight of us. We go a bit slower, hands faintly spread, but it's empty with no sign of being seen. There's a basketball hoop nailed useless to a tree when we're close.

— You think this is it?

— We can see. No reason to load up right now, though.

Yellow and white light has the way plugged with the lane barely wide enough for the both of us. Reed's movements are bound tight.

— This isn't it.

Balcony slats are visored above, making him stare with his nose raised. There's only air, cool and isolated.

Up to a spotlit clearing; what's there is small and fenced. It's more shed than house, though with pieces peaked in asymmetrical angles.

The fence is locked but easy to jump. He waits there while nothing happens.

Slowly to the front, I come to the glass, where there's a pile of shoes at the door, a stuffed couch, shipping container comfort. The knob doesn't turn. Reed goes around, soundless and deliberate. He comes right back.

— Later.

— Really?

He shrugs.

— Just if we have to.

We keep going. The mud of a work yard starts trampled through trees, and the path stops for another home taken by the forest. Everything is gone about it. The way in isn't vacant or abandoned; it's written over, there. I keep my voice hoarse between us.

— Not here.

An offshoot digs to the mouth of an animal shed, witch-dark with emerald grass and the gathered dust of pine needles above. The trees spike in pushy, undelineated masses at our side with the spectre of the house shrouded above.

A voice rises from its quiet, singing. The words are sent with care, feminine and about birds.

The shed is a warning through the portal as the voice stops and starts again somewhere back in the middle. We have to put ourselves at the opening to see, to be seen.

The singing ends before she looks right to us. We're too far from each other. Reed's hands are adrift on the bat, and I keep small, even as her shoulders come ready.

— Hi, there.

A rifle is propped behind that she sinks to without moving. Her focus keeps jarred from us, pinned just behind.

— There's no need. Didn't mean to scare you. We're just saying hi.

The words trace through till she tosses something back that falls short.

— What are you doing here?

Her jeans are wet at the knees in a garden that's thin with flowers.

— We saw the sign. Figured we'd have better luck poking around the mill than trying to go fishing without a pole.

The sagging post chain droops between us as her voice comes back, close to scolding.

— It's private property.

— Is that still a thing?

I put myself more in view, but there's nothing in her response.

— Don't go up there.

She stays in place, stripped of any sort of need. Reed's sudden warmth brings her glaring back at us.

— It was just an idea. Would you be willing to let us rest here for a bit? Could use some water, if you can and will.

She holds silent, a torrent coming underneath. I get repositioned.

— We'll be on our way right after.

She looks back again, changed.

— Yeah, I'd love to have a visitor. Come around, I'll meet you out front.

She waits with a smile chiseled underneath. We try to return it as each of us turns slowly back. She's towards the shed as we lose sight, and sun breaks back into the trees on the way up to the scaffold porch of the house.

She's not here yet. No one clearly inside. Her footsteps start as the forest air settles back in around us and the top of her rises into view. It's not shouldered; she holds it low and from on top.

She gestures to the porch, and the buffer stays between us with each padded crunch.

What's there is acrid with an ashtray and left out bottles. There's also a can that isn't empty.

She waits for us to sit. The response stalls, but Reed drops his bat against the railing.

— Much obliged.

She heads through the unlocked door as we try to get comfortable in the wicker. The chair Reed takes can rock, but he doesn't move. Eyeing him gets nothing. The window is cracked where our heads are bare to the living room, and I can't get away from it. She comes back with a pitcher and plastic cups. There's a Pyrrhic move to help as she sets down against the ash pile and pours, leaving them there for us to take. He goes ahead, and I wait for her.

— Oh, this is good. Really good. We still can't get the taste out no matter how much it's boiled. Even the water's burned, huh.

Reed catches me, but I'm unworded. She doesn't pay much attention.

— At least here you're drinking more trees than house, right?

There's a small cluster of carrots twisted in their own roots and tops. A paring knife. They sit there.

— You have a nice place.

She's close to glaring as she goes into her front pocket for a rolled cigarette, watching us as she puffs it lit. One long inhale and a stream of smoke gives her somewhere else to turn.

Reed looks down at the bottles. None of the labels are intact.

— Pretty cozy, huh? Your, uh, spot in the storm.

She stares off. The stillness of the woods holds the house hushed behind us. Reed comes in shifts for the carrots, taking one, then the knife, and he squares to shave the growing edges back onto the board. She stops looking.

The skunked weight of the smoke takes her place. Wafts. Stays. I press my shoulders back where they come against the worn-in smell of a dog.

No one looks at each other.

I get my own and bite into the fringe, getting the locked nectar and taste of dirt.

Her heels cross at the ankles. The porch space between has us isolated. Lets us be.

She puffs out in one long exhale above.

— You come from town?

She watches from the side and nods before there's an answer.

— Cabe, huh?

We come more still, all of us. His voice darts troglobitic back.

— Not a friend of yours?

She stays on the well viewed side of the closest tree.

— You tell me.

Between the tray, the water, the smoked husks, the bottles, there's nothing.

— No, I wouldn't say so. What difference does this mill make, anyway?

— I don't know. It's just a place.

She drags deeply in and slowly lets out, still not looking at us. Reed's distant.

— Well, all the man was going to pay for was reconnaissance. That an issue?

She doesn't turn back.

— What more's there to know?

No answer.

— Suppose you could have tried to hide it a bit more, but truth's its own cloak.

Her arm comes down for one of the unfinished beers and brings it up to drink. I'm forward, and Reed keeps talking.

— It's nice if you can afford it.

Silence. The crushed mouthful is wet at the front and she still doesn't look.

I'm ready, the paring knife quicker than my own. Reed is in his knot with her only puckered. She stretches blind for the tray and doesn't stop until she lands on a carrot. It swirls up into her fingers with the greens rattling underneath, and she brings it close, feelers reaching back until she takes a bite.

— You two got to relax.

She keeps eating and either sighs or laughs. Another deep drag, and she passes what's left back to me. I put it in with eyes still looking, and the skunk heat is an immediate familiar that takes something as it goes. There's nothing for Reed, but I offer.

— I don't need any more fire.

I kill what's left and add it to the pile. The calm of the woods presses closer, impenetrably thick. Cool air comes in and says hi. She starts rolling another.

— I'll get more. Home-brewed.

She gets up without an answer and returns with bottles that hiss open, cool but not cold. It's too sour.

— Fucking mill.

LIFE

THE FIRST TREE-CHOKED cabin has the door smashed past the jamb, untoothed. We step in on empty air, and every household nicety is piled high with garbage. Layers on layers of lived through junk. Different kinds of rot mixed in packaging, most of it down to a black smudge. The furniture is swallowed, the paths eroded, the smell gone. Only the cold holds my nose wet.

Our movements get smaller. Reed starts checking, but I only open a drawer. Ripped mail stuffed in with silverware. Something is torn out in the other room, and I look to the next house in the woods. Reed comes behind me.

— Think it's them?

I shake my head.

— It's just another cabin.

He shrugs and doesn't show his find.

— We'll see.

He puts a hand to the door that won't stay open or shut, and my eyes need to adjust.

More hollow and disposable houses join in a campground connection. The first step creaks, and inside the same life waste is featureless without furniture. A sharp hiss gets me down and running back to the trunk, wet in its moss.

The rise of a cabin is fortressed in the trees ahead. Grey window peaks watch against the animal wandering of where we are. It's one long porch above the gate, a place for someone to bark down orders or shoot. The fence is too high, and everything stays completely still.

— That way.

Reed sinks us back into the forest, where we lose the sun between the other white-gutted frames. An American flag hangs in our wake. Something else on the balcony too.

The brush we move into makes us slow, and each forest house that mushrooms into view is another monster to watch. The road keeps along in glances as we get deeper through. Ivy, tall grass, a creek if we keep going. We come into a long driveway where a porch light is dimly lit.

Reed's wildgrown cheeks chew it over. Nothing's different in the cream siding, no defense. It's right where grandparents would be lying dead or a locked door has travelers to be butchered limb by limb. We stay in the brush and begin to sidestep our way back to the road.

— We just had to move on.

Our pneumatic movement binds to the jestered attempt. He keeps on.

— You want to head back for more beer, we can.

My ankle gets scraped under flowers that haven't fallen, and the fence leaves us in view of the creek.

— We'd have heard if this wasn't safe.

— Well, that's optimistic.

Our eyes are locked on the empty joke.

A manicured set of cabins comes next, deep brown and totally open. River rocks line everything in cement—the foundations, fire pit, pine tree flower beds.

— This is right where all the partying camp counselors end up slashed; creatively.

He slows into its middle. I start after.

— Maybe back in the eighties. Now it'd have to be something meta.

— And if there's no more meta?

His smile fades without turning for a response. Black is caught above us in the eaves.

— I think this one's a maybe.

— How good's a maybe?

— Good enough to say hi.

The road is quiet on nothing ahead, the same and different from the incipient horror show. I turn back into it with my arms flung.

— I'm just here for a walk.

He throws his head to the canopy.

— This is a walk!

On, and a side path shoots too deep into the forest. There's an adjacent house, but that's not what it's to. Reed leans into my hair as we pass.

— And this one's a coven.

The road splits to a maw, holding each disjointed house in the same view where deep-scored trees are left in their dirt. People are out. One far off with a dog. Another hammering something together on a table. We're slow, and their movements are dense in arboral pockets. Reed starts for the first and the carpenter stands still. The dog walker waits. We're silent as our plastic passivity melds to theirs. Reed steps small again to the one with the hammer, and I hold electric behind.

— Hi.

His voice stays beneath where the hammering was, though it's too far to talk.

— We're passing through.

The torso is dredged up in the soft needles of the driveway, something like a shell in hand, strange to inspect.

— Anything we should know?

His movement is indistinct, shoulders not knowing where to go. The dog walker is just close enough to get involved and Reed takes the space between us.

The man is older up close. A faded trucker hat holds a frizzed shock of white and the jacket puff adds girth that's not there. It's his bones that keep him from falling bent.

— Haven't been out since the fire, but the town holdouts ran off, far as we know. Whoever stayed is now one of them.

— You don't deal with that here?

His head shakes tight and controlled.

— They're taking their time.

Reed looks around. The woman with the dog is fine where she is.

— They'll get right through your door.

They make eye contact.

— Yeah.

He turns to his work, the shape of it unclear.

— Do you, uh, have a fishing pole?

They see each other differently.

— I could cut you some line and a hook. Plenty of sticks out here.

Reed lightens inward.

— What are you looking for?

The man shakes his head with much more of a sway.

— Nothing. Just wait here.

He puts down the hammer with some regret and walks back to the open shed. He's a figure to us, and the dog walker swallows her dappled shadow with the dog. She speaks only to me past Reed's forced through hello.

— Are you okay?

Her weariness, her layers of clothing, her distance make her impossible to look at.

— Sure. How are you?

She nods lightly to herself and falls stony back through water. The man hands over a fistful of curled line, then a hook and knotted lure. They only nod to each other.

We leave everything that we pass until we're back to the whisper of creek and forest. Reed watches it follow.

A platform crests sharp all over with vegetation before us. Everything is empty, green space and corners.

— I think those are berries.

— It's berry season?

— Maybe.

He passes the weight of his bat to me and jumps the chain link. The framed void jingles and shudders, and I stay low watching him tromp through, all green around him.

He hits the stairs, quiet each one, and stops alligatored at the top. There's light movement at the gravel across the street, but nothing to see other than the back of a car. He's still stopped in place, and I let myself bend further into view. There are legs locked straight and wavering. They don't do anything. I sink back into the undergrowth and only listen.

It's minutes before Reed comes back with a dirty handful of lettuce.

— Comfortable?

I start and he follows, extending the better of the two and biting into his.

— I'll wash it.

— If you want.

The next opportunities pass by.

The trees change their ghosts. The nothing that's there is all sunlight and the shadows coming in gaps. Reed checks and checks the shoreless creek. It stays a small scribbling of ferns.

Part of the way clears to a peaked cabin peopled over with animal lawn art. We shrug and jump the gate, quick in the open. Uphill, and there's the back of a head inside. The hair is thin, shoulders hanging over. There's nothing in the woodpile behind as I catch on the stone dust of Reed's look. Everything pushes right back, and I swallow the air, taking it and gliding muscled back in the step.

A door shuts behind as we go.

What's left along the way is heavy with forest dirt and all junk, empty at each step.

Reed looks through at a utility station that's gated and barbed from before. A gas tank is bright with warning signs where the field office is long closed.

— You think anything?

He doesn't respond. A trail into the mountains takes his attention, and I keep to what's ahead, behind. The river is quiet on a ruptured shoal below, and we go.

The submarine focus of something coming makes us run awkwardly off the road. Plants trying to grow bend at my shoes and dirt-grey hands until the falling stops in a trickle. Reed hits the water with the bat branched in above him, crumbling the edge as the viscous swell of what's coming draws closer. He lets slip a light smile, and my hands are dug in where it's cold. Something I do makes him keep the grin. The surging is close and slower than it would have been, but there's no stop. He's calm, looking past me at the water, which isn't that high. It's all surface and the sound of it not with us. He sees me again, just looking. We start to climb.

Where we arrive splits at a bridge and another turn right into the mountain. Lime light shivers on all sides, fern to maple, until the looking breaks in the pines. There's a roof buried far ahead, another across the bridge.

— Let's try this way.

The sign warns of a narrow winding road for the next three miles.

— There's going to be nothing up there.

Something both sharp and soft is caught in his eye, pressing, feeling its way out.

— Isn't that the point?

The wooded offshoot is narrow and steadily up. Dirt stands mineral close. Trees are fenced in at the unpeopled distance, ending where mist and daylight hang over unfinished construction.

Shattered branches under, over thatched needles pad the treesides. The canopy has its own air, bringing the topsoil into an outgrowth that can only be had in fragments and blurs. We're lichen through it. Green shears all but a glimpse of the too-far road below. Bend after bend puts nothing against us but the way forward.

It's colder and alone up here, and the mountain meanders into the skin-cracked pavement.

A falling stream trickles in moss-clumped rocks. My teeth cringe quick and we rub it hard into our faces before filling bottles. I dip the lettuce and the leaves bend and bend with the flow.

The tunnel continues. Continues. A fenced off cabin appears in a downy clearing. It's small but on stairs where the windows glow mothball white.

— You like it?

— We need to eat.

It's far back and dim with mountain dust. An overhanging branch comes gently between us.

— Not the most promising sort of abandoned.

— I know.

He smiles. I grab the chain link and shake it. It's all stillness inside. I step over to where the fence ends in the mountainside and dig into the leaves to get the rest of me spacewalked over the edge.

Reed crushes behind and bends the top closer until he can fall in. The bat scrapes after, and he takes up too much of the space with me.

A pile of branches by a water heater is all that gives the clearing function. The stair boards creak indistinguishable from the cabin, trunks on all sides. Its windows are only portholes for keeping your bearings, covered in corpse white. They stay waiting for something that isn't us.

Reed clears the glass neatly from the door, then lowers his face to the edge and waits at the dark. His hand shoots through and has to stay there as metal scratches come from the other side, muffled until it separates and drifts in.

Everything is stale and dark. A couch waits there, fully somatic and inert. We split for the surfaces, floor, countertop, dead sink, quilted bed. All that's in the cupboards is salt and pancake mix. Packets of tea.

He's on the couch going for our food that keeps lightly clung. Dried corn, dried fruit, some nuts from before. A wrapping of baked cakes comes gently undone. I start there, and he leaves his.

— There's really nothing.

He looks into one of the few nailed up frames. It doesn't show anything.

— Yeah, well, we'll keep going.

The lettuce is a ball now and I keep at it until nothing's left. The water is all that's filling, but the rest goes down too and starts its work.

— Why? We're just going to end up with moss. Pine needle tea.

Everything is crunched away but his biscuit.

— We're happier.

The oil-rich curls keep his gaze away. He leaves my reaction and keeps gnawing. I'm done and head for the bathroom, and he's standing against a wall when I'm back.

— Surprised it's like this.

I turn for loose floorboards that aren't there, back to the bedroom. His talking's in segments.

— There's still enough day left to see that town. We can always come back, if we want.

We leave and Reed gets the door locked behind.

The creek joins us again downhill with the way turning muddy to meet it, keeping us slow between another cluster of cabins. Something was here, but we keep on until we're scraping our shoes back on pavement.

The water winds to a false lagoon with the hue of mold on bread. Rocks show through at the surface where nothing dances, just the clarity. There's a recreational shore on the other side that Reed faces along the bend.

A jutting of shacks makes us stop and come armed. The angles break our descent tight between mud and shore. Boarded porch, each curtain easy sniping. It's ahead or the water if we don't turn and climb.

The trees are cleared to stumps except for what's spiked against the house. Closer, a string of cans guards the clearing. There's room for mines.

Reed drifts into the ferns for the widest view. The water hums just out of sight.

— It's fine.

Past the first, a window is left open onto the road. The dark in the drapes is too there to ignore. An outgrown wisp climbs the hard-packed dirt.

The door of what's next is ajar, the cabin nothing but a room.

— Not a fan.

We pick up pace and get through.

The path divides, leaving us and every other step to a talpine up or down. Acrylic air has each movement dense and locked on itself.

The green-soaked either/or buffets chance, buffets anything but the movement. A longhouse shows more ornament than site far below.

Redwood that's turned white rises high enough to take the air; space that's still on its way farther up. The mist at the top dances as I see it, and a telephone pole keeps dwarfed and flayed in wire at its feet.

Everything narrows to detritus that keeps the dirt in place. Up, again up.

The climb ends in a set of homes turned at the cliff edge. They're tree houses, simple and right there on the road. Nothing to stop us. We come close enough for something to burst out and have us pinned against the rock.

Herbs and citrus spot the porch, parts yellow and brown. I step gently up to where the blinds split. Nothing. The mint's twisted over and the rest has dried away.

Pavement clutches up and down within an entire community. The first rises to a wooded peak. Downward edge over edge is overtaken in platforms, each house piece tight with beetle feet.

The sky breaks wide and right to us between oak and the aimless undergrowth. Anything pine is far off, and the white in the middle of everything reaches on straight to blue.

Vacancy is locked all over in forest soot, the blinds or panels. It's with me too, down to my balance.

— Why is no one here?

He keeps on in gravity to the closest built outcropping.

— Nothing happened.

He waves for quiet, close to sniffing the door. He turns back.

— It's kind of perfect, right?

Reed doesn't really look.

— It's not sustainable.

— We don't know that.

He faces me for my contours, hue, the way I'm filled in. I smile.

— Come on, it's nice.

And he takes it to a stone in hand.

— It's ghosted.

There's nothing in him. No emotion or its lack. Just the words. I make a small step closer without intending.

— We can do what we want to.

He stays straight on it, then sees me and rolls his eyes.

We go to the one that's most defended. High point, sturdy uphill fence that cuts at neck height. Segments rise across the property, and a moist set of tracks is where a vehicle used to be.

Inside, the pine-yellow ceiling leaves the rooms wincing. The furniture is clean and comfortless, and the windows are impossible to get through. I turn the knob and the stove clicks clicks clicks to a blue ring of fire and I cut it off.

— Why don't you keep looking? I'll check the rest outside.

There's hardly anything. I sit down for a small view and the buzzing of my feet.

When he's back, he's empty-handed and quiet with the door. Bat comes down, shoes come off, and I look at mine tight with dust and losing shape.

— The water doesn't work.

He stares down at the counter.

— That's fine.

Reed walks to the chair with the most cushion and sits, eyes clamped, and I'm back to the dust and bent edges.

I wake against the cold. His stony weight is laid out next to me, full, untouching and too close to see. Our shared sweat passes the quilt, keeping its heat but given over in grease. It puts me in harmony.

I get up from the lump, the still breathing face locked above it, and go on quiet feet to the first window. Morning sun has the room lit and warming, and just past the trees shine. Everything is strange and static. I put the edge of myself looking out and stay as the possibility shrinks to nothing.

All of our water falls into the moka pot and I drop in coffee that's not enough. My arm throbs from not being on my back, giving me just my half, which is more now than it's been. I stretch the fossilized ache from my feet, toe to arch, heel to ankle. The ends are either bright red or bloodless. Steam comes up as the dark shape stands from the room.

He doesn't look or speak when he comes in.

— You didn't wake me.

His eyes are low with the weight of having eaten from the wrong plate.

— There's really nothing out there. Now you're better off for next time.

He stares outside and is right back to it. The cup's too hot.

— Still not worth it. We can't forget about watch.

What we have will force us to look.

The forest has a head start on the day. Moisture keeps the light shining where it gets through, and we go.

The last of the slope gives us the empty shapes of a playground and other fenced nothings until we curve all the way down to what's next.

The main street advertises auto parts first. Structures are damp in the growth, rough with meat grinder stairways packed close and far away. There's a garage slabbed on the other side, and something's draped and waiting within.

The only thing human is a stenciled sign for restrooms.

We come into the middle, nothing ahead or behind. The valley is low in complete view around us, every point accessible and already traversed.

The windows above windows of an inn open on nothing. No forms, furnishing, only doors and walls with the murmur of something deeper and not leaving. A cobblestone wall hides the entrance and puts us to an Old West general store.

The dilapidation is intentional; rust so dense that it needs to mean something. And it still works. Reed waits for my readiness, laying it open.

He raises his hand to a simple, short handle thrust. The flat covered windows and double door make the whole thing shelled. I inhale, exhale, pull out the pocketknife against the holster. He eases into the platform, where the bat head joins him.

The boardwalk is cracked but firm to the door. Reed leans in until the seal breaks with only a sliver of floor and the counter in front. Air comes warm and spoiled, dancing in its disintegration.

Reed has the opening and waits with it. A bodiless wheeze starts small on its own path, and the space seals gently back shut. Reed mouths without turning.

— Two. Third grounded. Counter. Take the aisle.

I breathe and keep my thumb steady until the blade is pried open. He goes with the tip of the bat, leaving me to shut us in where we're low and exposed in the barred-off light. He has the listless back beyond the counter, and the other is the same at the end of the aisle. I move liquid-on-rocks, absorbing the change to come and the thickset crack that will set her in motion. She's hunched, and the mass in her hair hasn't dried out. It starts, and I jump into her turn, taking the mess right in my hand and twisting hard. The point rises to the cheek and goes in at the temple. She stumbles caught into me, and I brace as a hand takes my sodden grip, immediately scraping. There's no leverage and I push it again as the shelf breaks me free. Canisters come down hard around me as she twists the gap closed with her face immediately down on me as I stumble, trying, still, for an initiative that's gone.

The only other place for her to go is the shelf, which gores my lower back with the morning cold of her forehead hitting me, leaving me nothing. I press with her, shoulders and the soft of my back giving in to the metal until something falls behind. She goes with me and I throw myself blind and rolling until I can't anymore.

I stop on something inert and almost don't get up before she's back in. In the movement, Reed is still standing against the one that's coming to him.

I run to the counter, where the surge hits after me and I scramble further and further in from it. The body that's there is a deflated mass of clothing and barely raised bones. I shake it and keep moving. A loud ringing of either bone or metal throbs high in front as I'm smeared over to the other side.

Everything's blurred, and I throw a crate of what used to be fruit into the path of her; and she steps wrong into it and falls. I can't place them, only have their movement choking close as I turn. I get back on the handle with my wrist taken in the motion. Her flailing seeks me out, putting pain and torsion where I can't stop it. I push by the tip, somehow deeper. It's digging back on me and her mouth is gone, but I keep through where her pulling begins to drive itself back by the point in her head. The unpupilled eyes are up in the writhing, twisted on my wrist and slowly falling stiff in place. I jam it mashed and mashed, using all of me through the grip until something stops.

The floor rattles behind me, and I can't turn back.

She looks straight up, ready to be worked on further. A slime has the handle wet, and it's only my wrist that's bleeding within the fingers. Nails are dug into me where they're coiled. I whimper on top of her, but there's no leaving. I twist and keep at it for reprieve. It hurts more, close to something worse, and I push back in on the knife and the shut-hinge fingers until it's searing. A stack of bottles crashes behind me, and I can't react. I have to stay with her.

A hand has me at my shoulder. It pulls again but stops to work at my wrist instead. His fingers are brown with sweat, and when they touch where she's locked, the hurt's back, burning over and in.

She's forgotten, a thing made for selling and throwing away.

I'm looked at though the hand is still on me. He pushes me to face him but I stay. I stay, and I bring all of myself back again into the blade and its home, in, in and over until I've moved enough to fall. I land on someone's foot and keep moving to the counter.

Reed is in my face but I don't look at him and he doesn't go for my wrist. He leaves staggered for the windows, where all there is to do is listen.

The blood in my head keeps me from more than half looking at the thing that I touched. The face is smushed to the side and I stop. Its mass remains in view.

Reed is back at me again and drenching my wrist, making it burn and cut itself fresh all over. I flinch closed with the dampness getting past my jacket. The urge to hit and hit comes to dead extremities. He rubs it with a shirt he's got from nowhere and makes me hold it myself.

He leaves and starts taking things without any closer look. I get up heavy and wait for something to go wrong. It doesn't. I bend to put my fingers to what's now a nub. The knife stays and I pinch it by the rivet, which barely holds back at my nails. Suction keeps it until it slides immediately out with a sound. It doesn't come clean on her pant leg, but I shut it anyway and put it back where it's been.

Hard breathing fills the shop. He hurries to another part, starts one way and comes back. There's a light crunch outside. It draws steadily towards the front, maybe finding the steps. The lumps are resined together, the two just more concise than what's at the counter.

I stand up and shake back against the way I'm wrenched. There is food, hardware essentials. Hammer. Saw. No hatchets. A heavy flashlight and crowbar on the floor. I don't see batteries.

Reed stops to listen. The noise isn't there, and it's calm, how it was. A creak runs through the floorboards with small movements to the door. Reed exhales and catches me unmoving. I only have the crowbar when I'm to him, and we step gently, readied. The bat rises braced in front, and I keep mine in both hands, where it droops uncertain. We go.

It's a child. Reed's too high and immediately caught. Thin fingers bring him down and in, and I swing into them, putting the teeth of the crowbar into the boy's cheek and through where the hand stays held. We keep together and push him into the banister, where he crushes wild and indelibly in the shape of pain. Reed yanks the bat on to safety, and the boy comes with it until he drags to his knees in the street.

There are more too. Someone who died in coveralls. Two who are linked in friendship. We avoid them past a post office and the mouth of a repair shop. We stay close. The town ends with the valley and a small church over the bend. It's boarded, and one last zombified local watches us on the knoll and does nothing.

We're back in the trees, back to the creek. We keep on until the last houses are gone and there's a clearing.

I put the crumpled shirt into his hands and take the bat, which stays until I pull. His pack spills over when it's open and makes me drop for the disinfectant. His eyes stay vacant on a lone shed. There's a gash with nowhere deeper to go, and I press inside with the cloth after getting it dripping again on the road. He groans, growls as I keep it there, weak.

We're alone and shaded. Reed takes a small step, then turns to what fell. I scoop and stuff them back in as he keeps in place.

— I'm sorry.

He looks ahead until the jagged zip pushes him on.

— It's alright. Thank you.

— I'm sorry.

He sucks in and lets the air leave on its own. He turns open on me.

— And thank you.

The same forest line follows ahead. The stream water goes faster and farther down. Reed's stride is nearly a stomp, but his voice is light.

— Next time we burn it down.

He blankets himself in my gaze.

— Or we give them it. All of it.

The bright marks on my wrist burn in the air.

WHERE WE'VE MADE IT DARK

OUR BREATH HAS FALLEN into each other, shooting faster and catching back on dry viscera, an empty mass again and again. There's nothing to look at but what the trees have.

The forest keeps overhead as the colors bend from kiwi to grey jade. Chartreuse in the moss is right in place, and the valley of trees on trees is there if we could just see past them. We go to jungle emerald with a haze that's close and running from us. Earth breaks in powdered adobe. Mud, a wall. There'll be nothing on the road for as long as we're on it.

The shock of cream is high ahead. Windows keep Argused on empty space with the hard expanse of cut grass and the sky right back again. We stop short and stare.

A circle of pines leaves the back twisted, but a boxed pen draws us in. It's still and all texture where the ground is cool and dark from the day. They've been here too long, the bodies down to feathers. A wing or other parts still catch the gusts. It's canvas, no pile or story to it. Just a penned abandonment of what's left.

Reed sours and looks to the door until the weight of what he's carrying turns him gently back and we go.

The rest splits to something manicured and high behind trees, and we keep low from it, back to needles.

We're at the top. The clearing's flat and could be a stop for elsewhere. It rounds from the path to a cetaceous tear that throws the end of the valley in complete view. We're just one small opening across from others, and a dark hole in the nearest trees is barred with a farm gate. The pit of it hides what it actually is, just trees and a somewhere. We head in, sheared of the climb that brought us before the one black spot in the world.

It's its own path, and a cabin in the trees is dead on us.

The peak of the attic is bright where it sees the valley, everything under thick with shade and made for use. We get in at a window that's cracked with forest calm. A fur is big on the wall, but it's the same emptiness everywhere that greets us. Nothing behind the couch or under the bed that's up small stairs. The only creaks are us. Nothing works, but plastic jugs are sealed full in a closet. The bat comes down in the middle of the room and we eat what's here. Cold soup and chili. Green beans with the juice. Meat that misses the picture. It's all filling once it's there and getting warm.

The sun leaves before it sets. He covers the windows and I take a last look in the yard before coming back to the locks. We're quick to go upstairs, where the space doesn't do anything and there's an attic door with a string right above.

The cloth is still part of him, and he doesn't look when I get close. His hand is thick with it. The outside is dusted and the folds stuck red. The gash has darkened with yellow and dried black, though it's small in swelling that has the fingers stiff.

He touches my forearm and looks where I'm stung, feeling the muscle, staying for the heat to arrive. We move for the sink and wash in slow cupfuls. Above the swollen mess where the trace of her thumb and forefinger keeps fighting, his other hand keeps back from the unsurfacings that become burns, gouges. My skin's dark. A cut is gummed on the knuckle and he wipes at the bright red of it that keeps coming back.

I get out in jellyfish bends. It can't just be washed, but that's where I start, getting a lather that goes right in and seeps back red. A broken word drops in my ear. I stop, and he brings in more, starting again himself. I slowly unbind from him and wait at the towel. He sets the meat of it in. A clean sheet and a clothespin take it away, not telling whether bones need to be pressed or if rotting is what comes next.

We break back to where we've made it dark and sit on cushions. He makes room. The wind is active on the house and trees. Worn-in currents come graceful and chaotic where we're swallowed. What's between us is mostly shapes. I only have my breathing, which swells bursting up front. He's looking down or right at me, and the white of the bandage is a reef fish below. He exhales gently, and it falls between us in bird wings that don't stop. I move in the gap, fitting until our mouths have found each other. They almost cut with the movement. All I taste is asphalt and I swallow it down. I get my hand on his shoulder and hang inward, briefly back. He holds the break and I wait, right there. His lines are something to jump into. A nastic split becomes a smile outside my lips, and I press back in fully, feeling the slow climb of him rise back into our pocket. He grabs me now and gets over so that I have somewhere held in and ours. Our chests come together and more fits. One of us laughs. I pull at his clothes, and they don't give yet. He's on my neck with a hand at my chest. The movement wet against teeth, full in hand and turning me pliant, swallowed. I grab back at him too and have the base of him now. Parts scream back on. One of us is coming down and one of us is easing free. Each flavor, each sound is gulped as it's given. Layers new and old turn on each other as soon as they arrive.

Every giving is a taking more that leaves us new.

We're each other's place to be.

FISHING

THE RIVERBED RIPPLES at the seams. What's there quivers without going anywhere. I step clouded through until the bottle can go under. He stays crouched.

— There was that spot from before, if you want.

The end of it twitches and bobs.

— There could be something here. If you'd keep yourself from splashing in.

A thin wash of yellow is glassy and close throughout. Moss has the edge dark with turquoise. It's empty. I'm out, and he still has the hook.

— I think we're getting to the coast.

He stays straight at the surface. The water is stony on my teeth. The bank is dry enough, but I don't sit. A sound with the hollow of bells starts upstream. It doesn't stay.

— Come on. There's not enough water.

He holds tight to the stick.

— Yeah, but. Fine, fine.

There's power in the rise, feet grounded flat between the open roots. The scowl sours to a smiling that clambers back to me without finding where it can stop. His jaw relaxes in the glimmer of lips and teeth that I know. I come through the wet surface and take his good hand. The stick scrapes.

— Let's go sea fishing, then.

His eyes shift and unearth until they've slipped wide to laughter. The sound melds with the water. With me. I get the taste of him again and let my teeth in too. He looks around and squeezes me before we go.

We move on hooks up into the path until we've climbed back on top of everything. The hills we're in are the shearing of clouds, and we go where the grass hasn't grown.

It ends flat against another valley. Part is paved with drying pools holding the path's edge. Something white is in the distance where there are no trees. Reed turns up instead of down.

The next hill crowds out the rest. It rises from the road in razor cut rows that break brown to send the expanse running. The tight lines continue from view.

Tiny flowers spread under both sides of the tube gate and they come underfoot. Inside, the vines have fallen from the wire and still point up.

We keep on in them until the row splits. Yard debris and work houses show where the road we left fades. The white from before is back, past the dead vineyard and surrounded by more at the next ridge. Forest is in between, and we keep on in the hardpacked dirt.

It's a slow stomping down.

River rocks lie alien except for where grass is scarred where the water was. Our clacking and clacking comes heavy into the tree line. We step in enfleshed. Immediately, it's harder up. Thickets give their own shape and wear into our perspective, but we don't stop.

It's louder in the branches. The hill's too high to do anything except break and snap through. We're borne free in shaking, dry limbs that scrape down flesh if we let them.

It clears back to rows of vines that are bright with green. Broad shoots wave against the trees and dead grass of everywhere else. Soft and prickly; the grapes are work to separate skin from seed in their anxious sweetness. The tendrils hold taut aside from the few that come to our faces.

Vats shimmer from the back of a production cellar. The black factory windows are too high for anything but light, and we watch them.

Gravel cuts across, endless either way. Driven-in grey locks the chlorophyll and burnt moss together under pewter. We take it, still walking higher as the vines come and drop from us in scales.

It appears in a wide stretch of sunlit nothing. Everything is high about it, the windows, the few oaks faded and on guard, its cupola with lightning rod cutting the skyline.

We come into the lawn, which crunches differently, nothing living in it up to the oak where the path comes. The front door is swung open, and someone is on the porch, standing, waiting.

New wood is everywhere, as empty as what's just outside. Hosting room, hosting room, kitchen for as many who'll fit, now no one but us. A mirror wide enough to take it all has me dark at the edge.

More food. An unopened bottle of wine. A fieldworker's machete with no way to make it cut yet.

There are vacant bedrooms upstairs.

Reed comes in again from the hallway, done washing now too. We go back and face where the ocean is hidden.

THE COAST

A HEIGHT of metal rises at the ocean end. It's overly tall, ten feet on ten feet of lines bright with rust. A drop of coastal succulents wedges it with sunlight.

The spaces between spin carouseled back until I stop. It's all asphalt to a therapeutic-looking inn. It stands, still taking environment into account. The metal opens onto itself and bird shit paints the end white.

Wind comes cold from the structure and into us. Reed's creases are dragged into satisfaction, gathered and warmed at the built nothing in front of us.

I put my hand to the quiet split and swing in. An earth-brown roof is lighthoused by the salutatory height of a totem. It waits as the mist moves avian overhead. There's nothing in the parking lines, the landscaping. The ocean and sky are the same except for the sharp and fading white that keeps them apart. It's nice.

We're slower towards the entrance. Doors are shut, two floors, all to take the rubbed-out view. Prismatic glass shows a great hall where the ocean's held in place and covered dark within. Plants graze at our eyes.

The door is black glass where only the first few steps show through. The shapes of lounge seats and side tables lie within. We keep still as the ocean gets louder. It hits a rock somewhere and loses force immediately.

We push in and the air is wrong. Sodden, burying to acid and fat fallen together. I strain on the nothing in front of us with only the upturn of rug that we're on and the windows to put an end to the dark. The coastward white is blurred and humming with the weight of stars. It's jettisoned close, high up and illuminating nothing. The white moves. Mounds of black bend and pulse underneath. There's no fixed point, only undulations and turning. They don't come stopped but swell. Swell forward, away, going somewhere in the worm's hole.

The wall of black begins to break. The white stays fuzzed on what was against it, and it lingers. The hushing of the waves is still met with dead air locked in with us as the great room is full on all sides, black space, shifting edges, the white. They're coming in front, from the bar, already into a chair that's loud back down on the floor. The door is gone behind us. Nothing yet, and the chair falls over and keeps moving. The only opening from the dark is an outline of stairs. We go up. Each step shows as we take it with lines waiting to be filled until they already are. Reed pushes down with the bat but I'm touched too by something that won't move. It wraps, and I drag it with me up a step, another. The third is too heavy and he's stuck prying straight down in front of me. I fire in the dark and it doesn't do anything. His weight gets us both forward, and I fall hard against the stairs and keep on. We're in a void blazing white at the top. Both ends of the catwalk close in bodies and Reed swings to send one into the rail. Another is right there that I fire into and into and charge shouldered on to push it hard and away. It hits back wall-thick, but I go. The weight of what must be Reed is with me to the end. The hall is flat with the glow of doors against the dim. The stair surges in flesh and limbs that are faster than us in the oversized echo of wave sounds and mouth sounds that we move through.

I twist the first knob and get nothing. The next is open but blocked. Reed pushes with me, and it's too slow. Something comes against it as it starts to budge, and we fall away. The next is either this or jumping over. It's locked. I scramble the crowbar out and hit it in, in, and pull. Part is metal for the key card and I crank, crank again, again, and it pops. I fall in, and Reed doesn't come behind me. Between empty and empty, I reach back out and grab the shoulder that's there and pull. He hits me coming in and it needs pushing for the swing bar. Things fall, and he has a desk that doesn't do anything to push back on them. The door thuds louder. There's bed and closet and sliding glass to the ocean. Reed runs into the bathroom and tries to shut the door but I follow through to the pitch dark.

BLACK

The table moves in short metal screeches. It creeps, breaks further, and gets swallowed with the sudden, thick movement of cloth on the wall and door. The pressure laps against us. Another is in, another, pushing. The door is hit by limb and table corner and on past. Something falls over. The rest doesn't stop.

Reed keeps moving. He drops his pack. The bat clinks hushed on the floor between us while the burrowing outside hides the rest. He's moved into what must be the shower.

I run my hand on the cold of the counter. Something soft falls over, and I come down slowly onto the toilet.

There's a stifled chatter of teeth. Reed's voice pushes small and deliberate in our hollow.

— I'm bit.

I go for the bag, pushing blind through clothes, containers for the hard of the machete.

— Where?

— Don't. Just help me tie it off.

I grab at the spa robe I've hit and tear the knot. His breathing holds back caught on something. I go down too quick, running into glass, the tile. His hand is reaching out for me and has my shoulder, takes me to his ankle and puts me onto a wet, torn spot that keeps me there. I feel up into the hair of his calf and lay the cloth carefully where it fits. The wrapping dances in the dark. The pocketknife meets the center and his breathing goes quick right before I torque into him. Object moves into animate. The groans and verberations sound with the others. I'm alone to tie it, and the other foot holds me with him into stillness.

— Let me do it.

Small copies of hissing go as he pushes himself back up. Our voices are smaller.

— No, the pain's bad enough. And I'm not going to be any use to you that way.

I hold him at the thigh, and he doesn't wince from it.

— And what good is dead going to be?

Our heads are damp together. He's breathing harder and I kiss him, take his air. He kisses sour back. I go for his hand and he fights to make it the right one.

The movement is sand coming together outside. Steps, dead breathing, little vocalizations. The room is big enough for twenty if they want.

I put my head to his shoulder. He holds me strong and gives kisses that immediately lose their print. My legs come into his and the binding between us.

I get up and go for the bag.

— No.

Things fall out that might be too loud. I'm quick to get it. There's nothing for my eyes to adjust to, but I come back.

— No, seriously. Don't. Just don't.

His voice is small and distant. Already it's falling away. The him that's there is also the him that's not. And the pain's what's already lost and lost again over and over. Already buried, already gone, but still left losing it.

I put it back to the tile.

The movement is heavy, quiet. A body lands bouncing into the bed and is still moving the springs.

I can't see. I can't see him. His breathing swells and falls with stillness blocked between. The space I had taken inside is gone.

— We're not going to stay here.

My voice makes him stop. Movement on movement is endless outside, always going somewhere. He's completely still.

— I'll do what you want.

My hand finds the wall and pushes flat. The noise behind me spindles right past the door, touching, taking. I bring two fingers to a short tap. It's firm through their movement. I move, wait, tap. The pulse of what they do is quieter. They move and go, still leaving the door. I feel for the crowbar.

It pries slightly in. The bending and chipping dusts me throughout their mute back-and-forth. It scrapes and slips needful in place as I keep the angle. A hole forms over the teeth. I lean in, pry, push; it's punctured. The end stops on something, and nothing's come to the door. There's no change when I try up or down. It draws free, and I set it to bore new again. Another. It goes back into the first hole and things start to crack. It's just a small part that moves, and dust is in my nose and mouth while I rip it down to the ground. I feel the broken spot for another way and keep going.

I can't tell that he's there.

It drives to the end and I scrape at it. It's soft and hard together. I press in and back for it to give, and something they screech makes me come to a quick stop. The door rocks back, still. I rake, rake, push black into nothing. Use my shoulder and only get it with fingernails. Drag small in place until what's there bends gently away. I do it all unmovably tight to the wall. And then I'm through.

It's just as dark.

The spot spreads to a hole, a gap. Their sounds and mine go together. I can't see anything. Parts come off. A beam stands fuller and fuller against me as I reach past.

I'm coming through. I stop for it to take a shape, but all I have is the dust. My hand goes in, gouges into something, and my fingers stop on the other side. It's close enough to hold. I break it further and further while the wall powders me. The desk stops one from coming to the door. I can put both hands in, maybe my shoulders. I keep going until I feel its lack go wide in front of me.

— Reed?

The first thing I reach is his shoe. He moans at it, suddenly loud, and the table slips free.

I reach his chest and stay.

— Reed, let's go.

He moves, but he doesn't speak. I breathe what comes out of him and reach for his face. He slips out of the way, and his words take the place.

— Just leave me here.

The dip of his chest puts me closer in. I finger and grip until I'm able to make him move. He keeps limp before putting a hand out to me, to the floor to move forward.

We're both bent in front of it. He moves for the bag, but I grab it alone, and he is slow to turn aside. I place it in but it won't go. I push and push the parts of it and the bottom rips as it's gone.

The rest slowly pushes it out of the way.

I face his darkness next to me. The door is being touched. I take his hand inert into mine. It's cold through the wrapping. I leave it limp at my ankle.

I fill the shape of it. Knee on the edge. Back swooping and scraped. I pull with everything else slow to follow.

The hand pushes to bone on my bottom, hard, and I fall out.

I'm alone with a sightless line of light. There's a static shuffling back in the hole, and my hands are locked under me. The rumble rises and slips and there's a buried gasp.

I get his shoulders first and they don't fit. His hands spread around me, my thighs. They don't stop anywhere.

I pull with his breath spouted against me. A slack, hurt moan slides the rest of the way out until I have him.

A broken, machine thudding fills the bathroom alone.

I'm as much hands as feet to the too-white line. The opening screech brings everything bright and in. Reed is still straining upright where the light stops right above.

Mangled skin is parts black and white. The red is gone, and it's dry and webbed past teethmarks. He sees me seeing it and leaves himself there.

Where he looks hangs half empty. The arms and hands of him are the same. They remain, and they don't stop moving.

— Let me help.

He's caught between me and the floor with words that are gravel sliding by.

— No, not the bed.

There's only the floor, a desk chair he'd fall out of.

— Nice view.

It's featureless beyond the glass. A line of green blue deepening to dark before it burns hazed away. Everywhere above is unchanged.

I sit next to him. He shoots plantlike up and winces against it.

— What do you need?

His mouth keeps still. There's a ruffled thud, and he makes himself turn to me before sliding back down.

— I want you to go.

Nothing else comes. His hand stops on the back of mine where I can't grab it.

— Not like I have anywhere else to be.

He doesn't return the smile. He only breathes. I lean, and it's bone and sand as I settle in. He keeps tight, holds. I pull back with him coiled to the absence, and he comes after.

— Here.

He pushes for his hand and pocket. It comes halfway to me.

— Go on, you'll need it. Memento parti.

I take the bottle opener quicker than he can tell, leaving the hand to drop back. He pushes again to find what's with us before settling back down.

— Go through it.

His breathing has lost the effort, and he stays on what's outside. I go slowly to the pile and the empty hole. The pink skin of my bag is cut through, and I lay everything out, move it by use. Use today, use tomorrow. More and more of it stays behind. Weight decides.

His is just more. What's hard to fit inside rips right out and rolls away. Nothing ahead for the pants, the dull machete. The lightening comes gripped out of me.

There's only his leg and the view. I drag what I'll take over with the crowbar. Then his bat.

— I'm sorry I can't stay.

I'm locked stiff in front, where I stop the sun. I drop for his face. His lips don't give as I work over them, lock their feeling to me. The small deep blue of the sea has us both.

— At least there's this.

The sounds against the wall blur under the waves.

He smiles short from laughter.

— Not the pole, huh?

— It is yours.

I get his water and hold him to drink. His mouth sputters into me with something thick.

— Whatever it is, it can't hurt like this.

— It?

He stays gutted on me, wordless.

— That's what you want?

He comes higher, unable to shrug.

— I won't keep these looks, but it beats the alternative.

The sounds make my ears ring.

— You won't be you.

The shoulders keep him in place.

— Something will. And I'll have that.

The square of light takes his face. He holds inside it but drifts to the bat. He doesn't move.

The ocean moans around us. His body sends its own groans, which come out swimming to our feet. His eyes only rise when they can to me, the sea, the bat. I stay there, and he pushes back. The side of his jaw is locked tight and his leg kicks me. I go, and he throws stiff with both hands into the floor. Fingers come and immediately clamp onto me and I fight him back.

The bat goes rolling away. Our glimpse leaves him adrift. Chest and shoulders knock back into the wall, drawing a response from the hole. He's liquid and locked stiff on top of each part, and he's stopped looking. He breathes hard, choked still and hard again. I begin to load the gun.

The thudding stays in the hole, and he calms with the clinking metal bits in my hand. There's no ground, only the surface where the sun has him white. His chest is rising. Rising. It's louder and there's still siliceous sweat on me.

He falls and his body comes long, pushing, moving itself back and towards the hole. His chest is stretched wide with ribs and spine crabbing him along. His head stops in the floor as the rest of him continues rising until he drops. He's stopped in the middle and his chest keeps moving.

The sounds in the hole are distinct, and I shoulder the bag, holster the gun, pick up the bat. It's heavy at the end and I leave it planted.

I'm stopped in the light, and the surface rises and falls with the driving of the organ. My hand is on the glass door, its untouched cold. My breathing doesn't steady and I turn to the glared seaview.

He tries to get up.

I get the door open and stand in front of the air. He's shoulders locked to what's coming in the hole. Hands take his weight as his feet linger into pushing, standing. Something breaks in the scratching and there are voices clear with it. He gasps tight too.

He turns paper white to me in the sun. He's there, warming, and he takes a step. I bring the bat sideways into his neck. The table rattles against him, and I'm narrow in place with the bed. I turn it overhead and come straight down onto him. The sound fills the room. Pieces move. He's closer and there's no room before he's touched me and I can't go back. The contact is placid before it comes crushing. Bat teeth grip low into his hamstring, and the sweep sends him ripping down my chest. I hammer straight back into him, hard and flying. His hands are moving to pull him up in it, and the deluge beneath takes my ankle as the wall stops me in place. I leap to the bed. I can't stop kicking and he's taken the edge and coming over. I roll free but the bat stays dug into his hands. I rip it out. Hitting him into the bed bounces him back and back again. There's something in the hole and he's in the way.

I hit him and the teeth dig in and I hit him again. It's red and flat on the bed, all surface. I make more of it and pry the parts further each time. The bed makes him move, and me.

Limbs and faces from the hole come in. The back of him bobs beneath the bat. It's all gap between us.

The first is coming. It touches him and breaks the space. I'm on the balcony and he begins righting himself. I'm over and stung hard, shins to feet. Scrapes keep me moving to grab what I dropped. The blue against blue is still together, and I'm alone with the crash and wind.

I go down sand to heavy rocks until the water hits me. It roils white in front with the larger parts beating rocks behind. I stand on the end, and I wait.

ACKNOWLEDGMENTS

Where We've Made It Dark exists because of the person who shows me what a life lived with love is, Juliana Ma Crawford. Each of my countless hours spent were yours as well, and the same goes for how we fall into the apocalypse.

Thank you to my parents for the support and structure that you gave, which helped bring this work into the world. Thank you to my in-laws for welcoming me to San Francisco, which has been such a vivid and wonderful point of connection with the world.

Where We've Made It Dark is a work with many relatives. Thank you to Cormac McCarthy, Neil Druckmann, and the creators of *Telltale's Walking Dead* for so endearingly setting the coordinates of who we are without world; and to George Romero for raising this most perfect monster to life.

Thank you, Slavoj Zizek, for providing the very means by which to engage how we desire in a dead world, the radical potential in seeing things through, and your steadfast commitment to who we are on the other side of revolution. Thank you, Todd McGowan, for your beacon of insistence on universality and how you keep it the point of all our efforts.

Thank you to Olivia Batker Pritzker and Meg Storey for giving the text such clarity and helping set it to stone. Thank you, Christina Kent, for your beautiful vision that I'll never stop enjoying, and to Naomi Clark for giving the book such life and form.

And thank you to you, reader, for giving this journey a shot.

ABOUT THE AUTHOR

Nicholas Crawford is an author and philosopher who pursues death drive and its undead correlates. He studied English at Vassar College and completed his master's degree at the University of Virginia. He lives in San Francisco with his wife and two children.

Sign up for the author newsletter and be the first to learn about releases as well as exclusive deep dives and sneak peeks.

NicholasCrawfordAuthor.com

Author Photo - Carolyn Fong

tiktok.com/@nicholas_crawford

BOOK CLUB QUESTIONS

Thank you for reading *Where We've Made It Dark*. The time you take to share a review on Amazon, Goodreads, and social media is essential to the support of a debut novel. Thank you!

Join the conversation on TikTok or Fable, or introduce *Where We've Made It Dark* to your book club with some of the prompts below.

1. When Imogen first goes shopping for supplies, all she walks away with is a compass that gets traded away later in the book. Other objects keep falling away as the story goes on. Is there anything that Imogen does hold onto? How have objects themselves changed as the world ends?

2. Part 1 ends with a reversal: Imogen no longer wants to go back to college, and her father insists that she go even if there's risk. What's at work here, and why is a car crash the ultimate decider?

3. What really makes Imogen's family stay when so many opportunities to leave present themselves? What makes their initial capability falter, or does it? Could Imogen have stayed?

4. While partying at the beach, Chloe tells Imogen that it's better to stay with Eshan till he gets himself killed than die somewhere together with you. Is she right? How does Imogen take this message to heart, or does she reject it?

5. How does identity change after everything that defines normal life is gone? What aspects of Imogen's character persist at the end?

6. Do the LGBTQIA+ characters react any differently to the end of the world? Do men react differently from women? What about Imogen's parents, and where does Imogen fall in response?

7. The book opens with a moment of unseeing as Imogen is woken too early by her alarm. Why is this important? What other kinds of unseeing are presented to the reader throughout the story? What is the reader left with instead?

8. There are three romantic relationships: Aidan, Chloe, Reed. How is Imogen different in each one? What is love by the end of her journey?

9. The dread of zombies becoming real centers on the need to become violent, and this violence plays itself out in gradual, constant steps. Is Imogen just doing what she has to to survive? Why or why not? Was there a point where you disagreed with her actions? If so, what do you think made her do it?

10. Imogen is abandoned by her friends for being unreliable. Is she? Would they still call her unreliable afterwards?

11. What makes Imogen's father insist that it wasn't weakness to let the people take their car? Is he thinking according to the logic of the old world or the new one? What about Imogen?

12. The zombies are slow, strong, and require hacking apart to die. What does it mean for Imogen to face them? Why does she keep doing it?

13. What moments of betrayal stuck out to you? Are the betrayals done for survival or something else? How does love persist, if at all, in these betrayals?

14. Imogen's father cannot accept that people (burners) could be killing indiscriminately so quickly. Is he right to reject what he knows to be true? How is Imogen's own descent into violence also a reaction to these broader horrors?

15. Imogen leaves the family who hosted her for the night to the zombie that is headed their way. Is this anything more than petty revenge for their treatment of her? Is Imogen wrong?

16. The friendships Imogen makes while out on her own are ones that she knows she will lose. So why does she keep making them, even when she tells herself that she doesn't want the attachment? How is what she does any different from Chloe and Eshan?

17. What is the life left to be lived at the end of Where We've Made It Dark?

18. Post-apocalypses question who we are without society, the extremes to which we're capable of change. The author has said that he strove to avoid the stand-in answers of who we are--the family unit, tribalists, vicious misanthropes. What is it that Imogen clings to instead?

19. After leaving her family, Imogen doesn't look back. Reed tried to go back to his wife and child to lay them to rest. After failing to do so, he traveled the country to be with his parents, who are missing from their home. Are Imogen and Reed at odds regarding family? How does this play out in the end?

20. Zombie apocalypses are famous for depicting capitalism past its breaking point--how the pleasure of consumption persists in the empty mall, how the freedom that's made available to survivors remains in a capitalist form. How do the people around Imogen cling to the forms of the old world? Does Imogen remain a capitalist subject, or does she become something different? How does this difference apply to today's world?

21. Imogen looks at a painting by Wayne Thiebaud and expresses the desire to rip the up-and-down highway from the canvas to get to what matters, where everything is headed. In what way does the change in the world, Imogen, and the people around her all link to Thiebaud's art? How does this also apply to Christina Kent's *Kitchen Window* on the book's cover?

22. Morality is the effort to remain faithful to each other. Ethics is how we remain faithful to ourselves. How are morality and ethics at

odds in the book? Is there a point at which harming another, even outside of self-defense, is no longer immoral, or is immorality itself the burden inherent to living without world? The book leaves the characters' immoral acts undepicted and unaddressed. What does this achieve? How should we feel about their choices?

23. Where does the book overlap with other apocalypses and where does it diverge? Is the story different from the zombie trend that was started by *28 Days Later* and *The Walking Dead*? What about *The Last of Us*? The author has said the book presses into the same radical space of *The Road*, *The Last of Us*, and *Telltale's Walking Dead Game* and pushes it further. What does this mean? Was it successful?